Praise for Our Authors

Anne McAllister

"This is a beautifully crafted story that deftly balances tragedy, sexual tension and the sweetness of falling in love."
—*RT Book Reviews* on *The Virgin's Proposition*

"*Hired by Her Husband* is an enchanting romantic tale that will touch your heart, tickle your funny bone and make you shed a tear or two. Anne McAllister writes magical, dramatic and heartrending romantic novels."
—*CataRomance*

Helen Brooks

"Helen Brooks pens a knock-out read in *A Whirlwind Marriage* (4.5 stars) with a deep, emotional story and gripping conflict."
—*RT Book Reviews*

"*The Billionaire's Marriage Mission* (4.5 stars) is wonderfully fun, flirty and full of romance, but it also has a serious side, just like the captivating hero. He'll make your heart melt."
—*RT Book Reviews*

Sara Orwig

"Convincingly written sexual tension as well as plenty of action and suspense make Sara Orwig's novel a real pleasure to read."
—*RT Book Reviews* on *The Playboy Meets His Match*

"First love, last love and new perspectives give Orwig fans another warm and heartfelt romance."
—*RT Book Reviews* on *Wild Western Nights*

Mistletoe Surprises

USA TODAY Bestselling Author
Anne McAllister

Helen Brooks

USA TODAY Bestselling Author
Sara Orwig

HARLEQUIN®ANTHOLOGY

ISBN-13: 978-0-373-83789-2

MISTLETOE SURPRISES

Copyright © 2013 by Harlequin Books S.A.

The publisher acknowledges the copyright holders of the individual works as follows:

BREAKING THE GREEK'S RULES
Copyright © 2012 by Barbara Schenck

A CHRISTMAS NIGHT TO REMEMBER
Copyright © 2011 by Helen Brooks

TEXAS TYCOON'S CHRISTMAS FIANCÉE
Copyright © 2010 by Sara Orwig

Recycling programs for this product may not exist in your area.

Printed in U.S.A.

www.Harlequin.com

CONTENTS

BREAKING THE GREEK'S RULES

Anne McAllister

For Nancy

Chapter 1

Alexandros Antonides studied the crumpled receipt, the one with the hastily scrawled name, address and phone number on the back, and was tempted to stuff it right back in his pocket.

Or better yet, throw it out.

He didn't need a matchmaker, for God's sake!

His fingers crushed the already frequently crumpled piece of paper and he stared out the window of the taxi as it headed north on Eighth Avenue. They weren't out of midtown Manhattan yet. It was nearly five-thirty. He should just tell the driver to forget it.

But he didn't. Instead he made himself lean back against the seat and, just as he had done a dozen or more times before, he smoothed out the paper against his palm.

Daisy Connolly. His cousin Lukas had scribbled down her name and address a month ago when he and Lukas had met up at the family reunion out at Lukas's parents' place in the Hamptons. "She'll find you the perfect wife."

"How do you know?" he'd asked Lukas, letting his voice

carry his obvious doubt. He'd looked around pointedly, noting Lukas's complete lack of not only a wife, but even a date for their family reunion.

"Seen her do it," Lukas said frankly. "I went to college with her. She did it then. She does it now. She has some uncanny sense of who belongs together." He shrugged. "Who knows how she does it? Hocus-pocus? Tea leaves? Beats me. Give her a call or go see her."

Alex had grunted, not a sound meant to convey agreement.

"Unless you really don't want to get married." Lukas had cocked his head, considering Alex. Then, "Maybe he's chicken," he had said to his brothers.

One of them had made a clucking sound.

Alex had masked his irritation and rolled his eyes. "Fine," he'd said curtly. "If I get desperate enough, I'll look her up."

"I'd say you're already desperate," Lukas had said, grinning. "How many fiancées have you gone through?"

"Two," Alex said through his teeth. "But Imogene doesn't count."

Imogene had been perfect. She hadn't loved Alex any more than he'd loved her. When her long-time boyfriend had got cold feet faced with a lifetime commitment, Alex had grabbed her on the rebound. Unfortunately two days after she'd said yes to Alex, the love of her life had come to his senses and begged her to marry him.

"What can I do?" she'd wailed at Alex. "I still love him!"

The more fool she, Alex had thought. But he'd been polite and wished her good luck. He still did. If she was that besotted, she'd need it.

"I don't know," Lukas had said slowly, studying him. "Two fiancées in a little over a year…" He'd arched his brows in speculation, then looked over at his brothers. "Sounds pretty desperate to me."

His brothers, Elias and PJ, had nodded sagely.

Alex had merely snorted. He didn't want a perfect wife, anyway. He just wanted a suitable one. He was thirty-five years old. Time to get married.

Of course lots of men would disagree. But not Antonides men. Antonides men married. All of them.

Not young, as a rule. Most all of them sowed their wild oats before settling down. But in the end, every last one of them took the plunge.

As a young man Alex had turned his back on the notion. He'd figured to be the exception to the rule. Besides, then the thrill of the hunt and endless variety had enticed him.

Now it often seemed more trouble than it was worth.

Sex? Well, that wasn't too much trouble. But picking up women who wanted a one-night stand seemed tawdry to him now. And while it was fine to play the field when they were young, Alex understood what every Antonides male understood—that there came a time to turn into a responsible, steady, dependable, mature man.

And that meant having a wife.

Elias might have been born responsible. But even PJ, who had been a beach bum for years, was respectably married now. In fact he had been secretly married for years. And Lukas, the youngest of them and definitely a free spirit, would get married, too.

Even Lukas knew it. It was just a matter of time.

Alex's time was now.

He had made up his mind last year. The hunt had begun to bore him and he found he preferred spending his time designing buildings than enticing women into his bed. It wasn't all that difficult, honestly. The difficult part was when he had to convince them he didn't intend to fall in love with them.

It would be easier and more straightforward, he decided, to find a woman he liked, spell out the rules, marry her and get on with his life.

It wasn't as if he had a lot of rules. Basically all he wanted was an easy-to-get-along-with, undemanding woman who wanted an easy-to-get-along-with, undemanding husband. He wasn't looking for love and he wasn't looking for kids. He wasn't looking to complicate his life.

He and his wife would share bed and board when they were in the same country and would attend each other's duty functions when possible. Presently he lived in an apartment he'd restored in Brooklyn above his offices, but it was a bachelor's pad. He wouldn't expect his wife to live there. They could get another place close to her work. She could choose it. He didn't care. He was perfectly willing to be accommodating.

So, really, how difficult could it be to find a woman willing to agree to his terms?

Harder than he thought, Alex admitted now.

His last three dates had seemed promising—all of them were professional women in their thirties. He'd met them at business social functions. They all had high-powered careers, fast-track lives, and nearly as many demands on their time as he had on his.

They *should* have been perfect.

But the lawyer had treated their dinner date as a cross-examination about his determination not to have children. The dentist bored on about how much she hated her profession and could hardly wait to quit and start a family. And Melissa, the stock analyst with whom he'd had dinner with last night, told him point-blank that her biological clock was ticking and she wanted a baby within a year.

At least Alex had had the presence of mind to say just as firmly, "I don't."

But that date, like so many of the others he'd had since he'd decided that it was possible to marry without anything as messy as love complicating the relationship, had gone downhill from there.

Which brought him back to the receipt he held in his hand. Daisy.

He stared at the name Lukas had scrawled on the crumpled paper. It brought with it flickers of memories, a frisson of awareness. Honey-blonde hair. Sparkling blue eyes. Laughter. Gentle, warm words. Soft sighs. Hot kisses. He shifted in the seat of the cab. Once upon a time, for one brief weekend, Alex had known a woman called Daisy.

So maybe this was fate.

The hot-kisses, soft-sighs Daisy had wanted to marry him. Maybe the matchmaking Daisy would find him a wife.

"Think of it as delegating," Elias had urged him pragmatically when he'd balked at Lukas's suggestion. "You do it all the time at work."

That was true. Alex had a whole staff at his architectural firm who did the things he didn't have time for. They did what he told them, checked availability, researched zoning and land use and materials, sorted and sifted through piles of information, then presented their findings and recommendations, and left him to make the final decision.

It was sensible. It was efficient. And Elias was right: a matchmaker could do the same thing. It would be smarter, in fact, than doing it himself.

He would be leaving less to chance if he deputized a disinterested employee to find appropriate candidates. And he'd be spared the awkwardness of future dinners like the one he'd shared with Melissa last night. With a matchmaker vetting the candidates, he would only have to meet the really suitable ones, then decide which one would make the best wife.

It suddenly sounded promising. He should have dropped in on Daisy Connolly before this. But Alex didn't ordinarily get to the Upper West Side. Today, though, he'd been working on a building project in the West Village and, finishing early, he'd had a bit of time to spare before he headed back to Brooklyn. So he'd plucked the paper out of his wallet and hopped in a cab.

Twenty minutes later he consulted it as he got out again on the corner of Amsterdam Avenue and the cross street on which Daisy Connolly had her office.

He hoped she hadn't gone home already. He hadn't made an appointment. It had seemed more sensible to leave himself the option of changing his mind if, when he saw the place, something about it made him want to walk straight on past.

But the street wore the New York City version of homey respectability. It was quiet, lined with four and five story brownstones, a few blocks north of the Museum of Natural History. The trees on either side of the street were all varying shades of gold and orange this early October afternoon, making it look like a photo op for an urban lifestyle magazine. Alex took his time walking up the block, the architect in him enjoying the view.

When he'd first bought a place to live in New York three years ago, changing his base of operations from Europe to this side of the Atlantic, he'd opted for an apartment in a high-rise about a mile south on Central Park West. Twenty-odd stories up, his aerie had given him a useful bird's-eye perspective of the city, but it had literally kept him above it all. He hadn't felt connected.

Two years ago, offered a chance to tear down a pre-war office building in Brooklyn not far from where his cousins Elias and PJ lived with their families, he'd found a purpose and a place where he was happy at the same time. He'd found another property on which to build what the owner wanted, and seeing a chance to make a useful contribution to the gentrification of a neighborhood in transition, he had snapped up the pre-war building for himself. Now he had his offices downstairs and his apartment on the fourth floor. He felt more like he belonged and less as if he were soaring above it.

He got the same feeling here on Daisy Connolly's street. There was a laundry on one corner, a restaurant on the other. Between two of the brownstones he passed an empty lot which now held a small local playground with some climbing equipment, a swing and slide. One brownstone had a small discreet plaque by the door of the garden floor apartment offering herbs and organic seedlings. Another had a small sign for a chiropractor's office.

Did matchmakers have signs? He felt an unwelcome flicker of awkwardness. When he found the address midblock, there was no sign. It looked like a version of all the rest—a tall, narrow, five story building with three stories of bay windows and another two stories above them of more modest windows— where once servants had dwelt no doubt. It was the color of warm honey, lighter than the traditional brownstone, and it sported lace curtains at the first floor bay windows making it look pleasant and professional at the same time.

Besides the lack of signs, there were no astrology signs or crystal balls in sight. No tiny fairy lights flickering in the windows, either. None of the "hocus-pocus" Lukas had mentioned. Alex breathed a sigh of relief.

He straightened his tie, took a deep breath, strode up the steps and opened the outside door. In the tiny foyer, on the mailbox for apartment 1, he saw her name: *Daisy Connolly.* Resolutely he pressed the buzzer.

For half a minute there was no response at all. Alex shifted from one foot to the other and ground his teeth at the thought of wasting the end of an afternoon coming all the way to the Upper West Side for nothing.

But just as he was about to turn away, he heard the sound of a lock being turned. The door opened into the shadow-filled front hall and he could see the silhouette of a slim woman coming to push open the door to admit him.

She was smiling—until their gazes met. Then the smile faded and the color drained from her face.

She stared at him, stricken. "Alex?"

Honey-blonde hair. Deep blue eyes. A memory of scorching hot kisses. *"Daisy?"*

Alex? Here? No!

No. No. No.

But all the time the word was banging around inside Daisy's head, the truth—all six feet of his whipcord-lean, muscular, gorgeous male self—was staring at her in the face.

Why in heaven's name couldn't she have looked out the window before she'd answered the door?

The answer was simple: Alexandros Antonides was so far in her past she never ever considered that he might turn up on her doorstep.

She'd been expecting Philip Cannavarro.

She'd done a photo shoot with the Cannavarro family—

Phil, Lottie and their three children—last month at the beach. A week and a half ago, they had chosen their photos, and Philip had called at lunch to ask if he could drop by after work and pick up their order.

So when the buzzer had sounded at twenty minutes to six, Daisy had opened the door with a smile on her face and an embossed portfolio of photos in her hand—a portfolio that the sight of Alexandros Antonides had let slip from her nerveless fingers.

"Oh, hell."

Her heart hammering, Daisy stooped quickly and began gathering up the photos. Focusing on that gave her a few moments of time and a little bit of space to get her bearings. Ha. *What was he doing here?*

She hadn't seen Alex in years and she had never expected to ever see him again. Only the fact that he seemed as surprised as she was allowed her to breathe at all.

She stopped doing that, though, when he crouched down beside her and began to help pick up the photos.

"Don't do that. Leave them," she said, trying to snatch them away from him. "I can do it!"

But Alex didn't let go. He simply kept right on. He only said, "No."

And there it was—the same single word, delivered in the same implacable tone that he'd said five years ago—that one that had pulled the rug right out from under her hopes and dreams.

Worse, though, was that his rough-edged, slightly accented, unconsciously sexy baritone still resonated all the way to the core of her exactly as it had from the moment she'd first heard him speak. It was as if he had been her very own personal pied piper of Hamelin. And foolishly, mindlessly, Daisy had fallen under his spell.

Then she'd called it "love at first sight." *Then* she had believed in the foolishness of such fairy tales.

Now she knew better. Now she knew the danger of it, thank God. There would be no falling under his spell again. She gathered the last of the photos, no longer in any shape to be presented to Philip Cannavarro, and got to her feet.

"What are you doing here?" she demanded, stepping away as he rose to his feet, too.

He shook his head, looking as dazed as she felt. "You're Daisy?" He glanced at a piece of paper he held in his hand, then frowned. "Well, of course you are, but…Connolly?"

Daisy lifted her chin. "That's right. Why?"

But before she got an answer, another man appeared outside on the stoop, just beyond the heavy front door and looked past Alex questioningly.

Daisy's knees went weak with relief. "Phil! Come on in!" He might as well have been the cavalry come to her rescue. She beamed at him.

Alex turned and stared over his shoulder, his brows drawing down. "Who's he?" he demanded as if he had more right there than her client.

Fortunately Phil was already pulling the door open, glancing in quick succession at Daisy's relieved face and Alex's scowl and finally at the photos in Daisy's hands. "Sorry. Didn't mean to interrupt—"

"You weren't," Daisy said quickly. "But I heard the bell. I thought it was you, not—" she gestured helplessly toward Alex who was standing so she could almost feel the heat of his body "—and I accidentally dropped your photos. I am so sorry." She gave Phil a hopeful smile. "I need to have them redone."

"Don't worry about it. They're probably just a little frayed at the edges," Phil said cheerfully. "No problem." He held out his hand and doubtless would have taken them from her, but Daisy shook her head and clutched them against her chest like a shield.

"No," she said. "I guarantee my work. And I don't give less than my best. You and Lottie deserve my best." He and Lottie had been one of the first matches she'd made. Lottie had been a makeup artist she'd met when she first began working as a photographer after college. Phil used to do her taxes. She felt almost like their mother even though they were older than she was. And she wasn't giving them less than her best.

"I'll put a rush on it," she promised. "You should have them in two days. I'll have them couriered directly to your house."

Phil looked doubtful. "We won't mind," he said. "Lottie will want…"

"Take these then." Daisy thrust them at him. "But tell her they're just until the new ones come in. Tell her I'm so sorry. Tell her—" She shut her mouth, the only way to stop babbling.

Phil fumbled with the photos, too, then stuffed them in his briefcase, shooting Daisy worried sidelong glances. "Are you sure you're okay?"

"I'm fine," she lied.

But she knew why he was asking. Phil and Lottie were used to the unflappable Daisy, the one who rolled with the punches, adjusted on the fly, never worried if life threw pitchforks in her path.

"Daisy always copes," Lottie said. It was like a mantra.

Daisy wasn't exactly coping now. Alex's mere presence created an electricity in the air, a force field of awareness she could never manage to be indifferent to. Damn it.

"She'll be fine," Alex said smoothly now. "She's just had

a bit of a shock." He stepped even closer and looped an arm over her shoulders.

Daisy nearly jumped out of her skin. At the same time, though, her traitorous body clamored to sink into his embrace. Muscle memory was a dangerous thing. Daisy held herself rigid, resisting him, resisting her own inclination.

"She'll be all right. I'll take care of her." Alex's tone was all reassurance as he smiled and somehow put himself between her and Phil, edging the other man toward the door, making it clear that Phil didn't need to hang around.

Phil didn't hang around. He understood male territoriality as well as the next guy. "Right," he said, all smiles and cheerful bravado. "I'll tell Lottie."

And he was out the door and down the steps without glancing back.

"Thank you very much," Daisy said drily, slipping out from beneath his arm, which still managed to leave her with a sense that it was still there. She could feel the warm weight of it even though she'd stepped away. Instinctively she wrapped her own arms across her chest.

What was he doing here? The question pounded again in her brain.

"Daisy." The way he said her name was somewhere between musing and caressing. It sent the hairs on the back of her neck straight up. A slight smile played at the corners of his mouth. "It is fate," he murmured.

"What?" Daisy said sharply.

"I was just thinking about you." His tone was warm. He acted as if they were old friends. Well, maybe to him that was all they were.

"I can't imagine why," Daisy said, which was the absolute truth.

"I'm looking for a wife."

She stared at him, her jaw dropping.

He just smiled, expecting no doubt to hear her say, *Oh, yes, please! Pick me.*

Daisy hugged her arms more tightly across her chest. "Good luck with that." She could have said, *You don't want a wife. You made a huge point of telling me you didn't want a wife!*

Now Alex raised his brows. The smile still lurking. "I wasn't proposing," he said mildly.

Mortified, Daisy said stiffly, "Of course you weren't."

She wasn't going to bring up the past at all. It did her no credit. She'd been young and stupid and far too romantic for her own good when they'd met five years ago at a wedding reception.

Daisy had been one of her college roommate, Heather's, bridesmaids, and Alex had been pressed into service as a last-minute substitute for a sick groomsman. Their eyes had met—something wild and hot and amazing had sparked between them—and to Daisy's fevered romantic twenty-three-year-old brain, it had been one of those meant-to-be moments.

They had only had eyes for each other from the moment they'd met. They talked, they danced, they laughed, they touched. The electricity between them could have lit New York City day and night for a week.

So this was love at first sight. She remembered thinking that, stunned and delighted to finally experience it. She had, of course, always believed. Her parents had always told Daisy and her sister that they'd known from the moment they'd met that they were destined to be together.

Julie, Daisy's sister, had felt that way about Brent, the moment she'd met him in eighth grade. They'd married right out of high school. Twelve years later, they were still deeply in love.

Daisy had never felt that way—wasn't sure she believed it—until the day Alex had walked into her life.

That afternoon had been so extraordinary, so mind-numbingly, body-tinglingly perfect that she'd believed. It was just the way her parents had described it, the way Julie had described it—the sense of knowing, of a belief that all the planets were finally lined up, that the absolutely right man had come into her life.

Of course she hadn't said so. Not then. She'd just met Alex. But she hadn't wanted the day to end—and he hadn't, either. She was the bridesmaid who had been deputized to take Heather's car back to Manhattan after the reception.

"I'm coming, too," Alex had said in that rough sexy baritone, and his eyes had met hers. "If that's all right with you."

Of course it had been all right with her. It was just one more reason to believe he was feeling the same thing, too. Together they had driven back to Manhattan. And all the way there, they had talked.

He was an architect working for a multinational firm, but eager to strike out on his own. He had his own ideas, a desire to blend old and new, to create both beauty and utility and to design buildings that made people more alive, that spoke to their hearts and souls. His eyes had lit up when he'd talked about his goals, and she had shared his enthusiasm.

He had shared hers about her own professional hopes and dreams. She was working for Finn MacCauley, one of the preeminent fashion and lifestyle photographers in the country. It was almost like an apprenticeship, she'd told him. She was learning so much from Finn, but was looking forward, like Alex was, to finding her own niche.

"People definitely," she'd told him. "Families, kids, people at work and play. I'd like to shoot you," she'd told him. She wanted to capture the moment, the man.

And Alex had simply said, "Whenever you want."

When they got to the city, she had left the car in the parking garage by Heather's Upper East Side apartment, then she'd taken Alex downtown on the subway to the Soho flat she was subleasing from a dental student on a semester's internship abroad.

On the subway, Alex had caught her hand in his, rubbing his thumb over her fingers, then dipping his head to touch his lips to hers. It was a light touch, the merest promise, but it set her blood on fire. And when he pulled back, she caught her breath because, looking into his eyes, she had seen a hunger there that was as deep and intense as her own.

It had never happened before. A desire so powerful, so intense just grabbed her—and it wouldn't let go. Daisy wasn't used to this sort of intensity. She didn't fall into bed at the drop of a hat, had only once before fallen into bed with a man at all. It had been fevered groping on his part and discomfort on hers.

With Alex, she'd tried telling herself, it would be more of the same.

But it wasn't.

His kisses were nothing like any she'd tasted before. They were heady, electric, bone-melting. They'd stood on the sidewalk nearly devouring each other. Not something Daisy had ever done!

She couldn't get him back to her apartment fast enough.

Once there, though, she'd felt suddenly awkward, almost shy. "Let me take your picture," she'd said.

And Alex had given her a lazy teasing smile and said, "If that's what you want."

Of course it wasn't what she wanted—or not entirely what she wanted. And it wasn't what he wanted, either. It was foreplay. Serious and smiling, goofing around, letting her direct him this way and that, all the way watching her—burning her up!—from beneath hooded lids.

He wanted her. He didn't have to say it. They circled each other, moved in, moved away. The temperature in the room rose. The temperature in Daisy's blood was close to boiling.

Then Alex had reached out and took the camera from her. He aimed, shot, posed her, caught the ferocity of her desire, as well. He stripped off his jacket, she unbuttoned his shirt. He skimmed down the zip of her dress. But before he could peel it off, she had taken the camera back, set the timer and wrapped her arms around him.

The photo of the two of them together, caught up in each other, had haunted her for years.

But at the time she hadn't been thinking about anything but the moment—the man. Within moments the camera was forgotten and in seconds more the rest of their clothing was gone.

And then there was nothing between them at all.

Alex bore her back onto her bed, settled beside her and bent his dark head, nuzzling her breasts, tasting, teasing, suckling, making her gasp and squirm.

And Daisy, shyness long gone, had been desperate to learn every inch of him. She'd prowled and played, made him suck in his breath and say raggedly, "You're killing me!"

But when she'd pulled back he'd drawn her close again. "Don't stop," he'd said.

They hadn't stopped—neither one of them. They'd driven

each other to the height of ecstasy. And it wasn't at all like that other time.

With Alex there was no discomfort, there was no second-guessing, no wondering if she was doing the right thing. It had been lovemaking at its most pure and elemental, and so perfect she could have cried.

After, lying wrapped in his arms, knowing the rightness of it, she had believed completely in her mother's assertion that there was a "right man"—and about knowing instinctively when you met him.

She'd met Alex and—just like her parents, just like her sister and Brent—she had fallen in love.

They'd talked into the wee hours of the morning, sharing stories of their childhood, of their memories, of the best and worst things that had ever happened to them.

She told him about the first camera she'd ever had—that her grandfather had given her when she was seven. He told her about the first time he'd climbed a mountain and thought he could do anything. She told him about her beloved father who had died earlier that winter and about the loss she felt. He understood. He told her about losing his only brother to leukemia when he was ten and his brother thirteen. They had talked and they had touched. They had stroked and smiled and kissed.

And they had made love again. And again.

It was always going to be like that, Daisy vowed. She had met the man of her dreams, the one who understood her down to the ground, the man she would love and marry and have children with and grow old with—

—until she'd said so.

She remembered that Sunday morning as if it had been yesterday.

They'd finally fallen asleep in each other's arms at dawn. When Daisy had awakened again it was nearly ten. Alex was still asleep, sprawled on his back in her bed, bare-chested, the duvet covering him below the waist. He was so beautiful. She could have just sat there and stared at him forever, tracing the strong lines of his features, the hollows made by his collarbone, the curve of muscle in his arms, the long, tapered fingers that had made her quiver with their touch. She remembered how he'd looked, naked and primal, rising above her when they'd made love.

She would have liked to do it again. She had wanted to slide back beneath the duvet and snuggle up against him, to rub the sole of her foot up and down his calf, then let her fingers walk up and down his thigh, and press kisses to the line of dark hair that bisected his abdomen.

But as much as she wanted to do that, she also wanted to feed him before he had to catch his plane. She knew he had an early evening flight to Paris where he would be spending the next month at the main office of the firm he worked for. She'd hated the thought of him leaving, but she consoled herself by hoping that when he started his own company he would bring it stateside. Or maybe she would follow him to Paris.

Daisy had tried to imagine what living in Paris—living in Paris with Alex—would be like while she made them eggs and bacon and toast for breakfast. The thoughts made her smile. They made her toes curl.

She'd been standing at the stove, toes curling as she turned the bacon when hard muscled arms had come around her and warm breath had touched her ear.

"Morning," Alex murmured, the burr of his voice sending a shiver of longing right through her.

"Morning yourself." She'd smiled as he had kissed her ear,

her nape, her jaw, then turned her in his arms and took her mouth with a hunger that said, *The hell with breakfast. Let's go back to bed.*

But she'd fed him a piece of bacon, laughing as he'd nibbled her fingers. And she'd actually got him to eat eggs and toast as well before they'd rolled in the sheets once more.

Finally in the early afternoon he'd groaned as he sat up and swung his legs out of bed. "Got to grab a shower. Come with me?" He'd cocked his head, grinning an invitation that, despite feeling boneless already, Daisy hadn't been able to refuse.

The next half hour had been the most erotic experience of her life. Both of them had been wrung out, beyond boneless—and squeaky clean—by the time the hot water heater had begun to run cold.

"I need to go," he'd said, kissing her thoroughly once more as he pulled on a pair of cords and buttoned up his shirt.

"Yes," she agreed, kissing him back, but then turning away long enough to stuff her legs into a pair of jeans and pluck a sweater from the drawer. "I'll go out to the airport with you."

Alex had protested that it wasn't necessary, that he was perfectly capable of going off by himself, he did it all the time.

But Daisy was having none of it. She'd smiled saucily and said, "Yes, but now you have me."

She'd gone with him to the airport, had sat next to him in the back of the hired car and had shared long drugging kisses that she expected to live off until he returned.

"I'll miss you," she'd told him, nibbling his jaw. "I can't believe this has happened. That we found each other. I never really believed, but now I do."

"Believed?" Alex lifted his head from where he'd been kissing her neck long enough to gaze into her eyes. "In what?"

"This." She punctuated the word with a kiss, then looked

deeply into his eyes. "You. Me. It's just like my mother said. Love at first sight." She smiled, then sighed. "I just hope we get more years than they did."

There was a sudden stillness in him. And then a slight movement as he pulled back. A small line appeared between his brows. "Years? They?"

"My parents. They fell in love like this. Took one look at each other and fell like a ton of bricks. There was never anyone else for either of them. They were two halves of the same soul. They should have had fifty years. Seventy-five," Daisy said recklessly. "Instead of twenty-six."

Alex didn't move. He barely seemed to breathe. The sparkle in his light green eyes seemed suddenly to fade.

Daisy looked at him, concerned. "What's wrong?"

He'd swallowed. She could remember the way she'd watched his Adam's apple move in his throat, then the way he'd shaken his head slowly and said, "You're talking a lifetime, aren't you?"

And ever honest, Daisy had nodded. "Yes."

There had been a split second before the world tilted. Then Alex had sucked in a harsh breath. "No." Just the one word. Hard, decisive, determined. Then, apparently seeing the look on her face, he'd been at pains to assure her. "Oh, not for you. I'm not saying you won't have a lifetime…with someone. But…not me."

She remembered staring at him, stunned at the change in him. He seemed to have pulled inside himself. Closed off. Turned into the Ice Man as she'd watched. "What?" Even to her own ears her voice had sounded faint, disbelieving.

Alex's jaw set. "I'm not getting married," he'd told her. "Ever."

"But—"

"I don't want to."

"But—"

"No." His tone was implacable. Yet despite the coldness of his tone, there was fire in his eyes. "No hostages to fortune," he'd said. "No wife. No kids. No falling in love. Too much pain. Never again."

"Because…because of your brother?" She had only barely understood that kind of pain. Her parents had been gloriously happily married until her father's death a month before. And she had witnessed what her mother was going through after. There was no doubt it was hard. It was hard on her and on her sister, too. But her parents had had a beautiful marriage. It had been worth the cost.

She'd tried to explain that to Alex in the car. He hadn't wanted to hear it.

"It's fine for you if that's what you want," he'd said firmly. "I don't."

"But last night…this morning…?" Daisy had been grasping desperately at straws.

"You were great," he'd said. Their gazes had met for a moment. Then deliberately Alex looked away.

By the time they'd arrived at the airport, there were no more kisses, only a silence as big and dark as the Atlantic that would soon stretch between them. Alex didn't look at her again. His fingers were fisted against his thighs as he stared resolutely out the window.

Daisy had stared at him, willed him to reconsider, to believe—to give them a chance!

"Maybe I was asking for too much too soon," she ventured at last as their hired car reached the airport departure lanes. "Maybe when you come back…"

Alex was shaking his head even as he turned and looked at her. "No," he said, his voice rough but adamant.

She blinked quickly, hoping he didn't notice the film of unshed tears in her eyes as she stared at him mutely.

"I won't be back, Daisy. A lifetime is what you want," he'd said. "I don't."

It was the last thing he'd said to her—the last time she'd seen him—until she'd opened the door a few minutes ago.

Now she dared to stare at him for just a moment as she tried to calm her galloping heart and mend her frayed nerves, tried to stuff Alexandros Antonides back into the box in the distant reaches of her mind where she'd done her best to keep him for the past five years.

It wasn't any easier to feel indifferent now than it ever had been. He was certainly every bit as gorgeous as he had been then. A shade over six feet tall, broad-shouldered in a pale blue dress shirt and a gray herringbone wool sport coat, his tie loosened at his throat, Alex looked like the consummate successful professional. His dark hair was cut a little shorter now, but it was still capable of being wind-tossed. His eyes were still that clear, light gray-green, arresting in his tanned face with its sharply defined cheekbones and blade-straight nose. And his sensuous mouth was, heaven help her, more appealing than ever with its hint of a smile.

"Why are you here?" she demanded now.

"Lukas sent me," he said.

"Lukas?"

Alex's cousin Lukas had been her official "other half" at the wedding where she'd met Alex. He'd insisted she stay by his side at the reception long enough so that his mother and aunts wouldn't fling hopeful Greek girls at his head. Once he'd established that he wasn't available, he'd given her a conspiratorial wink, a peck on the cheek and had ambled off to drink beer with his brothers and cousins, leaving her to fend for herself.

That was when she'd met Alex.

Now Alex pulled a piece of paper out of his pocket and poked it in front of her face. "He said I should talk to his friend Daisy the matchmaker."

Yes, there it was—her name, address and phone number—in Lukas's spiky handwriting. But she was more arrested by his words than what he was waving in front of her face. "You're looking for a matchmaker? *You?*"

Alex shrugged. "No doubt you're amazed," he said easily. "Thinking I've changed my mind."

She didn't know what to think.

"I haven't," he said firmly. "I'm not looking for hearts and flowers, kindred spirits, the melding of two souls any more than I ever was."

She wondered if he was being so adamant in case she decided to propose. No fear of that, she wanted to tell him. Instead she pressed her lips into a tight line.

"I want a marriage of convenience," Alex went on. "A woman with her own life, doing her own thing. She'll go her way, I'll go mine. But someone who will turn up if a business engagement calls for it. And who's there…at night."

"A sex buddy?" Daisy said drily.

Was that a line of color creeping above his shirt collar? "Friends," he said firmly. "We'll be friends. It's not just about sex."

"Hire a mistress."

"I don't want a mistress. That *is* just about sex."

"Whatever. I can't help you," she said flatly.

"Why not? You're a matchmaker."

"Yes, but I'm a matchmaker who does believe in hearts and flowers, kindred spirits, the melding of two souls." She echoed his words with a saccharine smile. "I believe in real marriages. Love matches. Soul mates. The kind you don't believe in." She met his gaze steadily, refusing to look away from those beautiful pale green eyes that she'd once hoped to drown in forever.

Alex's jaw tightened. "I believe in them," he said harshly. "I just don't want one."

"Right. So I repeat, I can't help you." She said the words again, meant them unequivocally. But even as she spoke in a calm steady tone, her heart was hammering so hard she could hear it.

Their gazes met. Locked. And with everything in her, Daisy resisted the magnetic pull that was still there. But even as she fought it, she felt the rise of desire within her, knew the feelings once more that she'd turned her back on the day he'd walked out of her life. It wasn't love, she told herself. It was something else—something as powerful and perverse and demanding as anything she'd ever felt.

But she was stronger now, and no longer an innocent. She had a life—and a love in it—that was worth resisting Alex Antonides.

"I hope you find what you're looking for," she said, holding his gaze. "It was nice to see you again."

It was, she hoped, a clear dismissal. It was also a blatant lie. She could have gone the rest of her life without seeing Alex again and died a happy woman. She didn't need a reminder of the stupidest thirty hours of her life. But in another way, she was aware of owing him her unending gratitude.

That single day had forever changed her life.

"Was it?" he asked. His words were as speculative as his

gaze. He smiled. And resist as she would, she saw in that smile the man who once upon a time had melted her bones, her resolve, every shred of her common sense, then broken her heart.

She turned away. "Goodbye, Alex."

"Daisy." His voice stopped her.

She glanced back. "What?"

The smile grew rueful, crooked, far too appealing. "Have dinner with me."

Chapter 2

"What? *No!*" She looked panic-stricken. Horrified.

Not at all like the Daisy he remembered. And yet she was so much the Daisy he remembered that Alex couldn't just turn and walk away. Not now. Not when he'd finally found her again. "Why not?"

"Because…because I don't want to!" Her cheeks had grown red in the throes of passion. Her whole body had blushed when he'd made love to her. His body—right now—was already contemplating doing the same thing again.

Which was a profoundly stupid idea, considering what he wanted, what she wanted, considering the present—and their past.

"Do you hate me?" he asked. He remembered the way they had parted. She'd looked devastated, about to cry. Thank God she hadn't. But what she'd wanted—the hope of a lifetime of love—was his worst nightmare. It brought back memories that he'd turned his back on years ago. What had begun happening between them that weekend was something he wasn't ready for. Would never be ready for.

So there was no point in making her hope in vain. He regretted having hurt her when he'd left her. But he could never bring himself to regret that weekend. It was one of the best memories of his life.

"Of course I don't hate you," she said briskly now. "I don't care at all about you."

Her words were a slap in the face. But he supposed he had it coming. And it was just as well, wasn't it, that she didn't care? It meant he hadn't hurt her badly after all.

"Well, then," he suggested easily, "let's share a meal." He gave her his best engaging grin. "For old times' sake," he added when he could see the word *no* forming on her lips.

"We don't have old times."

"We have one old time," he reminded her softly.

Her cheeks grew brighter yet. "That was a long, long time ago. Years. Five or six at least."

"Five," he said. "And a half." He remembered clearly. It was right after that weekend that he'd made up his mind to stay in Europe, to buy a place in Paris.

It made sense businesswise, he'd told himself at the time. But it wasn't only business that had made him dig in across the pond. It was smarter to put an ocean between himself and the temptation that was Daisy.

She was still tempting. But a dinner he could handle. "It's just a meal, Daisy. I promise I won't sweep you off to bed." Not that he wouldn't like to.

"You couldn't," she said flatly.

He thought he could, but emotions would get involved. So he wouldn't go there, as tempting as it was. Still, he wasn't willing to walk away, either. "We have a lot to catch up on," he cajoled.

But Daisy shook her head. "I don't think so." Her smile was brittle. He saw none of the sunny sincerity he'd always associated with his memories of her. Interesting.

He studied her now, wondering what her life had been like over the past five years. He'd always imagined she'd found the true love she'd been seeking, had found a man who'd made her happy. And if the thought occasionally had made him grind his teeth, he told himself a guy couldn't have everything. He had what he wanted.

Now he wondered if Daisy had got what she wanted. Suddenly he wanted to know.

"Another time then," he suggested.

"Thank you, but no."

He knew he was going to get "no" if he asked a hundred times. And the knowledge annoyed him. "Once upon a time we had a lot to say to each other," he reminded her.

"Once upon a time is for fairy tales, Alex. Now, if you'll excuse me, I have to go."

"Let's," he said readily. "I'll walk with you."

"I don't mean go somewhere else," she said. "I mean I have to go back inside. I have work to do. In my office."

"Matchmaking?"

She shook her head. "Not tonight."

"Photography?" He remembered the camera, how it had been almost a natural extension of who she was.

She nodded, smiling a little. It was a real smile.

"You've got your own business then?" he pressed.

"Yes." She nodded. The smile stayed.

"Families? Kids? People of all shapes and sizes?" And at her further nod, he said, "Show me."

She almost moved toward the door, almost started to invite him in. But then she stayed where she was, gave her head a little shake. "I don't think so."

"You took photos of us." Sometimes he'd wished he had one. To take out and remember. But that was stupid. It was better to forget.

She shrugged and looked just a little uncomfortable. He wondered if she still had the photos.

"Why matchmaking?" he asked her suddenly.

She shrugged. "Long story." And no invitation to ask her to tell it.

He lifted a corner of his mouth. "I've got time."

"I don't."

"You're scared."

The color in her cheeks bloomed again. "I am not scared! What's there to be scared of?"

"I don't know. You tell me." He cocked his head. "Temptation maybe?"

She shook her head adamantly. "I'm not tempted. I'm busy. I have things to do. I haven't seen you in five years, Alex. I barely knew you then. We don't have a past to catch up on."

"We had a hell of a lot." He didn't know why he was persisting, but he couldn't seem to leave it alone.

"And we wanted to do different things with it. Goodbye, Alex." She turned away and started to go back inside.

But before she could, Alex caught her arm, and spun her slowly back, then did what he'd been wanting to do ever since he'd realized who she was.

He dipped his head and kissed her.

It was instinct, desire, a mad impetuous hunger that he couldn't seem to control. It was a roaring in his ears and a fire in his veins. It was the taste of Daisy—a taste he'd never forgotten. *Never.* And as soon as he tasted her, he wanted more.

And more.

For a second, maybe two, Daisy seemed to melt under the touch of his lips. She went soft and pliable, shaping her mouth to his. And then, in another instant, it was over.

She jerked away from him, stared at him for one horrified moment, cheeks scarlet, mouth still forming an astonished O. Then she pulled out of his grasp and bolted back inside the foyer.

"Daisy!"

The door slammed in his face.

Alex stared after her, still tasting her. Jolted, intrigued, stunned. Aroused.

Five years ago Daisy had been like a siren he'd followed eagerly, mindlessly, hungrily. He'd wanted her on every level imaginable. And having her that weekend over and over hadn't assuaged his hunger. He'd only wanted more.

Leaving, thank God, had removed the temptation.

And now—within minutes of having seen her again—it was back. In spades.

It was the last thing he wanted. The last thing he needed.

Alex turned and walked down the steps, pausing only to drop the paper with her name and address in the trash.

She had been right to say no. He would be smart and walk away.

Ten minutes later Daisy was still shaking.

She sat at her desk, staring at the photo she was editing, and didn't see it at all. Eyes closed or open, she only saw Alex—older, harder, stronger, handsomer—in every way *more*, even more compelling than the younger Alex had been.

She shuddered and scrubbed at her mouth with her fingers, trying to wipe away the taste of his kiss.

But all the scrubbing in the world wouldn't do that, and she knew it. She'd tried to forget it for years. It hadn't done a whit of good.

She hadn't even tried to forget him. That would have been impossible. But as time passed, at least she'd managed to put him on a shelf in the back of her memory's closet. He was still there, but he couldn't hurt her.

But now Alex was here.

She'd just seen him, talked to him. Been kissed by him. Had almost, heaven help her, kissed him back. It had felt so right, so perfect, so exactly the way it had felt the first time.

But she knew better now.

He had come. He had gone. The other shoe had finally dropped. He wouldn't come back.

"And it wouldn't matter if he did," Daisy said aloud.

Because if one thing was completely obvious, it was that however much more he had become, in fundamentals, Alex hadn't changed a bit.

He might want to get married now, but he obviously didn't want anything more than "friends—with benefits." He didn't want love. He didn't want a real marriage. He didn't want a family.

He didn't want her.

For a nanosecond her traitorous heart had dared to believe he'd finally come to his senses, had learned the value of love, of relationships, of lifetime commitment.

Thank goodness, a nanosecond was all the time it had taken her to realize that there was no point in getting her hopes up.

Of course he had proved he still wanted her on one level— the one he had always wanted her on. She wasn't such an innocent that she didn't know desire when she felt it. And she had felt it hard and firm against her when Alex had kissed her and pressed his body against hers.

But physical desire was just that—a basic instinctive response. It had nothing to do with things that really mattered—love, commitment, responsibility, sharing of hearts and souls, dreams and desires.

It was nothing more than an itch to be scratched.

And she wasn't about to be a matchmaker for a pairing like that. If he was interested in nothing more than a woman to share his bed—but not his heart—he wouldn't be interested in the sort of marriages she believed in. So he wouldn't be back.

And thank God for that—because if her heart still beat faster at the very sight of him and her body melted under his touch, at least her mind knew he was the last person she needed in her life.

Not just in her life, but in the life of the person she loved most in all the world—the one who, at this very moment, she could hear pounding his way up the stairs from the kitchen.

"Mom!" His voice was distant at first, then louder. "Mom!" And louder still as the door banged open. "Mom! Aren'tcha finished working yet? It's time to go."

Charlie.

Four and three-quarter years of sunshine and skinned knees and wet kisses and impatience all rolled up in the most wonderful person she knew.

He skidded to a stop in front of her and looked up at her, importuning. "Mom!"

"Charlie!" She smiled at him, echoing his tone, loving him with all her heart.

"Are you ready?" he demanded.

"Almost." She turned back to close the file she hadn't done

a thing to since Alex had shown up on the doorstep. "Almost," she repeated, taking a deep breath to steady her nerves, then shutting the file.

She wished she could shut her memories of Alex down as easily. She couldn't. Particularly she couldn't right now—faced with the small boy staring up at her, all quivering impatience.

Impatience wasn't Charlie's middle name, but maybe it should have been. He'd been eager and energetic since the moment of his birth. Before his birth, in fact. He'd come almost two weeks early, right before Christmas. And he'd been taking the world by storm ever since.

He had a chipped tooth from a fall out of a tree back in May. He had a scab on his knee beneath his jeans even now. Daisy had told him last week she was going to buy stock in the Band-Aid company, and after he'd wrinkled his nose and said, "What's stock?" he'd listened to her brief explanation and said, "Good idea."

His stick-straight hair, the color of honey shot through with gold, was very close to the same shade as her own. But his light eyes were nothing like her stormy dark blue.

He didn't look like Alex—except for the shape of his eyes.

And after nearly five years, she was inured to it. She didn't see Alex in him every time she looked at him. She saw Charlie himself—not Alex's son.

Except today. Today the eyes were Alex's. The impatience was Alex's. The "let's get moving" was Alex down to the ground.

"In good time," she said now, determined to slow Charlie down—a little, at least. But she managed a smile as she shut the computer down. And she was sure she was the only one who noticed her hands were shaking.

"You said we'd go at six-thirty. It's almost six-thirty. The game's gonna start." He grabbed one of Daisy's hands and began to tug her back toward the stairs.

"Coming," Daisy said. But she straightened her desk, made a note to reorder the Cannavarro files, put her pencil in the drawer. All very methodical. Orderly. Step by step. Pay attention to detail. From the day that she'd learned she was pregnant, it was how she'd managed to cope.

Charlie bounced from one foot to the other until she finished and finally held out a hand to him again. "Okay. Let's go." She allowed herself to be towed down the stairs.

"We gotta hurry. We're gonna be late. Come on. Dad's pitching."

Dad. One more reason she prayed that Alexandros Antonides didn't darken her door again.

"Hey, Sport." Cal dropped down beside Charlie on the other side of the blanket that Daisy had spread out to sit on while they watched the softball game.

They had been late, as Charlie feared, arriving between innings. But at least Cal, Daisy's ex-husband, had already pitched in his half, so he could come sit with them until it was his turn to bat.

"We made a fire engine," Charlie told him. "Me 'n' Jess. Outta big red cardboard blocks—this big!" He stretched his hands out a couple of feet at least.

Cal looked suitably impressed. "At preschool?"

Charlie bobbed his head. "You an' me could make one."

"Okay. On Saturday," Cal agreed. "But we'll have to use a cardboard box and paint it red. Grandpa will be in town. I'll tell him to bring paint."

Charlie's eyes got big. "Super! Wait'll I tell Jess 'bout ours."

"You don't want to make him jealous," Cal warned. He grinned at Charlie, then over the boy's head at his mother.

Daisy smiled back and told herself that nothing had changed. Nothing. She and Charlie were doing what they often did—dropping by to watch Cal play ball in Central Park, which he and a few diehards continued to do well after the softball leagues ended in the summer. Now, in early October, there was a nip in the air, and the daylight was already going. But they continued to play.

And she and Charlie would continue to come and watch.

It was the joy of a civilized divorce, Daisy often reminded herself. She and Cal didn't hate each other—and they both loved Charlie.

"—you?"

She realized suddenly that Cal was no longer talking to Charlie. He was talking to her. "Sorry," she said, flustered. "I was just…thinking about something."

"Apparently," Cal said drily. Then he looked at her more closely. "What's wrong?"

"Nothing." She looked around. "Where's Charlie?"

Cal nodded in the direction of the trees where Charlie and the son of another one of the players were playing in the dirt. "He's fine. You're not. Something's wrong."

"No. Why should anything be wrong?" That was the trouble with Cal. He'd always been able to read her like a book.

"You're edgy. Distracted. Late," he said pointedly.

"I didn't realize you were timing me. I've got things on my mind, Cal. Work—"

But he cut her off. "And you're biting my head off, which isn't like you, Daze. And you must've come on the bus."

"The bus?" she said stupidly.

"You always walk, so Charlie can ride his bike." Cal looked

around pointedly. There was no bike because, he was right, they hadn't had time to bring it. Charlie wanted to ride his bike everywhere. It was the smallest two-wheeler Daisy had ever seen, but Charlie loved it. Daisy was sure he would have slept with it every night if she hadn't put her foot down. Cal had given it to Charlie for his fourth birthday.

Daisy had protested, had said he was too young, that no four-year-old needed a bike.

"Not every four-year-old," Cal had agreed. "Just this one." He'd met her skeptical gaze with confident brown eyes and quiet certainty. "Because he wants it more than anything on earth."

Daisy couldn't argue with that. If Charlie's first word hadn't been *bike* it had been in the first ten. He'd pointed and crowed, "Bike!" well before his first birthday. And he'd been desperate for a bicycle last winter. She hadn't thought it would last. But Cal had insisted, and he'd been right.

Charlie's eyes had shone when he'd spotted the bike that morning. And over the past six months, his love for it had only grown. Since Cal had helped him learn to balance and he could now ride it unaided, Charlie wanted to ride it everywhere.

Usually she let him ride to the park while she walked alongside him. But they had been late today because…because of her visitor.

She was suddenly aware that Cal was watching her, not the game. "He doesn't have to ride his bike every time," she said testily. "And it's nearly dark."

"True." Cal stretched his legs out in front of him and leaned back, resting his weight on his elbows and forearms as his gaze slowly moved away from her to focus on the game, yelling at the batter to focus. Then, still keeping his gaze on the batter, he persisted quietly, "So why don't you just tell me."

He wasn't going to leave it alone. She'd never won an argument with Cal. She'd never been able to convince him of anything. If he was wrong, he couldn't be told. He always had to figure it out himself—like his "I can love anyone I will myself to" edict. He'd been as wrong about that as she had been about her "love at first sight" belief.

Clearly, when it came to love, the two of them didn't know what they were talking about.

Now he stared at her and she plucked at the grass beside the blanket, stared at it. *Nothing's changed. Nothing's changed.* She tried to make it into a mantra so she could convince herself. But she was no better at lying to herself than she was at lying to her ex-husband. Finally she raised her gaze to meet his as he turned away from the game to look at her. "I saw Alex."

There was the crack of bat hitting ball. Whoops and yells abounded.

Cal never turned his head to see what happened. His eyes never left Daisy's. He blinked once. That was all. The rest of his body went still, though. And his words, when they came, were quiet. "Saw him where?"

Daisy ran her tongue over dry lips. "He came to my office."

Cal waited, not pressing, allowing her to tell the story in her own way, in her own time.

And she couldn't quite suppress the ghost of a smile that touched her lips. "Looking for a matchmaker."

"What!" Cal's jaw dropped.

Hysterical laughter bubbled up just as it had threatened to do when Alex told her. This time Daisy gave in to it. "He's looking for a wife."

"You?" Cal demanded.

"No. He was as surprised as I was when he knocked on my door. He didn't know he was coming to see me."

"Then how—?"

"Lukas sent him."

Cal's eyes widened. His teeth came together. "Lukas needs to mind his own business."

"Of course. But Lukas never does. Besides, he didn't have any idea what he was doing. He never knew about Alex and me. No one did." No one ever had except Cal—and only because when she'd discovered she was pregnant, she'd had to talk to someone. "Don't blame Lukas. He thinks he's doing me a favor sending clients my way. And he is, I suppose. Most of the time. Not this time," she said quietly.

"No." Cal stared down at his fingers plucking at the grass for a moment. Then his gaze lifted and went toward Charlie who was still playing with his friend in the dirt. The question was there, but unspoken.

"I didn't say a word."

"But he—"

Daisy shook her head. "No. That hasn't changed. He wouldn't want to know."

"Still?" Cal persisted.

"No. He doesn't want relationships any more than he ever did," Daisy said firmly. "He doesn't want a real wife—he wants a woman to take to social events and go to bed with. It will save him the effort of having to go out and find one, charm one."

"He charmed you," Cal pointed out.

Cal, of course, knew that. He knew the whole sordid story.

She had met Cal Connolly when she'd taken the job with Finn after college. Cal had been the photographer she'd replaced, Finn's assistant before her.

Even after Cal hung out his own shingle, he had regularly come by Finn's to talk shop. Daisy had been included in the conversation. She learned a great deal from both of them.

Finn was brilliant, mercurial—and impatient. Cal was steadier, calmer, more methodical. He didn't yell quite as much. Finn had a wife and growing family. Cal was single, on his own. So it was Cal she began to spend time with. And while Finn had always remained her mentor, Cal had quickly become her best pal.

When she wasn't working for Finn, she had spent hours working with Cal, talking with him, arguing with him. They argued about everything from camera lenses to baseball teams to sushi rolls, from free will to evolution to love at first sight.

That had always been their biggest argument: did you love because—bang!—it hit you between the eyes? Or did you love because you decided who the right person was and made up your mind?

Because of her parents, Daisy had been a staunch believer in the "love at first sight" notion.

"I just haven't met the right person," she had maintained over and over. "When I do, I'll know. In an instant. And it will be perfect."

But Cal had scoffed at that. Ever the logical realist, he'd said, "Nonsense. I don't believe it for a minute. That makes you nothing but a victim of your hormones."

"It's not hormones. It's instinct."

But Cal had disagreed. "You can will whom you love," he'd told her firmly. "It's a rational decision."

So when he'd proposed to her, he'd been determined to demonstrate just that. "Obviously your way doesn't work," he'd pointed out. "So we'll try it my way now."

And Daisy, because she did love Cal—just not the way she

thought she loved Alex—had faced the truth of her own folly. And she'd said yes.

It turned out they were both wrong. But they'd given it their best shot. And Daisy still did believe in love—now she had a codicil: it was apparently for other people.

Now Daisy let out a sigh and wrapped a blade of grass around her finger where Cal's wedding ring once had been.

"So, are you going to do it? Matchmake for him?" Cal asked.

"Of course not."

He grunted. "Good." He stared out across the field. "Was it...the same? Did you feel...this time...what you felt before?"

It was all Daisy could do not to touch her tongue to her lips. Instead she pulled her knees up and wrapped her arms around them, in full cocoon mode. "He's still charming," she admitted.

Cal had been watching the next batter swing and miss. But at her words he turned his head and shot her a sharp glance.

Daisy gave him a quick humorless smile. "Speaking objectively. Don't worry. I'm not a fool anymore."

"So I should hope."

The batter swung and missed. Cal hauled himself to his feet to go pitch another inning. "You all right? Anything I can do?"

"No. He won't be back."

Cal cocked his head. "No?" He didn't sound so sure.

"Why would he? I didn't invite him in. I didn't encourage him at all." *I didn't kiss him back!* "And he doesn't want me. He wants some woman who won't care."

"And Charlie?"

"He doesn't know about Charlie. I'm doing him a favor, really," she said firmly. "He doesn't want kids. He never did."

"Because he doesn't think he has any," Cal pointed out. "What if he finds out he does?"

"He won't."

"But if——" Cal persisted. It was what she hated about him.

"Charlie is mine! And yours."

She had always told Charlie—not that he understood yet really—that he had two fathers—a birth father who had given him life, and Cal, the father he knew. Charlie didn't question it. Someday he would, no doubt. But by then it would be ingrained in his mind. There would never be a time when she had to "tell him" his father was not Cal.

Because in every way that counted, his father was Cal. Cal was the one who had been there for her. He'd been her husband when Charlie was born. Charlie bore his surname. He was the only father Charlie knew.

If someday he wanted to know about Alex, she'd tell him. If someday in the distant future, Alex learned he had a child, perhaps they would meet. But not now. Now Charlie was a child. He was vulnerable. He didn't need a father who didn't want him.

"You don't know what he'll do, Daze," Cal said heavily, "if he finds out."

"He won't find out." She would make sure of that.

Cal's smile was grim. "We hope."

Chapter 3

A day went by. Two.

Daisy still kept looking over her shoulder—well, out the window, actually—feeling skittish. Apprehensive.

She checked the caller ID every time the phone rang. Her breath caught whenever she saw a shadow on the front steps.

She actually dropped the kettle she was filling this morning, even though it was just the FedEx man bringing an order to Mrs. Kaminski upstairs.

Now she was filling it again for her friend Nell, who had just brought Charlie home from preschool and was staying for a cup of tea and regarding her curiously all the while.

"Something wrong?"

"No. I just…dropped the kettle this morning. I'm trying to be more careful now." Daisy set it on the burner and turned the gas on.

"Cal giving you trouble?" It was always the first thing Nell thought of because her own ex-husband, Scott, was a continual source of irritation.

"Cal never gives me trouble," Daisy said. She glanced out the sliding door to the garden where Charlie and Nell's son Geoff were playing with trucks.

Nell grimaced. "Lucky you. Scott's driving me crazy."

Daisy wasn't glad to hear that Scott was creating difficulties in her friend's life, but talking about it did avert Nell's further interest in Daisy's edginess. She gave Daisy an earful about her ex while they drank their tea and ate biscotti. Daisy made soothing sounds, but Nell was still grumbling when she decided it was time to go. She called Geoff in and they headed out the front door.

Relieved that her life was nowhere near as complicated as her friend's, Daisy was feeling much more sanguine when the phone rang as the door shut behind Nell and her son.

"Daisy Connolly," she said brightly into the phone.

"Daisy." The voice was warm, slightly gruff and instantly recognizable. The intimate tone of it made the hairs on the back of Daisy's neck stand straight up. Why hadn't she checked the ID this time?

"Yes. This is Daisy," she said crisply. "Who is this?"

"You know who it is." There was a smile in his voice as he called her bluff.

"Alex," she said flatly because playing the fool any longer wasn't going to help matters a bit.

"See. I knew you'd figure it out." He was grinning now. She could hear that, too.

"What do you want?"

"Are you married?"

"What?"

"I remembered you weren't Daisy Connolly back then. Wasn't your last name Harris? Morris?"

"Harris."

There was a brief silence. "So you did marry." It wasn't a question.

"Yes," she said firmly.

"And now?"

"What do you mean, and now?" Why did he have to ask? What business was it of his?

"Are you still…married?"

What kind of question was that? Damn it. She wanted to lie. But she'd never been a good liar, and though her acquaintance with Alex hadn't been long, it had been intense. She was sure he would be able to tell if she did.

"I'm divorced." She bit the words out.

"Ah."

Which meant what? Never mind. She didn't want to know. "Alex," she said with all the patience she could muster. "I'm working."

"This is work."

"No. I told you, I'm not matchmaking for you."

"I got that. You don't want what I want." He parroted her sentiments back to her. "This is photography. Or are you going to turn me down for that, too?"

She opened her mouth, wanting desperately to do exactly that. But she wouldn't give him the satisfaction of knowing he'd rattled her. "What sort of photography?" she said. "I do family stuff."

"And weddings. And bar mitzvahs. And some professional head shots. Some editorial. Recreation. Ice skating," he added. "Frisbee in the park. Baseball games." He ticked off half a dozen scenarios that were all shoots she had actually done.

"How do you know that?"

"You have a website," he reminded her. "The internet is a wonderful thing."

Daisy, grinding her teeth, wasn't so sure. Her fingers tapped an irritated staccato on the countertop. Outside Charlie was making vrooming noises as he pushed his cars around the patio. Any minute he'd slide open the door and want a snack. To prevent it, she latched the sliding door and got some crackers out of the cupboard and cheese from the refrigerator, preempting his demand. "What did you have in mind?" she asked.

"I need photos. An architectural journal is doing a piece on me and some of the work I've done. They've got photos of my projects from all over the world. Now they want some of me on one of the sites." He paused. "They said they could send a photographer——"

"Then let them."

"But I'd rather have you."

She wanted to say, Why? But she didn't want to hear his answer. Besides, asking would open a whole new can of worms.

"Not my line," she said briskly as she slapped cheese between the crackers and made little sandwiches for Charlie.

"You do editorial. I've seen magazine articles."

"Yes. But I don't traipse all over the world. I work in the city."

"The building is in Brooklyn." He gave her a second to digest that, then added, "I seem to remember you cross the river."

They had crossed the river together coming back from the wedding on Long Island. Daisy felt the walls closing in.

"Yes, I cross the river. *If* I have time. I'm busy."

"Any time in the next two weeks," he said smoothly. "And don't tell me that every minute of your life is booked."

Daisy heard the challenge in his voice. It was just another way of saying, *I don't believe you're really over me at all. You still want me. And now that you're divorced you might not believe in that ridiculous "love at first sight" notion anymore. You might be glad for a roll in bed.*

And, if it weren't for Charlie, heaven help her, she might.

"Are you still there? Daisy?" he prompted when she didn't reply.

She drew a breath. "I might have something next week. Let me check." It was the only way she could think of to prove to him—and to herself—that she wasn't a weak-willed fool.

She put the cracker sandwiches on a paper plate, flipped up the latch and slid open the door. Charlie looked up and, at the sight of the plate, grinned and jumped to his feet.

Daisy put a finger to her lips to shush him before he could speak, grateful that she'd taught him almost since he could talk not to blurt things out where people on the phone could hear him. That way, she'd explained, he wouldn't have to have a babysitter as often if she could take calls as if she were in her office when, in fact, she was at home.

Charlie had learned quickly. Now he stuffed a cracker sandwich into his mouth, then carried the plate back to his trucks. For a moment, Daisy just watched him and felt her heart squeeze with love. Then quietly she slid the door shut and went to look at her appointment book.

"Where in Brooklyn? What sort of photos?" she asked as she flipped through the pages of her day planner.

"Park Slope." Alex gave her the address. "It's a pre-war building."

"I thought you were an architect. Don't you design new buildings?"

"Not this one. I built this one from the inside out. The outside is pretty much intact, except for the windows. I fixed the windows. The place was in really awful shape and the guy who owned it wanted it removed. He wanted me to put up a new building there. But when I got into it, I couldn't see tearing it down. Structurally it was sound. And it had some really strong period architectural features. It fit the block, the surroundings. So I made him a deal. I bought it from him and he bought land a couple of miles away. Then I built him what he wanted there, and I kept this one for myself."

The eagerness and the satisfaction in his voice reminded her of when he'd talked about his hopes for his career. He'd already done some big projects for the company he'd worked for then. But those had been projects he'd been assigned, ones that had been the vision of someone else. Now it sounded like he had taken the reins and was making his own choices, his own decisions.

"Are you your own boss now?" she asked, unable not to.

"For the last five years." He hesitated, then went on so smoothly she might have imagined the brief pause. "There was never going to be the perfect time to leave, so I just… jumped in."

"You like it?"

"Couldn't be happier," he said. "What about you? You've obviously left the guy you were working for."

"Finn? Yes. And I like what I'm doing, too."

"You can tell me all about it—if you can see a way to work me into your schedule?"

He made it sound very straightforward. A job. No more. No less. Maybe this really was all business.

Daisy could almost—but not quite—forget the way he'd kissed her. Deliberately she shoved the thought away. "What sort of thing does the writer have in mind?" she asked. "What do they want to feature?"

"Me," Alex said ruefully. "Up-and-coming architect, blah,

blah, blah. I designed a hospital wing—first one I've done—and it's up for some award."

"That's great." And not surprising, really. She imagined that Alex would be good at whatever he did. "Where? Nearby?"

"Upstate a ways. Same side of the river, though," he added drily. "They used staff photos for that. They want ones of me and of the place in Brooklyn because it's a new departure for me. So you'd be shooting it now—plenty of awful 'then' photos already available. And then they want some of me 'in my environment.'" His tone twisted the words wryly. "With a pencil protector in my pocket." She could hear his grin. "Playing with blueprints. I don't know. You will."

If she did it. And maybe she should. Maybe it was exactly what she needed to do—learn about the man, demythologize him, turn him into some digital files and eight-by-ten-inch glossies.

"I can spare a bit of time next Thursday afternoon. Say, around three?"

"Great. I'll pick you up."

"I'll meet you. Just give me the address again." It was business. Just business.

He gave her the address. She wrote it down.

Then he said, "See you Thursday. Bye."

And he was gone. Just like that.

She had second thoughts. And third. And thirty-third. By the time Saturday rolled around, it was all she could think about.

"So call him and tell him you can't," Cal said when he came by to pick up Charlie Saturday morning. Charlie had already given her a smacking kiss goodbye and bolted out the door eager to tell his grandfather about the fire engine they were going to make.

But Cal hadn't followed him. He was eying her curiously as Daisy told him about Alex's call and his offer of the photography job. She also admitted to her qualms.

"It's just…distracting!" She stuck her hands in her hair and tugged.

"Why do it then? Call him up and tell him no."

"He'll want to know why."

"You're not obliged to tell him."

"If I don't, he'll get suspicious."

"About what? Is he going to think you're hiding his son from him?"

"No, of course not. He'll think—" Daisy hesitated "—that I'm still in love with him. That I don't trust myself around him."

"Possible," Cal agreed. "Or maybe you don't trust him."

Maybe she didn't trust either of them. The attraction was still there on a physical level. She hadn't told Cal about Alex's kiss. Or her reaction to it. There were some things better left unsaid. Now she just shrugged. "It'll be all right," she murmured.

Cal gave her a long hard look. She tried to remain indifferent under his gaze, but Cal was a photographer, too. He saw things that other people couldn't see.

"Is it just hormones?" he said at last. "Or something more?"

Daisy flushed, giving him yet another telltale sign. "I'm curious about what he's done with the building. About the sort of work he's doing."

"Uh-huh." Cal wasn't having any of it.

"Really. I wouldn't jeopardize Charlie's future. You know that." She looked at him steadily.

"Keep it in mind," Cal warned.

"No fear. I'm not an airy-fairy fool anymore."

Cal looked as if he doubted that. But at last he shrugged. "If you say so."

"In fact," Daisy added, "I think this may be a good thing. I can learn more about his real life, so I'll be able to tell Charlie about it someday."

"Oh, there's a plus," Cal muttered.

"It'll be fine." She put a hand on his sleeve. "Really, Cal. Don't worry."

Cal let out a slow breath. "I'm trying not to." He started toward the door and then turned back. "Charlie hasn't seen him? He hasn't seen Charlie?"

"No!" She smiled her best reassuring smile.

"Someday…"

"Someday they'll meet. Someday when Charlie is older. Grown-up. Settled. And if he has questions in the meantime, I'll answer them. But I'm not setting him up to be hurt! You know that. We've discussed it." When a man felt about having kids the way Alex did, deliberately introducing him into Charlie's life wasn't a risk she wanted to take.

Besides, he had a perfectly fine father in Cal. And one father was enough—for the moment at least.

"C'mon, Dad!" Charlie poked his head out of the window of the car.

"Go on, Dad," Daisy urged him. "And don't you worry. I'm doing enough for both of us. And it's silly, really. I will be fine. I'll shoot his photos, admire his handsome face and come home. End of story. Trust me. I can take care of myself."

The building Alex had restored wasn't far from Prospect Park. Daisy found it easily. It sat on the corner of a residential street filled with brownstones and trees and a business cross street that was wider, had fewer trees to block the view, and gave her plenty of scope.

She'd arrived early to scope out the neighborhood, wanted to get herself in work-mode before she ever laid eyes on him. The day was cool and crisp, the trees in their full autumn glory as she walked down the block, studying the building side on.

At a few minutes before three the sun was low enough that the shadows picked out some of the ornate carved relief on the facing of the top floor, sharpening the detail, showing the building to best advantage. Daisy took out her camera before she was halfway down the block, framed and shot. She took a dozen or more, then crossed the main thoroughfare to study the angles.

The building was tall and narrow, a four story redbrick like others in the neighborhood, but, unlike the rest of them, it seemed somehow to draw in the light.

She studied it more closely, trying to understand what she was seeing. The ground floor housed an electronics store which seemed an odd tenant for an old building. But somehow it fit the space easily and looked as if it belonged. Studying it, she began to realize why. The windows were taller than those in other buildings on the block and she remembered Alex saying he had changed the windows. But they still fit the period; they belonged. But he'd made the proportions just that little bit more generous.

Now they fit twenty-first century people. It made all the difference.

The second floor echoed the look with a series of gothic-arched windows and cream-colored facings that contrasted with the dark red brick. Stenciled just above waist height across the central largest window in black sans serif was Antonides Architectural Design. Simple, spare, elegant.

She could see possibilities forming as she moved quickly along the sidewalk. She would shoot Alex standing in that window, looking out, master of his kingdom. And another at his drafting table. She could envision him in her mind's eye bending over a drawing, black hair drifting across his forehead as he studied his work intently.

There would doubtless be plenty of other possibilities inside; an open staircase perhaps or a period elevator or maybe a skylight and, she grinned delightedly—enough light to make it happen.

Suddenly enthused and feeling like a real competent professional photographer for the first time since Alex had asked her to do it, Daisy turned—and came up hard against a solid male chest.

Chapter 4

"I saw you wandering back and forth across the street. I thought you might be lost." Alex had caught hold of her when she'd turned and crashed into him. He was still holding on now. Their bodies were touching.

Daisy's heart was going a mile a minute. Hastily she pulled away from his hard chest. "I wasn't lost," she said, hating her sudden breathlessness. "I was studying the building. Looking at all the angles."

She squinted up at him, trying not to be bowled over by the casual magnetism of the man. What was it about Alexandros Antonides that drew her like a moth to a flame?

Well, he was still gorgeous, there was that. Tall, whip-cord lean, broad-shouldered. Masculinity defined. Alex didn't have to flaunt the testosterone. It wasn't a veneer he put on. It was clearly bedrock in him.

"Well, if you're done assessing all the angles, let me show you around." He gave her one of those smiles, too, the one that had, from the beginning, undermined her common sense.

But she was older now, Daisy reminded herself. Made of sterner stuff. And she knew what he was made of, too.

"Fine," she said briskly. "Lead on."

He did just that, but not before he plucked her camera bag and one of the tripods out of her hands, leaving her with only her purse and the smaller tripod. "You could have left that in the building while you were looking around," he said over his shoulder as he crossed the street.

"I suppose."

"How'd you get here?"

"Subway."

He turned as he stepped up onto the sidewalk in front of his building. "With all this stuff? For God's sake, Daisy! They have cabs in Manhattan!"

"It's more efficient to take the subway."

"I'd have paid the cab fare."

"I don't need your cab fare. It's a business expense. When I want to take a taxi, I take one. I prefer the subway when I'm coming to Brooklyn. No bridge tie-ups. Now can we get going?"

She didn't want him fussing over her. He had no right. She didn't need him—of all people—thinking he knew best what was good for her.

Alex grunted, but still he shook his head as if despairing of her as he pushed open the door to the building. The electronics store she'd already spotted had its entrance off this interior vestibule on one side of the building. On the other was a stationer's shop—all fine paper and cards and pens.

"The old and the new," Daisy remarked, looking from the stationer's to the electronics store, nodding. She'd work that in, too.

Meanwhile he was leading her into the electronics store,

pointing out the new windows and the old oak paneling, the new built-in oak cabinets and the old tin ceilings now restored. It was an artful blend of the best of both, and it showed off the latest electronic devices spectacularly well. After a quick tour there, he took her into the stationer's shop, and the same was true there, as well.

The exquisite paper products looked appealing against the same oak cabinetry. The displays of calligraphic pens and multicolored inks and artists' tools were equally appealing.

Against the tall narrow windows Alex had created window seats which the proprietor had set up as inviting nooks for one or two people to sit and try out the various products. They were all full—and many of the customers were as young and hip as those in the electronics store across the vestibule.

"I'll show you photos of how it was before when we go upstairs," he said. "In the meantime, shoot whatever you want. Den and Caroline—the owners of the stores—have given their permission."

"Great. Thanks. You don't have to hang around," she said when he made no move to go. "I'll shoot down here. Then I can come to your office."

"I've cleared my calendar." He set her bag down, then propped his shoulders against the wall and watched every move she made.

Daisy was used to going about her work single-mindedly forgetting everything and everyone else but the focus of her shots. She was, this time, aware every second of Alex's eyes on her. She tried to tell herself he was just being polite. But he didn't simply watch while she took photos in the stationer's shop and in the electronics store. He followed her outside so she could shoot a couple from down the block.

Daisy shot him a hard look. He smiled back blandly.

"Fine," she muttered, "if you're going to tag along…" Then she raised her voice loud enough for him to hear and motioned him to stand in front of one of the heavy oak and etched glass doors. "Stand there and look 'lord of the manor-ish.'"

He was Greek. What did he know about lords of the manor?

But apparently some things were universal, and he understood perfectly, leaning casually against one of the walls by the front door, a proprietorial air about him that said exactly what she wanted it to—that this was his domain. He owned the place.

"Got it," she said, clicking off half a dozen so she could have her pick.

"Come on upstairs, then." He led the way back inside.

The elevator was utilitarian, so she wasn't sure what to expect when the doors opened—a hallway and doors to offices, she would have guessed. But that wasn't what she got.

The elevator opened into one big room facing north. There were expanses of gleaming oak flooring broken up by areas covered with dove-gray carpet. In one of the carpeted areas, a woman sat at a desk making some notes while she talked on the phone. Not far away, on another carpet there was soft furniture—sofas and armchairs that invited you to sit and peruse books from floor-to-ceiling bookcases.

Where the floor was wood, she saw several large tables with projects on display, detailed architectural models in place. Around the sides of the room, in their own spaces but accessible to everyone, there were drafting tables, a couple of which had people working at them. They had glanced up when the elevator doors opened, but seeing Alex, they'd nodded and gone back to work.

Daisy's gaze swiveled to take in the whole room. "Wow," she said, impressed. "Very nice."

"I like it. Let me show you around." He introduced her to Alison, his middle-aged office manager. Then he took her to meet the two at the drafting tables. A young dark-haired woman, Naomi, was deeply involved in whatever she'd been assigned and barely glanced up to smile. But the other, an intern named Steve, had some questions about his project, so Daisy was able to take some shots of Alex and Steve, leaning over one of the drafting tables, studying blue prints.

Then, while Alex answered Steve's questions, she wandered around, taking other shots of the room, of Alex on the job.

It was just the way she'd imagined him—in his element, his easy competence apparent. He drew her gaze as he bent over the table, his dark hair falling across his forehead as he pointed out something to Steve. She snapped off a couple of shots. But even when she lowered the camera, she couldn't seem to look away.

"Sorry," he said, coming back to her. "I didn't mean to spend so long with him."

"No problem. I got some good shots. Which is your table?" She nodded toward the vacant drafting tables.

"Upstairs. I'll show you."

He led her to a spiral staircase that ascended in one corner of the room. "We could use the elevator, but this is faster."

It was also a treat. It had caught her eye earlier, a bit of wrought-iron frivolity in stark utilitarian surroundings. And yet it belonged.

"Was it original to the building?" It was a little added lagniappe, and she had already taken a number of shots of it.

"No. But I wanted something to catch the eye," Alex said. "Something that was from the original period. I went to every salvage place in the boroughs, looking. I knew it when I saw it."

"It's perfect." She motioned him to precede her up the steps.

"Turn around," she said when he was halfway up. She took several shots of him on the steps, and was seriously tempted to take one of his backside when, afterward, she followed him up. But she didn't need any more reminders of how tempting Alex Antonides was.

His office was out of the mainstream, but connected to it. "I don't let them up here," he said frankly. "I need my space."

"A perk of being the boss," Daisy acknowledged. But she had to admit she liked his private aerie, too. The room in which he had created his office wasn't large. Like the bigger room downstairs, it had tall, narrow, gothic arched windows and polished oak flooring. Floor-to-ceiling bookshelves held vast arrays of architectural titles, books about design, and a lot of history, art and photography books. Daisy studied the titles.

It was disconcerting to find many of the same titles she had on her own shelves. So, whatever it was, it wasn't just physical.

She wished it were. He would be so much easier to resist. Forcing herself to focus on the task at hand, she gave a little wave of her camera, asking permission to take photos. "May I?"

He nodded. "Of course."

"I've heard that there's a movement to minimize windows for energy conservation," she said as she pointed the camera in his direction. "You obviously don't believe that."

"There's a place for that. But light is good, too. And while you can conserve energy by building dark, I like light. So I try to make sure the windows are doing their job, too." He stopped. "Sorry. Boring."

Daisy lowered the camera. "It's not, actually. And I'm a photographer. I like light, too."

"Come on," he said suddenly. "I'll show you the best light of all."

Without looking to see if she followed, he started up to the next level on the same spiral staircase. Daisy followed, expecting more office space. But when he reached the landing and unlocked the door, she knew better.

This was where Alex lived.

If he hadn't said, "Welcome to my place," she would have known it anyway. The light walls, the earth tones, the casual modern but not stark furniture, the plush dark rust and blue and gold oriental rug centered on the polished oak floor created a visual backdrop for the man she had known. Even if he weren't standing there watching her take it all in, she would have known this was where he belonged.

There were, in the furnishings, in the books and papers on the coffee table, in the framed architectural drawings on the walls, signs of Alex everywhere. She was shaken by how instantly she felt at home, as if she, too, belonged here.

No. No, she didn't.

She took a breath, steeled herself and tossed his words back at him, "So show me the best light of all."

He smiled. "Right this way."

Wouldn't you just bloody know that it would be the skylight in his bedroom!

Daisy stopped dead at the door, realizing a split second before she crossed the threshold exactly where they were going. "I didn't mean—"

Alex turned, flashing her a grin. "You asked for it."

Daisy read the challenge in it—the very challenge she'd told Cal she could handle. And she could, damn it. So, deliberately, she stepped in and looked around. The skylight was above the bed. The bed looked to be the size of, perhaps, the Sahara Desert—but vastly more comfortable with its buff-colored duvet and a quartet of dark brown pillows.

"Very nice," she said, doing her best to keep her gaze fixed on the skylight until she turned back to the living room again. "Let me shoot some photos out here."

He smiled, but didn't challenge her further, just let her wander around and look her fill.

Daisy resisted looking her fill. She'd have been here for hours, curious about the man, wanting to know him better, at the same time she knew she shouldn't want to know him at all.

Alex's apartment was not some sterile showplace. There were dishes in the sink, a newspaper on the counter. Two pairs of athletic shoes, a gym bag and a racing bike sat by what she supposed was the main front door—the one that didn't lead down to his office. And one wall of the kitchen was painted as a mural of something that looked like the Greek islands—lots of blue sea and sky, white-washed buildings and blue domed churches. It drew her attention.

"Did Martha paint that?"

Martha was Lukas's twin sister. Daisy had met her several times over the years. She knew Martha now lived part of the year in Montana—of all places—and part of the year on Long Island and wherever her husband, Theo Savas, was sailing boats.

It seemed an amazing exotic existence to Daisy who had been born in Colorado, came to the big city for university, and never left—except to go back home occasionally.

"She did," Alex agreed. "Kind of bowls you over, doesn't it?"

"I like it," Daisy said.

"I didn't," Alex said, surprising her.

"What? Why not?"

He shook his head. "Memories."

That startled her until she remembered him telling her about his childhood, about his brother who had died young.

"You could paint over it," she suggested.

He shrugged. "I got used to it. I just wasn't expecting it. I was heading out of town and I told her to paint whatever she wanted. She thought it would make me happy. Can we get on with this?" he said abruptly, gesturing to her camera.

"Oh! Yes, of course!" Daisy grimaced, feeling a flush of confusion engulf her. That would teach her.

She pointed to the armchair near the window. "Go sit there and look at one of your books."

Alex picked up a book and sat down with it, opened it at random, studied it as if he cared what was in it while Daisy moved and shot, moved and shot.

He turned a page. "I hired a matchmaker."

Daisy's finger slipped on the shutter release. Then, taking a slow careful breath so as not to jar the camera, she clicked off several more shots and lowered it again.

"Did you?" she said, heart pounding. "Good for you. I'm sure you'll find exactly what you're looking for. Turn a little more this way."

He turned. "I found her on the internet."

A breath hissed through Daisy's teeth. "The internet? For heaven's sake, Alex! How do you know she's legitimate? She might be a charlatan—someone hanging out her shingle, looking to make money off poor unsuspecting fools."

He looked up from the book and raised a brow. "Poor unsuspecting fools...like me?"

Daisy's cheeks burned. "I didn't mean that! I never said—" She retreated behind her camera again. "I just meant that not everyone is reliable, honest. Did you get letters of recommendation? What do you know about her background?"

"She has a degree in human relations. She was born and raised in Virginia. She came to the 'big city' when she was just out of college. Reminded me a little of you."

"I'm not from Virginia," Daisy bit out. "And I don't have a degree in human relations."

"So maybe she's more qualified than you are," Alex mused, giving her a sly smile.

"Maybe she is. I've got enough here. Let's go back down to your office." Someplace less intimate. Someplace where she could focus on her work. She didn't want to hear anything more about his matchmaker.

Alex picked up her camera bag, then started down the stairs again. He glanced back. "I went out with one of her suggestions last night."

Daisy pasted on a bright smile. "How nice. Maybe you'll have a wife by Christmas."

He nodded. "Maybe I will. She's a stockbroker. Nice enough. Intense, though," he mused.

Daisy pointed him toward his drafting table. "Put out a drawing and focus," she directed. She did not intend to get sucked into analyzing his date.

"Too intense for me," he went on, even as he obediently pulled out a drawing, spread it on the table and stared down at it. "She'd talked nonstop about everything from chandeliers to parakeets to stock options to astronomy."

"Well, it's early days yet," Daisy said briskly. "Maybe the next one will be better."

If he'd been her client she'd have talked to him about that, tried to learn what he hadn't liked, what was "too intense." But she wasn't finding a wife for Alex Antonides. He was someone else's problem.

He kept his gaze on the drawing. "Maybe. I'm going out with another one tonight."

"Another one?" That fast? Where was the "matchmaking" in that? It sounded more like trial and error.

He glanced around. "Amalie—that's the matchmaker—has got a whole list."

A list. Daisy wasn't impressed. "Is she French? Or fake?" she added before she could help herself.

Alex raised a brow. "Her mother's French. Is that a problem?"

Daisy raised her camera again, refusing to admit she was taking refuge behind it. "Of course not. I just wondered. I suppose she's introducing you to French women then." It made sense. He spent a good part of every year in Paris.

"Career women," Alex corrected. "And I'm not looking for a French one. I live here now."

That was news. Daisy stayed behind the camera. She kept moving.

Alex picked up the drawing and rolled it up. Whether she was finished or not, it was clear that he was. "She has a list as long as my arm," he reported. "She said I need options."

Daisy grunted noncommittedly. She didn't think much of "options." But then, when she helped people find the right mate, she was trying to find their soul mate, not a sex partner who was willing to share a mortgage.

"So," Alex said, "I just have to find the right one."

Good luck with that, Daisy thought. But she kept her skepticism to herself. If she expressed it, he'd tell her she should do it herself.

"All done," she said, and began disassembling her camera and stowing it in her bag. "I'll get to work editing these early next week. I'm going to be out all day tomorrow, and I'm not working this weekend. If you'll give me your business card, I'll email you when I've finished. Then you can let me know whether to send you a disk or email you files or send them directly to the magazine."

Alex fished a card out of his wallet, started to hand it to her, then took it back and scribbled something on the back before pressing it into her palm again. "You can reach me at this number anytime."

Not likely. But Daisy just pocketed it and smiled as she zipped her bag shut, stood up and hoisted it onto her shoulder. Then, deliberately, she stuck out her hand to Alex for a businesslike shake. "Thank you."

He blinked, then stared—at her, at her hand. Something unreadable flickered across his face. Then in slow motion, he reached out and took her fingers in his. Flesh on flesh.

Daisy tried not to think about it. But his palm was warm and firm and there were light calluses on it, as if he didn't only sit in his office and draw. She remembered those calluses, those fingers—the way they had grazed her skin, had traced the line of her jaw, the curve of her hip, the hollow of her collarbone. Other lines. Other hollows.

She swallowed hard.

Still he held her hand. Then abruptly he dropped it. "Thank you, too," he said, his voice crisp. As businesslike as she hoped hers was.

"Goodbye." One more polite smile and she'd be gone.

Alex nodded, his gaze fixed on hers. The phone on his desk rang. He grimaced, then picked it up. "What is it, Alison?" There was barely concealed impatience in his tone. Then he grimaced again. "Right. Okay. Give me a sec." He turned back to Daisy. "I have to take this."

"Of course. I was just on my way."

She was down the steps and out the door without looking back. There. She'd done it—beard the lion in his den.

And survived.

Just like she'd told Cal she would.

Staring at the skylight in his ceiling in the dark didn't have much to recommend it. There were stars. There were a few small clouds scudding along, silvery in the moonlight.

There was Daisy.

Alex flipped over and dragged the pillow over his head. It didn't help. She was on the insides of his eyelids, it seemed.

The whole day had been a bloody disaster. Well, no, that wasn't true. Before 3:00 p.m., things had been pretty normal. He'd been a little distracted, there had been a lot to do, but he'd got some work done.

And then Daisy had shown up. Exactly as he'd planned.

She was supposed to come, take her photos, and leave again. He was supposed to smile and look professional and competent and disinterested, and see her on her way. Asking her to take the photos was supposed to settle things between them, put them on a business footing.

It was supposed to pigeonhole her—and convince Alex that he wasn't really attracted, that he hadn't been thinking about her fifty times a day since he'd seen her again, that she didn't draw his gaze more than any other woman, that he was perfectly happy to watch her walk out of his office and out of his life.

The operative word was *supposed*. The truth was, well, something else altogether.

And the day hadn't been all that normal before three o'clock, either. He might have got some work done earlier in the day, but shortly before Daisy was due to arrive, he'd found himself walking over to look out the window every few minutes. It was a nice day, sunny, brisk. He was enjoying perfect fall weather. No more, no less.

So why had his heart kicked over at the sight of her down there on the sidewalk, pointing her camera up at his building? Why had he stopped Steve abruptly halfway through a question to go down and intercept her before she came in? Why had his fingers itched to reach out and touch her? And why had he had to fight to suppress the urge to kiss her when she'd turned and bumped straight into his chest?

She drove him crazy. She got under his skin. The minute he saw her, he couldn't seem to focus on anything or anyone else.

The feeling persisted the whole time she was there—this desire to touch her, to smooth a hand over her hair, to pull her against him, to touch his lips to hers. His heart had begun hammering the moment he'd seen her, and it was still banging away when he'd had to take that phone call and she'd left.

He'd wanted to stop her, to say, "Hang on. Wait," because it was too soon, there had been so little time, he had not had enough of her yet.

But at the same time, he knew it was stupid—*he* was stupid.

Daisy Harris—Connolly!—was *not* what he wanted—or needed—in his life.

And it didn't matter that she was divorced now. She still apparently wanted things he didn't want. Wanted things he wasn't prepared to give. So the one bit of common sense he had, had kept his mouth shut.

He hadn't said, "Wait." Hadn't stopped her or called her to come back.

It was better she had left. And better still that he had had a date that night with one of Amalie's "options."

Whoever she was, she would erase Daisy from his mind.

Except she hadn't.

Her name was Laura or Maura or Dora. Hell, he couldn't remember. She had been pleasant enough in an airheaded sort of way. But he'd spent the evening making mental comparisons between her and Daisy.

Suffice to say, Dora/Maura/Laura had come up short on all counts.

She didn't have Daisy's charm. She didn't have Daisy's ability to listen. She didn't have Daisy's smile or Daisy's sparkling eyes or Daisy's eager enthusiasm.

She wasn't Daisy. He was bored.

He'd been polite enough. He'd listened and nodded and smiled until his jaw ached. He'd dutifully told her a bit about himself, but his comments were flat and uninteresting even to his own ears. It wasn't hard to tell she was bored, too.

"You win a few, you lose a few," she'd said, smiling and shaking his hand when they'd left the restaurant to go their separate ways.

It was nine-thirty. Shortly after ten he was home.

And that was when he began to realize his mistake. He'd not only lost, he'd lost big-time.

He hadn't vanquished Daisy from his mind by having her come take photos this afternoon. On the contrary he now had a whole host of new images of Daisy—on his turf.

Now when he stood at the window, he could look down at where he'd first spotted her, camera to her eye, taking pictures of his building, her hair loose in the wind. And when he grew tired of pacing his apartment and went back down to his office to do some work, the minute he sat down at his drafting table, he could almost feel her presence just over his right shoulder where she had been that afternoon.

He crumpled up half a dozen attempted drawings before

he gave up, stomped back upstairs, stripped off his clothes and took a shower.

She hadn't been in his shower, at least.

Not this one, anyway. But he'd shared a shower with her five years ago, and the memories flashed across his mind with such insistence that he'd cranked the hot water down till only the cold beat down on his body. But his arousal persisted.

He wanted to go for a bike ride, burn off the energy, the edge. But not in Brooklyn. Not at midnight. There was stupid—and then there was stupid.

He was stupid, not suicidal.

He should have known better than to think he could see her again and forget her. He'd never been able to forget her. And he wouldn't be able to, damn it, until Amalie finally found him the right woman.

In the meantime he'd flung himself onto his bed, stared up at the skylight—and discovered the depth of his folly.

Daisy had been in his bedroom. He'd deliberately brought her in here—to show her the "best light"—wanting to get a rise out of her.

Well, she wasn't the one who was rising. Pun intended, he thought savagely. The joke was on him.

The trouble with doing an hour-long shoot with Alex was that the hour was just the beginning.

Oh, it was over for him. But Daisy had to work with the images, study them, analyze them, choose the best ones, correct them. Spend hours and hours and hours contemplating them.

It drove her insane.

She didn't want to see him in his element hour after hour. She didn't want to feast her eyes on that handsome face. She didn't want to focus on the lithe muscular body as he stretched across the drafting table to point something out to Steve. She didn't want to study the strong profile, the sharp angles, the hard jaw, and hawklike nose as he stared out the window.

He was everything she'd thought he would become.

And she couldn't bear to look at it.

She put the photos away and went to read books to Charlie. The next night she watched a movie instead. The following night she had a new shoot, some high school senior pictures to work on. She'd get to Alex's when the memory of being in his office, in his apartment—in his bedroom—wasn't quite so immediate.

She would do them.

Not now. Not yet.

She needed time. An eon or two.

She needed space. Would a galaxy be enough?

The trouble with the "options" Amalie was providing him with, Alex decided after his fifth disastrous date, was that not one of them—so far—had been worth the trouble.

He'd gone out with half a dozen since he'd contracted with her, and since the intense Gina whom he'd mentioned to Daisy and the airhead whose name he couldn't recall, there had been phlegmatic Deirdre and twitchy Shannon and a politician called Chloe.

But if they'd been bad, tonight's "flavor of the evening" was absolutely no improvement, though Amalie had sworn they would be perfect for each other.

"She's an architecture student. You'll have so much in common!" Amalie had vowed.

He met her at a restaurant near the Lincoln Center. She was at the bar when he got there, a red scarf looped around her neck. That's how he would recognize her, she'd told him on the phone.

He did a double take when he saw her. She looked so much like Daisy. Maybe a little blonder than Daisy, maybe a little taller. And her eyes were a sort of faded gray-green. She beamed at him when he arrived.

"I knew it was you!" She was like bubbly champagne. "You're even more handsome than your picture."

She might have meant it. He didn't know. Didn't care. Her eyes didn't sparkle like Daisy's.

They took their drinks to a table and he said, "Amalie says you're studying architecture."

Not quite. What Tracie knew about architecture she appeared to have memorized from Wikipedia. She started talking about the Acropolis before they ordered and had barely reached the Colosseum by the time their entrees arrived.

It was always interesting to learn which buildings inspired another architect, but Tracie wasn't an architect—or even a student of architecture, Alex was willing to bet. After two hours of her nonstop talking, he'd had enough. If she hadn't looked so much like Daisy, he doubted he'd have lasted that long.

But the truth was, the longer he spent with her, the less like Daisy she seemed. Tracie was nervous, edgy. She had a shrill laugh. Her voice grated on him.

Daisy's laugh made him feel like smiling. Her eyes always sparkled—either with joy or annoyance. It didn't matter which. They drew his gaze. When she was with him, he couldn't stop looking at her. Her voice was always like warm honey.

Not, of course, that he'd heard it since she'd walked out of his place a week and a half ago. She'd taken his picture and said she'd be in touch and he'd never heard from her again.

He set down his fork sharply.

"You're bored," Tracie accused, staring hard at him over his empty plate. He hadn't had to talk, so he'd eaten everything in front of him.

Now Alex shook his head. "No," he lied. "I'm distracted. I just realized I have to be somewhere. I have an appointment."

"Tonight?" Her eyes widened.

"I have to pick up some photos," he said. "I need to get them to an editor in the morning." It wasn't entirely true. But the editor did need them. She'd called him yesterday inquiring about where they were. He'd thought Daisy had sent them in so she wouldn't have to contact him again.

Tracie pursed her lips, then pouted. "But we've only reached the Duomo." Which meant they had about six hundred more years of architecture to cover.

"I'm sorry," Alex said firmly. "I really need to go."

He did finish his coffee, but then called for the bill, saw her into a taxi and watched it drive off. Not until it disappeared around the corner did he breathe a sigh of relief. He was free.

For what?

It was just past nine. Not really late—unless you'd just spent the past two hours being systematically bored to death. Then you wanted some excitement, something to get the adrenaline going.

But the adrenaline was already going—and so were his feet.

They knew exactly where they were headed, and before Alex even realized it, he was on the corner of the street where Daisy's office was.

Daisy—who was, let's face it, the reason he'd been willing

to go on five dates in the past ten days—so he would bloody well stop thinking about her.

But he hadn't stopped.

Every night he lay in bed and stared at the damned skylight and remembered her sparkling eyes, her smooth golden skin, her warm smile. And because he was in bed, he remembered other things, too.

He remembered touching her skin—all over. He remembered kissing her smiling mouth. He remembered stripping off her clothes and running his hands over her body, teasing, tasting—

Hell! He couldn't show up on her doorstep halfway to wanting to bed her. Not that she'd even be there. It was her office, for God's sake. Why would she be burning the midnight oil editing photos? Presumably she had a life.

She probably even went out on dates now that she was divorced. Maybe she had a boyfriend. His jaw tightened and he shoved his hands in the pockets of his jacket as he started walking down the street.

He didn't expect she would be there. So he was taken aback to discover lights on in the bay window of the apartment that was her office.

She didn't have a life, after all? He stopped across the street and stared.

Now what? Turn around and walk back to Columbus? Catch a cab home? And stare at the damn skylight again?

Abruptly Alex crossed the street, took the steps to the front door two at a time, opened the door to the vestibule and punched the doorbell.

He waited. And waited. He shifted from one foot to the other, and wondered if she left the lights on all the time. Maybe she wasn't even there.

He was ready to turn around and leave when all at once he heard the sound of the lock twisting and the door handle rattling. The door opened.

Daisy stared out at him, nonplused. *"Alex?"*

"I came for the photos."

"What?"

"The editor called me. She wants the photos. You said you'd have them ready."

"I said I'd call you when they were ready." She was gripping the door, glaring at him, and by God, yes, her eyes were sparking fire.

He almost smiled as he snaked past her into her office before she could object, then turned and let his gaze run over her again.

She was wearing a pair of jeans and a sweatshirt—about as inelegant as imaginable—and she looked as sexy as hell. Her blonde hair was hanging loose around her face. It was disheveled, as if she—or someone else?—had been running fingers through it.

"Am I interrupting something?" he snapped.

"What?" She frowned. Then she shrugged. "My work. If you want the photos, let me get back to them. They're not done yet. I'm sorry. I've been busy. I'll have them for you tomorrow. I—"

"Let me see them."

"No. Not while I'm still working."

"Why? Afraid of someone else's opinion?"

"Do I offer you opinions about the buildings you design?" she countered with saccharine sweetness. "Of course not. So go away."

But Alex didn't want to go away. He wanted to drop down in the chair and watch her work. He wanted to run his fingers through her hair and pull her close. He wanted to slide his hands down the curve of her spine, cup her buttocks—

He groaned.

"What's wrong?" She was looking at him intently, worriedly.

He ground his teeth, then turned away, knowing he should get the hell out of here, but somehow he couldn't go. It was as if she'd bewitched him, cast some spell that wouldn't let him find the woman he knew had to be out there, the woman who would actually be right for him.

"Alex?" she pressed in the face of his silence.

Finally he snapped. "I've had five dates, and they've all been disasters!"

Daisy's eyes widened. She stared at him, then let out a sound that might have been a laugh. Or a snort.

"What a shame," Daisy said in a tone that told him it had been both a laugh and a snort.

"It is, damn it! And it's a waste of time." Alex cracked his knuckles and spun away to pace irritably around her office. But every step brought him closer to her. And he wanted her. Badly.

She stepped past him and moved toward her desk, and he wheeled to follow her when he found himself face-to-face with the photos on her walls.

None of them, of course, was Daisy.

But they all spoke of Daisy. Of what she wanted and he didn't.

Families. Children. Pets.

He looked at her. Her cheeks were flushed. She ran her tongue over her lips. She watched him warily, worriedly.

"Never mind," he said abruptly. "I have to go."

Ignoring his desire, forcing himself to turn away from the

most beautiful woman he'd ever made love to, he stalked out the door. He was halfway down the steps when he turned his head, his heart still hammering. "Send me those photos, damn it."

Chapter 5

The next day Alex got an email with a link to a site where he could download the photos Daisy had taken.

Here you are, the email said. Sorry it took so long. Hope they meet with your editor's satisfaction. Thank you for the opportunity to work with you.

Kind regards, Daisy Connolly.

Kind regards? Daisy *Connolly?*

As if he would need her last name to distinguish her from all the other Daisys in his life.

Blast her, anyway! Alex smacked a hand on the desk next to his computer screen. So all it had needed was for him to turn up on her doorstep and make an idiot of himself and Daisy was suddenly inspired to finish editing the photos, send them along and get him out of her life.

Swell.

He'd lain awake half the night—staring at the damned skylight and cursing his own misplaced desire—and wishing Amalie would come up with a viable "option."

In the morning he called her and demanded a better selection. "The last one was a charlatan," he said. "If she was an architecture student, I play center field for the New York Yankees."

"I'm talking to another young woman today," she promised. "You're very discerning. It takes time."

It didn't take time, damn it. That was the trouble. If Daisy wanted what he wanted there wouldn't be any problem at all.

But she didn't. That was perfectly clear. She probably hadn't been stalling. She'd probably actually been busy, too busy to get right to his photos. But once he'd turned up on her doorstep, making demands, she'd outdone herself getting the photos finished so she didn't need to have anything more to do with him.

They were amazing photos, though.

He stood in his office, staring at them now. He'd spread them out on his drafting table, studying them, seeing himself through her eyes.

They were every bit as sharp and insightful as the ones he'd seen on her wall last night. She'd taken most of the shots in black and white which, on first glance, surprised him.

But the more he studied them, the more he saw what she was doing: she had used the monochrome scheme to pare him down to his essence, exactly the way an architectural drawing or a blueprint did.

She caught him clearly—a man who had little patience with subtlety, who knew what he wanted.

He wanted her.

She had to know that. Didn't she know that?

He sighed and scraped the photos into a pile and put them back into the envelope. Of course she knew it.

She didn't want him—not on his terms.

So he'd seen the last of her.

End of story.

Daisy was still taking deep breaths and letting them out slowly a week later. But it was her own fault. She knew she should have got the photos edited and sent off right away. She hadn't.

And so Alex had turned up on her doorstep. An intense, edgy, irritated Alex. An Alex who had looked at her with fire in his normally cool green gaze. An Alex who had shot into her office so quickly, she hadn't even thought about how to stop him. And once he was there, it had felt like being trapped in a cage with a full-grown, very hungry panther.

A panther who had complained about the meals he was being offered at the same time he was looking at her like he intended to make her the next one.

She'd skittered away, crossed the room, needing to put space between them, because the mere sight of him had set her heart to pounding. All her senses went on alert with Alex. Her body wanted him no matter what her brain—and her mother's-heart—told her was wise.

She had been determined to resist—not just Alex, but her own desire.

Then abruptly he had turned and walked out!

And Daisy had been left staring after him as he strode off into the cold dark windy night. Then she'd shut the door and leaned against it, her heart still slamming against the wall of her chest, her pulse racing.

The adrenaline had kept her working half the night.

It took a week to wear off, more for her to be able to say with confidence to Cal that life was back to normal, and still more until she believed it herself.

So it was a blow on the first Saturday evening in November to hear a knock on the door, expect to get the Thai takeaway she'd ordered, and find Alex standing on her doorstep again.

She stared at him, dumbstruck.

"Good evening to you, too," he said cheerfully. His tone was mild, friendly, completely at odds with the Alex who had shown up last time.

"Good evening," she replied cautiously, trying not to look at his smooth-shaven face, his quirking smile, that groove in his cheek she always itched to touch. Deliberately she curled her fingers into the palm of her hand.

He hesitated a split second, then said, "I just wanted to say that I may have found the one."

Daisy blinked. "The one? The one what?"

His smile widened. "Woman." There was a pause. Then, "Wife," he clarified.

Daisy's stomach did an odd sort of somersault. She swallowed, then mustered her best polite smile. "Really. How nice."

She shut her eyes for an instant, and opened them to discover that he'd done it again—slipped past her and was suddenly standing in her office. How did he do that?

"She's a vice president in marketing for an international cosmetics firm," he reported, his handsome face looking very pleased. "She runs campaigns in half a dozen places all over the world. Always on the move. She has two phones. A red one for emergencies." He grinned, as if this were a good thing.

"Does she?" Daisy said drily. "Sounds perfect for you."

"You think so, too?" He was still grinning, so she didn't know if he heard her sarcasm as it had been intended or not. "That's what I thought. I read Amalie the riot act after the first bunch, said if that was as good as she could do, I was finished. And then she came up with Caroline."

Caroline. Even her name was right. Sophisticated, but approachable. She did sound perfect.

"And," Alex went on with considerable enthusiasm, "there are other things, too—she's beautiful, bright, funny, articulate, well-read."

Daisy shut the door but stayed by it, keeping an eye out for the Thai deliveryman and thanking God that Charlie was at Cal's this weekend. "So have you asked her to marry you yet?" she asked Alex flippantly.

"Considering it."

Her jaw dropped. "On the basis of a couple of dates?"

"Three," Alex corrected. He was moving around her office in panther mode, but looking better fed. He picked up an alabaster cat on the bookcase, and examined it while he talked. "Well, two and a half." His mouth twisted wryly. "The red phone rang tonight. She had to leave in the middle of dinner. She's on her way to San Francisco right now."

"You're joking." He had to be joking. *Didn't he?*

But when he didn't immediately agree that he was, Daisy shook her head, torn between despair and the prickling of awareness and wholly useless desire she always felt faced with Alexandros Antonides. Still. Damn it. "You're insane."

He put the cat down again and looked at her quizzically. "Insane? Why?"

"You can't make a decision like that in a few weeks' time!"

"Why not? She's what I want."

"But are *you* what *she* wants?" Daisy didn't know why she was asking that. Didn't know why she was arguing with him.

"That's her problem."

"Yours, too." She couldn't seem to help herself. "If you get married without knowing each other well, without thinking things through—"

"I could end up like you did?"

Daisy rocked with the punch of his words. *"What?"*

"That isn't why your marriage didn't work?"

"No, of course it isn't!" Daisy felt the heat of his accusation. But she denied it, and it wasn't a lie, either. "And we're not discussing my marriage." She wrapped her arms across her chest, as if they would defend her. Fat chance.

"Why didn't it, then?" he persisted.

"This is not about me!"

He raised his brows. "Maybe I'm trying to learn from your mistake."

"You and I are not likely to make the same mistakes."

Alex shrugged. "How will I know if you don't tell me?"

"I'm not going to tell you, Alex! My marriage is none of your business." She shoved away from the door and jerked it open. "I think you should go."

But Alex didn't go anywhere. On the contrary, he turned and flopped down into one of the armchairs, settling in, folding his arms behind his head. "Not yet. I want to hear why I shouldn't pop the question."

Daisy wanted to strangle him. But the quickest way to get him out of her life was to answer his questions. So she did. "Because," she said slowly and with the articulation of an elocution teacher, "you don't want to get a divorce. Do you?" she challenged him. "Maybe you don't care whether you do or not because you won't care about her."

"I don't want a divorce," he said evenly. The green eyes glinted.

Daisy shrugged. "Fine. Then take your time. Make sure you're on the same page. That you want the same things.

That… Oh, hell, why am I telling you this? You don't understand!"

He cocked his head. "Weren't you on the same page, Daisy?" He sounded almost sympathetic now.

She pressed her lips together and didn't answer.

He gave her a little half smile. "Are you going to marry again?"

"I doubt it." She turned away, then turned back and shrugged. "Maybe someday. It depends."

"On?"

"On whether or not I'm in love with him."

Alex's jaw clenched.

Daisy smiled. It was a painful smile, hard-earned. "Yes, love. Still. I want the whole package, Alex. Now more than ever."

Alex didn't move. A muscle ticking in his temple was the only betrayal of anything beyond casual interest in what she had to say. Then, with studied nonchalance, he rose slowly. "I wish you the joy of it then."

"And I you," Daisy said automatically.

He gave her a sardonic look.

"No, truly." She almost put a hand on his arm as he passed. But then she laced her fingers together instead. Still, she looked up at him earnestly. "I mean it, Alex. You deserve a wonderful life. I hope…Caroline is the right woman for you. I hope she gives you what you want."

He had stopped and was standing now, quite close. She kept her gaze on the rise and fall of his chest, knew that she could reach out and touch him. Knew she should back away.

But she didn't. She stayed quite still and met his gaze. "Regardless of what you think, marriage is more than you expect.

You should…take your time, get to know this…woman you're considering marrying. Make sure it's right for both of you."

Alex stood staring at her as if he couldn't believe the words coming out of her mouth.

Daisy couldn't believe them, either. It wasn't any of her business. But she couldn't seem to stop herself. And maybe she did owe him the benefit of her experience with Cal. Certainly it had taught her something.

"No matter what you think you want out of marriage," she finished, "it can surprise you. You shouldn't take it lightly."

Alex's eyes narrowed further, and she expected he would tell her to mind her own business. But his jaw just tightened again, then he nodded. "I'll keep it in mind."

Their gazes locked—all the electricity flowing through New York City at that moment had nothing on what arced between them.

Then, carefully, consciously, Daisy swallowed. "Have a good life, Alex."

For a long moment he didn't reply, and she couldn't read his gaze. Then he said flatly, "I will. Shall I invite you to the wedding?"

No! It was her gut-level response. But she squelched it. "When you're sure she's the right one," she said slowly, "I would be delighted to come."

Alex's lips pressed together in a thin line. He nodded, then walked past her wordlessly out the door.

She closed it after him, leaned back against it, knees wobbling. Only after the sound of his footsteps had long faded away, did Daisy breathe again.

Moving on.

That's what her father always used to say when Daisy or her

sister got all wrought up about something they could do nothing about. He'd listen to them anguishing for, oh, maybe thirty minutes, and then he'd say, "Can you do anything about it?"

They'd say, "No."

And he'd flash them his sunny grin and say, "So…moving on…"

He didn't mean, *get over it.* He meant, *stop dwelling on it. Get past it.*

You might still ache with disappointment. You might remember it forever. But you'd done all you could do. Now it was time to pull up your socks and move on.

Daisy moved on.

She still thought about Alex. How could she not? She had loved him once. He was the father of her child, even if he didn't know it. She owed him for that—for Charlie. And she wished things could have been different.

But they weren't.

Life moved on, and determinedly Daisy moved on with it. She did her work. She introduced a great couple, Debbie whom she'd met at a yoga class and Mark, who played baseball with Cal, and was delighted when they seemed to hit it off. She wasn't losing her touch with other people at least. Cal bought Charlie a point-and-shoot camera, and she went with the two of them for walks in the park and on the streets and took loads of pictures. It was fun to discover Charlie's interest, and restful to be with him and Cal.

Every time her thoughts drifted to Alex and she wondered if he'd proposed yet, she deliberately focused them elsewhere. So she wasn't even thinking about him the Sunday evening before Thanksgiving when Cal came into the kitchen and asked, "Whatever happened with Alex?"

Her ex had stopped by that afternoon to take Charlie for a

bike ride in the park. When they'd come back, Daisy had invited him to stay for leftovers. After, he'd helped Charlie build a fire station with his Legos. Now Charlie had gone upstairs to get ready for his bath while Daisy put dishes in the dishwasher.

She felt a moment's jolt at the sound of his name. But then she just shrugged. "No idea. Haven't seen him for a while. I believe he's got a woman in his life. He seems to think she's 'the one.'" Daisy couldn't help adding that.

Cal looked at her closely. "I'm sorry."

"I'm not," Daisy said, dropping forks in the silverware slots. "He was never the man I thought he was. He still isn't."

"Life sucks," Cal said with a faint grin.

"It has some good bits," Daisy countered, nodding toward the stairs where they could both hear Charlie banging around in the upstairs hall.

Cal's grin widened. "You're right. It does." He shoved away from the doorjamb and flexed his shoulders. "I'll be going then. Thanks for letting me take him to the park."

"Anytime." She walked to the front door with him and kissed him on the cheek and he gave her a hug. Then he shrugged on his jacket.

"I'll pick Charlie up Thursday morning. I told my folks we'd be up there by noon."

Daisy nodded and forced a smile even as she felt her throat tighten. "He'll have so much fun."

Cal was taking Charlie to his parents' upstate for Thanksgiving. They wouldn't be back until Sunday morning. The thought of rattling around by herself for four days was horrible. But it was good for Charlie and for Cal and his family. It was a part of the life they'd made.

"My folks are really looking forward to it," Cal said. He

looked at her closely. "You can come if you want." He must have seen some of the hollowness she felt.

Daisy shook her head. "Thanks, but I can't. You know that."

If she did Cal's parents might think there was hope of them getting back together. They had been upset when she and Cal divorced. Now they seemed to be coming to terms with the way things were. It wouldn't do to get their hopes up again.

"You're probably right. No, you are right. It's just—I'm sorry. Especially this year."

Daisy shrugged. "Don't worry. I'll be fine. I'm going to Finn and Izzy's. It will be chaos. I'll never miss you. What do you have planned?"

"Going fishing if the weather stays warm enough. Chopping wood otherwise. Getting ready for winter." He grimaced.

"You'll have fun."

"Charlie will make it fun. He and Dad are something else when you get them together." Cal shook his head, grinning. "Like two kids."

"I'd guess there were three." Daisy cocked her head and smiled at him.

Cal rubbed a hand against the back of his neck. "Well, yeah."

Their eyes met, both of them rueful.

"Moving on," Daisy said with all the briskness she could muster.

And Cal nodded resolutely. "Moving on."

He went out, and Daisy locked the door after him. Then she went back into the living room, rubbing her hands up and down her arms. Was Alex having Thanksgiving with the woman in his life? Or was he working on one continent while she was on another?

What did she care? Daisy asked herself irritably.

She didn't, damn it. But sometimes moving on felt curiously like walking through molasses with her shoelaces tied together. Hard and lonely.

She felt suddenly very, very cold.

Chapter 6

Finn and Izzy's at Thanksgiving *was* chaos. Finn's nieces, Tansy and Pansy, were both there, along with Rip and Crash, Finn and Izzy's sons, and a dozen or so other friends, several slightly giddy from having spent the night before over by the Museum of Natural History where all the gigantic balloon floats for the annual parade were being inflated.

Daisy had gone to the MacCauleys' early and she'd stayed late. Friday she'd spent the entire day catching up on photo editing. More often than she'd liked, she'd been tempted to open the folder where Alex's photos were.

Every time, she'd steeled herself against it and had resisted.

Saturday was harder. Her backlog of work was gone. The house was reasonably clean. The laundry was done, folded, put away. The rugs vacuumed, the furniture dusted. She supposed she could clean the oven, but that seemed like taking things too far.

Instead she took the dog Murphy for a long walk in the park, then decided to do some Christmas shopping. Closer to

Christmas, stores would be jammed. Of course, they were on Saturday, too. But it wasn't as lonely as being home by herself, wondering if Charlie and Cal were having a good time.

Wondering what Alex was doing.

It was a relief when Cal and Charlie got back late Sunday afternoon. Charlie was full of stories about hiking in the woods and stacking firewood.

"No, I didn't let him chop it," Cal said before she could ask.

"An' we caught fish," Charlie told her, hopping from one foot to the other. "We got pictures. Look."

Daisy admired the pictures Cal had taken of Charlie and the fish. One of them, though, startled her as his expression in it was so much like Alex's. She never thought he looked like Alex. She really didn't know who he looked like, except that he had her color hair. But in that photo of him grinning up at his grandfather she could see that he had Alex's profile. It made her catch her breath.

"What's wrong?" Cal asked.

"Nothing," she said, papering over her surprise. "I was just amazed at the size of the fish."

"It was huuuuuge," Charlie told her proudly. He spread his arms to their fullest extent.

"Well, maybe not quite that big," Cal said.

But to Charlie it was the biggest fish in the world, and he'd had the best time in the world. And he proceeded to tell Daisy all about it after Cal went home and all through dinner and during his bath.

And Daisy nodded and smiled as she listened to her son's nonstop commentary. He'd had a wonderful time. She was glad he had gone. Glad Cal and his parents had had the joy of him.

Mostly, though, she was glad he was home again.

And when she went to bed that night, she thought, *I can do this. I'm going to be fine.*

She and Cal could cope with trading Charlie back and forth. Charlie wasn't a basket case. He was a normal happy little boy. Life was good.

She didn't think about Alex—or his perfect woman.

At least she tried not to.

"How much longer till Christmas?" Charlie asked. He'd been asking for the past four days, ever since he'd got back from Cal's parents'.

"Oh, a long time," Daisy said, tucking him into bed. She'd been saying the same thing every day since, too, because a person who was Almost Five had no concept of time, and she'd quickly discovered that if she said "soon," Charlie expected it to be "right after lunch."

"And my birthday?"

"Not quite as long."

Charlie made a face. "They should hurry up."

"All in good time." Even though she had caught up on things over Thanksgiving already, four days later, she felt her to-do lists getting longer by the minute. Lots of people suddenly remembered they wanted family photos for Christmas, and Daisy, understanding the desire, tried not to disappoint any of them.

She had other jobs, too. Most were from repeat customers who wanted her to do some editorial work, and a promo for a boutique in Soho. But one phone call the day after Thanksgiving had surprised her.

"This is Lauren Nicols," the woman had said when Daisy answered. "You did the photos for my piece on Alexandros Antonides."

"Oh! Yes, of course. I hope they were suitable," Daisy said, her heart quickening.

"More than," Lauren Nicols said warmly. "I was delighted. Alex told me you'd be good, but they were better than I'd hoped. The black and white surprised me, but it was perfect. You caught the man."

"I hope so," Daisy said honestly. "I tried."

"Oh, you did," the other woman assured her. "I wondered if you'd be willing to do some more for me."

"Of Alex?" Daisy asked, startled.

"No, Alex's article is in production. But I do other personality pieces for trade periodicals, usually three or four a month. Would you be interested in working with me on a couple of them at least?"

"I—" Daisy stopped herself before she could refuse, because really, why should she? She had enjoyed doing the photo shoot of Alex, and what better way to make sure her brain kept him in the "business" folder of her mind than to start filling it with other assignments, as well? "Yes," she had said. "I'd like that."

And so she had two shoots for Lauren to do before the holidays, as well.

"Go to sleep," she told Charlie now. "It will get here sooner."

"How much sooner?"

Daisy bent and kissed him good-night. "You'll just have to wait and see."

Charlie made a face. But eventually he screwed his eyes shut, and Daisy, knowing that was going to be his best attempt, smiled and turned out the light. "Night, Chaz," she said softly. Then she pulled the door and went down the hall to her office where she'd be working until midnight at least.

First on the docket were the wedding photos she'd taken last night. Wednesday night weddings weren't common, but this had been a small intimate affair to which Daisy had been thrilled to be invited—and eager to take the photos.

They were her wedding present to the couple because both the bride and the groom were "hers."

Seeing Rafaela Cruz, a tech at Murphy's veterinarian's office, and Gino Martinelli, a cop who lived in Finn MacCauley's building, standing at the altar together made Daisy's heart sing for she had helped them find each other.

When she'd learned that besides being a photographer, Daisy was a matchmaker, Rafaela had said, "Huh. Not sure I believe in that."

"Some people don't," Daisy had replied. She wasn't in the market to twist anyone's arm. But Rafaela had wanted to know more because, as she said, "I don't believe there's any good men left." So Daisy had spent time talking to her, trying to discover who, beneath her bluster, Rafaela really was.

Even when she finally said she wanted to try it, Rafaela had had her doubts.

And she and Gino had definitely not been "love at first sight."

Gino, who was Rip MacCauley's soccer coach, had been badly burned in an earlier relationship. But somehow he was the one Daisy had thought of when Rafaela had challenged her to "prove there's one good man."

"Come watch him coach," Daisy had suggested.

Rafaela had dismissed the idea. "I don't want a coach. I want a husband."

"You want a patient man," Daisy said. "A man who works hard and values kids and will be there for you and your family no matter what."

"Yes, but—" Rafaela had protested.

"Maybe Gino could be that man. Unless you're afraid to

try?" Daisy had challenged her right back. Then she'd turned around and challenged a reluctant Gino, too.

"She's too pretty," Gino had said. "She'll want some hot-shot stud."

Daisy had just looked him up and down. "And you're not a stud?"

Gino had laughed at that. "All right. Bring her on."

They'd been cautious to the point that Daisy sometimes wanted to bang their heads together. But gradually Rafaela and Gino had faced their doubts, had given each other a shot. Had discovered in each other what Daisy had seen from early days. Over the summer they had fallen in love.

And now they were married.

Daisy's gift to them was going to be a book of photos she'd taken throughout their courtship and at their wedding. She just needed to get it finished. The pages from the courtship were done. Now she picked up the wedding invitation and set it on the flatbed scanner. It was high rag content paper, heavy and elegant.

Daisy remembered when she'd plucked it out of the mailbox right before Thanksgiving. She had stared at it, feeling an odd sinking sensation in the pit of her stomach because she hadn't thought it was Rafaela and Gino's invitation at all.

She'd thought it was Alex's.

She'd been shocked at the relief she'd felt upon opening it to discover Rafaela's and Gino's names inside.

Of course, she'd told herself logically, even if Alex had run right out and asked his perfect woman to marry him the minute he'd left her that night, they wouldn't have been sending out invitations right away.

But logic had never had much to do with anything where her relationship with Alex was concerned.

Now, taking an expansive breath, Daisy smoothed the invitation flat and lowered the lid, then pushed the scanning button.

The phone rang as it was appearing on her screen. She picked it up absently. "Daisy Connolly."

"Daisy." The voice was gruff and instantly recognizable. "I have a favor to ask."

"Alex," she said as soon as she could breathe again. "What do you want?"

"A date."

Once more Daisy's breath caught in her throat. Then she realized what he was really asking for. "I am not matchmaking for you."

"I don't want you to fix me up with a date. I want you."

I want you. She knew he didn't mean it the way it sounded. She didn't *want* him to mean it the way it sounded. But she didn't know what he did mean, either. "What are you talking about?"

"I need a date for Saturday night."

"*Need* a date?" That had to be a first.

"There's a big charity fund-raising dinner and dance at the Plaza. Remember I told you I designed a new wing for a hospital? Well, I'm on the guest list—and they're giving me some plaque or something—so I have to show up. With a date."

Daisy waited a beat. "What happened to Caroline?"

"Caroline had to fly out to Hong Kong this afternoon. Unexpected breakdown of some project she'd been overseeing. She won't be back for a week. I can't show up alone. I've already committed for two. They expect me to bring someone. Head table and all that."

"Head table?"

He grunted. "So I need a replacement." And apparently in

his mind it was perfectly logical that she would drop eve
thing and accompany him to some society event in anoth
woman's place.

Daisy focused on the wedding invitation on her screen.
"Get your matchmaker to find you one."

"Can't."

"Of course you can."

"No," Alex said tersely. "I can't. Thanks to you."

That startled her. "Me? Why me?"

"Because, damn it, you're the one who told me to take it
slow. 'Don't ask her to marry you yet. Get to know her,' you
said. Make sure she's 'the one.'"

He'd listened?

"So I have been. It isn't easy because half the time I'm out
of town or she is. But we've gone out more."

"As well you should," Daisy said firmly, still surprised that
he'd done it.

"So I can't ask Amalie to find me a date, can I?" Alex said.
"If I went out with someone else now—someone new—what
would that say to Caroline? Not to mention that I'd be creating false expectations in whoever Amalie found."

Daisy was somewhere between dazed and amazed. "You
thought of that all by yourself?" Since when had Alex put
thought into the repercussions of relationships?

"Can I help it if you put ideas in my head?"

"Good for me." She grinned in spite of herself.

"So you see the problem. It has to be you."

Daisy pressed back against the desk chair she sat in and
asked, "Why won't I upset Caroline?"

"She knows I need a date. I told her I was going to ask you.
She'll be glad I've found an old friend to go with."

"Old friend?" Daisy echoed.

nean. So," he went on briskly, "Satur-
equivalent for you. I'll pick you up
where do you live?"

Wait. I didn't agree."

don't stand behind your own advice?"

usy opened her mouth to object, and couldn't find words
to convince herself, let alone ones that would convince as stubborn a man as Alex.

"I can't," she said feebly.

"Why not?"

Because I don't have a babysitter. She didn't say that, even
though it was certainly true. "I— My wardrobe doesn't run
to that sort of thing."

"Get something suitable," he directed. "I'll pay for it."

"You will not. I can't—"

"Did you or did you not tell me to take my time, get to
know Caroline?"

"Yes, but—" She stopped, waiting for him to cut her
off, but he didn't. He waited in silence for her next reason
she couldn't go. And she didn't have one—other than self-
protection.

Maybe she was protesting too much. Maybe going with
him would be the best self-protection there could be.

Maybe spending an evening with Alexandros Antonides,
going on a date with him, would actually force her to "move
on" once and for all.

Last time she'd felt like Cinderella going to the ball—and
she'd believed she'd found Prince Charming. If she went now,
she would go with no illusions at all.

She could even dance with him—but know it ended
there—know that her happy ending was waiting at home in
her life with her son.

She would be in no danger of succumbing to airy-fairy fantasies. She would enjoy the evening and come home at midnight—unlike Cinderella—with both shoes on and her heart intact.

Daisy took a breath. "Yes, all right. I'll do it."

"Great." He sounded pleased. "What's your address?"

"I'll meet you there."

Alex argued. Daisy was adamant. He said she was being silly. She said she didn't care.

"I'm not your real date. I don't need to act like one. I will see myself to the Plaza and I'll see myself home afterward."

"Daisy, that's ridic—"

"Take it or leave it."

There was a long silence, then an exasperated sigh. "Fine. Quarter to eight. Front steps of the Plaza. This Saturday. Don't be late."

She was out of her mind.

Absolutely insane.

She couldn't go out with Alex! She didn't have a babysitter. And even if she could find one, she didn't have a dress. Nor did she have a fairy godmother and some talented singing mice who could whip one up in an afternoon.

She was in a complete dither the next afternoon when Izzy and the boys stopped by for a visit after Rip's orthodontist appointment.

Izzy took one look at Daisy pacing around the kitchen and demanded, "What's the matter with you?" Her boys went running out back to play with Charlie, but Izzy stood right where she was and studied Daisy with concern.

"Nothing's wrong with me."

"Really?" Izzy's tone dripped disbelief. "You're pacing the floor. You're tearing your hair."

True, but Daisy stopped long enough to put the kettle on. "I have to go out tomorrow night. To the Plaza."

Izzy's eyes widened. "A date? At last!" She beamed and rubbed her hands together.

"Not a date! Nothing like that," Daisy said quickly. "It's business. Well, sort of business." She couldn't quite explain.

"Who with?" Izzy demanded.

"A cousin of Lukas's. An old…friend." Which was the truth, wasn't it? Alex had even called her "an old friend." "I knew him years ago. He's interested in getting married. Wanted me to matchmake for him. I said no. Now he's got a serious girlfriend, but she's out of town. So he asked me to go in her place."

It sounded quite believable to Daisy.

Izzy immediately caught the snag. "Why wouldn't you matchmake for him? I thought you loved matching people with their soul mates."

"Yes, but—" She wasn't going into what Alex thought about soul mates. "I didn't feel I knew him well enough." Daisy turned away and started rearranging the forks in her silverware drawer. A Tarzan-like yodel from the backyard turned her around in time to see Izzy's oldest son, Rip, hurtle out of the tree at the end of the garden. He and his younger brother, Crash, were Charlie's heroes.

"Mountain goats," Izzy muttered. "I can make them stop if you want."

Daisy shook her head, grateful the conversation had veered away from Alex. "It's all right. Charlie loves trying to keep up with them. And it's good for him to have them. He needs older brothers."

"Not these two." Izzy winced as Crash followed his brother's leap with one of his own. "What's he like? This cousin of Lukas's," Izzy elaborated at Daisy's blank stare. "Your 'old friend'? One of the dark handsome Antonides men, is he?"

Daisy did her best at a negligent shrug. "I guess."

"Not a wild man like Lukas, I hope."

"No. He's not like Lukas," she said. "He's very...driven."

"Is that why you're chewing your nails?"

"I'm chewing my nails because I can't find a babysitter. I already called your girls."

"Tansy and Pansy are hopeless now they're in college," Izzy agreed cheerfully. "They have lives." She sighed. "But no worries. I'll keep him."

Daisy blinked. "You will? Are you sure?"

"Absolutely. If you don't mind me having him at our place." Izzy picked up the kettle and began pouring boiling water because Daisy wasn't doing it. "He can even spend the night. In case you don't want to turn into a pumpkin right after the Plaza." She grinned.

Daisy flushed and shook her head. "Not a chance. I am a pumpkin. Home before midnight. This is not a date. But Charlie would love to go to your place, if you're sure."

Izzy waved a hand airily. "I'll never notice he's there." She zeroed back in. "What are you wearing?"

"That's my other problem," Daisy admitted. Nothing in her wardrobe lent itself to upscale fund-raisers at the Plaza. And despite his brusque "Get something. I'll pay for it," she had no intention of allowing herself to feel beholden to Alex.

Izzy was thoughtfully silent for a long moment. Then, "I might have something," she said, looking Daisy up and down assessingly. "Ichiro Sorrento," she said.

"What?"

"That new designer whose collection Finn shot last year. Japanese-Italian. You remember him?"

Daisy did. But she shook her head. "No way I can afford anything with his label."

"You don't have to. You can wear mine. Remember that gorgeous dress and jacket I wore to Finn's opening last spring?"

Daisy's eyes widened. "*That* dress?" The dress had been a deep-sapphire-blue silk, spare and elegant, with an exquisitely embroidered jacket in the same deep blues, emerald-green and hints of violet. "You don't want me wearing your gorgeous dress. I'd spill something on it."

"I already have. It doesn't show," Izzy said cheerfully.

"I'm taller than you are."

"Everyone is taller than I am," Izzy countered. "So what? You'll just show more leg. I doubt anyone will mind. Especially—" she grinned "—not a male Antonides."

"Not. A. Date," Daisy reiterated firmly. "I'm not trying to show off my legs."

"Of course not. But you're not a nun, either. You need to knock Mr. Driven Antonides's socks off. Make him forget all about his serious girlfriend and run off to Vegas with you!"

It was as if a little devil called Izzy was sitting on her shoulder tempting her. "Dream on," Daisy scoffed.

"A little dreaming never hurt anyone," Izzy retorted.

Daisy let her have the last word.

But in her heart she begged to differ.

Where the hell was she?

Dozens of hired cars and limos and taxis slid up to the Plaza's entrance Saturday evening while Alex stood on the steps, shifting from one foot to the other, watching and waiting. There were snowflakes in the air. Alex could see his breath, and his shoulders were getting damp as the snow melted, but he couldn't bring himself to go inside and wait and pace.

There were scores of black-tie-clad men and elegantly dressed women getting out of taxis and limos—and not one of them was Daisy.

He'd told her quarter to *eight*. It was almost ten after. He'd got here early, to be sure he was here when she arrived, and she was nowhere to be seen.

He should never have given in to her demand that she come on her own, that he neither pick her up nor take her home after. He'd agreed only because she would have refused to come otherwise. The sweet and malleable Daisy he had known five years ago might still be somewhere inside this Daisy Connolly, but he hadn't caught a glimpse of her in a long, long time.

Was this her revenge? Was standing him up payback for his having said he wasn't interested in marriage all those years ago?

He shouldn't have asked her to come. It was a damn fool idea. When Caroline had said she couldn't make it, but suggested he invite his friend Daisy, he'd been surprised.

"My friend Daisy?" he'd echoed, puzzled.

Caroline had shrugged. "I assume she's your friend. You talk about her all the time."

Did he? Surely not. But he could hardly deny their friendship if it came across that way to Caroline because how could he justify talking about her if she wasn't a friend? What would Caroline think if he said she wasn't a friend at all, she was…a thorn in his side, an itch he never quite managed to get rid of. Like poison ivy, perhaps.

So he'd shrugged and told Caroline he'd ask. And, hell, why not? He could prove to Daisy that he'd listened, that he hadn't gone straight home and asked Caroline to marry him. He'd done what Daisy suggested and got to know her.

He hadn't fallen in love with her. That wasn't going to happen. He knew it. Caroline knew it.

They had seen each other as often as their schedules allowed. They always had a good time. Relationship-wise they were on the same page—and perfectly happy to be there. And if they still hadn't managed to make it to bed together, well, the time had never been right.

She'd had an early meeting or he was flying off to Paris. She was in Rio or he was in Vancouver. It had nothing to do with memories of Daisy in his bed. She hadn't been in this bed.

Only in his bedroom. And the fact that he couldn't forget that was still driving him nuts.

"Alex!" A hearty booming voice from the doorway startled him back to the present—back to the lack of Daisy anywhere in sight. He turned to see Tom Holcomb, the hospital's vice president in charge of building development.

Tom was grinning broadly, holding out a hand to shake. "Good to see you. Big night for you." He pumped Alex's hand, then looked around. "Where's your date?"

Alex opened his mouth, hoping that a suitable polite reply would come out when, all of a sudden, from behind a hand caught his.

"Sorry," Daisy said, catching her breath.

Alex turned his head, saw her smiling up at him, and felt his heart do some sort of triple axel in his chest. There was a glow to her cheeks, as if she'd been running, but she was smiling.

And so was he. His heart which, after the triple axel, had seemed to stop all together as he looked at her, began beating again. "About time," he said gruffly, swallowing his relief. She was gorgeous. She wore a long black wool dress coat and he could barely get a glimpse of the dress beneath it, but what he could see seemed to sparkle—just as Daisy did. Her eyes were alight, electric almost, taking in everything. She'd pinned her hair up in some sort of intricate knot which reminded him of the way she'd worn it at the wedding when he'd met her. He remembered taking it down, running his fingers through it. Felt a quickening in his body at the temptation to do it again now. It was, after all, already slightly askew, as if she had been running.

"My cab got stuck in traffic. Think I stood you up?" She laughed.

"No." He wiped damp palms down the sides of his trousers. He wasn't admitting anything.

"Your date, I presume?"

Alex was suddenly conscious of Tom Holcomb still standing beside him, looking with interest at Daisy.

Alex nodded and drew her forward. "This is Daisy Connolly. Daisy, Tom Holcomb. He is the VP in charge of building development, the man I worked with on the hospital design."

"The man who rubber-stamped his terrific ideas," Tom corrected, shaking the hand Daisy offered. "I'm delighted to meet you. Are you an architect, too?"

"No. A photographer," Daisy said, shaking the hand he held out. "I recently did a photo shoot of Alex at a building he restored in Brooklyn."

"A man of many talents," Tom agreed. He drew Daisy with him into the hotel, asking questions about her own work which she answered, still smiling. And Daisy, with a glance back at Alex, went with him.

Alex stood watching, bemused, and somehow a little dazed.

Dazed by Daisy. Dazzling Daisy, he thought, smiling wryly

at his own foolishness. But it was true. And he didn't mind following, it gave him a chance to admire her from another angle.

From any angle tonight she was elegant, sophisticated, tailored, stylish. She would never be the stunning classical beauty that Caroline was. Daisy's nose still had a spattering of freckles, her cheekbones were not quite as sharply pronounced. Her mouth was less sculpted than impish. And you could never say that Daisy had every hair in place.

But everything about her was alive—from her unruly hair to her lively sparkling eyes to her kissable lips.

Alex tried not to think about her kissable lips. It wasn't as if he was going to be tasting them again this evening. Furthermore, he reminded himself, he shouldn't even want to. He was this close to buying Caroline an engagement ring.

But Caroline's kisses had never intoxicated him. They'd never made him hot and hard and hungry in a matter of an instant. He'd lost every bit of his common sense that weekend with Daisy—and she hadn't had any at all.

There had never been anything cool, calm and collected about her. She was a lead-with-her-heart, damn-the-torpedoes, full-speed-ahead sort of woman.

Basically the anti-Caroline. And Caroline was what he wanted.

Wasn't she?

"Are you coming?"

Alex jerked his brain back into gear to see that Tom had disappeared into the hotel, but that Daisy was still standing at the top of the stairs by the revolving door, waiting.

"Got distracted. Sorry." He bounded up the steps, feeling awkward, caught out. And feeling that way, he challenged her. "Been running?" he asked her gruffly.

"I told you," she said with some asperity. "The cab was caught in traffic. I left it in the middle of Columbus Circle."

"You *walked* from Columbus Circle?" Wide-eyed he stared at her high pointy-toed heels.

"No," she said flatly. "I ran."

Definitely the anti-Caroline. Alex shook his head, dazed and amazed, and unable to keep from grinning. "Of course you did."

Daisy glared, her eyes flashing. "You said not to be late!"

"So I did." His grin widened briefly, then he met her gaze. "Thank you."

Their eyes locked. And Alex felt the electricity arc between them exactly the way it always did. It didn't seem to matter that she was all wrong for him. He jerked his gaze away from hers, but it only went as far as her lips. Nervously she licked them.

Alex's body went on full alert.

Daisy tore her gaze away. "It sounded like the sort of occasion where it wouldn't do to waltz in late," she said, a little ragged edge to her voice. "Not if you're at the head table."

She was right, of course. He was being a fool—again.

Impatient with his own weakness, Alex gestured her brusquely into the revolving door. "Well, let's not waste your sacrifice, then. We'll go in."

Daisy was in complete control.

She might as well have had a squadron of singing mice and a fairy godmother the way everything had fallen into place. Izzy was keeping Charlie, the glitzy shimmery dress fit perfectly, the sophisticated black dress coat her mother had given her for her birthday was beautifully appropriate. Other than the stupid traffic jam and having to run quarter of a mile and that she could feel her hair slipping from its knot, she didn't have a care in the world.

Granted her first glimpse of Alex in formal attire, complete with black tie, pristine white shirt, checking his watch impatiently as he waited for her, had made her mouth dry and her heart gallop. But, Daisy assured herself, that was because she'd just been running, not because of the man himself.

Still, once in the hotel, on the arm of the handsomest man in the room, it was hard not to believe she was channeling Cinderella.

Daisy had been to the Plaza before. But she'd never been to An Event.

This was An Event—in a cavernous room that despite its immensity, managed somehow to seem warm and appealing and elegant with matte gold walls, burgundy drapes, glimmering sconces and crystal chandeliers. The dozens of tables wore pristine white damask linens, sported napkins folded by origami experts, and had settings of gleaming china and rows of delicate stemware.

Not a bowl of mac and cheese in sight.

When she worked for Finn, Daisy had gone to plenty of glitz-and-glamour events. In the fashion industry they'd been brasher and flashier, not to mention, thousands of decibels louder than this one. A girl from small town Colorado had been very much out of her league. But after the first half dozen or so, she had become blasé and soon she began waltzing through them without batting an eyelash.

Of course those rarely required her to look suave and elegant and remember which fork to use. Tonight there looked to be a surfeit of forks. But it wasn't the number of forks that was making her blood race. It was Alex.

"Can I get you something to drink? Wine? A cocktail?"

"I'll have a glass of wine," Daisy decided. "Red."

They'd drunk a smooth dark burgundy when they'd first met. If she was going to rewrite the ending of their encounter, she would begin tonight the way they'd begun before. But this time she wouldn't let herself embroider the circumstances with airy-fairy fantasies of happily ever afters.

"Burgundy," Alex said, surprising her. Did he remember? But she couldn't—wouldn't—ask.

"I'll be right back." He headed toward the bar.

When he returned, drinks in hand, Daisy was standing near the wall right where Alex had left her. She drew his eye clear across the room. The dress he'd glimpsed before she'd shed her coat definitely lived up to its promise. Its blue-green iridescence sparkled like northern lights as it molded her every curve. The short embroidered jacket covered more than he wished, hinting at bare shoulders beneath, smooth shoulders he remembered kissing all too well.

But it was more than the dress that drew his gaze, more than the dress that made the woman. There was a warmth and a vibrant energy in Daisy—as if she were the only person there in three dimensions. Everyone else seemed flat by comparison.

She had been alone when he'd left her, but now she was chatting with hospital CEO Douglas Standish and his wife. Daisy's expression was animated, interested. He remembered her that way from the moment he'd first seen her. She engaged with people, drew them out. She had drawn him.

Never particularly social, Alex had attended the wedding with the intent of leaving as soon as it was reasonable to do so. He'd drifted around the periphery of the room, keeping his eye on the exit—until he'd seen Daisy.

Then he'd only had eyes for her. It was still that way.

Now he wound his way through the crowds of people, heading toward her as determinedly as he had that long-ago day.

"Here you go." He handed the drink to Daisy, then turned to Standish's wife. "May I get you a drink?"

"No, thank you, dear. Douglas will do that. I just wanted to meet your lovely lady—and tell her how lovely you are—" her eyes twinkled merrily when Alex opened his mouth to protest "—and what an amazing gift you've given us with the design for the hospital wing."

"Thank you for saying so."

She patted him on the sleeve. "Have a wonderful evening. You deserve it. So nice to meet you, dear," she said to Daisy, before taking her husband's arm and guiding them into the crowd.

"So," Daisy said, looking him in the eye when the other woman had left, "you're the guest of honor. And you couldn't be bothered to tell me?"

Alex shrugged. "It's no big deal."

Daisy's eyes glittered. "It's a huge deal," she contradicted him. "Huge. Apparently your hospital wing has broken new ground in patient services. It's celebrated worldwide." She had gone beyond glitter to glare now. "They're giving you an award."

"I told you that when you did the photos for the article."

"An award, you said. You didn't tell me anything about it. It might have been for perfect attendance at meetings for all I knew! This is wonderful!" And now her wonderful eyes sparkled with warmth and delight, and in spite of himself, Alex felt a rush of pleasure. "Did you tell Caroline?"

"No," he said, surprised.

"Why not?"

He shrugged. "It's nothing to do with her."

"Of course it is!"

Baffled, he shook his head. "Why?" She hadn't done anything. He hadn't even known her when he'd done it himself.

"Because *you* did it! Because you're her man."

But he *wasn't* Caroline's man. He wasn't anyone's man. But he wasn't going to have that argument with Daisy now. Fortunately people were beginning to head to their seats. So he just said, "Come on. We need to go sit down." He took her arm, more aware of touching her than he was whenever he touched Caroline. He led her to the table where they would be sitting, then pulled out her chair.

Daisy flounced down into it, but she still wasn't done. She looked up at him, her expression annoyed. "She'd be thrilled," she told him. "And proud. I am—proud," she said, "and it's nothing at all to do with me."

Alex felt a warm flush of pleasure at her admitting that. What he didn't do was tell her that it wasn't entirely true.

He would never have taken the commission at all if something she'd said to him hadn't stuck with him for the past five years. Initially he'd said no. He had no interest in hospital design. He didn't like hospitals. Hated them, in fact.

After his brother had got leukemia, Alex had spent far too much time in hospitals watching his brother suffer and become more and more remote. It had devastated him. Even now Alex associated hospitals with the most painful period of his life.

After Vass's death, Alex had never set foot in one again. Even when he broke his arm playing lacrosse in college, he'd insisted on having it set at a doctor's office. "No hospital," he'd said firmly. It was the last place he wanted to be.

He didn't talk about hospitals, either. Didn't talk about Vass.

Never had to anyone. Except that weekend when Daisy had got under his skin.

He supposed it was because she was just getting her equilibrium back after losing her father. Barely fifty, he'd been born with a heart defect that had grown worse over time. He'd been in and out of the hospital often, she'd said. And the sad wistful look on her face had prompted Alex to confide that he, too, hated hospitals.

"They take away your life," he'd said harshly, remembering how remote and sterile they had seemed, how they'd isolated his brother, how Vass had wanted to come home so badly, to be out, to be anywhere but there. "They don't save it."

He'd expected her to agree.

Instead she'd shaken her head. "It wasn't the hospital's fault. Without the care my dad got there, we'd have lost him sooner. But it was hard for him to feel connected. He felt so isolated, like he wasn't really a part of things anymore."

Vass had said the same thing.

"There was only one window," she'd gone on. "But he couldn't see outside from his bed. So we used to pretend. We'd close our eyes and pretend he was home or we were going fishing in the San Juan or even doing chores, chopping wood for the fireplace. He loved that fireplace…" Daisy had swallowed then, and her eyes had glistened with unshed tears. She'd blinked them back rapidly. "It wasn't the hospital's fault," she repeated. "But it could have been better. It could have been more."

Her words had made Alex think.

What if Vass had had a chance to spend time in a hospital that had allowed him to feel connected. What if he'd been able to do, at least virtually, the things he wanted to do—like go back to the beach near their island home, or drive a race car, or sail over the Alps in a hot-air balloon?

Once Alex opened the floodgates, the ideas wouldn't stop coming. And what hadn't been possible twenty-five to thirty years ago was within reach now.

Alex's hospital wing was full of windows—floor-to-ceiling in many rooms. Even treatment rooms, wherever possible, brought the outside in. If a patient wanted to see the world beyond the walls, he could. The semirural setting just across the river north of the city provided views of the countryside as well as the city skyline. And it wasn't just about the visuals. Alex worked in sound systems and even olfactory ones, connecting senses to the world beyond the hospital's confines.

He had provided virtual worlds, as well. Patients in the wing he'd designed could close their eyes as Daisy's father had, but they could also use modern electronics to create the sights, sounds and smells of the seashore, the woods, the inside of a race car or the ballroom of a fairy-tale palace.

He told her about it now, aware of the way she looked at him, as if he could hang the moon. The salads that had been in front of them when they'd sat down remained virtually untouched.

"It sounds like an amazing place." Daisy smiled, a smile that went all the way to her eyes, that touched—as it always did—a place hidden somewhere deep inside him that no one ever reached but her.

He cleared his throat. "If you have to be in a hospital," he agreed gruffly, "if you can't have what the rest of the world takes for granted, I guess it will do."

Their eyes met. And Alex knew that whether or not he mentioned his brother or her father, Daisy remembered. Daisy knew.

What surprised him, though, was her withdrawal. One minute she'd been gazing at him with warmth and admiration. The next some shadow seemed to settle over her, her expression shuttered.

"I'm sure that all the children will appreciate it." Her tone was polite, but she seemed suddenly more remote. She turned to her salad and began to eat.

Alex was more nettled by her withdrawal than he would have liked. But really, what difference did it make? He hadn't done it for her. He'd done it for people like her father, his brother. He dug into his own salad.

Neither of them spoke until the salads were taken away and the entree was set before them. Then Daisy turned toward him again. "What sort of building are you working on now?"

So they were going to be polite and proper and distant. Fine by him. Alex was glad to talk about the present so he told her about the office building he was designing on the edge of Paris.

Daisy had never been to Paris. And as he talked, he saw her eyes begin to sparkle again. Her remoteness vanished. Her questions came more quickly, and her enthusiasm was contagious. He wanted to make her smile, wanted to have her cock her head and listen eagerly. Alex found himself telling her not just about his work in Paris, but about the city itself, about places he liked, things he'd seen, galleries he visited, buildings he admired.

"You used to live there, didn't you?" It was the first time she'd alluded to the past.

"Yes. And then I was here for a while. But I went back four or five years ago," he said. He knew precisely when he'd gone—and why. After the disastrous end to his weekend with

Daisy, New York had more memories than he wanted. Paris seemed like a far safer place to be.

It was only in the past six months or so—when he'd made up his mind to marry, in fact—that he'd returned to live more or less permanently in New York. Even now, though, he kept his small flat in the fifth arrondissement.

Their talk moved from Paris to the Riviera, to other places he'd been. Daisy asked about all of them. The women Amalie had set him up with had asked questions, too, but not like Daisy. Not as if they cared about the answers.

Daisy did. And her interest and enthusiasm drew him out. He would have liked to show her Paris, to walk the wide boulevards and narrow lanes with her, to sit at a tiny table in an outdoor café and drink strong dark coffee with her, to wander through the museums and the galleries hand in hand with her, to walk along the Seine with her and kiss her there, to run through a rainstorm with her.

To take her back to his little garret flat and make love with her. He could imagine Daisy there, letting him strip off her little embroidered jacket, then letting him find the zip at the back of her dress and lower it slowly. He'd kiss his way down—inch by luscious inch and—

"And what?" Daisy was looking at him, curious and impatient.

Hot. God, he was hot. And hard. And suddenly aware that he was in the middle of a crowded room with the object of his fantasy studying him worriedly. Her eyes were still bright and eager, but she was looking at him with puzzlement.

"What happened? You stopped talking," Daisy said. "Did you just get distracted?"

Alex's heart was still hammering, his body still feeling the effects of what he'd been thinking about—her. He shifted in his chair and cleared his throat. "I did, yes." He gave a quick shake of his head. "Sorry about that."

He didn't let it happen again, even though he was still intensely aware of her. It was almost a relief when dinner ended. Except then the speeches began, and Alex knew he would have to say something when the award was presented.

Public speaking wasn't his forte. He preferred to speak with his work, with his design, with his buildings, not his words.

But when the time came, Daisy clapped madly and beamed at him encouragingly when Douglas Standish beckoned him to the podium to accept his award.

Alex made it brief. He gripped the podium and stared into the bright lights as he thanked the hospital board who had given him the opportunity to design the wing and the committee who had given him the award. It was what he had prepared, and it was all he had intended to say.

But before he could walk away, his gaze slid across the hundreds of people in the room and, looking down, he didn't see the lights. He saw Daisy.

His mouth went dry at the sight of her upturned face, at her avid expression, her tantalizing smile. And he didn't walk away. He looked at her, spoke to her.

His voice was less stilted and more ragged as he said, "I hope this wing makes a difference to the patients. I hope it gives them the safe haven they need to get well and—" he paused, his eyes still locked with hers "—the connections to the world outside to keep them strong."

Like your father never had. Like my brother never had. And you're the only one who knows why I did it.

He could see that in her eyes, the realization dawning, her lips parting in a silent O.

Alex jerked his gaze away and abruptly shut his mouth.

Then, clutching the award in a sweaty hand, he said hoarsely, "Thank you all," and strode back to his chair and sat down.

His heart was crashing in his chest. He didn't look at Daisy. He didn't have to. He could sense her eyes on him. The awareness, the emotion vibrated between them. So damn much emotion it felt like being swept off by a tidal wave. He kept his gaze resolutely on the platform where Douglas was coming back to speak.

With a few brief words he thanked Alex again, then thanked all the hospital's staff and benefactors for their support. Then the doors opened to the adjoining ballroom and the small live orchestra just beyond those doors began to play.

People stood up, couples headed toward the dance floor. Alex breathed again.

Abruptly he stood and held out a hand. "Let's dance."

Chapter 7

Putting her hand in his was like touching a live wire.

A current of electricity seemed to flow between them, one even stronger than the flickering awareness she'd felt all night.

Daisy was aware of the pressure of Alex's strong fingers wrapping around hers as he led her through the doors and onto the dance floor. But it was nothing compared to her awareness when he took her in his arms.

She almost stumbled against him as she tried to do the opposite and keep a respectable distance between them. It was a battle because every instinct in her went to him like a moth to the proverbial flame.

Every touch was memorable. His fingers encased hers warmly. She was exquisitely aware of his hand pressing lightly at the small of her back. She was close enough that she could catch a faint hint of soap and aftershave. And a quick glance showed her how smooth-shaven his jaw was. She remembered it rougher, had loved to stroke her hand over it, stubbled one way, smooth the other.

Abruptly she turned her head, trying to follow his lead at the same time and nearly tripped over his foot. He caught her, pulled her closer. And Daisy knew the sensation of her body melting into his, as if she belonged there, wrapped in his arms.

She had danced with lots of other men. She had felt other men's hands on her body. None—not even Cal's—evoked such strong reactions.

Even now, knowing he was not for her, knowing for a fact that she and Alex had no future, Daisy could not deny that Alex's touch, Alex's smile, Alex's gaze brought to life something inside her that no other man's ever had.

Dancing with Alex was, just as it had been five years ago, the Cinderella experience that Daisy had remembered.

She understood now how she had been swept away by it. There was a feeling of rightness, of perfect understanding, that she'd never had with anyone else. And it scared her to feel it again and know how wrong it had been.

She forced herself to remain clearheaded and sane. She looked away from his hard jaw to study the room, determined to commit it to memory. She focused on the music, tried to think of the title, the composer, to isolate the instruments. And all the while she was aware of the man who held her in his arms.

His breath teased the tendrils of her hair. His trouser-clad legs brushed the silk of her dress. And every touch, every brush set off a hum of something electric. And the study of the room and the music and everything else faded away.

It was all right, she told herself. Nothing was going to happen on a dance floor. He couldn't sweep her off her feet. She couldn't slide a hand between the buttons of his shirt.

So where was the harm in appreciating the feel of hard muscles under her fingertips? Why not give in, just for the moment, to the instinctive rhythm they seemed to engage in when they moved to the music? As long as she didn't allow herself to remember the instinctive rhythm they'd brought to their lovemaking…

There was a point beyond which lay foolishness. Daisy had been there once. Never again.

Careful, she warned herself. Be careful.

But her head turned and so did his. Her lips brushed his jaw. His touched her ear. A shiver ran from the hairs on her neck to the tips of her toes. Her body trembled. Her knees wobbled. And deep in the center of her, something ached with the desire she refused to admit.

She took a breath. "So," she said, "tell me about Caroline."

She was gratified when Alex seemed briefly to stumble. But then he caught himself and without even looking directly at him, she saw his jaw ease as if he were smiling.

"Caroline is amazing," he said. "She's quick. Witty. Beautiful."

His voice was warm, animated. Of course it was. Caroline was his woman. *Remember that,* Daisy told herself sharply and kept asking him Caroline-related questions.

Maybe it was masochistic. Maybe it was just the only way to keep her common sense. Whatever it was, it helped. Daisy made herself listen as he told her all about the ad campaign Caroline was developing that had taken her to Hong Kong. Alex told her about how Caroline had been headhunted by five different companies in the past two years.

"She's amazingly successful. Definitely making her mark. She's even thinking she might go out on her own in the next couple of years." He clearly approved of her ambition and her talent. Daisy forced herself to think about that and not about the way his legs brushed against hers.

"So what are you waiting for if she's so wonderful?" She ventured a glance at his face, wanting to see his expression.

A tiny crease appeared between his brows. The muscles in his shoulder tensed beneath her hand, and hard green eyes looked down into hers. "I thought you weren't in favor of quick decisions these days," he said sharply.

"Yes, well, I'm not you."

Alex grunted. He didn't say anything else. Didn't answer. Didn't talk about Caroline anymore, either.

Daisy tried to stifle her irritation. She told herself it didn't matter, but for some reason it did. It would be easier if he were engaged. Easier to stop thinking about how damned appealing he still was.

Well, fine, if he wouldn't help her out by talking about Caroline, she'd talk about the pulmonologist whose photos she'd taken for Lauren Nicols.

"I have to thank you for sending Lauren my way," she said. She didn't really want to be beholden to him. But it was her own work that had caused Lauren to call, nothing he'd done. So she talked about that. And Alex seemed grateful enough to take up that topic of conversation. Then the dance was over, and Douglas Standish asked to partner her for the next one.

She danced with half a dozen men, and only reaffirmed that no one's touch affected her the way Alex's did. She seemed to be aware of him—where he was, who he was dancing with— even when he was nowhere near. Actually though, he always seemed to be somewhere fairly near. Wherever her partners danced her, Alex was never far away.

She tried not to look at him, tried not to envy the women he held in his arms, tried not to gauge if he had held them as closely as he'd held her. But she couldn't help noticing that while he danced and chatted with them, his gaze often sought her.

It didn't mean anything. It couldn't.

But she couldn't quite stifle the gratification she felt every time she felt his eyes on her. She didn't dare catch his eye, though. It would be playing with fire. And Daisy had no intention of playing with fire, though there seemed to be one kindling somewhere just south of her midsection, and every time she looked his way, the fire grew.

The evening passed quickly. It was nine-thirty. Ten. Then nearly eleven. They danced. They visited with people Alex had worked with. They danced again. And this time the flames burned even hotter than before.

His eyes seemed to bore into hers whenever she looked at him. Their legs brushed. Their bodies touched. Against her breasts, she could feel the beat of his heart. With everyone else they spoke easily, casually. But when they danced, they had little to say to each other, and the conflagration continued to build.

It wasn't yet midnight, not even eleven-thirty. But Daisy knew she needed to be sensible. While she wouldn't turn into a pumpkin at midnight, and Izzy was keeping Charlie until the morning, a woman could stand just so much temptation.

But one more dance wouldn't hurt, she thought as the music began again and, wordlessly, Alex drew her once more into his arms. They hadn't danced with each other two dances in a row. But it seemed natural now. Right.

Inevitable.

Just as, inevitably, in a few minutes she would say thank-you for a nice evening and take her leave.

But now—just for a few moments more, Daisy allowed herself the luxury of lingering close to him, to luxuriate in the warmth and the nearness of his body, to relish the shiver she felt at his warm breath against her hair.

It's all right, she assured herself. It's just now. Just this moment. Not forever. She had no expectations this time. She was only making memories that would last her through the years.

Her body trembled. Vibrated. Particularly her hip.

Her hip? For a moment she didn't know what was happening. The vibration stopped, thank God. But almost instantly, it started again.

Daisy stumbled, realizing that this vibration had nothing to do with the nearness of Alex and everything to do with the tiny mobile phone she'd tucked into the on-seam pocket of the dress.

"You won't need it," Izzy had said.

But Daisy had insisted. Most glitzy high-fashion dresses clung so tightly that anything more than underwear—and sometimes even that—was too much. But Izzy's gorgeous kicky swirly dress flared at the hips, and Daisy had put her phone into one of its tiny pockets.

"Just in case," she'd said, patting it.

"Suit yourself. I won't be calling you," Izzy had vowed.

But someone was calling her now.

Alex caught her when she stumbled. "What's wrong?"

"It's my phone."

His brows drew together. "Your *phone?* Who the hell do you need to talk to tonight?"

Daisy didn't answer that. "Sorry." She shrugged, half apologetic, half worried as she slipped out of his arms and moved to the edge of the dance floor. "I have to get this."

Alex followed her. "One of your clients out on a hot date and need advice?" he growled.

Daisy glanced at the caller ID. It was Izzy. She answered at once. "Is it Charlie? What happened? What's wrong?"

"He's fine," Izzy said quickly. She sounded as out of breath as Daisy felt. "Well, not entirely fine. But nothing life-threatening. Really. Don't panic."

"What *happened?*" Daisy pressed the phone hard against her ear, trying to hear above the music.

"He was following Rip," Izzy reported ruefully. "Doing what the big boys do. They were climbing on the bunk beds. Rip has this notion that he can move all around their bedroom without touching the floor—"

"Oh, God."

"Well, he can," Izzy admitted. "Of course he's bigger than Charlie. He has longer arms and legs. More wingspan."

Daisy didn't need to have it spelled out. "Oh, God," she said again, knees wobbling.

"Charlie's a pretty impressive climber," Izzy said with the calm that came from having got sons through the first decade of their adventurous lives. "And jumper—but he didn't quite make it to the top of the chair from Rip's bunk. He's broken his arm. I'm so sorry, Daisy. I feel terrible. I—"

"Where is he? St. Luke's?"

"Yes. Finn's taking him. We're on a first-name basis with the emergency room staff."

"I'll meet him there." Daisy was already headed for the nearest exit so she could grab her coat and then a cab.

"I'm so sorry," Izzy repeated. "And Rip is devastated."

"Tell him not to worry. I'm sure it will be fine." She just needed to get there. Now.

"I feel so responsible. Or, as Finn says, irresponsible."

"Don't. It's not your fault."

"It is. I forget how much younger Charlie is. Call me as soon as you've seen him. Promise?"

"I promise." Daisy stuffed the phone back into her pocket and headed for the cloak room.

"What is it? What happened?"

Dear God, she'd forgotten about Alex!

Daisy shot him a quick glance and apologetic smile over her shoulder. "I— It's…an emergency. A friend…" She gave a vague wave of her hand as she skirted around groups of people in the foyer. "I'm sorry. I have to go."

"I figured that out," Alex said gruffly. "Not a client."

"No."

"Your ex?" he bit out.

Daisy blinked at him. "What?"

"Guess not. A new boyfriend?" His gaze narrowed. When she didn't answer, it narrowed further. "Did you tell him you were coming out with me?"

There were no answers to anything he was likely to ask now. "I need to go, Alex," she repeated, then forced herself to stop and face him squarely, even managing to paste a smile on her face. "Thank you for this evening. I enjoyed it."

"I did, too," he said, a grim set to his mouth. Then he stepped around her to present the claim check for her coat to the lady behind the desk.

"Thank you. You don't have to wait. I'll just catch a cab."

He didn't reply. But he didn't leave, either. And moments later, when the lady brought her coat and she reached for it, Alex was there first, shaking it out and holding it so she could slip it on.

"Thank you." As the coat settled on her shoulders, Daisy flicked a grateful smile in his general direction. "I'm sorry to run off. I did have a lovely evening." She paused, hoping he'd say, *Of course, I understand. Thank you for coming.* Then, niceties observed, she could dart away.

He said, "I'll come with you."

"No! I mean, no, thank you. It's not necessary. Really, Alex. I mean it," she said when she saw his jaw tighten. "Thank you for everything, but I'll say good-night here." There was a moment's silence. Then, not knowing what else to do, she thrust out a hand for him to shake.

He looked at it as if she'd offered him a poisonous snake.

Hastily Daisy withdrew it. "Good night, Alex." And without giving him time to reply she turned and darted out of the hotel to catch a cab.

He should just let her walk away and get on with his life.

It was clearly what she wanted. Whatever the hell she was doing, dropping everything and running off at the drop of a hat, it wasn't any of his business.

Alex knew that.

She didn't want him there. He knew that, too.

But he couldn't let her go and face whatever the hell she was about to face when the mere thought of it turned her white-faced and stricken.

So what if it was a boyfriend? Once he saw that she was all right, he'd leave her to it. To him—the boyfriend. Though he couldn't help grinding his teeth at the thought.

The cab he'd grabbed outside the Plaza took a right on Fifty-seventh and headed west. It was Saturday night in midtown, and the traffic was bumper-to-bumper traffic. The theaters had just disgorged people by the hundreds onto the streets. Progress was excruciatingly slow.

He should have just followed her straight out the door. But she'd got a head start on him, and then Standish had called his name. There was no way to pretend he hadn't heard, and impossible to be impolite and brush the older man off—not without being able to offer a convincing excuse.

And what was he going to say? "My date had to rush to the hospital because she thinks her ex-husband...or maybe her boyfriend...or some guy she knows called Charlie needs her?"

Damn it. Didn't she have any pride?

He glared out at the traffic, willing it to move. At least Standish had told him where St. Luke's was. It wasn't that close to Daisy's office, though perhaps it was near where she actually lived.

He didn't even *know* where she lived. Something else she hadn't shared with him. And something else to fume about until the driver dropped him off outside the emergency services department and sped away.

Facing it, Alex's feet suddenly felt rooted to the pavement.

He didn't do hospitals. Of course he'd been in and out of the hospital he'd designed the wing for. But he'd never been in it other than for work. He'd never been in a hospital for anything resembling a medical reason—for anyone—since the day Vass died. Everything in him wanted to walk away.

Only the memory of Daisy's stricken face made him take a breath, then another deep one, and stride straight in.

It was a zoo. There were people everywhere, sitting, standing, crying, bleeding, filling out forms.

Not one of them was Daisy.

Alex stood by the door, cracking his knuckles. He didn't even know who to ask for. Charlie Somebody.

Hell, he didn't even know the guy's last name. He got in line anyway. Maybe he'd spot her before he had to come up with a name.

He was two cases from the desk when he heard the sound

of her voice. His head jerked around, his heart lurched at the sight of her drawn pale face.

She stood in the doorway of one of the examining rooms, her expression intent as she listened to a white-coated doctor. Whatever he said, she nodded, still looking fragile. The doctor patted her arm, then went into the room. Daisy started to go after him.

Alex went after her. "Daisy!"

She jerked as if she'd been shot. Then she spun around, white as a sheet.

He started to go to her, but instead she hurried toward him. "What are you doing here?" Her voice was thready, strained.

He just looked at her. "You're here."

She swallowed. Something shuttered in her gaze. "You don't need to be here."

"You look like hell."

"Thank you so much."

He moved closer. She moved back until he'd cornered her between a chair and the wall. Then he put a hand on her arm so she couldn't pull away. "I came to see if I could help, Daisy."

She shook her head almost fiercely. "I don't need your help. I told you that. It'll be all right."

"Charlie will," he clarified, needing to see her reaction to his name. He tried to keep his voice even, nonjudgmental, but he didn't like it when she flinched.

Her jaw tightened. Her fingers knotted.

"Is it bad?" he asked. He didn't want the guy to die, for heaven's sake. He just didn't want Daisy dropping everything to race across the city for him.

"He has a broken arm."

"A broken arm?" Alex almost laughed with relief at the

same time he felt a surge of annoyance. "All this hysteria for a broken arm?"

"I'm not hysterical!" Daisy said indignantly. There was color in her cheeks again.

He couldn't help grinning. "No? Taking a phone call in the middle of a dance? Rushing out of the hotel? For a broken arm?"

"I apologized," Daisy said tightly. She hugged her arms across her chest. "You didn't have to come. I certainly didn't invite you!"

"I thought he might be dying. You looked devastated. I didn't want you to have to face it alone."

Something flickered across her features. She hesitated for a moment, as if she was giving him the benefit of the doubt. Then she nodded. "That was kind of you. Thank you. But it really wasn't necessary." She straightened, pulled her arm out of his grasp, and gave him what he supposed was a dismissive smile. "It will be fine. *He* will be. I just… Maybe I overreacted. Don't worry. No one's going to die. Now, please excuse me." She tried to slip around him.

But Alex was in no mood to be dismissed and he blocked her way. "Who is he, Daisy?"

She didn't answer. He didn't think she was going to. But then a nurse poked her head out of the examination room. "Mrs. Connolly, Charlie's asking for you. Doctor is going to put the cast on now."

Once more Daisy started to move away, but Alex caught her arm. "He's *asking* for you?" he said mockingly. "To what? Hold his hand?"

Her teeth came together. Her eyes flashed. "Maybe. He's a little boy," she snapped, her eyes flashing anger. "He's my son."

Her *son?* Daisy had a *son?*

But before he could do more than reel at her words, Daisy had jerked her arm away, cut around him and stalked back into the examination room. The door shut behind her with a resounding bang.

A dozen people stopped talking and looked around in surprise.

Alex felt as if he'd been punched. *Where the hell did she get a son?*

Well, of course, he supposed she'd got the boy the time-honored way—she and her ex. But why hadn't she mentioned him?

Not that it was his business. But still…

Alex glared at all the people who were still murmuring and staring at him as if it were his fault she'd stormed away and slammed the door. He wouldn't have minded slamming one or two himself. Instead he stalked over to an empty chair by the windows and flung himself down.

He didn't know how long he waited. Long enough to have plenty of second thoughts. Daisy wasn't going to be happy to come out and find that he had waited. She'd made that perfectly clear.

And did he really want to meet Daisy's child?

It was annoying enough to think that she had professed to love him, then turned around and married someone else. To be honest, Alex had felt a certain satisfaction knowing her rebound marriage hadn't lasted.

That it had resulted in a child was somehow disconcerting. A child. Charlie.

Alex tried to imagine a little boy who looked like Daisy. Would he have her mischievous grin, a dimple in one cheek, freckles across his nose and a mop of honey-colored hair?

Or would the boy look like her ex-husband? Was the ex

holding Charlie's other hand in the exam room with them now? Alex straightened in the chair, scowling at the thought.

Maybe he was going to be sitting here when all three of them came out of the room together. And wouldn't that be awkward as hell?

The noise of a crying baby, a croupy cough, a parent and teenager arguing washed right over him. Alex paid no attention. So it would be awkward. So what? He'd walked out on her and their child, hadn't he?

Alex almost hoped the S.O.B. was here. He'd like to see what was so wonderful that Daisy had ever married him. Scowling, he shifted irritably in the chair, then looked up to see Daisy coming out of the examining room.

On her hip was a little boy with a mop of brownish-blonde hair and one arm in a bright blue cast. He'd expected a two- or three-year-old. But this boy looked bigger. Alex leaned forward, studying him intently. But he couldn't see much. There were people in the way.

Daisy was listening to the nurse. They were standing just outside the exam room door. The boy was listening, too. Then he turned his head to look out at the waiting room.

Alex's breath caught. His heart seemed to stutter even as he stared.

Charlie's jaw was squarer than Daisy's, his lower lip fuller, his nose a little sharper, his cheekbones higher. His eyes weren't blue, they were green.

He didn't really resemble Daisy at all. Even his hair was actually a deeper gold than Daisy's. But Alex knew exactly who he was. He had known another boy with those eyes, that jaw, whose hair had been exactly that color.

His brother. Vassilios.

Chapter 8

For a moment Alex couldn't move. Couldn't think. Could only stare.

And understand the implication. It hit him like a fist to the gut.

He moved on automatic pilot, putting himself between Daisy and the door. And all the while, he couldn't take his eyes off the child.

The boy was Vass all over again. Alex's heart squeezed in his chest. His throat tightened. He couldn't swallow. He barely had a toehold on his composure when Daisy finished talking to the nurse and turned—and saw him.

She stopped, rooted right where she was.

Their eyes locked and he watched her color fade. Her lips parted and trembled. Her arms tightened around the boy in her arms and she glanced around as if looking for another way out.

Bad luck, Daze, Alex thought grimly. Nowhere to go but through me.

She understood that, for a second later she straightened her shoulders, lifted her chin and walked straight toward him.

"I told you that you didn't need to wait."

Alex felt a muscle in his temple tick. He swallowed, seeking words. There were none. Only a well of pain.

How could you? His eyes asked her. The boy—his son!—was close enough to reach out and touch.

He balled his fingers into fists, every fiber of his being wanted to reach out to the little boy, to take him in his arms and never let him go. But the boy didn't know, wouldn't understand. Even Daisy seemed to think he was behaving oddly.

"Are you all right?" she asked when he didn't reply.

She had no idea. Didn't realize what he knew. Of course, she wouldn't. She had no idea Charlie could've been Vass's clone. Alex managed a curt nod. "Fine." Poleaxed, in truth.

"Good." She smiled briefly. "It was kind of you to bother," she said. "But not necessary."

It was necessary. Alex knew that down to his toes. He just looked at her. For a moment neither of them spoke, neither moved.

"Mommy."

Daisy shifted at the sound of the small plaintive voice. She hugged the little boy close. "This is Charlie," she said. "Charlie, this is Mr. Antonides."

Your father.

God, how he wanted to say the words. He didn't. He just studied the boy up close. His cheeks were fuller than Vass's had been. But at that age, maybe his brother had had round cheeks, too. Alex would have been too young to recall. But Charlie had the same freckles across his nose that Vass had had, the same long lashes.

"I got a brok'n arm," the boy told him in a froggy little voice.

Alex nodded and met his chocolate gaze. "Yeah, I see that you do."

Daisy shifted under the boy's weight. "I need to get him home. Thank you. I'm sorry that the evening ended this way."

I'm not. Alex didn't say that, either. He dragged his gaze away from the boy long enough to meet hers. It all made sense now—her distance, her coolness, her determination to shut him out.

But he wasn't out any longer—and he had no intention of ever being out of this child's life again.

"Come on," he said. "Let's get you into a cab." He stepped back to let Daisy go through the door. It was late, well after midnight, and the snow was still falling. Charlie couldn't put his arm in his jacket, and Daisy was trying to pull it more closely around his shoulders.

"Let me." Alex took the boy's puffy red down jacket and settled it around small bony shoulders. His hands trembled as he brushed them over him, then tucked the jacket close between Charlie's body and his mother's. "There you go." Even to his own ears, his voice sounded hoarse.

"Thank you." Daisy flicked him a quick smile.

There were no taxis right outside. So he strode off to the corner to flag one down. He half expected Daisy to have vanished by the time he got back with it. But sanity must have prevailed. Either that or she was too shattered by the events of the evening to pull a disappearing act.

Alex opened the door to the taxi. "After you. I'll take him." He held out his arms.

"I can manage." She tried to get in with the boy in her

arms, but she nearly lost her balance, and Alex scooped him away.

And the moment the boy's solid body settled in his arms, Alex felt something in him change. Something strong and protective took root, dug in. Instinctively he moved his face closer to the boy's soft hair, drawing in the scent of antiseptic, bubble-gum shampoo, laundry soap and earthy little boy.

His breath caught, his grip tightened.

"I can take him now." Daisy's hollow-eyed gaze locked with Alex's as she held out her arms to the little boy.

Slowly, carefully—reluctantly—Alex settled him on the seat next to her. Then, not giving her a chance to tell him he didn't need to come along, he slid into the backseat as well and shut the door.

There was silence except for the taxi's public service babbling. The car didn't move.

"You'll have to tell him where we're going," Alex said at last. "I don't know."

Daisy hesitated for a split second, then in a low voice gave the cab driver the address. It was the same address as her office.

As the cab lurched forward, he narrowed his gaze at her. Daisy kept hers focused straight ahead. Charlie huddled between them. Alex could feel the little boy's bony shoulder pressed against his arm. He angled his gaze down to see the top of the boy's head, the burnished gold of his hair, the sharp little nose and what looked like a stubborn chin. Looking at him, Alex felt his throat tighten with so many emotions he couldn't name them all.

Charlie.

His son.

Alex turned the notion over in his mind. Tested it. Tasted it. Wrapped his entire being around it. Then he lifted his gaze and looked over the top of Charlie's head at the woman who hadn't even bothered to tell him and felt his whole body stiffen with anger.

As if he were aware of something wrong, Charlie stiffened, too. He edged closer under his mother's arm.

Was he scared? Certainly he sensed something was amiss. Kids could do that, Alex remembered. He certainly had.

He'd read his parents' body language for years. He had sensed their worry about Vass, even when they'd tried to say everything would be fine. He'd felt their pain, their hurt at his brother's illness. He'd felt, without needing words, their emotional withdrawal.

He didn't blame them. His brother had been his idol. His hero. He knew as well as they had that Vass was the best person in the world. And he instinctively felt what they felt: that if they had to lose one of their sons, it should not have been Vass.

Moody, temperamental, fidgety, less-than-perfect Alex was the one who should have died.

Of course no one said so. No one had to. Kids could read body language. They could hear the feelings in the silences—as Charlie could no doubt hear his now.

Consciously Alex relaxed his body and stopped glaring at Daisy. Instead he shifted slightly away so that he could look down at Charlie more easily.

"I'm not Mr. Antonides. I'm Alex," he said.

The boy flicked a quick glance up at him and dipped his head in acknowledgment.

"Want to shake left hands?" Alex asked.

Charlie's gaze lifted again to meet his. Alex could feel Daisy's eyes on him, as well. Wary, suspicious. Charlie hesitated a moment, then nodded and stuck out his left hand. Small fingers gripped his.

And Alex knew that this first mutual touch was momentous, and that the feel of that small warm hand in his was a memory he would carry with him to his grave.

"I broke my arm once, too," he told the boy, "when I was ten."

"Did you jump off a bunk bed?"

So that was what Charlie had done. Alex smiled and shook his head. "I was climbing some cliffs. One crumbled and I fell."

If he had been on the cliffs near their Santorini home, he didn't think it would have happened. He knew those cliffs like he knew the inside of his bedroom. He and Vass had climbed them their whole lives.

But they hadn't been in Santorini. They had been at a place they were renting in Athens while Vass was in the hospital for treatments. Alex had hated it there, hated the hospital, hated the house, hated having to play by himself all the time because Vass was too ill to do anything.

And he'd only made things worse when he fell.

"You don't think!" his mother had raged. "You never think!"

"You should be glad it hurts," his father had said sternly. "Maybe you will not be so inconsiderate again."

"I wish I'd been with you," Vass had whispered when Alex finally got to see him. His brother's eyes had had dark circles under them. But they had still glittered with urgency and desire.

And Alex had said fervently, "Me, too."

Now, trying to push aside the painful memory, he smiled at the little boy who was looking up at him with Vass's eyes. "Did you break yours jumping from a bunk?"

"I was tryin' to get to the dresser like Rip does."

"Who's Rip?" Whoever he was, Alex liked his name.

"One of Finn and Izzy MacCauley's boys," Daisy said. "Rip is Charlie's hero. He tries to do whatever Rip does, in this case, apparently, to get around the house without touching the floor," she said despairingly.

Alex grinned. "I used to do that, too."

Charlie's eyes widened. "You did?"

"It's something all boys do?" Daisy looked dismayed.

"It's a challenge," Alex told her. "Boys like challenges. How old is Rip?"

"Almost twelve," Daisy said. They were speeding down Central Park West. There was little traffic now and they were hitting the lights. It would be a matter of minutes until they were at Daisy's office.

"That explains it," Alex told the little boy. "You've just got to get bigger."

"Mom says I can't do it again."

Daisy looked mulish. "I don't want him killing himself."

"He won't," Alex said. He smiled at Charlie. "You look like a pretty tough guy."

The boy's head bobbed. "I am. My dad says so."

"Your dad?" Alex lifted his gaze to look from Charlie to Daisy. "His dad?" he said to her.

"His dad." Daisy's look was even more mulish and her tone even firmer than before. "My ex-husband. Cal."

Alex's jaw tightened at the lie. He stared at her.

And just as if she were telling God's own truth, Daisy stared defiantly back. Their gazes were still locked when the cab turned the corner on Daisy's street and pulled up midblock in front of her place. He understood it was more than her office now. She damned well lived here, too.

"Here's where we get out," Daisy said briskly. She reached into the pocket of her coat and pulled out money for the cab.

"I'm paying," Alex said flatly.

Daisy opened her mouth as if to protest, but then shrugged. "Thank you."

He paid the driver, then opened the door and got out, reaching back in and lifting Charlie carefully up into his arms, settling him against his hip. Charlie looped an arm over his shoulder.

Daisy scrambled out and looked disconcerted to see the boy in Alex's arms and not standing on the sidewalk where she had apparently expected to see him.

Alex nodded toward the building. "After you."

He wasn't surprised when Daisy fished a key out of her pocket and, instead of going up the stoop, led the way through a wrought-iron gate and down the steps to the door below. Her movements were jerky as she fumbled the key, but finally unlocked the outer door and pushed it open, then did the same with the lock on the front door, and turned to hold out her arms for her son.

Still carrying Charlie, Alex pushed straight past her into a tiny foyer filled with jackets and boots and roller skates and the smallest bicycle he'd ever seen.

"Yours?" he asked Charlie.

The boy's head nodded against Alex's shoulder.

"Can you ride it?"

Another nod, this one firmer than the last.

"Good for you. I had a bike when I was your age." Alex smiled. Bikes had been his thing—never Vass's. And already Charlie rode one. So there was that bit of himself in his son. "We'll have to go riding."

"He has a broken arm," Daisy said sharply.

"Not now." Alex turned and faced her. "There will be time." He watched that register in her brain before he said to Charlie, "Plenty of time."

"Alex," Daisy protested faintly.

He turned his stare back on her until her gaze slid away.

"You got a bike?" Charlie asked, interested.

"Yep. I race bikes."

Charlie looked fascinated. Daisy looked dismayed. She shook her head, as if resisting everything. Then quickly and deliberately she stripped off her coat and hung it on one of the hooks in the foyer and crossed the room, holding out her arms.

"Give him to me. He needs to get ready for bed. Now."

Alex wanted to argue. Wanted to defy her, hang on to his son. But for all that he was furious with Daisy, none of it was Charlie's fault. But his jaw was tight, his whole body felt rigid as he loosed his grip and eased the boy into his mother's arms. He took special care not to jar Charlie's arm. And once he'd let go, he smoothed a hand over Charlie's hair, letting it linger.

"You're a brave guy," he said, keeping his gaze on Charlie. The boy nodded solemnly.

"We'll ride bikes together sometime soon," Alex promised, his smile crooked. "Okay?"

Another nod and a tentative smile.

He could hear Daisy's indrawn breath. "Good night, Alex." She paused, then added evenly, "Thank you for…everything."

For everything? His eyes asked her.

For giving you a son?

"Who's he?" Charlie asked as Daisy carried him up the stairs.

"A man I used to know. A…friend." But she was distracted

as she spoke, remembering Alex's narrowed gaze as he'd watched her carrying Charlie across the emergency room.

He didn't know, she assured herself. He couldn't.

It was Charlie's mere existence that had surprised him—that *she* had a son. And his terseness simply meant that he was annoyed she hadn't told him.

In Charlie's room, she flicked on the light and deposited him gently on the bed. She rarely carried him anywhere these days, and having done so now, she was almost out of breath, surprised at how big he'd gotten since she used to carry him all the time.

"My arm hurts."

"I know. I'm sorry." She bent to kiss his soft hair, then smoothed her hand over it, pulling back as she remembered that Alex had just done the same thing. "I guess maybe you won't leap from bunk beds anymore?"

Charlie pursed his lips, considering. "Not till I'm bigger," he decided. "Crash can do it."

"Maybe you should wait till you're nine or ten then." She got his pajamas off the hook behind the door.

"Maybe." Charlie took the pajamas, then tried to wriggle out of the jacket he still had over his shoulders and one arm.

"I'll help you tonight," Daisy said. "But you're going to have to figure out how to do it yourself, too." She eased off the jacket, then lifted the hem of his shirt and began to slide it up and over his good arm and his head.

"Maybe Alex could teach me."

"What?" She jerked back, then stared at the pair of bright eyes that popped into view as the shirt came off. "Why would he?"

"'Cause he broke his arm," Charlie said simply. "He'd know how."

"Oh. Well…" Daisy made a noncommittal sound. "I'm pretty sure you can figure it out without Alex's help." She finished getting his clothes off and his pajamas on. "Go wash your face and brush your teeth."

Charlie flopped back on the bed. "But I'm tired. Do I hafta?"

"Yes. Even boys who fall off bunk beds have to maintain a minimum of civil decorum."

"I didn't fall," Charlie protested. But he allowed her to pull him up. "I jumped. An' what's 'civil deck-somethin'?" Charlie loved big words.

"Civil decorum," Daisy repeated. It was what she had tried to maintain for the past hour and a half. She said, "Behaving like a well-brought-up *clean* child."

"Ugh." But Charlie slid off the bed and padded toward the bathroom while Daisy gathered up his clothes. "Oh!" she heard him say brightly. "Hi."

"Hi." The unexpected sound of Alex's voice right outside the door sent Daisy hurrying out. She skidded to a halt a second before she collided with his chest.

"You didn't leave."

"No." He had propped a shoulder against the wall outside Charlie's bedroom door and stood there meeting her gaze, then his eyes dropped to Charlie, and Daisy felt more than a flicker of unease.

He didn't say anything. But even quiet and unmoving, his presence seemed to overpower everything else. He was too big. Too close. The space was too intimate. And the situation didn't bear thinking about. She didn't want him here.

But she didn't know how to get rid of him without causing Charlie to wonder what was going on. He already had to wonder. No man but Cal had ever been upstairs.

But Alex was, right here in the hallway, his dark hair disheveled, as if he had run his fingers through it. He looked incongruous here in his formal evening wear, but even as she thought it, she realized the formal evening wear wasn't so formal anymore. He'd removed his tie—it dangled from his pocket—and he'd undone the top two buttons of his shirt.

It had the effect of making him look more masculine and primal than ever—with the added misfortune of reminding her of how he'd looked five years ago when she'd brought him into her tiny apartment after the wedding. He was all the things he'd been then and all the things she'd been at pains to resist earlier this evening—too broad-shouldered, too imposing and too damned predatorily male.

"I came to say good night to Charlie." His tone was measured, his words easy, understandable and, to Charlie, unthreatening.

But Daisy knew a threat when she heard one. She took a quick breath. "Say good night, Charlie."

Charlie tipped his head back to look up at Alex, but instead of saying good night, he said, "Can you teach me to get my shirt on an' off over my cast?"

Alex nodded. "I can."

"No, he can't. It's after one in the morning. You need to go to bed," Daisy said firmly.

"I'll show you," Alex promised smoothly. "Tomorrow."

"But—" Charlie began.

"Your mother's right," Alex said firmly. "You need to sleep."

"I can't sleep. My arm hurts," Charlie argued.

"But you're tough," Alex reminded him. The two of them looked at each other. Two men understanding each other—even though one of them was only four.

"Teeth, Charlie," Daisy said firmly. "And wash your face. Now." She took hold of his shoulders and steered him past Alex, doing her best not to brush against him in the narrow hallway. If she'd hoped he'd take the hint and go, she was out of luck.

He didn't budge, just waited until Charlie had brushed his teeth—awkwardly because he had to do it left-handed—and scrubbed at his face with a washcloth. He didn't use soap, but Daisy didn't make him do it again. She just wanted him in bed.

"Right," she said briskly. "Off to bed."

Obediently Charlie headed back down the hall, but stopped directly in front of Alex. He looked up again. "G'night."

And Daisy remembered when she'd seen the photo of Charlie looking up at Cal's father and had realized how similar her son's profile was to Alex's. They were indeed remarkably alike.

Was that how Alex had known? Or was it some scary primal innate recognition between father and son? She didn't know. She only knew that the still-deep emotion that she could sense simmering in Alex was more elemental than just a response to discovering she had a child she hadn't told him about.

The question was no longer: *Did he know?*

The question was: *What was he going to do now?*

He reached out a hand and brushed the top of Charlie's head once more. "Good night," he said gravely. "It was nice meeting you, Charlie." His fingers lingered for a moment, then he withdrew them and tucked them into the pocket of his trousers and brought his gaze up to meet Daisy's. "At last."

She suppressed a shiver, then swallowed. With her eyes she beseeched him to be silent, and was relieved when he didn't say anything else. Giving him a fleeting grateful smile, she slipped past him to follow Charlie into his bedroom where she shut the door with a solid click.

Whatever Alex might have to say to her—and she had no doubt he had plenty to say—he could say it tomorrow. Or next month. Not now.

Her priority was Charlie. It was the middle of the night and he'd been hurt, and it didn't matter that her brain was whirling a million miles a minute. If she pushed him, he would balk and take even longer.

So she did everything in his bedtime routine. She tucked him in, then read him a bedtime story. She listened as he told her about his day, including a long involved account of everything he'd done at Rip and Crash's house, what he didn't like about the emergency room, and ultimately, as she'd feared, questions about Alex.

"Do you think he'll ride bikes with me?"

"I don't know," she said. "He's a busy man."

"He said he would."

"Yes. And maybe he will."

"Remind him."

Daisy made a noncommittal sound. "Prayers," she reminded him, and when he'd finished, she added a desperate silent one of her own. Then she kissed her son good-night.

Charlie clutched her hand when she got up to leave. "Stay."

"Charlie."

"My arm hurts. Sing to me," he pleaded.

That wasn't part of the regular nightly routine, but sometimes when he was sick and irritable, she could calm him with some silly songs. "You're tired."

His big eyes drooped even as he nodded. "I'll sleep. Sing."

So Daisy turned out the light, determinedly shut out the turmoil roiling around in her mind, and sat back down on the bed beside him.

Maybe it would soothe them both, she thought as she began

to sing. There was a boat song, and a campfire song, and a bus, train and truck song. She had made them up about Charlie's life when he was a toddler. He knew them by heart. Now he settled against her, his eyes shut, the blue cast dark against the pale blanket that covered him. His breathing slowed.

Her voice slowed, too, and finally stopped. Waited. Watched him. And finally when she was sure he was asleep, she dipped her head and kissed him.

"I love you," she whispered, brushing a hand over his hair. Then she put out the bedside light and slipped quietly out of his room, shutting the door after her.

The clock in her bedroom said five minutes of two. Daisy felt as if she'd been up for two days. Or weeks.

Wearily, she stripped off Izzy's dress. It still sparkled in the soft bedside light. It had made her sparkle in the beginning. She didn't sparkle now. She felt as if she'd been run over by a truck. She flexed her bare shoulders and shivered as she stared into the mirror over her dresser. A pale, hollow-eyed, haunted version of herself stared back.

She felt ill. Exhausted. And scared.

Alex knew. And soon he would confront her about Charlie. He would say whatever he had to say about the son he hadn't known he had. The son he never wanted. She felt a tremor run through her.

Whatever he said, he could say it to her. He wasn't going to say it to Charlie. Charlie wasn't ever going to hear that he wasn't wanted. Ever!

Maybe, with luck, Alex would pretend he didn't know. Maybe he would simply walk away. She could hope.

Quickly pulling on her nightgown, she wrapped up in her fuzzy chenille robe and tiptoed down the hall to brush her teeth and wash her face. Then she went downstairs to let Murphy out. She would have done it when she first got home, but Charlie had taken precedence.

Murphy wagged his tail, delighted to see her. She rubbed his ears and kissed the top of his head. Then she slid open the door to the back garden, Murphy went out, and she slid it closed against the snowy December night. Then, while he was out there, she went to put the dead bolt on the front door. Alex couldn't have done it when he left.

If he had left.

He hadn't. He was sprawled, eyes closed, on the sofa.

Chapter 9

For a moment Daisy didn't even breathe, just pressed a hand protectively against her breasts and felt her heart pound wildly beneath it.

She dared hope he was asleep—because hoping he was a figment of her imagination was not a possibility. But even as she did so, Alex's eyes fluttered open and he rolled to a sitting position.

"What are you doing here?" she asked.

Alex rolled his shoulders, working the stiffness out. He had taken off his coat and the stark white of his shirt made his shoulders seem broader than ever. He looked at her levelly. "Waiting for you."

"It's late!"

His eyes bored into her. "Five years late."

"I don't know what you mean," she said. Her fingers knotted together.

"You know." His gaze was steady, his eyes chips of green ice.

"Alex," she protested.

"We're done playing games, Daisy."

"I'm not—"

"We're going to talk." There was a thread of steel in his voice now, and as he spoke, he stood up. Slightly more than six feet of whipcord muscle and testosterone somehow filled the room.

Daisy stepped back. "I have to let the dog in."

He shrugged. "Go ahead. I'm not going anywhere."

Exactly what she was afraid of. She hurried through the kitchen and fumbled with shaking fingers to open the sliding-glass door for Murphy. It wasn't just her fingers shaking, her whole body was trembling, and it had nothing to do with the cold December night. The cold in Alex's stare was a different story.

Murphy trotted in, wagging his tail cheerfully. Daisy shut the door and slid the bolt home, then cast a longing look at the stairs that led up to her room. But retreat wasn't an option. So, wiping damp palms down the sides of her robe, she went back to the living room.

Alex was standing by the mantel, holding the photo of her and Charlie and Cal taken last Christmas. At her footsteps, he took one last look and he set it back on the mantel, then looked over at her. "Is this your ex?"

She nodded. "That's Cal."

"Very cozy."

"It was Christmas. Christmas is cozy."

"You look happy."

"We were happy." She hugged her arms across her chest.

"You were still married to him then?"

"No."

One dark brow arched in surprise. "But you had a picture taken together?"

"Yes." She wasn't giving him any explanations. She didn't owe him any.

"He's not Charlie's father."

"Yes, he is." She had been married to Cal when Charlie was born. He was the father on Charlie's birth certificate. He was the father that Charlie called Dad. He was a father to Charlie in every way that mattered.

"Not by blood, he's not."

Daisy swallowed, then lifted her chin. "And you know this how?"

He reached into his back pocket and pulled out a thin black leather billfold. Opening the wallet, he took out a photo, crossed the room and handed it to her. It was a small color snapshot of two young boys, grinning at the camera.

Daisy saw only one. He could have been Charlie.

He was older than Charlie, maybe nine or ten. But his eyes were Charlie's—the same shape, the same light color. He had the same sharp nose, spattered with freckles, the same wide grin. He even had the same straight honey-blonde hair that she'd always assured herself had come from her side of the family.

She clutched the photo so tightly, her fingers trembled. Her throat tightened and she shut her eyes. She couldn't breathe.

Alex didn't seem to be breathing, either. He was stone silent and unmoving. Waiting for her to speak?

But what could she say?

Slowly she opened her eyes again and began to study the picture more carefully. The two boys were standing on a beach, bare-chested and wearing shorts, the sea lapping bright blue behind them. They had their arms slung around each other's shoulders and they were laughing into the camera. The older boy was the one who looked like Charlie. The other was younger, maybe six or seven, with a front tooth missing. He had dark shaggy hair and light eyes. Daisy knew those eyes.

Slowly, cautiously, she looked up at them now. "It's you..." she said so softly she doubted he could hear her. Her thumb stroked over the dark-haired boy's face. "And your brother."

A muscle ticked in his jaw. He nodded. "Vassilios."

Of course it was. His beloved brother, his hero, the beautiful loving boy whose death had destroyed his family looked almost exactly like Charlie.

Dear God, what a shock seeing his son must have been.

Outside a siren wailed as a fire truck went up Central Park West. Inside, the room was so silent she could hear the old oak mantel clock tick. She could hear Murphy two rooms away in the kitchen lapping up water. It was the calm before the storm.

"Why the hell didn't you tell me?" His voice accused her, anguished, ragged, furious. He plucked the photo back out of her hand, his fingers fumbling as he slid it back in his wallet and shoved it into his pocket.

She heard the pain, the anguish, the accusation. On one level she understood them. But she remembered pain and anguish of her own.

"Why the hell should I?" she countered, stung by his fury. "You didn't want a child. You said so! I babbled about marriage and family and you were quite clear. No marriage. No family! Why should I have told you?"

"That was before I knew I had one! How could I say I didn't want my son when I didn't even know he existed?"

"You didn't want him to exist!"

His nostrils flared and his jaw clamped shut. He balled his fingers into fists, as if he were trying to control what he did with them. Like strangle her. "You kept my son from me!"

"I took you at your word!"

"Damn it!" Alex let out a harsh breath. He glared at her, then raked his fingers through his hair and paced the room. At the far end, he whirled around. "You knew how I felt about my brother!"

Yes, she had known. She knew that Vassilios had been the favorite son, the star, the heir. She knew that everyone had loved him. Even Alex. Especially Alex. Vassilios had been bright, funny, caring, social. Everything, Alex had told Daisy five years ago, that he himself was not.

But Vass had been so wonderful that Alex hadn't envied him. He'd only wanted to be like him. He had loved his brother deeply. Vassilios's death had irrevocably changed his life.

She had known that losing his brother was the main reason Alex never wanted children. It was the reason Alex had originally never wanted to marry. He didn't want to love, he'd told her. Love hurt.

Dear God, she could agree with that. She'd hurt more in the aftermath of his leaving and her discovering she was having his child than she could ever have imagined. She'd loved him—and lost him—and for nearly five years now had Charlie to remind her of that loss.

But she couldn't regret it. She couldn't even regret marrying Cal. At least they'd had some sort of love. They'd tried.

Alex had refused to even try. Not then. Not now. He still wanted a marriage on his terms, a marriage without love. And children had still been a deal breaker. He'd made that clear.

So now she met his accusation squarely and told him the honest truth. "Yes, I knew," she agreed. "But mostly I knew you didn't want children. I did what I had to do. I did the best that I could for my son."

"Really? And you and dear Cal have such a spectacular marriage." His tone mocked her, infuriated her.

Daisy had to fight her own inclination to look away. Even so she felt her face heat. "Cal is a great father."

"And I wouldn't have been?" His challenge was loud and clear. Mostly loud.

"Not if you didn't love him! And be quiet. You'll wake him up."

Alex's teeth came together with a snap. She could hear his harsh breathing, but he didn't claim he would love Charlie. How could he? He'd already hardened his heart.

"Why would I think you'd be a good father to a child you didn't want?" she said. "Cal was. Cal was there when he was born—"

"Because you damned well didn't tell me!"

"Cal loves him," she finished quietly.

"And I've never had a chance to!"

"You didn't want one. You'd already made your choice. And when I found out I was pregnant, I had to make choices, too. I chose to do what I thought was best for Charlie. He needed love. He needed parents. A family. You didn't want that. You said, 'No entanglements, no hostages of fortune.'"

He had actually used those terms, and when she repeated them now, she saw him wince. "You said love hurt too much. You wanted nothing to do with it."

They glared at each other. Daisy wrapped her arms across her chest and stared unblinkingly at him. She knew what he had said, and Alex would be lying if he denied it now.

He didn't deny it. He didn't say anything at all. His jaw worked. His eyes reflected his inner turmoil. Seconds passed. Daisy could hear Murphy's toenails clicking down the hallway as he came out from the kitchen to look at them inquiringly.

Alex didn't notice. He was cracking his knuckles, then kneading the muscles at the back of his neck. He paced the room like an agitated animal trapped in a cage. Finally he flung himself down on the sofa and rubbed his hair until it stuck up all over his head. He dragged his palms down his face and stared at her bleakly over the top of them. "Hell."

In a word, yes.

It was a hell she was already familiar with. The confusion, the anguish, the damned-if-you-do, damned-if-you-don't choices she had faced when she'd discovered she was pregnant. She remembered the hollowness she'd felt at Alex's flat-out rejection of any sort of relationship. In the face of her hopes and dreams and—let's face it—fantasies, he had been crystal clear.

She hadn't even wanted to imagine what he would have said if she'd turned up on his doorstep and announced she was expecting his child. The very thought had made her blood run cold. Even now she shivered inside the thick robe she was wearing. Tucking her hands inside the opposite sleeves, she chaffed her arms briskly, trying to warm them.

Alex just sat there. He didn't speak. He didn't move, except for the rise and fall of his chest. His expression was grim as he stared across the room. He wasn't looking at her now.

She wondered what he was seeing in his mind's eye. His dying brother? His unknown son? The parents who had rejected him and each other? His life, as carefully designed as any building he'd ever planned, going down the drain?

She couldn't imagine. Didn't want to.

Murphy stood between them, looking from one to the other as if wondering what they were doing in his living room in the middle of the night. Finally, accepting it as dogs always did, he curled up on his bed in front of the fireplace and put his head between his paws.

Alex looked up and met her gaze. "I want my son."

"Want your…?" Daisy stared at him, breathless, as if he had punched her in the gut. "What does that mean? You can't take him!" she blurted, anguished. "You don't have any right!"

"I didn't say I was going to take him." Icy green eyes collided with hers. "But I'm not walking away, either."

Daisy swallowed, tried to think, to fathom what Alex's "not walking away" meant. For Charlie. For her. She didn't have a clue.

She only knew what she must not let happen. "You're not hurting him," she said fiercely. "I won't let you."

Alex rubbed a hand over his hair. His brows drew down. "Why the hell would I want to hurt him?"

Daisy had started to pace, but she stopped and turned to face him. "I didn't say you would intend to. But it could happen. He's only four, Alex. He won't understand. Besides, he has a father."

Alex's jaw tightened. "Cal." He spat her ex-husband's name. "Did you marry him because of Charlie?"

Daisy ran her tongue over her lips as she tried to decide how to answer it, how to be honest and fair to both Alex and to Cal.

"Did you?" Alex persisted when she didn't reply.

She sat down in the armchair across from the sofa where he was leaning toward her, his elbows on his knees, his fingers laced. "Yes," she admitted. "But it wasn't as simple as that. I didn't go find the nearest eligible man and ask him to marry me."

"No?" He mocked her.

Daisy tried not to bristle. "No," she said firmly. "Cal asked me."

"And you jumped at it."

In fact she'd been shocked. It had never occurred to her.

They'd been friends. Nothing more. "I thought about it. He insisted we could make it work."

"Sounds passionate," Alex drawled.

"Cal and I had been friends for a long time. He said love wasn't just a matter of passion. It was a matter of choice. I thought he was right. He wasn't. But—" she met his mockery defiantly "—I love Cal."

"You thought you loved me."

"I did," Daisy agreed. "But that was before I found out you didn't give a damn."

Alex stiffened as if she'd slapped him, then surged to his feet and loomed over her. "So you fell out of love with me and in love with What's His Face in, what? Six weeks? Less?"

"It wasn't like that."

"No? So, what was it like?"

She knew he didn't really want to hear the answer. He was angry and he just wanted to put her on the defensive, pick a fight.

But Daisy wasn't buying into that. "Sit down," she said, and pointed at the sofa when he didn't move. "Sit down and I'll tell you what it was like," she repeated sharply.

His gaze narrowed on her, but when she kept pointing, he dropped onto the sofa, still staring at her unblinkingly.

When he had settled again, Daisy tucked her feet under her and tried to find words that would make him understand.

"I was hurt when you didn't feel what I did that weekend," she began.

Alex started to interrupt, but she held up a hand to stop him. "I know you think I shouldn't have been. You think I presumed too much, And—" she took a steadying breath "—you were right. I presumed far too much. But I was young and foolish, and nothing like that had ever happened to me before."

Alex's mouth was a thin line, but he was listening at least.

Daisy twisted the tie of her bathrobe between her fingers, staring at it before lifting her gaze again. She shrugged and told him helplessly, "I fell in love with you. It was a mistake, I admit that." She laced her fingers in her lap and dropped her gaze to stare at them. If she looked at him, she'd realize that she was actually saying these things—and she didn't want to be saying any of them.

She wanted her life back—the way it had been before she had gone to the dinner with him tonight, the way it had been before everything she'd worked so hard to build and hold together for the past five years had all come apart at the seams.

"When you walked out, I was humiliated," she said. "I felt like an idiot. Sick."

Alex's jaw bunched. She knew he wanted to argue. He shifted uncomfortably. Daisy didn't care. She was uncomfortable, too. They could suffer through this together.

"Weeks went by," she continued. "Two, three, four—and instead of being able to put it behind me, I just felt sicker. And sicker. I started throwing up every morning. And that," she said, lifting her eyes to look at him squarely now, "was when I realized that it wasn't the memory of my idiocy that was making me sick. It was being pregnant."

He flinched, then let out a slow breath.

"I didn't even think about trying to find you," she said levelly. "You'd made it quite clear you weren't interested in any sort of involvement at all."

"You could've —"

"No," she said flatly. "I couldn't." She hesitated, then just told him the truth. "I was afraid you might want me to get an abortion."

He stared at her, shocked. "How could you think—?"

"Why wouldn't I?" she demanded. "You didn't want to care! I was afraid you'd say, 'Get rid of it before *anyone* cares.' Well, *I* cared. Even then I cared!" She could feel tears stinging the back of her eyes.

"Jesus," he muttered.

"Exactly," Daisy said, understanding the desperation that made him say it. "I did a lot of praying. You can believe that. I was scared. I didn't know how I was going to cope. I could keep working for Finn while I was pregnant, but after the baby came, I thought I might have to go back to Colorado and stay with my mother till I could work something out. And then—" she breathed deeply "—Cal proposed."

"Your savior. He was just standing around, waiting in the wings, for exactly that moment?" Alex demanded bitterly. "Ready to take some other man's woman?" Alex ground out. "His *pregnant* woman?"

"I was *not* your woman! And he was my friend. He *is* my friend."

"And yet you couldn't stay married to him," Alex said derisively.

Her jaw tightened. "It didn't work out." She folded her hands in her lap.

"Why not?"

"That's not your business."

Alex scowled blackly. "He married you, then dumped you? It doesn't make sense. None of it makes sense."

"He didn't dump me! And it made sense," Daisy insisted. "We hoped it would work. We wanted it to work. Cal's a good man," she said, looking over at the photo on the mantel. She stared at it for a long moment, then turned her gaze and met Alex's, smiling a little sadly. "He's been a good father."

"But not Charlie's only father!" Alex insisted.

"He knows he has a biological father. Well, as much as any four-year-old understands that. He knows he has two fathers. I figured I could explain you more to him as he got older."

"I'll explain myself to him now."

"No," Daisy said. "Not until I know how you feel."

"You know damn well how I feel. I want my son!"

Their gazes locked, dueled. And in the silence of battle, the stairs creaked.

"Mommy?"

Daisy's head jerked up to see Charlie peering over the bannister halfway down them. Alex stared up at him, too. Dear God, had he heard?

Daisy hurried up the stairs and scooped him up into her arms. "What is it, sweetie?"

"My arm hurts," he whimpered, and tucked his head between her jaw and her shoulder. He clung to her, but his gaze was fixed on Alex who was slowly coming to his feet.

Daisy shifted so that her body blocked his view. "I know." She kissed his hair and cuddled him close. "I wish it didn't. I'll take you back upstairs and sing to you. Okay?"

Charlie nodded. "Can Alex come, too?"

"Alex was just leaving." But she turned and carried Charlie down the stairs. "We'll just say good-night and see him out the front door." She smiled into Alex's suddenly narrowed gaze. "That will be nice, won't it?" she said to her son.

Solemnly Charlie nodded. He looked at Alex.

Alex looked back with an intensity that made Daisy quiver. Then Charlie lifted his head off her shoulder. "Night, Alex."

Daisy held her breath as, slowly, Alex shrugged into his suit jacket and crossed the room, stopping mere inches from them. He didn't look at her. He had eyes only for Charlie. To Daisy he looked dark, forbidding and positively scary.

But then he lifted a hand to touch Charlie's cheek and his expression softened, a smile touched the corner of his mouth. "Good night, son."

Chapter 10

It was like waiting for the other shoe to drop.

Daisy half expected to find Alex standing on the stoop when she got up. But a peek out the curtains as soon as she got up proved that no one was there.

He didn't call, either, though she jumped every time the phone rang.

Charlie, pushing his scrambled eggs around his plate, wanted to know what the matter was with her. "You're all jumpy," he remarked when a sound on the sidewalk made her flinch.

"Nothing's the matter." Daisy turned away, busying herself putting the dishes in the dishwasher. "Izzy said she and the boys were coming by."

Izzy's had been the first phone call she'd got this morning.

"How is he?" her friend had demanded even before Daisy had dragged herself out of bed.

"Still asleep," Daisy reported. In fact he was asleep on the other side of her bed. She'd got him back to sleep after Alex had finally left, but he'd awakened and come into her room again at five-thirty. Barely able to pry her eyes open, Daisy had taken the easy way out and let him clamber into bed with her. Fortunately he'd gone straight back to sleep, and when Izzy had rung at eight, he was still dead to the world.

"Sorry. We've been up for hours thinking about him."

"He's going to be fine," Daisy assured her. At least his arm was. How his life was going to change now that Alex was going to be part of it, she didn't know. But at least Alex had been kind last night. He'd actually behaved—toward Charlie—very well. Maybe, given that, he would be fine. And kids were resilient.

It was her own resilience Daisy was worried about.

How was she going to deal with Alexandros Antonides in her life?

She didn't want to think about it. So when Izzy asked if they could come and see Charlie in the afternoon, Daisy said yes without hesitation. The distraction would do them both good.

By midafternoon with no Rip and no Crash, Charlie was getting restless. Daisy had watched a Disney DVD with him, then read him a couple of dozen picture books. She tried unsuccessfully to talk him into a nap.

"I'm too big for naps," he told her. "An' I'm not tired."

No, just cranky. She had a photo shoot to finish editing before tomorrow afternoon. So she brought her laptop down to the living room and worked on it there while Charlie played with his cars and his Legos on the floor.

"Maybe that Alex will come back," he said hopefully, looking up from his cars.

"Mmm." Daisy didn't encourage that line of thinking. A man who had been as adamant as Alex had been about not wanting children might have had a brief change of heart when faced with a little boy who looked very much like his beloved deceased brother.

But having a son was a huge responsibility. And it wasn't one that you could just pick up and put down as the whim struck you. Alex wasn't a fool. He had to realize that. It was possible that Alex had gone home in the early hours of the morning, thought about the implications of having a son, and come to the conclusion that he'd made the right decision five years ago. Whatever he decided, Daisy was determined that she wouldn't let him upset Charlie's life to suit himself.

She didn't have time to think about it more because finally the doorbell rang.

"They're here!" Charlie scrambled up from the floor and raced to open the door.

Daisy unlocked the door, and Charlie tugged it open.

Rip MacCauley took one look at Charlie's cast and said, "Oh, wow. Your cast is blue? That's cool."

The first smile of the day flickered across Charlie's face. "You think?"

"Oh, yeah," Rip said, coming in and taking off his jacket. "I only ever had a white one."

"Mine was purple when I broke my ankle," Crash announced. "Here. This is for you." He thrust a package wrapped in newspaper comics into Charlie's hand.

"A little something to keep him busy," Izzy told Daisy as the boys headed instinctively for the cars and the Legos on the floor and she followed Daisy into the kitchen. "Rip and Crash have been really worried. They seem to think they're indestructible, but when Charlie got hurt, they were, like, 'Oh, no! What if he dies?' They felt very responsible. As well they should, Finn says."

"Finn being such a pattern card of model behavior." Daisy grinned.

Izzy laughed. "That's what I said." She perched on a bar stool while Daisy made them coffee. "I was amazed when Finn got home so quickly last night. Why didn't you let him stay for a bit and help you with Charlie?"

"No point. We were fine." And she was very glad he hadn't been there to witness the meeting of Alex and his son.

"I'm sorry we interrupted your evening. How was the Plaza? Tell all." Izzy leaned forward eagerly.

It took Daisy a moment to even begin to remember the details, so much had happened in the meantime. "It was… fine," she said vaguely. "The Plaza is elegant, of course. The dinner was wonderful," she added dutifully, because "fine" wasn't going to satisfy Izzy.

"And the dress?"

"It was fantastic."

"Knocked his socks off?" Izzy's eyes were bright.

"It wasn't supposed to knock his socks off," Daisy reminded her. "He's got a girlfriend."

Izzy looked disappointed. But then she shrugged philosophically. "So you had a good time."

Daisy did her best to sound bright and enthusiastic about the evening. She didn't tell Izzy that Alex had turned up at the hospital. She didn't mention anything that happened after that. Until she had some idea of what Alex intended, she wasn't borrowing trouble—or discussing him with anyone.

She was glad Izzy and the boys came because it took the edge off Charlie's boredom and irritability. The matchbox cars that Rip and Crash brought him were a big hit. But Daisy was, honestly, glad when they left again because it was hard to give the impression of cheerful equanimity when she felt edgy and stressed and as if her world was splintering into a million pieces. She left Charlie playing with his cars on the floor in the living room and retreated to the kitchen to wash up the cups and plates from the MacCauleys' visit.

And then the doorbell rang.

"It's Alex!" Charlie yelled, jumping up and running to the door.

Wiping nervous hands on the sides of her jeans, Daisy followed him to answer it. She dragged the door open a few inches and, as always, felt her heart do a somersault in her chest at the mere sight of him.

Gone, of course, was the formal wear of last evening. This afternoon Alex was in jeans and a hunter-green down jacket, his dark hair windblown and dusted with snowflakes, his jaw stubbled. His eyes were bloodshot, but they met hers squarely.

"Daisy." His voice was soft but firm, and gravelly as if he hadn't slept.

"Alex," she replied, holding herself rigid, trying to relax, but unable to. Still she swallowed and tried to sound cordial and polite.

"Hi, Alex." Charlie poked his head around to beam up at the man on the doorstep. "Come 'n' see my new cars."

"Cars?" Alex grinned and stepped across the threshold.

Daisy backed up hastily. "Charlie's much better," she said as he brushed past. "You didn't have to come."

He gave her a look so intense it could have leveled buildings. "I wanted to come." Then he turned his attention to Charlie. "You're better, are you?" he said, his tone far lighter. "Good. I thought maybe we could go to the park."

"The park?" Daisy echoed doubtfully.

But Charlie cheered. Obviously no one had told him he was an invalid.

"But let's see your new cars first." Alex was already shedding his jacket, dropping down onto the floor next to Charlie, making himself at home.

Charlie was clearly delighted to have the attention. He showed Alex the new set of Matchbox cars that Rip and Crash had given him. "Sports cars," he told Alex eagerly. "They go really fast. See?" He raced them around on the floor, making car noises.

Alex stretched out his long legs and leaned back on an elbow, watching, not just indulgently, but with real interest. He picked up the cars by turn, examining them, commenting knowledgeably because, of course, he knew all about cars. It must come standard issue with the Y chromosome.

Daisy stood there, watching, unable to pull herself away. Seeing the two of them together—father and son—was something she'd barely ever dreamed of. Hearing Charlie's eager chatter and Alex's low baritone in reply set something deep inside her quivering, aching.

Wanting. Far too much.

Abruptly she wheeled away. "I'll be upstairs," she said. "I have work to do."

He had come to see Charlie, not her. And while it was hardly an honest introduction to the demands of fatherhood, if he came looking for reinforcements in fifteen minutes, she'd know it wasn't going to last.

Charlie came in half an hour later. "Alex an' me want to go to the park. He says to ask if you want to go along."

Annoyed that he would presume to decide what he and Charlie were going to do without consulting her, Daisy hurried downstairs.

The Legos and Matchbox cars had been neatly put away

and Alex was zipping up his jacket. "Good," he said. "You're coming, too."

"You don't presume. You should have asked!"

"Charlie did ask."

Charlie bobbed his head. "I said we wanted to go, and did you want to come."

Daisy opened her mouth, then closed it again. "Fine," she said shortly. "I'll come."

It was torture, seeing him with Charlie, being with him herself, acting as though they were some lovely happy family, all the while knowing it was a sham.

"Take it easy," Alex said in an undertone as she jerkily shoved her arms into her jacket. "I'm not going to steal my son."

My son, she wanted to correct him. *And no, you're damned well not!*

But Alex had turned and was helping Charlie with his jacket. Daisy wanted to push him away and do it herself. But one look told her that Charlie was more patient with Alex helping than he would have been with her. And Alex did take the time to show him how to do it himself—except for the zipping up part.

"Guess we'll have to help with that," he said easily, then zipped the jacket up to Charlie's chin. Then rising again, he reached down to ruffle the little boy's hair.

It was a casual movement, but it already spoke of a connection that made Daisy's insides clench, especially when Charlie flashed him a happy grin.

Turning abruptly, she called Murphy and snapped on his leash. Then the four of them went out the door and headed to the park—just like a family.

She shouldn't have come. She should have stayed back in

her office and got more work done. But the temptation of watching Alex with Charlie was too great. It was terrifying, too. But Charlie was having such a good time.

There was still lots of snow on the ground. Once they got to the park, they built a snowman. And they had a snowball fight. Then Charlie made snow angels.

"A snow devil more like," Daisy said, laughing as she watched him, then taking photos with the small pocket-size camera she always carried. She got quite a few of Charlie and Alex rolling balls to make the snowman, then more of Alex lifting Charlie onto his shoulders so he could put an old hat on the snowman's head.

They were laughing as they did it, Alex lurching around in the snow while Charlie gripped Alex's hair with his free hand and laughed madly. Then Alex tipped his head back to grin up at his son, and the look they shared made Daisy feel as if she'd caught a snowball square in the heart.

Later she nearly did as she helped Charlie pelt Alex with snowballs. She got several shots of Charlie and Alex throwing them at each other. Then Alex took the camera out of her hand.

"What are you doing?" She tried to grab it back.

But Alex held it out of her reach, his green eyes mischievous. "Go play with your son."

Self-consciously at first, Daisy did. But then she got caught up in Charlie's enthusiasm. And while she pushed Charlie on a swing and helped him build a little snow dog to go with the snowman, Alex took pictures. Finally, when Daisy said it was time to leave, he set the camera's timer and hauled them all into a picture together, scooping Charlie up into one arm while he flung the other around Daisy.

And once more when his arm pulled her close, Daisy felt

the hum of electricity between them. She felt desire all over again, and knew it for the hopeless feeling it was. It was a relief when the timer went off, the shutter clicked, and he let her go, slung Charlie onto his shoulders and they all walked home.

On the doorstep, when Alex set him down, Daisy smiled politely. "Thank you. He enjoyed that."

"Did you?" Alex asked.

She heard the pointedness of his tone and chose to ignore it. "Of course." She fumbled to get the key in the lock. He was wearing sunglasses and before she'd turned away she couldn't read his expression, but she could still feel the intensity of his gaze.

"Good." He took the key out of her hand and opened the door himself. Then he pushed it open, let them go in, then followed and shut it behind him.

"I need to get dinner started. Don't let us keep you. I'm sure you have things to do." Daisy said briskly and, slipping off her jacket, started toward the kitchen.

"We can get takeout. What do you like?"

"I'm making stew. Charlie likes it."

"So do I." Alex smiled guilelessly.

"Alex can stay, can't he?" Charlie asked.

What was a mother to do? Of course she had to be polite. She was teaching Charlie to be polite.

The evening was interminable. Dinner. Then Charlie's bath. Then bedtime stories. And awareness of Alex at every single moment. Watching him with Charlie, catching him looking at her when he thought she wasn't noticing. Charlie's stories took forever, even though Alex read several of them. Prayers were longer, too, because Alex, of course, was added to them.

"No singing tonight," Daisy decreed before Charlie could

even suggest it. "You need to go to sleep. Remember, your class is going to the zoo tomorrow." The preschool trip to the Bronx Zoo—and a program about animals in winter—had been much anticipated.

Now Charlie looked up from his pillow and asked, "Can Alex come?"

"No," Daisy said without giving Alex a chance to reply.

"But—"

"I have to work," Alex said, sounding regretful. "But we had fun today. We'll do this again."

Charlie popped up. "When?"

"That depends on how well and how fast you go to sleep now," Daisy said, no stranger to manipulative children. She gave him a speaking look.

Charlie sighed, sank back against the pillow and shut his eyes. "I'm sleepin'."

"So I see," Daisy said drily, bending to kiss him. "Good night, Mr. Sleepyhead."

"Night," Charlie murmured, not opening his eyes.

She stepped back, and found that Alex had taken her place at Charlie's bedside. He brushed a hand over Charlie's head, then dropped to one knee and pressed a light kiss on Charlie's forehead.

The boy's eyes popped open and small hard arms and one very hard blue cast wrapped themselves around Alex's neck.

Alex stiffened. And Daisy held her breath.

Then slowly his posture eased, and his arms went around Charlie, too. He scooped the boy up for a fierce hug, burying his face in the crook of Charlie's neck. Then slowly he drew back and lowered the boy to the pillows again. "G'night, sport." His voice was rough. He straightened and stood looking down at the little boy for a long moment.

Then his gaze turned to Daisy. Their eyes met. She shut off the light and headed down to the kitchen.

If he wanted to talk, he could do it while she washed the dinner dishes. But frankly, she didn't know what else there was to say. She began to run water in the sink, all the while aware of exactly where he was, hip propped against the counter beside the refrigerator, watching her.

"Sorry I didn't get here earlier," he said over the running water.

"You didn't need to come at all." Daisy set the plates in the soapy water.

"Of course I needed to come. But I had to get hold of Caroline. I needed to tell her first."

Daisy did turn then. "That you had a son? How did she take that after your 'no children ever' edict?"

Alex's mouth twisted wryly. "She was…surprised."

"I'll bet." Daisy turned away again, picking up a mug and scrubbing it so furiously that the tiny sprays of yellow primroses on it threatened to disappear.

"But she understands."

Daisy's teeth came together as she swallowed half a dozen remarks that were far snarkier than the previous one. "I don't want her *understanding*. If she's like you, she doesn't want kids around!"

"She won't have them. We've broken it off."

Daisy stared at him. "What?"

Alex lifted his shoulders. "Circumstances changed. I called Amalie, too. Told her I was cancelling the rest of our agreement. My matchmaker," Alex said when Daisy stared at him blankly.

She was still processing Caroline's departure. "Why?"

"Because I don't need one now. Obviously. She gets her

money anyway, so she doesn't care. She wished me all the best." He paused, then exhaled slowly and said, "So, the decks are clear."

There was a moment's stark silence as the implication of his words set in. Daisy felt a sudden chill but it started inside her, not out.

"Clear," she echoed. "Clear for what?"

But as soon as she asked, she knew she couldn't let him answer. She already knew—and she didn't want to hear it. "For you to be noble? For you to do something stupid like ask me to marry you?"

Alex stared at her, taken aback. "Damned right I want to marry you. Why the hell not? It makes perfect sense."

Exactly what she wanted to hear. Daisy wasn't cold any longer, she was burning up. She wouldn't have been surprised if steam was coming out of her ears.

"You're just like Cal! What is it with men, anyway? Why do you always think you can make the world act the way you want it to?"

"Daisy—"

"It's all control with you, isn't it?"

"Daisy, stop it! Stop being stupid. And this has nothing to do with your ex or anyone else." He shoved away from where he was leaning against the countertop and came toward her. "Be sensible, Daisy. I want to—"

"No. Don't do it, Alex," she said fiercely. "Don't say it. I don't want to hear it." She flung the sponge away and put her hands over her ears. "I won't!"

Of all the bloody-minded females!

Alex couldn't believe it! But Daisy was glaring at him, her cheeks flushed, her eyes flashing. She'd flung the sponge into the sink and put her hands over her ears, defying him to…what?

Propose?

Of course he was damned well going to propose. It was the right thing to do. If he had fathered a child—and he quite obviously had—it was his duty to marry his child's mother, be her husband, a father to their child and…and then what?

Live happily ever after?

He wouldn't let himself think about that.

Because in his experience, people didn't get to. Well, maybe some did. But how did you know? How could you ever be sure?

You couldn't. But the decision was no longer his. He'd made it five years ago when he'd made love to Daisy. He'd spent all night coming to terms with what that meant, and he was ready to do it. Determined to do it.

And now…

Now he didn't have to.

Just like that, Daisy had popped his balloon of self-righteous nobility before he'd even had a chance to let it fly.

He should be relieved, Alex told himself. Somewhere deep down, he supposed he *was* relieved. But at the same time, he was madder than hell. He didn't like being dismissed, being told his presence wasn't needed, wasn't valued.

And if she expected he would just turn around and walk away, she was bloody well out of her mind. At least she'd taken her hands off her ears now and had turned back to the pots and pans with which she was making an almighty racket.

Alex scowled at her back. "I seem to recall," he pointed out, "that you wanted marriage."

The pots continued to clatter. She shot him a quick furious glance over her shoulder. "Five years ago, yes. When I was besotted, yes. When I thought you loved me, too. Not now! I don't want you now!"

It surprised him that her words actually hurt. They made him stiffen as if he could defend himself against them, against her. His jaw felt as tight as a steel trap. "Fine," he said tersely. "You don't have to 'have' me."

Daisy turned, a look of consternation flicked across her features, followed by a faint sheepish smile of relief. "Well, um, good. Thank you," she said gruffly.

"But that doesn't mean you're getting rid of me."

She blinked. "But—"

"For God's sake, Daisy. You have my son! You might not have seen fit to tell me, but I know it now. And I'm not going to walk out of his life. I want to be part of it. I want him to be part of mine."

"For how long? Are you going to be buddies like you were today? For as long as it suits you? Are you going to be here when he needs you or are you going to walk when the going gets tough? Do you imagine you can be here and not *care,* Alex? You said—you told me plainly—brutally—that you didn't want to care—about anyone!" Her eyes flashed with accusation.

"You never let me care," he pointed out, trying to sound calmer than he felt. "You didn't even tell me he existed!"

"To protect him! To protect him from the knowledge that for you love is a one-way street!"

Stung, for a moment Alex didn't reply. Deliberately he swallowed his discomfort at the truth of her words. But at the same time, he lashed back. "Is that what it is?" he challenged her. "Or maybe—" he flung at her because, damn it, he wasn't the only one in the wrong "—it's all about protecting yourself!"

"I don't need to protect myself from you anymore. I know

the score now. But Charlie doesn't. He'll give his love, wholly and completely, to you! To a man who can't let himself care— to a man who thinks love is worth nothing! And how do you think that's going to make him feel? I know what that's like, remember? And I wasn't four! I know what's right for my son!"

"And you're the arbiter of all things 'right' in Charlie's life?"

"I know him better than anyone. I love him more than anyone. I want the best for him."

"The best thing would be if he had a family," Alex told her flatly. "And you know it."

Daisy didn't reply. She just stared at him stonily. Then she reached for a towel, dried her hands on it, and marched past him, heading straight into the living room where she twisted the locks and yanked open the door. "I think it's time you left now."

Alex followed her into the living room, but he stopped there, staring at her, trying to fathom what was going on in her head. She wasn't being sensible, wasn't being rational.

"You know I'm right, Daisy."

She just looked at him, then at the door. When he still didn't move, she yanked his jacket off the hook where he'd hung it and thrust it at him. "Goodbye, Alex."

Wordlessly he reached out and took it, shrugged it on and zipped it up. "Fine. I'll go. But this isn't over. I'll be back. And while I'm gone, don't just think about Charlie. Think about what you want, too."

And he pulled her into his arms and took her mouth with his.

He'd been wanting to do this all day, all yesterday, every minute, it seemed, since he'd kissed her last. The hunger was so fierce he ached with it.

Now he felt her whole body stiffen. She raised her arms

between them, her forearms pressing against his chest as if to hold him off. It didn't matter. While he would have liked to feel her body melt against him, to have her arms wrap around him, to know her eagerness matched his, he didn't need it to prove his point.

He had his lips to convince her, to taste her, to tease her. He had his tongue to touch her lips, to part them, to slip between and find her sweetness. God, she made him crazy, made his whole being quiver with need, made the blood sing in his veins.

He wasn't going to let her pretend that it meant nothing. Kissing Daisy *never* meant nothing. Kissing Daisy was amazing, wild, always potent, always drugging. Kissing Daisy always made his heart slam against the wall of his chest, made his loins tighten and his body hum with desire.

And damn it, he knew—absolutely knew—it was the same for her.

She fought it. He could feel her resisting. But she was fighting herself, not him. Her lips trembled, pressed together, denied him. But she denied herself, as well.

So he touched them anyway. He drew a line with his tongue, coaxed, teased. And they gave, opened just a fraction. He took advantage, darted within. He heard her whimper, and her fingers opened to clutch his jacket, hanging on. Her lips softened, parted farther. And he felt a jolt as her tongue tangled with his.

Yes, like that. It was always like that between them. Always had been. Alex wanted to cheer, to exult, to press his advantage and take them where they both wanted to go. He wanted to slide his fingers beneath her sweater and stroke her curves, her breasts, her very bones. He wanted to tease beneath the waistband of her jeans, slide his fingers south, touch her—there. Damn she was killing him. His breath came hard and fast. He wanted to taste, to tease, to sample and suckle. He wanted to devour. He wrapped her in his arms, thrust his fingers in her hair, kissed her hard one more time.

Then he pulled back, dragging in lungfuls of air as he looked down into her stunned feverish gaze. "While you're thinking," he said roughly, "think about that."

Her palm connected with his cheek so fast he didn't even see it coming.

"What the hell was that for?" he demanded. His fingers curled. He jammed his hands in his pockets.

"What was the kiss for?" she countered furiously.

His gaze narrowed. *"That's* why you slapped me? For reminding you that we had something good?"

"I don't need any reminders, thank you very much. And it turns out we didn't have anything at all."

"You don't believe that."

"I do. And I don't need you trying to bribe me with sex."

He gaped at her. "Bribe you?"

Her eyes flashed. "Bribe me, get around me, coerce me, make me do what you want because I'm somehow susceptible to you! Call it what you like. It's not going to work."

"For God's sake, Daisy." He raked fingers through his hair. "I was trying to show you it isn't all about Charlie."

"No, it isn't. It's all about you—what you want, when you want it, and not when you don't. You don't love Charlie. You don't love anyone. You don't want to. You push people away. At least Cal wanted to," she spat at him furiously.

"Cal?" he retorted. "This is all about Cal? All about your 'failed' marriage? Has it really made you that bitter?"

"I'm not bitter at all. Not at Cal. Not at our marriage." She lifted her chin as if defying him to argue. "We went into it with our eyes open."

He watched her, saw a host of conflicting expressions cross her face. Then she lifted a shoulder as if shrugging off a burden and said, "Cal is gay."

Alex stared at her.

"He's my friend. And he didn't have a lover. So when he saw what I was going through, he tried to make it easier for me." She ran her tongue over her lips. "He was convinced that he could will himself to love whoever he wanted to love." She shrugged. "He believes in the same things I do—commitment, long-term relationships, responsibility. Love."

Alex's gaze narrowed.

"He never lied to me. And I didn't lie to him. He knew I loved you. He knew you didn't love me. He offered his name, his support, everything he could. And I did the same for him. But—" she lifted her shoulders "—it wasn't enough. We tried to make it work. It didn't. In the end we knew that. We'll always be friends. But there's more to real love, real marriage than that. And we both wanted…more."

"I'm offering you more," Alex pointed out indignantly.

Daisy just looked at him. She took a slow breath, then swallowed and shook her head. "No, Alex. You're not. You're offering far, far less."

She pushed him out the door and closed it after him.

Chapter 11

Daisy leaned against the door, tears blurring her eyes. She dashed them away with a shaking hand. Of course he thought she was mad. The way he'd looked at her, patent disbelief in his eyes.

He was offering her marriage, wasn't he? Hadn't that been her heart's desire five years ago?

Yes, then. Not now.

Because this was exactly the sort of "marriage" he would have been offering Caroline. A wedding, a legal, convenient version of friends with benefits. Now as she stood with her back to the front door, still hearing Alex's footfalls moving quickly away, Daisy wiped a hand over her face, touched the tears, wanted to deny them. Knew she couldn't.

They were as real as the truth she'd just told Alex: marriages of convenience didn't work. Not for her. She and Cal had done their best. But friendship and responsibility only went so far.

They were only a part of the deep abiding fullness of heart, soul, mind and body that real love was.

She knew it wasn't easy. She knew, just as Alex knew, that real love hurt.

She didn't care. If she could have the love, she could endure the pain. She'd been raised in the real love of her parents' marriage. She remembered their joys and their sorrows. She remembered all too well her mother's pain at her father's death.

But she remembered, too, the sight of her mother smiling through her tears as she'd said, "I don't regret it for an instant. Loving Jack was worth all of this."

This was sometimes heartache, sometimes pain, sometimes joy, sometimes the simple act of heart-deep sharing.

Daisy wanted that.

She had the pain part down pat, she thought, tears streaming down her face.

But she knew she'd done the right thing—even if Alex had been right, that she'd been protecting herself. If marrying Cal had been a mistake, marrying Alex would be a disaster—because she could not stop loving him, and he didn't know what real love was.

He couldn't draw a straight line.

He broke the lead in all his mechanical pencils. He snapped the nib off his best drawing pen. His hands shook so badly as he sat at his desk and tried to find the calm he always felt designing, that he crumpled up page after page of the paper in his sketchbook.

Finally Alex threw the whole damn thing out and went to stand and stare out the window, dragging in deep breaths. But for once even the sight of the spectacular Manhattan skyline didn't soothe his furious soul.

He pressed his forehead against the cold glass of the window, then lifted a hand and rubbed it against his stubbled cheek.

The physical sting of Daisy's palm was long gone. But the emotional sting was imprinted on his soul. So were the words she'd flung at him: *It's all about you. You don't love Charlie. You don't love anyone. You don't want to.*

His throat tightened. His eyes blurred. He sucked in another breath and shook his head, wanting to deny it.

But he couldn't. Not entirely. At least a part of what she said was true: He *hadn't* wanted to.

For years—ever since Vass's death and his parents' divorce— Alex had done his best to make sure that anything as messy and painful as love would not be a part of his world. He'd deliberately built himself a life without it. He had his business, his design projects, his friends, and recently he'd figured that he could do marriage as long as it was on his terms, where his wife didn't want anything deeper or more demanding than he did.

He'd wanted a world he could control.

Which was why he had turned his back on Daisy five years ago.

She had threatened his control. She had bowled him over that weekend, had loved and given and enchanted in equal measures. He'd never met anyone so unguarded, so genuine, so warm and real.

Letting Daisy into his life would have been opening himself up to a tidal wave of emotions he couldn't control, a future he couldn't predict, the possibility for pain he didn't ever want to experience again.

God knew what would happened if he let down his guard.

So he hadn't. He'd turned away from her warmth, rejected her love, shut her out of his life. And having done so, he'd thought he was safe.

He was wrong.

But she was wrong, too.

Daisy had thought he *couldn't* love, and Alex had believed he *wouldn't*.

But God help him, he did. He loved Charlie. He'd only had to see the boy, watch the joy of life in his eyes, listen to him, hold his hand, touch his hair—and he loved. But more than that, before he recognized that he loved Charlie, he knew he loved her.

Daisy.

In spite of himself and his determined intentions, the day Daisy had come into his life, she had created a tiny rent in his armor. She had pierced his defenses, had touched his heart and planted a seed deep in his soul. For two days she had given him a glimpse of what life could be like if he had dared to let it grow.

He hadn't. He'd turned his back. But while he thought he'd walked away heart-whole, it wasn't true.

The minute he'd seen her again this autumn, everything he had felt when he'd been with her the first time—the need, the emotion, the connection—the sense that the world was a brighter, warmer, fuller, more welcoming place—had broken through.

He hadn't given in, of course. Though he had felt the attraction all over again, he'd still tried to do it his way—to control it. To control her.

He couldn't.

She wouldn't let him.

He knew what she wanted. Demanded. A real future, a no-holds-barred willingness to love and, admitting that love, to face the possibility of pain, of loss of control, of helplessness—all the things he'd said no to.

He didn't know if he could do it now.

But he loved. He had no choice. It was simply there—in him. For better or worse. But he knew he couldn't face the future until he was able to face the past.

Rubbing a hand over his face, Alex turned away from the window, from the cool remote perfection of the distant skyline, to the emotional minefield that he carried inside him. He padded into his bedroom.

The room was spare, unadorned. It held a wide bed, a tall oak chest of drawers, a closet. Nothing more. He went to the chest of drawers, then crouched down and pulled open the bottom drawer.

It was empty except for one thing—a single sturdy, flat, dark green cardboard box, perhaps a foot-square, two inches deep.

For a long minute, he just looked at it. Didn't immediately reach for it. Didn't really want to touch it even yet.

He hadn't touched it except when he'd moved it, since he'd left for university at the age of eighteen. He hadn't opened it since he'd put the lid on it when his parents separated, when they sold the house, when his mother moved to Athens and his father to Corfu.

"Don't look back," his father had said as he'd sold off everything and buried himself in his scholarly books.

But Alex had put the things that mattered in that box, the things he couldn't let go of, even if he couldn't bring himself to look at them.

He'd carried the box with him ever since. He'd taken it to university in London, to his first job in Brussels, to the dozen or so places he'd lived in his adult life. He had brought it with him here.

Wherever he was, he always put it carefully in its own drawer where he wouldn't accidentally stumble across it when he was looking for something else. He didn't want to be blindsided when he wasn't prepared.

Someday, he always promised himself, he would open it. When the time was right he would once again let himself remember. But as time had passed, he'd learned to cope, he'd shut off the past, had refused to give it the power to hurt him. It was easier to forget. The time had never been right.

Until now.

Now he hurt anyway. Now Daisy's words had cut right through his protective shield, had looked inside him and found him wanting.

His hands shook as he drew the box out of the drawer and carried it over to sit on the bed with it. He was surprised how light it was. In his imagination it was the heaviest thing he owned.

He ran his fingers over the top, then carefully eased the lid off and set it aside. There were only a handful of things within—and just as he had feared, the sight of them brought a thousand memories flooding back.

There was the postcard of the Matterhorn that Vass had sent him when he was six and Vass was nine. Vass had been with their father in Switzerland. "It's s'cool," he had written. "You and me will climb it someday."

They hadn't, of course. But when Vass came home, they'd begun climbing the cliffs by their island home with eager purpose. Just as they'd earnestly practiced tying ship's knots in the two feet of line that lay in the box, as well.

"Learn to tie the knots and I'll teach you to sail," their father had said.

Now Alex drew the piece of line out of the box and his fingers moved automatically to make a Spanish bowline, a clove hitch, a figure eight while in his mind's eye he saw the summer days they'd spent on the water, the three of them. He remembered the heat and the sun and the wind—and the stories and the laughter that came with them.

He picked a small reddish-brown pottery shard out next, rubbing his thumb over its worn contours and remembering Vass finding it and saying he was going to grow up and be an archaeologist like Indiana Jones. And there were two very well-used Star Wars figures—Luke and Han, of course—they'd played with for years. There was a painstaking drawing of the Battlestar Galactica that Vass had drawn while he was in the hospital, and a far more precise elegant one that Alex had drawn at the same time because, after all, he was the one who was going to be the architect, not Vass.

And then there was a single silver Porsche Matchbox car.

Alex had faced all the other bits of memorabilia with a tight jaw, a strained smile, blinking eyes.

But the silver Porsche felt like a dagger to his heart.

They had fought over the silver Porsche, he and Vass. It had been his brother's, but Vass had been indifferent until Alex wanted it. And they had fought—actually came to blows—and Vass had punched him in the stomach and he had given Vass a bloody nose.

He stared at the small car now, picked it up and ran his hands over the lines of its frame. Then he closed his fingers around it until he felt the cold metal bite into his hand. He wanted to feel it. Needed the pain.

It hadn't been Vass's first bloody nose. He'd had several that summer. But this one they hadn't been able to stop. Not until they'd taken him to the doctor. And then there had been murmurs of concern. His mother's worry. His father's pacing. More doctor visits. A flight to Athens to see a specialist. A hospital. Tests.

A diagnosis. Leukemia.

Because of a bloody nose. A bloody nose that was Alex's fault.

It wasn't, of course. He knew that now. But at the time, he was not yet nine years old. He hadn't known—and no one had bothered to reassure him. They'd all been far too worried about Vass. He had been worried, too.

But he'd swallowed his worry and his guilt because there hadn't been time for it, there hadn't been room for it. His parents hadn't even seen it.

When Vass had come home from the hospital the first time, Alex had been scared to go into his room, afraid he might do more damage.

But Vass had said scornfully, "You can't give somebody leukemia. You're not that powerful, brat." Then he'd grinned, Vass's old wonderful "I can do anything" grin, and Alex had had his brother back.

Then he'd believed Vass would recover. Then he'd hoped for the best. Two and a half years later, there was no best.

The last time he'd been in Vass's hospital room, Vass had said, "Keep the Porsche. It's yours."

"I don't want it," Alex had protested, tears streaming down his face.

Now slowly, painfully, he unbent his fingers, and stared at the little car. He rubbed his fingers over it, remembering Vass doing the same thing. He squeezed his eyes shut and saw Vass's frail body and thin pale face, and he let the pain wash over him.

But other memories came, too. Along with the pain, he remembered the good times, the joy, the sharing and laughter. And he knew you couldn't have one without the other.

For years he'd put the Porsche and the memories in a box and tucked them away, unable to face them.

You don't love anyone. You don't want to. Daisy's words echoed in his mind. He heard them again, along with her parting shot: *You're offering far, far less.*

Alex knew what he had to do.

He just hoped to God he could do it.

"'S Christmas!" Charlie jiggled Daisy's shoulder, waking her, peering wide-eyed into her sleep-gritted ones. "An' Santa came!"

The pure joy of youth and belief beamed at her. She rolled over and shoved herself to a sitting position, then reached out to pull him into a fierce hug. "Of course he did. Were you worried?"

Charlie gave her a quick, hard, fierce hug in return, then wriggled out of her grasp, his head shaking to and fro. "Nah. I knew he'd come." He held out a hand to her and Daisy let him pull her to her feet.

"I did, too," she confided, snagging her bathrobe as he dragged her toward the living room, toward the Christmas tree which was already lit with small bright multicolored lights, because obviously Charlie had been there first, poking around.

But he hadn't opened any gifts. He had waited for her. Now he looked at her expectantly.

And deliberately, mustering all the joy she could manage, Daisy put her game face on. "Let me put the coffee on. Then we'll see what Santa brought."

There was no time to brood on Christmas morning. There were gifts to unwrap and ooh-and-aah over. Santa made a just-turned-five-year-old boy very happy. There was a set of Legos and some action figures, three new books, a soccer ball, and a floor mat with the outline of streets and buildings—a city to drive his cars around in. Daisy's mother had sent him a build-it-yourself racetrack for his little cars and a stash of art supplies for rainy days.

Charlie was thrilled. He wanted to play with all of it now. Daisy wanted to let him. But Cal was coming to get Charlie at noon. His parents were already here from Cooperstown and were looking forward to spending the day with Cal and their grandson. All of Cal's siblings and their families were coming, too.

"They'd be happy to see you, too," Cal had assured Daisy last week when they'd discussed plans. "You don't have to be alone."

But Daisy had shaken her head. "I'll be all right. I've booked a photo shoot." She had done it deliberately, agreeing to a plea from one of her old college classmates that she do a four-generation family shoot on Christmas afternoon.

"They're all only here for the day," Josie had apologized when she'd asked. "I know it's probably impossible being Christmas and all...but just in case..."

"Sounds great," Daisy had said firmly. It would keep her from sitting at home alone and miserable. "It'll be fun." She'd pasted a bright determined smile on her face. "If it's nice and there's snow on the ground, we can shoot it in the park."

It was nice. There was even, amazingly enough, a few inches of new snow on the ground. And more was drifting down by the time Cal appeared at the door.

He was smiling and looked happier than she could remember. She knew he'd met someone. It was early days yet, he'd told her last week. But there was a light in his eyes she hadn't ever seen before.

He took one look at her pale face and the dark circles under her own eyes and said, "You look awful."

Daisy laughed wryly. "Thank you very much."

But Cal frowned. "I shouldn't be taking him away from you today. Come with us."

Adamantly Daisy shook her head. "I'm meeting Josie's family at their place at one to do some indoor shots, then we're going to shoot at the Bow Bridge in the park if it's still snowing."

"Come after you finish."

"I'll be fine," she insisted. "Go on. Have a good time." She gave Charlie a hug and a kiss. "Behave."

"I always behave," he said stoutly. "I'm bringin' my new guys to show Grandpa."

"He'll like that." Daisy gave him one more squeeze, then stood up. Her smile was strained. Of course Charlie didn't notice. She hoped Cal didn't, either. "See you tomorrow," she said with all the cheer she could manage. Then she shut the door behind them, leaned back against it, and pressed her hands to her eyes.

It was letting Charlie go, she told herself. This was, after all, the first Christmas that she hadn't had him with her all the time. Always before, after their divorce, Cal had come here and they'd celebrated together. But they both knew that couldn't last. He had a life now—and she had to get one.

Now she scrubbed at her eyes and took a deep, hopefully steadying breath, then she went upstairs to get ready to go, picking out the lenses and filters she wanted to take, determined to keep her mind busy so she wouldn't think about where Charlie was and what he was doing and…

…about Alex.

She *had* to stop thinking about Alex.

It had been two weeks since they'd had their confrontation. Two weeks since she'd spurned his offer of marriage before he could even make it, since she'd told him exactly what she thought of it—and of him—and had shoved him out of the door and out of her life.

He hadn't been back.

Was she surprised? Of course not. It was for the best, really, and she knew it.

What surprised her was how much she cared.

She didn't want to care! She didn't want to miss him, didn't want to remember him sitting on the floor playing with Charlie, didn't want to think about him telling their son a story, didn't want to close her eyes and be plagued by images of him with Charlie in his arms or on his shoulders, the two of them grinning at each other.

She didn't want to remember how proud she'd felt the night he'd got the award for his hospital design, how intently she'd listened when he'd told her about his inspiration for it, how much she heard and understood what he didn't ever say.

She didn't want to think about him—and she couldn't seem to stop.

Now she finished packing her gear bag, slipped on her puffy, bright blue down jacket and headed toward the park.

It was Christmas. A time of hope. A time to put the past behind her and move on. She squared her shoulders, and picked up her bag. Maybe after she'd finished Josie's family's photo shoot, she would go ice skating, meet the man of her dreams, fall in love.

Fairy tales. Would she never learn?

Daisy sighed and headed for Josie's place.

Four generations of the Costello family were ready and waiting. Josie swept Daisy into their Fifth Avenue sixth floor apartment overlooking the park, equal measures eager and apologetic. They were so glad to have her take photos of their family holiday, they were so sorry they were taking her away from her own family today of all days.

"It's all right," Daisy assured them. "I'm glad to do it."

It was every bit the distraction she had hoped. The seven children—cousins who didn't see each other often—along with their parents, grandparents and two great-grandparents, were a noisy energetic mob. And Daisy, intrigued by the possibilities, threw herself into the work.

She did a series of family groups, then gathered them around the table, shot Josie's grandfather slicing the turkey, her grandmother helping the youngest grandson fill his plate. She caught two cousins playing chess in front of the fire, three little girl cousins playing dress-up with the small trunk of fancy clothes one had got for Christmas.

It was the perfect family Christmas, the kind she'd seen in movies and on TV. The kind she'd always wanted for herself. And especially for Charlie.

She shot their preening and their giggling. She shot four generations of Costello men watching football on television, simultaneously cheering or groaning. She had all the children make a human pyramid that mimicked the Christmas tree.

Then, as soon as she shot that, she said, "Let's go to the park," before things got rowdy, which the human pyramid showed signs of becoming.

The snow was still falling, picture-perfect, when they got to the Bow Bridge. She posed them there and did a couple of formal shots for posterity while passersby, walking off their Christmas dinners, stopped and watched then, smiling, moved on.

Daisy didn't pay them any mind. She glanced their way,

then turned back to shoot a series of photos of great-grandpa and grandpa and two little grandsons building a snowman. The girls were making snow angels, their colorful scarves flung out against the snow as they moved their arms and legs. They danced and played and she captured it all—the grace, the laughter—mothers and daughters, grandmothers, great-grandmother and granddaughters. The boys were wrestling in the snow now, pelting each other with snowballs, laughing madly.

Family.

How she envied them their family. She tried to shove the thought away even as it tightened her throat, made her swallow hard. She blinked hard and stopped shooting for a moment, needing to turn away.

Several people who had been watching, smiled at her and scuffed their feet and moved away. She got a grip, started to turn back, then caught a glimpse of someone else out of the corner of her eye.

Her gaze stopped, jerked back, dismissed it. She turned to shoot the snowball-throwing boys again. But her heart was beating faster as she edged around to get a different angle, to look west without turning her head.

He was still there, standing in the shadows beneath the trees.

Lean, tall. Dark wind-blown hair. Wearing jeans and a hunter-green down jacket.

"Lookit me!" one of the Costello boys shouted. He had scrambled up into the crook of a tree and peered down at her.

Daisy turned, focused, shot. Then she swivelled again, taking more shots of the snowball fight, but not even looking at what she was shooting.

She was trying to squint past the camera, to get a better

look. He was too far away to be sure. But the last time she'd seen Alex he'd worn a jacket like that.

Surely it wasn't. It couldn't be. It was her stupid fairy-tale-obsessed mind playing tricks on her.

She turned and aimed her shots at the snowman builders now. Grandpa had the littlest boy on his shoulders to loop a scarf around the snowman's neck. Daisy shot it all. That was what she was here for.

When she turned around again, she expected the man to be gone. He was leaning against the tree, hands in his pockets, staring steadily at her.

Daisy raised her camera and pointed it. She zoomed in, and caught her breath.

Slowly Alex nodded at her.

But he didn't move, didn't come closer. Just leaned against the tree, as if he was waiting for a bus or something!

"Are your fingers freezing? Daisy? Daisy?"

She turned, realizing that Josie had been talking to her. "N-no. I'm fine. I— Fine." She glanced back.

He was still there.

"I think we'll call it quits if you've got enough," Josie said. "The little ones and great-grandma are getting cold. I am, too," she admitted, blowing on her hands. "But it's been such fun. Will you come with us? We're going to make cocoa for the kids and hot toddies for the grown-ups."

The panicky desperate part of Daisy wanted to jump at the invitation. Whatever Alex was doing there, he was there on purpose. He had something to say. And Daisy was sure she didn't want to hear it.

But if she didn't hear it now, he'd find another time. And at least she wouldn't have to worry about Charlie overhearing.

"Thanks," she said to Josie. "But I'll just go on home. I

loved doing it, though. I'll have the proofs for you by the end of the week."

"Fantastic." Josie gave her a hug. "You were brilliant. And we had a blast. We'll remember it always."

Daisy smiled wanly. She had a feeling she would, too.

With cheery goodbyes and fierce hugs from several small children and a couple of great-grandparents, Daisy began to pack up her gear while the Costellos headed back across the park.

She focused securing the lenses in her camera bag. She didn't look around, ignored the sound of footsteps through the snow. But her heart was going like a jackhammer in her chest. She straightened just as a shadow fell across her.

"Daisy." His voice was soft and gruff, surprisingly hesitant.

Steeling herself, she turned. The sight that met her eyes was a surprise, too. This wasn't the smooth confident man she expected to see. This Alex's jaw was stubbled with at least a day's worth of beard. This Alex's eyes were bloodshot and shadowed. As she stared, his jaw bunched and tightened. He ran the tip of his tongue between his lips, then pressed them together again.

"Alex." She nodded carefully, determinedly giving nothing away, particularly encouragement. The last thing she needed was to fight this battle again.

For a long moment he didn't speak, either, and Daisy wondered if she ought to just step around him, head home. Maybe he'd just been walking in the park, had happened on her by accident. God knew perverse things like that could happen.

"You were right," he said abruptly. "What you said."

Daisy blinked. What she'd said? What had she said? Uncertainly she shook her head.

"That I didn't want to love. That I pushed people away."

He answered the question before she even had to ask. He said the words quickly, as if he needed to get past them. Then he said again more slowly, "I didn't want to. Then." Pale green eyes met hers.

Then? Which meant…what? Daisy felt herself tense, but didn't move. She searched his gaze, tried to hear the words he never said.

Then he took a breath and said them. "I loved my brother," he said, the words coming out on a harsh breath. "And I thought I killed him."

"What?" She stared at him, aghast.

He shook his head. "We had a fight…over a car. A toy. I was *eight*," he said harshly. "And I gave him a bloody nose. He bled and bled. They said he had leukemia. I thought…" He shook his head, anguished. "I wasn't even nine," he said. "I didn't know."

"Oh, Alex." She just looked at him. She'd known about his brother. She hadn't known this.

"He said I didn't. But he just kept getting sicker. And…then he died." Now she could hear him dragging the words out. "My parents were shell-shocked. Destroyed. They couldn't help each other. They couldn't even look at me."

"It wasn't your fault!"

"I know that now. But we don't talk much in my family, not about…" He swallowed, then looked past her over her shoulder, staring into the distance, his eyes bright with unshed tears. Whatever he was seeing, Daisy was sure it wasn't in Central Park.

He brought his gaze back to hers, his eyes filled with pain. "When I was ten years old I thought I'd killed my brother and ended our family." His throat worked. "I loved all of them."

And she had told him he didn't love anyone.

"I'm sorry." Her words came out as brokenly as his. She wanted to reach out, to touch his sleeve, to put her arms around him. She had no right. "I'm so sorry."

He nodded almost imperceptibly. He took a breath and then another. "I put it away, shut it out of my mind, didn't deal with it. I never talked to anyone about it—except you. Five years ago."

Her eyes widened. "You never—?"

"No. I shut it all out." There it was, the sharp hard edge. She could hear it. It was the way he always shut people out.

He bent his head. "But I couldn't shut you out." His voice was ragged. A faint smile touched his beautiful mouth.

"You certainly did," Daisy reminded him. She remembered his words all too well.

Alex had the grace to grimace. "I tried," he allowed. "Because you got under my skin. Made me feel things that scared the hell out of me."

"What?" Daisy blinked, confused.

"I was…falling in love with you—even back then, that first night." He pulled a hand out of his pocket and rubbed it against the back of his neck. "I was falling in love with you," he repeated, wonderingly, as if he was amazed he could admit it not only to her but to himself. "And it scared me to death. When you started talking about it like it was a good thing— loving—all I could think was, 'I've got to get out of here. I'll destroy her, too.'" His tone was harsh, anguished. And when she looked close she could see his eyes glistening. He blinked rapidly, then gave a quick shake of his head. "So I did." He swallowed. "Hell of a lot safer that way."

Daisy digested that. Drew in a breath, then another, and cocked her head, then asked him gently, "Was it?"

A corner of his mouth quirked up. "It was until I ran into

you again back in September. Then, short answer—no. You're under my skin. I can't get rid of you. Wherever I go, wherever I am, there you are." He made it sound awful, but Daisy suddenly couldn't stop smiling.

Despairing, Alex shook his head. "I couldn't get you out of my mind, though God knows, I tried. I told myself I needed a woman who didn't make me feel all the things you made me feel. But you must have noticed, I couldn't stay away."

"Every time I thought I'd seen the last of you, you came back," Daisy realized. "It made me nervous."

"Because of Charlie?"

"Partly. But really, I suppose, because I'd…never quite got over you." She didn't want to admit it, but if they were being honest, she owed him that. The heat of his gaze was warming her, making her tingle all the way to her toes. At the same time she was still trying to get a grip on the notion that five years ago he'd been falling in love with her, too.

"I wanted you as soon as I saw you again," he told her.

"On your terms."

"Hell, yes. Safer that way. And Caroline was safe. I never felt for her the tiniest bit of what I feel for you. I never wanted her. Never missed her. I knew I could live without her. I can't live without you."

"Alex." She touched his cheek with her palm and he turned his face to press his lips into it, his kiss making her shiver.

"I couldn't ask her to marry me," he admitted. "I was going to, but I never could."

"You must have realized she needed someone else."

He reached up a hand to press her palm against his cheek. He looked down into her eyes, his full of an emotion she'd never dared hope to see there. "Yeah, maybe that was it." He gave a self-deprecating laugh. "No, damn it. I was still in love with you."

Daisy stared at him in astonishment.

"And then I discovered Charlie."

"And you wanted Charlie."

"Yes. I love Charlie," Alex said with an intensity that made her believe it. "Not just because he reminds me of Vass, though God knows he does. I love him because he's yours. And mine. Because he's bright and inquisitive and fun and just knowing he's alive gives me joy." He shook his head slowly. "And I would give my life for him—and for you. I will go to the ends of the earth for you. I will slay dragons for you. I will get hurt for you. I swear it, Daisy." There was wonder in his voice.

Daisy opened her mouth, then closed it again. She didn't know what to say. Her eyes brimmed. So did her heart. Dear God, she'd loved this man for years, but never more than she loved him now, now that he had discovered the love he was capable of, the love he was willing to dare to share.

He reached out and touched her cheek, stroking away a tear she didn't even know was there. Then he wrapped his arms around her and drew her close, let her feel the pounding of his heart, the warmth of his love, the shelter of his embrace.

She leaned against him, letting herself sink into him, loving his strength, his steadiness. She rested her head in the crook between his shoulder and his chin.

"I would have been here sooner," Alex went on. He spoke softly, his lips against her hair. "But I didn't think you probably wanted to talk to me again after what you said the last time."

Daisy raised her eyes to look up at him, feeling guilty. "I didn't know—"

But Alex shook his head. "No, you were right. It was my problem. You gave me a reason to confront it, to deal with it. And I needed to before I could come back. So I did. I had to go to Paris for work anyway. It was a commitment. I spent ten days there. Then I went to see my parents."

Daisy took a quick look into his eyes.

He bent his head, held her closer. "We've…barely talked in years. It was, I suppose, easier for all of us that way. Not to be reminded."

Daisy slid her arms around his back, holding him close, feeling the tension in him.

He cleared his throat, scuffed his boot in the snow, then pulled back a little so he could look down into her eyes. "They're both in Greece these days. Not together. My mother's divorced a third time. My dad is still buried in his books. But I…talked to both of them. About Vass. About…what happened, about what I thought. They were shocked. They had no idea." His eyes were brimming again. He shook his head. "I'm glad I went. And I…expect I'll see them again." He hesitated. "I told them about you…and Charlie. They'd like to meet you both someday…if you're agreeable."

"Of course," Daisy said faintly, her heart spilling over with love for him, thrilled that he'd taken the step to reconnect with his parents, delighted that they might all now find a beginning to their healing.

Alex pressed a kiss into her hair. "Thank you."

Then he drew back and dug into the pocket of his jacket. "Will you give this to Charlie?" He took out a small silver Matchbox car and handed it to her. "I have real Christmas presents for him, but he's got them already. I left them with Cal."

"Cal?" She stared at him in wonder. "You've never even met Cal."

"I have now. I went to your place from the airport. You

weren't there. I didn't know where you were. I thought you might be with him."

"How do you know where he lives?"

"I told you once before—" Alex's mouth quirked "—the internet is a wonderful thing."

Apparently it was. "But I wasn't there."

"No," Alex said. "But he knew where you were."

"And he told you?" That didn't sound like Cal. He was generally very protective.

"After he'd threatened me within an inch of my life. Said I'd be sorry if I hurt you. And I believed him. I liked him. And...I don't ever want to hurt you, Daze." His voice was rough and warm and intense.

And he wasn't hurting her, he was killing her, Daisy thought desperately. She looked down at the tiny car in her hand. Without having to be told, she knew what it was.

"The car you fought over," she said.

He nodded. "It was Vass's. He gave it to me before...before he died." Alex choked on the words. "I've carried it with me ever since."

"Your hair shirt?" Daisy asked gently.

"I didn't think so then, but yes, it was. I lived with the guilt a long time. I might have lived with it forever—without you."

"Oh, Alex." She nestled close again.

"Charlie should have it. He doesn't need to know its past. Only that it's for him—a gift from the uncle he'll never know. Vass—" Alex swallowed "—would have loved him."

Daisy blinked furiously, her fingers tightening around the tiny car. "Yes." She tucked it into the pocket of her jacket. "Oh, yes."

"I have something for you, too." He fished in his other

pocket and pulled out a small box, the sort that jewelry came in. A ring box?

Daisy's heart hammered furiously. More manipulation? Or were they past that?

Alex held it out to her. "This is for you. I saw it at a little shop in Paris and I thought of you. Of us. It's the way I'd like us to be." He looked into her eyes and pressed it into her palm, then closed her fingers over it. Snowflakes dusted his dark lashes, settled on his midnight hair. He smiled gently. "I love you, Daisy. I hope someday you believe it."

Then he drew away from her, turned and set off through the snow.

Numbly, Daisy stared after him. *What?*

He was just going to leave her here? He was going to tell her he loved her, give her his heart, then walk away?

No insistence? No demand? No renewed proposal?

She looked down at the tiny box in her hand, then fumbled to open it. Inside was a silver necklace—real silver, unlike the Porsche—of two interlocking, entwined open hearts.

I thought of you, he'd said. *Of us.*

Two open hearts entwined.

Daisy bit down on her lip. Her fingers trembled. She clutched the box with the necklace in one hand and her camera bag in the other and broke into a run. "Alex! Alex, wait!"

He stopped, turned. Looked at her, half stricken, half hoping. She recognized that look now. She skidded to a halt bare inches in front of him, blinking furiously into the sun, into the dawning hope in those beautiful pale green eyes. "Ask me."

He frowned. "Ask what?"

"You know what!"

He raised a brow. A corner of his mouth quivered, almost smiled.

"Ask," Daisy demanded.

Then he took a breath. "Will you let me love you?" he asked. "Forever?"

"Yes." She threw her arms around him.

"Will you love me?" he asked as she kissed him. His voice was suspiciously hoarse.

"Yes!" She breathed the word against his lips.

"Will you marry me, Daze?" He barely got the words out because now he was kissing her back.

"Yes, Alex. Oh, yes, yes. Yes."

Daisy didn't miss Charlie that night as much as she'd thought she would. She took Alex home and didn't even open the other Christmas present he'd brought her from Paris.

She put on her necklace—or, rather, he put it on for her. Then she took him upstairs to her bedroom. There, slowly, he took off her sweater, her jeans, her shirt, her socks. Then he lowered her to the bed, and, smiling, began to take off everything else she wore.

Everything but the necklace. Daisy wouldn't let him take off that. But the rest—oh, yes. She shivered with pleasure at the way his fingers traced the lines and curves of her body, the way his lips followed and his tongue, as well.

When he unfastened her bra and slipped it off her shoulders, then bent his head to kiss her breasts, she lifted her hands and threaded them in the silky softness of his hair.

Alex kissed his way across her breasts, laved her nipples, made her tremble with longing. Then, smiling at her reaction, he dropped kisses down the line between her breasts, on down to her navel and beyond. And Daisy quivered with need for him.

"Alex!" She squirmed when he peeled her panties down,

tossed them aside, then ran his fingers back up her calves, then her thighs, then touched her—there. "Wait. My turn. You're overdressed."

He lifted his head and smiled. "Am I?"

"Oh, yes." And then Daisy set about unwrapping the Christmas present she wanted more than anything—him.

"I love you," she whispered as she tugged his sweater over his head. "I've never forgotten doing this." She tossed his sweater on the bedside chair, then quickly disposed of the buttons of his shirt.

"You're faster at that than I remember." Alex kept his hands at his sides as he watched her, but there was a flame of desire in his eyes.

"Practice," Daisy said, beginning to work on the zip of his jeans.

"Practice?" Alex frowned.

"Charlie couldn't always dress himself."

He grinned, then sucked in a quick breath when she made quick work of the zipper and her fingers found him. He swallowed hard, then shrugged off his jeans and came to her on the bed, settled next to her, stroked his hands over her with an almost hesitant wonder.

And Daisy felt the same. "I love you," she whispered, glorying in being able to say it, to acknowledge it, and to know that he wanted to hear the words.

"I know. But not as much as I love you," he said, a tremor in his voice and another in the hands that stroked her sensitive skin.

"I'll show you," she insisted, and rolled onto her back, drawing him on top of her, wrapping herself around him.

"And I'll show you," Alex countered, teasing, tasting, touching. He was so exquisitely gentle, yet possessively so.

His fingers found her, knew her, parted her. And then he slid in. "Daze!" His body tensed, froze. And then—at last—he began to move.

"Alex!" Her nails dug into his buttocks. Her head thrashed on the pillow. Her body tightened around him. He made her shiver, he made her quiver, he made her shatter. And he shattered right along with her, his face contorting, his body going rigid, then collapsing to bury his face against her neck.

She stroked his sweat-slick back, then turned her head and kissed his ear and along the whisker-roughened line of his jaw.

When at last he lifted his head it was to look down into her eyes with wonder. "Why did it take me so long to realize?" he murmured, sounding awestruck.

Daisy shook her head. She didn't need to ask why anymore. She had the answer she needed. "I'm just glad you did."

He rolled onto his back then and pulled her on top so that she rested her head on his chest and felt the gallop of his heart beneath her cheek. Softly, rhythmically, Alex stroked her hair.

Daisy didn't know how long they lay like that. She might have slept a little. She thought he did. But when they roused and began to touch, to love again, he raised his head from the pillow and peered down his nose at her. "Is this the sort of match you try to make?" he asked, giving her his heart with his eyes.

Daisy returned his gift full measure. But then she shook her head no.

"It's better," she told him, rising up to meet his lips, to love him, to share the wonder once more.

★ ★ ★ ★ ★

A CHRISTMAS NIGHT
TO REMEMBER

Helen Brooks

Chapter 1

How could you have longed for something with all your heart, lived through endless minutes and hours and days and weeks anticipating the moment it happened, and be numbingly terrified now it had?

Melody shut her eyes tightly, wrinkling her face as she told herself to get control. She could do this. She had to do it actually. There wasn't a choice. By tonight her hospital bed could be occupied by someone else, and topping and tailing was strictly against the rules.

The brief moment of dark humour helped to restore her equilibrium. She slowly unclenched her hands, which had been fists at her sides, and opened her eyes. The small room—one of four off the main ward—had been home for three months since the accident. Early on one of the nurses attending her had told her it was mostly long-term patients who were placed in the more private *en-suite* rooms. She suspected Sarah, the nurse in question, had been trying to warn her not to expect miracles. The damage she'd done to her spine and legs when she'd stepped in front of a lorry one morning wasn't going to be a quick fix. As it happened she hadn't needed it spelling out. She'd known she'd changed her life for ever when she'd looked into Zeke's contorted face as she'd emerged from the fog of anaesthetic after the initial emergency operation.

Enough. Don't think of him. You need to be strong this morning.

Obeying the inner voice, Melody reached for her thick, warmly insulated jacket. In spite of the hospital's hot-house central heating, she knew it was freezing outside. The experts had been predicting a white Christmas for days, and it seemed they were going to be right for once. There had already been an odd flurry of snow this morning, and the sky was low over the rooftops beyond the hospital precincts.

Melody walked across to the window and gazed at the view she would be seeing for the last time. The car park was busy— it was always busy—and beyond the walled grounds the streets of London stretched away full of houses and offices and industry and people going about their everyday business. Normal people. She bit hard on her inner lip. Girls who wouldn't have to think twice about wearing a short skirt in the summer or a bikini. She had been like that once. Now every advertisement on TV and every magazine she read seemed full of perfect women, girls with long beautiful legs and flawless skin.

Enough. She turned from the window, hating herself for the self-pity which always seemed to hit when she least expected it. She was lucky to be alive, she knew that, and she was grateful for it. The damage to her spine and mangled legs, not least the huge amount of blood she'd lost at the scene of the accident, had meant it was touch-and-go for days, apparently, although she hadn't known much about it. She had vague memories of Zeke sitting by her bed, holding her hand in Intensive Care, but it had been a full week before she had woken one morning and found her mind was her own again.

That all seemed like a long time ago now. As soon as she could be moved from the hospital in Reading she'd been transferred to this one, which specialised in spinal injuries. She hadn't known Zeke had been instrumental in accomplishing this, or that with her type of injuries expert care was essential for good long-term recovery until recently, when her consultant had mentioned it. Not that it would have made any difference to her decision to end their marriage.

Melody limped across to the narrow bed, staring down at the suitcase she had packed earlier that morning. She had all the relevant documentation and had said her goodbyes. It only remained for her to leave the place which had become comfortingly womb-like in its safety over the past weeks and months, even as she'd longed to be in charge of her own life once again. But here it didn't matter that she walked with an ungainly gait. The nursing staff were so proud of her that she'd fought to walk at all. They didn't wince at the sight of her scars, but praised her for the way she'd tackled the painful physiotherapy day after exhausting day.

Outside the walls of the hospital was the real world. Zeke's world. She swallowed hard. A realm where the rich and beautiful had the power, and nothing less than perfection would do. She had inhabited that world once—briefly.

She straightened her shoulders, telling herself such thoughts would only weaken her when she needed to be strong, but somehow today she found she couldn't control her mind the way she had done since she'd told Zeke their marriage was over and she didn't want him to visit her again.

Zeke James—entrepreneur extraordinaire, king of the show-business world he ruled with ruthless detachment. She

had heard of him long before she'd met him while audition-
ing as a dancer for a new show. Everyone in the show-business
world had heard of Zeke. He was the living embodiment of
a man with the Midas touch.

She had arrived late for the audition—an absolute no-no if
you were serious about a job. For every dancer selected there
was likely to be over a hundred or more who were disappointed—competition was fierce and jobs were scarce. But old
Mrs. Wood, the elderly widow who had occupied the ground-
floor bedsit of the house she'd been living in, had found her
beloved cat dead in the road first thing that morning, and had
been so upset she hadn't felt able to leave her until the frail little woman's married daughter had arrived. Consequently she
had raced into the theatre where the auditions were being held
breathless and red-faced, and had been given a dressing-down
by the dance director in front of everyone without being allowed to say why she was late. By the time she had ventured
onto the stage to dance her piece she had given up all hope of
gaining a place in the chorus line, much less that of lead female dancer which was what she'd applied for.

Perhaps that was why she had performed the routine she'd
practised every evening so perfectly—she'd had nothing to
lose. She had felt as if her body was a musical instrument,
tuned and played as finely as a violin, and she'd responded to
the piano, any nerves melting away as she'd flowed with the
rhythm, her timing faultless.

Melody's mouth trembled for a second. Never again would
she feel like that. One momentary loss of concentration and the
career she had worked so hard for had been smashed for ever.
All the training since she had been a child, the sacrifices, the
time spent pushing her body to reach levels of physical fitness
and agility greater than that needed by most top athletes had

been for nothing. The years dancing in clubs and pantomime and cabaret as she'd honed her craft, the waitressing and bar work she'd done to pay the rent between engagements, the lack of opportunity to put down any roots since most dance companies undertook tours both at home and abroad, the poor pay and constant discipline—all pointless now.

But none of that mattered as much as losing Zeke.

Melody continued to stand staring into the compact little room but she was miles away, lost in memories.

The first time she had seen Zeke was when she had finished the audition and someone had risen from the small group sitting in the auditorium and begun to clap slowly. She'd stood, panting slightly and unsure how to respond, and her gaze had focused on a tall, broad-shouldered man with dark hair and rugged features.

"Excellent, Miss…" he had consulted the notes in his hand "…Miss Brown. Better late than never. Or do we have a prima donna on our hands who expects us to be grateful that she bothered to turn up at all?"

She had instinctively known he was Zeke James; everyone backstage had been buzzing with the fact the great man himself was present. She had also disliked him on the spot. She detested sarcasm, and the deep, faintly husky voice had been oozing with it. Drawing herself up to her full five-foot-ten-inches—something which had spoilt her chances of becoming a successful ballet dancer but which hadn't interfered with her career as a modern stage dancer—she'd tried to keep her voice from betraying her when she said, "I'm sorry I was late but it was unavoidable."

"Really?" he'd drawled. "I would like to know what came before a place in my production, Miss Brown? I presume it was nothing less than a life-or-death matter?"

"Death, actually."

She could see she'd taken him aback—whether because of the hostile note she'd failed to keep hidden or the content of her reply she wasn't sure; whatever, it had been immensely satisfying to see him at a loss for a moment, even if she knew she'd just blown the faintest chance which had remained of being offered a job.

He'd recovered almost immediately, of course. "I'm sorry." His eyes had narrowed as he'd stared at her more intently before sitting down once more.

Once in the wings, a couple of the other dancers she knew had gathered round her and she'd filled them in on what had happened as they all waited to find out their fate.

"A cat?" Katie, a tall redhead who was easily the most ambitious person Melody had ever met, had stared at her in disbelief. "When we heard you say a death we thought it must be your nearest and dearest to stop you trying for the part of Sasha, but it was just a *cat*?"

"It might be just a cat to you, but it was Mrs Wood's companion and best friend and she was heartbroken this morning," she'd answered, knowing even as she spoke Katie would never understand. Like acting, dancing was highly competitive, and only about one in ten dancers registered with Equity was in work at any one time. Prospects were always poor. Every dance teacher she'd ever had had hammered home the fact that it was only the most dedicated and talented dancers who succeeded, and if you had a thick skin and were ruthless to boot it was all to the good.

Katie, who was also trying for the lead female dancer's role, had unwittingly confirmed her thoughts when she'd said, "Darling, you're a sweetie, you really are, but I wouldn't have kept Zeke James waiting if my dear old mother had kicked the bucket in front of my very eyes this morning. You have to look after number one in this world because no one else will, take it from me. It's dog eat dog."

One of the other dancers had chipped in at this point. "And we all know you'd step on any one of us, Katie, if it gave you an edge in getting what you want, never mind an old lady and her cat."

"Too true." Katie had grinned, completely unabashed. "And the only difference between me and you is that I admit it up front. You'd do the same, Sue. And you, Christie. We all would except perhaps Melody, our own little angel of mercy."

It was only at this point that they had become aware of Zeke James, the dance director and the producer standing having a cup of coffee some distance away. That the three men must have been able to hear their conversation became apparent when Zeke strolled over a few moments later, his face deadpan as he murmured softly, so no one else could overhear, "It's the first time I've played second fiddle to a cat, Miss Brown. A novel experience."

He had walked on before she could retaliate, and when she had glanced over at Katie something in the other girl's face had made her suspect Katie had known Zeke James and the others were within earshot all the time.

Ten minutes later they were all called back on stage. She had got the part of Sasha and Katie was her understudy. And when she had left the theatre later that day Zeke's black Ferrari had been waiting for her...

Enough. Melody shook her head, forcing the memories back into the little box in her mind where they remained under lock and key most of the time. Today, though, she didn't seem able to prevent them escaping.

Flicking her silky, shoulder-length strawberry-blond hair—

which just missed being Titian—free from the collar of her coat, Melody reached for her suitcase. Her hands were trembling. Taking several deep breaths, she composed herself, and when she studied them again they were steady. A small victory, but heartening.

She was going to be fine. She nodded to the thought. Her plans had been carefully made. All she had to do was take it a day at a time now. The hospital thought she was going to stay with friends, but once she'd known she could leave the day before Christmas Eve she had phoned numerous London hotels until she'd found a room, reserving it for a full week. Due to a mix-up with her paperwork her departure had been delayed for a day, but the hotel had kept her room when she'd let them know she would now be arriving on Christmas Eve instead. The room had been expensive, but with it being the holiday period she'd been lucky to find one at all. It would give her the breathing space she needed and that was all that mattered. She nodded again.

Once in the main ward Melody was touched by how the nursing staff gathered round, despite her having said her goodbyes earlier that morning, but then at last she was free to leave and make her way to the lifts. She hadn't expected to feel so shaky and overcome, and as the lift sped her downwards to the hospital lobby it was as though she was venturing into hostile alien territory. When it stopped and the doors slid silently open she had to force herself to move.

A large robust man brushed past her on his way to the lift, and although the action was slight it was enough to knock her off balance due to her injuries. Melody stumbled, the weight of her bulging case hampering her regaining control, and to her horror she knew she was going to fall. She had firmly resisted all suggestions of a stick or crutches, but walking the

length of the ward and pacing her room was very different
from negotiating a crowded hospital foyer.

And then suddenly a pair of strong arms was holding her,
steadying her, and the next moment the suitcase was taken
out of her hand.

"Hello, Melody." Zeke's voice was expressionless, his ebony
eyes unreadable as they stared down into her startled green
ones.

"What—?" She was so surprised her brain wouldn't compute. "How—?"

"Questions later." He was leading her towards the huge automatic doors with a firm hand at her elbow and she had no
choice but to walk with him. "For now let's get out of here."

Chapter 2

It was the impact of the freezing air outside the hot-house warmth of the hospital that jolted her out of her shock. Her wits returning along with her voice, Melody jerked her arm free, stopping dead as she faced him. "What are you doing here?" she bit out hotly.

"Isn't it obvious? Collecting my wife."

His voice was unruffled, even lazy, but Melody knew better than to be fooled that was how he was feeling inside. Zeke was a master at disguising his thoughts and emotions; it was one of the attributes which had made him so hugely successful.

There were plenty more.

At thirty-eight years of age, Zeke had been building his empire for twenty years with a ruthless determination devoid of sentiment. He was no respecter of persons; in the two years since they had been married—she had walked down the aisle on her twenty-fifth birthday—Melody had come to realise that, whether someone was a big star or a virtual novice, Zeke treated each artist exactly the same. He expected total dedication and one-hundred-per-cent commitment and if he got that he was charm itself. If he didn't...

Undoubtedly the charisma he exuded as naturally as breathing helped—especially with the ladies. He was tall at six-foot-four and big with it, although Melody knew for a fact there wasn't an inch of surplus fat on the muscled male body. His broad shoulders and tough physique dwarfed most other men, and his face was hard and rough-hewn, too strong-featured to be called handsome by any stretch of the imagination. But he had something much more powerful than pretty-boy good-looks: a magnetism that emphasised his raw masculinity and cynical, sexy appeal.

The sharply defined planes and angles of his face were un-softened by his jet-black hair and dark ebony eyes framed by thick short lashes, but it was his mouth which had always fascinated her. In repose it was deliciously uneven and stomach-quiveringly attractive, and his voice... On their first date she had felt she could listen to the deep, smoky tones for ever. She still did.

But she had made her decision and it was irrevocable. She didn't belong in Zeke's world any more. Perhaps she never had. And she wasn't going to cling onto him until even the memories of the happiest time in her life were soured by the present. She had never understood what it was about her that had made him love her in the first place—not when he could have had any woman he liked—but the Melody he had married was gone.

Forcing a strength into her voice that belied her trembling inside, Melody said, "How did you know I was leaving today? I haven't told anyone."

"But I'm not anyone. I am your husband." He smiled, but it didn't reach the coal-black eyes.

A sliver of ice ran down her spine. She recognised that smile that wasn't a smile, although it had never been directed at her before. But then she had never had occasion to challenge him in the past and come up against his inflexible will. "We're separated and I've told you I want a divorce."

"And I've told you only over my dead body," he said conversationally. "So, do we stand here in the cold, discussing this for the next umpteen minutes, or are you going to be sensible and come home with me?"

Now she felt a welcome flood of adrenaline as her temper rose. "I have no intention of doing either." She glanced over at the taxi rank outside the hospital gates. "I'm getting a cab to where I want to go, so may I have my case, please?"

He shook his head. "No can do."

She glared at him. "I mean it, Zeke."

"So do I."

"Fine. Keep it." She had her handbag over her shoulder, containing her credit cards and cash. "But just leave me alone."

"Stop this." The studiously calm pose vanished. "I've stayed away the last six weeks, as you asked. I thought that would give you time to come to your senses after the doctor said my presence was upsetting you and hindering your recovery—" the icy quality to his words told her how he had received that news "—but I'm damned if this ridiculous farce is continuing for another hour. You're my wife—we're in this for the long haul, remember? For richer or poorer, in sickness or health, till death do us part."

She only heard the "long haul" part. It suggested gritted teeth, a fulfilment of duty, doing the "right thing" when everything in him was crying out against it. It confirmed all her fears. She felt herself shrinking, dwindling away to nothing.

Zeke had never made any secret of the fact that he delighted in her body. Every night of their marriage and sometimes in the day too he had worshiped her with his lovemaking, taking her to heights she had never imagined as they gloried in each other. He was a skilful and generous lover, adventurous but infinitely tender, intent always on giving her pleasure even as he satisfied his own desire. She had never slept with anyone before Zeke because she had never been in love with any of the men she had dated, and she'd always known she wanted to wait for "the one". And then Zeke had blazed into her life like a dark, glittering meteor, and within two months of their first meeting she had been Mrs James.

Melody took a deep breath, and as she did so the first starry snowflake wafted by in the wind. "It takes two to keep a marriage together, Zeke. You can't force me to stay."

"I don't believe I'm hearing this."

"Believe it because I mean every word." She was amazed her poise was holding. "Things are different now."

His opinion of her last statement was decidedly profane, but she didn't flinch in the face of his anger. He stared at her after his outburst, conflict evident in every line and contour of his rugged features. "Are you telling me you don't love me any more?" he ground out finally. "Is that it?"

She lowered her eyes from the brilliant black orbs boring into her. She couldn't lie convincingly otherwise. Allowing her hair to swing forward and hide her face, she muttered, "Yes, that's it. I don't love you. All right?"

"Look at me and say it." His fingers forced her chin upwards. "Tell me you're prepared to wipe away the last couple of years and all we've shared together as though they never happened. Tell me that and look me in the face while you do it."

"Of course they happened, and I'll always be grateful for them, but things move on. People change." She could hear herself saying the words as though it was someone else speaking.

"*I haven't changed!*" He suddenly shook his head in rapid movement, signifying a silent apology for his raised voice. "I haven't changed," he repeated more softly, the sensual, smoky quality to his voice apparent. "And I simply don't believe you have either."

"Oh, I have," she said, with such bitterness he couldn't fail to believe her. He had married a young, whole woman. Now she didn't feel young any more and she certainly wasn't whole. She was a mess, inside and out. And there was no room in Zeke's world for emotional and physical cripples.

"You mean the accident? Your legs?" He was speaking so quietly she almost couldn't hear him. "That doesn't make any difference to me—surely you know that? You're still you—"

"No." Her voice was brittle but with a thread of steel running through it. "I'm different, Zeke. And you can't wave a magic wand and make me the old Melody, any more than you can pretend I'm not damaged. I'll never dance again. I'll never even walk without a limp. I have months of intensive physiotherapy in front of me and they've already warned me the chances of arthritis as I get older are high. I could end up in a wheelchair at worst."

"I know all that. I've been seeing the consultant on a regular basis and I have worked out a programme of treatment with him." Before she could react, he took her arm again, adding, "It's starting to snow and you're getting cold. Come and sit in the car at least."

"I've told you I'm getting a cab." He was wearing a black overcoat and he looked very big and dark as he glanced down at her. A part of her noticed the way his hair curled over his collar, unlike his usual short, almost military style. Was that intended or did he need a haircut? For some reason she found the thought weakening, and to combat this her voice had a sharp edge as she added, "And I don't want you talking to my consultant again, okay? Much less deciding on my treatment. I can look after myself. We're not together any more, Zeke. Deal with it."

Before she had met Zeke she had looked after herself for years after all. She knew from her grandmother that her father had walked out on her mother before she was born, but, her mother having died when Melody was little more than a baby, she had no recollection of her. Her maternal grandmother had brought her up, and as her mother had been an only child there had been no aunts and uncles or cousins in her life, and her grandfather had divorced her grandmother years earlier and moved away.

Consequently it had been a somewhat singular childhood, especially as her grandmother had discouraged friendships with other children. She had lived for the twice-weekly dance lessons she'd attended since a small child. At the age of sixteen she'd been accepted at a dance school and had just graduated from there when her grandmother had passed away, leaving her a small inheritance. She had moved from her home town in the west of England to the capital, finding a bedsit and beginning to look for dancing work while practising every day. Once her nest egg was gone she'd been forced to take other jobs between dancing engagements to pay the bills, but she had been happy enough while she waited for her "big break". And then the part of Sasha had come along and she had met Zeke and her life had changed for ever.

"You're being extremely childish, Melody," Zeke said, in a tone which one would use with a recalcitrant toddler having a tantrum. "At least let me drive you to where you want to go. What do you think I'm going to do, for crying out loud? Kidnap you and spirit you away against your will?"

It was exactly the kind of thing he *would* do, and her face was answer enough. Her green eyes were a perfect mirror of her thoughts.

Zeke clicked his tongue in exasperation. "I give you my word—how's that? But you must see we need to talk? You owe me that at least. The last time we talked you were all but hysterical and I had half the medical team at the hospital breathing down my neck and accusing me of delaying your recovery. I didn't understand what I'd done wrong then and I still don't. And I intend to get to the bottom of this."

"I wrote to you last week," she said flatly, knowing he had a point. But how could she explain to Zeke what she didn't fully understand herself? She just knew it was impossible for them to be together. "There's nothing more to be said."

"Ah, yes, a lovely little missive," Zeke said with heavy sarcasm. "A few lines stating you wanted a divorce, that you required nothing at all in the way of settlement and that in view of this kindness you expected the divorce to go through without contest. Well, I've got news for you. There's no way—*no way*—I'm going to let you walk away from me. You're my wife. When I made those vows they were for life. It wasn't some kind of nice little event that could be put to one side when it suited."

Her chin came up. "I'm not a possession, Zeke, like your Ferrari or your villa in Madeira. This acquisition can think and feel."

"Don't twist my words," he said with remarkable calm. "Now, are you going to let me take you where you're going without a scene or shall I put you over my shoulder and carry you to the car? The choice is yours. I'm easy either way."

She didn't make the mistake of saying *You wouldn't dare.* Zeke would dare. Drawing on what was left of her limited supply of dignity, she eyed him icily before allowing him to lead her in the direction of the car. It wasn't hard to pick it out. There weren't too many sleek black Ferraris crouching in the hospital grounds. The car was like its master—distinctive.

The few desultory flakes of a minute ago were thickening into a real snowstorm as Zeke helped her into the car. She watched him as he walked round the bonnet, her heart aching and her stomach churning. This was just the sort of confrontation she'd been hoping to avoid, but then she might have known Zeke wouldn't give up so easily. She *had* known it. Hoped, even? a little voice asked. Which was ridiculous and self-indulgent. Zeke was constantly surrounded by the cream of the entertainment industry, and it wasn't just the wannabes who offered themselves to him on a plate. Women were drawn to him like pins to a magnet. She had seen it so often at parties and functions. He had that undefinable something which would be worth a fortune if it could be bottled and which had nothing to do with his wealth. She'd often teased him and said he'd have made an irresistible gigolo if he'd decided on a different career. It didn't seem so funny now. Then she had been confident in her youth and perfectly honed body. Now...

He didn't start the car immediately, turning to her in the luxurious leather-clad interior as he slid an arm along the back of her seat. "I've missed you," he said huskily, the ebony eyes as soft as black velvet. "Every minute, every hour."

No, don't do this. His anger and irritation she could cope with; then he was the Zeke the world knew—hard, determined, ruthless. But with her he had always been the opposite to those things. And when a man as big and masculine as Zeke revealed his soft centre it was terribly seductive. From the first evening, when he had waited for her outside the theatre, he had been open and vulnerable with her in a way that had cut through her initial dislike and antagonism like a knife through butter. The more so when she had learnt his history.

Zeke had grown up in the care system from the age of eight, when his single mother had finally abandoned him after years of neglect and disappeared who knew where. He freely admitted to having been a troublesome child and an even more troublesome youth, and remembered one teacher predicting he'd either be a villain or a millionaire—or maybe both—by the time he was thirty after yet another of his misdeeds had come to light.

"That teacher did me a favour, although he didn't know it at the time," Zeke had told her one evening over dinner at a fancy restaurant, when she'd been seeing him for a couple of weeks. "It was one of those crossroads in life—a decision time, you know? It would have been easy to go down the dark route—I was already more than halfway there—but to make a fortune legitimately was harder. More of a challenge. And I've always liked a challenge. So I decided to prove something to him and to myself."

She remembered she had stared at him, fascinated. "And is that the only reason you veered on the side of law and order?"

"I should say no—that deep down I wanted to do the right and noble thing—shouldn't I?" he'd answered with the crooked grin which had already become so familiar to her. "But the truth of it is I didn't think that way then. I'd lived in dumps mixing with all kinds of types when I was with my mother, and once in care I developed a huge chip on my shoulder. I was an angry young man, I guess." His grin had widened. "I'd have been an excellent villain, though."

She'd laughed with him. "I'm glad you chose the route you did," she'd said a little breathlessly, somewhat overwhelmed.

His face had straightened and he'd reached across the table for her hand. "So am I," he said softly, "and never more than at this moment. I would have found it very hard to look into your eyes and ask you to love a man like that."

She'd blinked before murmuring, "And is that what you're asking me to do? To fall in love with you?"

"I've loved you from the minute you stood on that stage and put me in my place, and I've never told another woman I love her because it hasn't been true before. I don't want to rush you but I want to marry you, Melody. I want you to be my wife, the mother of my children, my partner through life. I love you, I want you, I need you and I adore you." He'd let go of her hand and leant back in his seat. "Does that answer your question?" he'd drawled self-mockingly.

They had got engaged that night and married six weeks later, and she had felt her life had only begun the day she had met Zeke. To have someone who was hers, who loved her, had been sweet.

She turned her head from him now, hardening her voice as she said, "You shouldn't have come here today, Zeke."

"The hell I shouldn't. Nothing could have prevented me."

The snow was coating the windscreen in a blanket of white, shutting them in their own little world. He was so close the faint familiar smell of his aftershave mingled with leather from the car's interior, evoking memories Melody could have done without. Memories that turned her fluid inside.

She knew he was going to kiss her, and when he turned her chin to face him she didn't resist, steeling herself instead to show no reaction as his mouth claimed hers. It was a slow, leisurely, sensual kiss, not the hard, possessive onslaught she'd half been expecting, and it took all her willpower not to respond to the magic of his lips. But she managed it. Just.

When his mouth lifted from hers she saw his eyes were narrowed as he searched her face. "I see," he murmured after a moment. "Do you think you can keep it up?"

His body warmth reached out to her, dark and compelling, as she swallowed hard before muttering, "I don't know what you mean."

He smiled faintly. "Of course you don't." He leaned forward again and kissed her thoroughly and with an enjoyment he made no effort to rein in, and by the time he finished Melody was not only kissing him back but trembling with desire.

"There." His voice was very soft as he tilted his head to look down into the clear green of her eyes. "That's better." He stroked a strand of blond hair from her cheek, his touch tender. "Can we go home now?"

Melody stared into the tough, furrowed face and suddenly a flood of anger burnt up all other emotion. Drawing away from him, she said bitingly, "Is that all you think it takes? A kiss and I'm putty in your hands?"

A muscle in his cheek twitched at her direct hit.

"I'm not going home with you, Zeke. Not today, not tomorrow, not any time." Ignoring the cloud of fury darkening his features, she continued, "Whether you accept it or not, our marriage is over. Now, if you're not going to take me to the hotel I've booked into, I'll get there under my own steam. Okay?"

There was a long pause when he turned from her and gripped the steering wheel as though he wanted to break it. Then without a word he started the engine and the powerful car growled into life. "Where do you want to go?" he asked coldly, his tone searing her, and after she'd given the name and street of the hotel he pulled out of the parking space.

She had won. He'd given in. As they passed through the hospital gates she sat still and numb, refusing to feel or let herself think. The time for that could come later, when she was alone. For now she had to remain in the bubble that had surrounded her. It was the only way to retain her sanity.

Chapter 3

Melody hadn't seen a photograph of the hotel; with most of the ones she had tried being full for Christmas it had been a case of beggars couldn't be choosers. Now, as Zeke pulled up in front of the somewhat shabby exterior of the building situated in a side street off the Bayswater Road, Melody took a deep breath. "I'm sorry," she said painfully, "I really am. But one day you'll see this was for the best. Thank you for meeting me today but I think it's better if we communicate only through our solicitors from now on."

Zeke said nothing, exiting the car and walking round the bonnet to help her out, his dark face grim.

It was a less than elegant emergence onto the pavement due to her damaged legs and as unlike her normal natural poise as was possible to imagine. Knowing Zeke's appreciation of grace and style, Melody cringed inside, before telling herself it was all to the good. This was reality, and if he was repulsed by her clumsiness it only underlined the sense of what she had been saying: that they had no possible future together.

She glanced at his face as he shut the passenger door, but the inscrutable features could have been set in stone and revealed nothing. When he extracted her case she reached out a hand for it but he ignored the action, taking her arm as he steered her towards the hotel's glass doors.

Once inside the lobby—which wasn't half as bad as she'd expected from the exterior of the building—she said firmly, "Thank you," as she extended a hand for the case once more. "I can take it from here."

"Sit down." He deposited her on one of the plump sofas the lobby held as he spoke. "I'll check you in and get the case sent to your room and then we're going to lunch. Is there anything in the case you need before it disappears?"

Melody shook her head. Her medication was in her handbag. "But I don't think—"

"Good. Don't think," he said with grim sarcasm. "For once in your life just listen."

She stared at his back as he walked over to the reception desk and muttered several words under her breath. Her head was spinning, her legs were hurting and her back was aching like mad. When she'd been cocooned in her little room at the hospital her proposed plans for this momentous day—her emergence into the big bad world once more—had seemed straightforward. The doctors had warned her it would be tiring after the weeks spent in bed or sitting in the chair in her room, and she had imagined taking a cab here and then retiring for most of the day and using Room Service if she wanted anything to eat. She hadn't expected to feel quite so weak and wiped out, though, but perhaps that was due more to seeing Zeke than her physical condition.

He was back in a couple of minutes. "All taken care of," he said with annoying satisfaction, "and they're serving lunch in the restaurant in an hour so I've asked the concierge to park the car. They have a few spaces reserved for staff but they were very helpful. Very helpful indeed."

She didn't doubt it. Money had a way of smoothing out such issues and Zeke was always generous.

"I thought you'd prefer to eat here than elsewhere," he continued, sitting down beside her. "You look tired. And I've ordered coffee while we wait."

Melody felt herself bristling. How dared he take over like this, and what did he mean by saying she looked tired? That she looked haggard and unattractive? Well, she didn't need him to tell her that. Her mirror did a perfect job every morning. She hadn't slept well since the accident and when she did nod off her dreams were mostly nightmares.

After glaring at him she turned to look out of the window next to the sofa. Big fat flakes of snow were settling on the ground and already rooftops were covered with a glistening mantle. It was going to be a white Christmas for sure. Last year they had spent the holiday skiing in Switzerland, returning to their wonderful little lodge each night and spending the evenings wrapped in each other's arms in front of the blazing log fire drinking hot toddies. She had been due to be involved in a big production in the West End in the New Year, likely to run for a good while, and life had been sweet. They had talked about having a family one day, of course, but not for years. Most dancers had to finish their career in their mid-thirties and Zeke had been content to wait until she was ready.

As though he could read her mind, he said quietly, "Looks like we wouldn't have to chase the snow this year like last. It's come to us instead."

"Except there's not much skiing down the Bayswater Road," she said as lightly as she could, knowing her days of such sports were over. "Not unless you want to be taken away by men in white coats."

Zeke chuckled, and then almost immediately his smile died and he leant forward. "Talk to me, Dee," he urged, unconsciously using his own private nickname for her. "Tell me how you feel, what this is really about. I need to know—you can surely see that? This excuse about not feeling the same isn't you."

It *was* the truth and it wasn't. And deep down she had known she would have to explain herself fully for Zeke to accept they were finished. She had hoped by shutting him out and refusing to let him visit her in hospital his resentment and manly pride would overshadow his feelings for her, but Zeke wasn't so shallow as that. At the same time she knew how he felt about sickness. In the years with his mother, before she had left, he'd been brought up in the most squalid of surroundings, often rubbing shoulders with drug addicts and down-and-outs, meths drinkers and the like. It had left him with an almost pathological resolve to take care of his own body and he couldn't understand people who were careless about their health. Her perfectly honed, supple dancer's body and extreme physical fitness had formed a large part of her attraction for him; she knew that although he had never spelt it out in so many words. And now...

Choosing her words carefully, she looked him full in the face. "Zeke, will you listen to me? *Really* listen and not interrupt until I've finished? Will you do that?"

He nodded, his face tense. "If you tell me the truth."

"You asked me earlier if I still love you and the answer to that is of course I do." At his sudden movement she held up her hand, palm facing him. "You promised," she reminded him.

He settled back, his ebony eyes intent on hers. "Go on."

"But now, after the accident, my loving you or you loving me is not enough. From a little girl all I've ever wanted to do was dance. It was my life. I was totally dedicated to and disciplined by the demands of ballet up until I grew too tall, but as long as I could carry on dancing I didn't mind too much. You know how fierce the competition is within the entertainment business, but it never caused me a moment's doubt because I *had* to dance. It was as simple as that. And now that is over."

The waiter arriving with coffee interrupted her, and Melody waited until he had bustled off before she went on. "I know I could have been killed that day, and I am grateful to be alive, but I can never go back to the way things were. I'm all at sea at the moment, I admit it, but one thing I do know is that if I don't want to drown in a sludge of self-pity I have to make a new life for myself far away from the world I've embraced for the last decade. And Zeke..." She paused, not knowing how to say it but then deciding there were no right words. "You're the embodiment of that world. You love it; it's food and drink to you; it's your whole life."

He again made a movement to speak and was stopped by her raised hand. "But that's only part of why I have to leave. You're surrounded by women who see you as the means of their getting on in the business. Beautiful women—talented, young, ambitious—and we've laughed in the past at what some of them will do to get your attention. I've been there when you've been blatantly propositioned. I know how far some of them will go. I didn't like it then and I like it still less now."

She was trembling and took a sip of her coffee, needing the caffeine. The next part was harder to say.

"Then I could be everything you need. Now I can't. We have to be honest here, to face facts. You have a crippled wife. You—the head of the entertainment business. When we would

attend functions and dinners and walk the red carpet and so on
I'd be hobbling along beside you. There might even come a
day when you'd be pushing me in a wheelchair. Or I'd stay at
home, watching from afar, wondering which starlet was trying her luck that night. I'd turn into someone I don't want to
be and in turn you'd change. I don't want us to end like that.
Far better a clean break now, while we still care about each
other and have good memories to look back on."

He was staring at her as though she were mad, and now
nothing could have stopped his next words. "This is rubbish—
absolute rubbish," he bit out with controlled fury. "This isn't
you and me you're talking about here. What we have is stronger and better than the people you've painted. And these supposedly beautiful women you've gone on about—what are you
if not beautiful? Inside and out?"

"But I'm not, Zeke, not any more." She was as white as the
snow outside the window but determined to make him see. "I
have scars—angry, red, puckered things that are gouged into
the skin you used to say was like honey-coloured silk—and
they'll always be there. Oh, they might fade some, but they'll
still be ugly until the day I die. This isn't going to go away."

"I don't care about your scars. Only inasmuch as they affect your perception of yourself," he added softly.

"You haven't seen them." She stared at him, dying inside.

"And whose fault is that? When I asked to see them you
went hysterical and I was thrown out of your room and warned
not to mention it again. You'd show me when you were ready,
they said. But the next thing I know I'm warned visiting you
at all is doing you more harm than good and if I care about
you I have to give you a breathing space. Well if the 'breathing space' resulted in these damn fool ideas you've got I should
have carried on visiting. I love *you*, dammit—every part of

you, scars and all—and I resent being labelled as some pathetic bozo who will bed any women on offer. That's not who I am and you know it."

Two spots of colour burnt in her ashen face now as her own temper rose. "I didn't say that."

"That's exactly what you said." He was breathing hard and still furiously angry. "Okay, let me ask you something. What if it had been me in that accident? What if I'd been the one having the operations and months in hospital? What if it was my legs? Would you be looking around for someone else?"

"Of course I wouldn't. You know I wouldn't."

"Then why the hell do you think I would? And what makes your love so damn superior to mine? Because that's what you're insinuating, however you dress it up, and I resent that."

"You're twisting my words," she said helplessly, on the verge of tears. "I never said my love is better than yours."

Zeke looked at her trembling lips, at the bruised blue shadows under her eyes from where she hadn't slept and her too-slim frame where the weight had dropped off her. Swearing softly, he pulled her into him, careless of where they were. "Don't cry," he muttered thickly. "I don't want to make you cry. I want to love you and care for you and make it all better, but you're driving me mad, woman. Stark, staring mad. I've nearly gone insane the last few weeks. I even resorted to coming to the hospital at night and sitting outside in the car park just to be near you. Crazy, eh? But that's how it's been."

Melody relaxed against him for a moment—but only a moment. Far from reassuring her, his words had hammered home the fact that Zeke wasn't seeing things clearly. He couldn't make it all better—no one could—and the words he'd spoken earlier, about being in it for the long haul, were at the forefront of her mind. He felt staying with her, supporting her, protecting her, was his duty. And duty wasn't a bad thing, even if there were folk these days who regarded it as a four-letter word; she just didn't want it to be the reason for their marriage to continue. She couldn't live with pity. His pity.

Drawing away from him, she made herself finish her cup of coffee. After a moment or two he did the same, but the ebony eyes remained fixed on her delicate features as he drank. "This is partly to do with your grandmother," he said after a little while. "You know that, don't you? A damn big part too."

Caught unawares, she shot her gaze to meet his. "What on earth are you talking about? My grandmother has been dead for years."

"I know she brought you up and you loved her," he said tersely, "but she wasn't exactly a fan of the male of the species, from what you've told me. She never let you forget that your father walked out on your mother, and your grandfather's affairs were mentioned every day. Isn't that right?"

"Every day is an exaggeration."

"Not much of one. She drip-dripped the poison of her own bitterness for years. You know she did. She couldn't get over the fact that he left her in the end, even though she'd put up with his roving eye most of their marriage."

Melody lifted her soft chin and glared at him anew. "And why should she have forgiven him? He was a hateful man. I'd have taken him to the vets for a certain operation if he'd been my husband," she declared stoutly.

A flicker of a smile touched Zeke's mouth. "I'll bear that in mind," he said gravely. "But the truth is her jaundiced view did some damage and made you very insecure in certain areas. Admit it. It's the truth, Dee, and you know it. Face it."

"I'll do no such thing." How dared he criticise her grandmother like this? "And my father and grandfather's actions have absolutely nothing to do with this situation."

"It isn't a situation, Dee," Zeke said grimly. "It's our marriage and, regardless of what you say, their unfaithfulness has a huge bearing on how you see it and me. Did you ever expect us to make old bones together? Did you? Deep, deep inside, in your subconscious? Because I don't think you did. I never have. But that didn't matter because I intended to prove you wrong and I wasn't going anywhere. I'm still not."

He was confusing her, muddling everything up, and it wasn't fair. She had prepared herself for the inevitable over the past torturous weeks, steeling her heart against any hope, and she couldn't go back to the terrible time just after the accident when she hadn't known what to do. That had been worse than after she'd realised leaving Zeke was the only way she could retain her dignity and who she was in the future. She couldn't watch him slowly fall out of love with her as their life together went wrong. Their work and colleagues, their friends—*everything* was tied up in a world in which she had no part now. The very thing that had joined them was now the gulf forcing them apart. The ultimate irony.

"I just know I can't do this any more, Zeke," she said wearily. "Us, our marriage. I can't."

The entrance doors to the hotel opened as she finished speaking and a young Japanese couple came in with two small and clearly very excited children, gabbling away in their own tongue. The little girls were so cute in their matching red coats and hats that in spite of how she was feeling Melody had to smile as she caught their mother's eye.

"It's the snow," the young woman called across in perfect English. "They so wanted snow at Christmas, so Santa and the reindeers could land their sleigh here and feel at home."

"That's very important," Melody agreed, glancing at the little tots as she added, "And don't forget to leave some carrots for those reindeers, will you? They get very tired delivering so many presents in one night."

The children giggled; whether they understood her or not Melody wasn't sure, but as she turned back to Zeke he was watching her with unfathomable eyes.

"And what about the family we said we'd have one day?" he said quietly. "Where do children fit into this future of yours?"

She looked down at her hands, letting the heavy wings of soft strawberry-blond hair hide her face from him. "They—they don't," she whispered, knowing if she didn't have babies with Zeke she wouldn't have them with anyone. Just the thought of another man touching her was unthinkable. She was Zeke's and she'd always be his—body and soul—even though she couldn't be with him.

"I see." His voice was low and tight. "So you've made the decision on my behalf. How kind. And am I allowed to protest at losing the chance of fatherhood?"

"You don't have to lose it. You could have children with someone else." She still didn't look at him.

"If it wasn't for the fact we're in a public place I'd tell you exactly what I think of that little gem," he ground out with hot, fuming fury. "Do you seriously imagine anyone else could take your place? Do you? Hasn't anything I've said in the past meant something? I fell in love with *you*. I don't want anyone *but* you. Not ever. Listen to what I'm saying, damn it."

She had never seen him so angry when she made the mistake of glancing up. His face was that of a stranger—a dangerous, outraged stranger—as black as thunder, and his words were underlined with the same furious energy.

Her heart threatened to give way but somehow she kept

her voice steady when she said, "This is what I was trying to avoid by not seeing you. I don't want to fight with you, Zeke, but I mean what I say and you won't change my mind. If you want to forget about lunch and leave now that's fine."

She watched him slowly rein in his anger, his self-control formidable. She had seen it before, this ability to master his emotions, and it was almost scary. After a few moments he was able to smile slowly, and you would have to know him very well indeed to recognise it wasn't a real smile. But she did know him well.

"I'm here and I'm staying," he drawled lazily.

And Melody had the feeling he wasn't only talking about lunch.

Chapter 4

They sat in a quivering silence that vibrated with things said and unsaid, until a young, pert receptionist came across to inform them smilingly that their table in the restaurant was waiting for them.

Melody had steadfastly kept her eyes on the view outside the windows, where the snow continued to fall thickly from a heavy, laden sky, but she was vitally aware of Zeke's black, brooding gaze fixed on her profile. In spite of his relaxed, nonchalant pose—one leg crossed over the other knee and his arms draped along the back of the sofa—she knew Zeke was as tense as a coiled spring.

The restaurant was pleasant enough, but nothing like the grand, expensive eating places Zeke had always taken her to. Nonetheless, the Christmas decorations were tasteful and brought a festive charm to the room, and their table for two was pretty, with a tiny beaded Christmas tree taking centre stage on a white linen tablecloth encrusted with sparkling silver stars.

After the waiter had placed two embossed menus in their hands and left them to decide on their meal, the wine waiter appeared. Zeke smiled at her. "As we're celebrating, I think a bottle of your finest champagne," he said to the waiter, but with his eyes on Melody. The waiter beamed. This was obviously his type of customer. And at Christmastime too, when everyone tended to tip well.

Melody let the man bustle off before she said quietly, "Celebrating?" keeping her voice expressionless.

"Of course. You're out of hospital and life can start again." His smile was challenging. "Isn't that worthy of good champagne?"

She wasn't going to rise to his bait, she told herself silently. Raising her small chin a notch, she shrugged. "I didn't think you approved of drinking and driving."

"Quite right," he said with aggravating aplomb. "I don't." Fighting the urge to ask what he was going to do about the Ferrari, because she knew he wanted her to do just that, Melody gritted her teeth and concentrated on the menu. No doubt he'd get one of his minions to pick up the car and he'd get a taxi home. He wouldn't care about spoiling someone's plans for Christmas Eve.

And then she immediately felt ashamed of herself. Whatever else Zeke was, he wasn't high-handed with his staff. She was just being nasty, and it wasn't like her. But then she'd come to realise over the past months since the accident that she didn't know herself at all.

She had always thought she was quite a focused, well-balanced person on the whole—the type of woman who would take whatever life threw at her and get on with things. But the accident had knocked her for six—not just physically but mentally, and more importantly emotionally too. It had been one of those cataclysmic events—one of those disasters that she hadn't imagined in her worst nightmares—and she hadn't known how to handle the fall-out. She still didn't. It had brought to the surface a whole host of emotional blocks which had begun to dissolve to reveal the insecurities and pain inside, starting from as way back as her father walking out on her and her mother. He obviously hadn't wanted the responsibility, so had he abandoned her mother because of that? Had she been the cause of their break-up?

Melody suddenly became aware that the waiter was back and pouring sparkling champagne into two crystal flutes. Once he'd placed the bottle in an ice bucket he sailed off again, and Zeke raised his glass to her. "To you," he said very softly. "My beautiful, vulnerable, exasperating, sweet, incomparable wife. The centre of my universe."

She had raised her own glass. Now she put it down without taking a sip. "Don't, Zeke." Her voice was quiet and pained.

"Don't what? Say how much I adore you? But I do, Dee."

"You—you don't have to say that." Her legs were hurting, reminding her of how she looked beneath her leggings.

"Have to?" His tone was quizzical rather than annoyed. He shook his dark head. "When have I ever done anything because I have to? Okay, that toast clearly isn't to your liking. How about—" he raised his glass again and paused until she did the same "—to us?" he suggested mildly.

"Zeke." She frowned at him but he merely smiled back.

"The season then. A merry Christmas to one and all. Is that sufficiently impersonal? Surely you can drink to that?"

Melody tasted the champagne. It was delicious, Dom Pérignon at its best, smooth, seductive and sophisticated—very much like Zeke. She glanced at him. "Very nice," she said primly, trying not to notice how his mouth was curving.

"Isn't it?" he agreed softly. "Are you hungry?"

Surprisingly, for the first time since the accident, she did have something of an appetite. She nodded. "A bit."

"Good. You need feeding up." Ignoring her grimace at the criticism of her thinness, he went on, "I'm going to pass on the Christmas fare and save the turkey dinner till tomorrow. How about you? The salmon *en croûte* looks good for a starter, and the lamb shanks with redcurrant and rosemary to follow for me, I think. I'll think about dessert later."

Melody would have chosen the same, but felt the need to assert her independence. "I'll have the wild mushroom pâté and then the beef in black bean sauce." She put the menu down and took another sip of champagne. The bubbles danced in her mouth as the wine fizzed and she reflected she would have to be careful. She hadn't drunk any alcohol in the past months whilst in hospital, and this excellent vintage was as dangerous as it was delicious. With Zeke in the mood he was in she needed all her wits about her. She had never been able to resist him in the past, with or without alcohol.

The waiter glided to their table and as Zeke talked to him Melody was able to really study Zeke's face for the first time that morning. He looked as attractive as ever, but tired, she thought, a little dart of concern piercing her heart. Had he been working too hard? Before their marriage she'd heard it wasn't unknown for him to work round the clock when some drama or other necessitated it, and even after they'd wed there had been the odd occasion when she hadn't seen him for twenty out of twenty-four hours. He found it impossible to delegate, that was the thing. Having carved out his small empire with blood, sweat and tears, he was fiercely proud and protective of it, and not always so sure of himself as he'd like people to believe. Particularly so with regard to her.

It had been that which had first captivated her when they had begun dating, she acknowledged. He'd been mad for her but touchingly unsure of how she felt about him, which had surprised her. He rarely talked about his early days, but when he did she'd come to realise he'd had massive issues about love and commitment in the past and trusting the female of the species.

The thought bothered her. She had been trying to push such truths to the back of her mind these past weeks.

But Zeke *would* find someone else easily enough, she told herself in the next breath. Her grandmother had always said that love meant something entirely different to men and women, and that men's love was altogether more earthy and transient. "Even the best of them will look for a younger, fitter model in time, Melody. Just you remember that and protect yourself against the day it happens."

For a moment it was as though her grandmother was right there with her and Melody blinked, mentally shaking herself. Zeke had said her grandmother's jaundiced view of life and love had affected her, and she hadn't liked it at the time, but could there be some truth in it? Had it affected her adversely?

The idea felt like a betrayal of the woman who had raised her and sacrificed much to give her the dancing lessons she'd craved, and Melody immediately repudiated it. Men *did* obsess on a woman's body and looks. The number of middle-aged women who were dumped during their husbands' "mid-life crisis" was proof of that. Men simply weren't naturally monogamous.

She came out of her reverie to find she'd inadvertently finished her glass of champagne and that Zeke's gaze was tight on her face. Silently he refilled her glass. "What were you thinking just now?" he asked quietly. "It was about me, wasn't it?"

There was no way she was going to tell him, but she had to say something to satisfy that razor-sharp mind. She made herself glance across the restaurant, which was gradually filling up, her stance studiously offhand, before she said, "Just that today hasn't gone the way I'd planned, I suppose."

"Did you really think after three months or so of being incarcerated I'd let you do this on your own?"

"I am more than capable of taking care of myself," she said tersely. "I'm not a child."

His voice carried more than a touch of self-deprecation when he drawled, "Believe me, Dee, I've never seen you as a child. Exasperating, unfathomable on occasion, but never a child."

She flushed at the sensual desire in the ebony eyes. She'd walked right into that one. Flustered, she sipped at her champagne, before realising what she was doing and putting the glass down so abruptly it almost toppled over.

"Relax." He took her hand, as if he had the perfect right to touch her whenever he wanted to and her talk of separation and divorce had never happened. "You're like a cat on a hot tin roof. This is me, remember? Your husband."

He slid his thumb into her curved palm, softly stroking her silky skin before turning her hand over and raising it to his lips. A bolt of electricity shot up her arm and she gasped before she could stifle her reaction to his mouth on her sensitive flesh. Jerking her hand away, she glared at him. "Don't do that," she said, a mite too fiercely.

"Another don't." His mouth curved wryly. "But you like me touching you. Don't deny it. And I like touching you, Dee. Remember how it used to be?" His gaze drifted to her lips and she felt them tingle, the tips of her breasts hardening as a flood of sexual need raced through her. "We'd make love anywhere, any time, remember? And that's what we did, Dee. We made *love*. We didn't just have sex, great though that was."

She wanted to say *Don't* again, and stopped herself just in time, but his voice was evoking memories she could have done without—memories that persisted in surfacing in dreams at night that rent her in two when she awoke and he wasn't there.

"Like that time in Madeira when you were cooking us pancakes for breakfast and we found another use for the maple syrup," he murmured throatily. "I swear I've never tasted anything so good. We never did have the pancakes, did we...?"

They had ravished each other right there on the sun-warmed wood of the kitchen floor, and later, when they'd showered away the stickiness of the syrup together, washing each other with silky-soft suds, they had made love again, slowly and languorously, making it last. Heady days. Magical days.

Aware that she was in a public place, and couldn't give way to the anguish the terrible enchantment of his words had induced, Melody grappled for self-control. It didn't matter how good they had been together. That was then and this was now. The girl who had revelled in winding her smooth, honey-coloured limbs round his, who had delighted in the pleasure he got from her perfect body, was no more. Never again would she feel so uninhibited, so full of joy, so *his*. She didn't expect him to understand—she barely understood herself—but self-survival dictated she had to leave him before she withered and died trying to be the person he'd fallen in love with. She couldn't face the prospect of kindness and pity replacing the desire and passion he'd had for her.

"You want me, Dee. Every bit as much as I want you." He refused to accept her transparent self-denial. "You need to feel me inside you as much as I need to be there. I want to make love to you for hours again. Nothing hasty or rushed, because we have all the time in the world now you're with me once more. Every doubt you have, every concern, I can make it better. I can sweep them all away and make you believe we're okay."

"No, you can't, and I'm not with you again—not in the way you mean," Melody said feverishly, trying to fight the ache of sexual need his words had called forth.

"You're mine, you'll always be mine, and you know it." He leant closer, not touching her yet enveloping her with his body warmth. "Our home is waiting for you and it's killing me to live there alone. I can't be there without imagining you in my arms, making love in every room like we did the first week we moved in." His ebony gaze watched the way the memories he'd called up were sinking in, and his voice was husky as he continued softly, "This is the first day of the rest of our lives together—"

"Stop it." Her tone was sharp enough to check anything further he might have said. "Stop it or I'm leaving right now."

He stared into her eyes, large and tragic against her pale features, and then swore under his breath. Leaning back in his seat, he drained his glass of champagne.

The waiter brought their first course to the table in the next few moments, and it was another minute or two, after they had begun to eat, that he said, his voice conversational, "I don't know whether I want to kiss you or strangle you right now." His voice was low, but she knew he meant every word.

"You don't need to worry about it because I wouldn't let you do either." She deliberately kept her voice light and her face expressionless. "This is wonderful pâté, by the way."

Zeke's eyes were hard black stones as he tried to assimilate the change in her. She could see she had thrown him, and because he was always perfectly in control he wouldn't like that.

She didn't think a woman had ever said no to him before either; until he had met her he had always been the one to end his relationships, and they had invariably been conducted exactly the way he decreed. Having said that, most of his exes seemed to have a soft spot for him still.

"So you are determined to continue with this ridiculous farce?" he said mildly, after he had finished his salmon.

Melody looked at him squarely, blessing the strength that had come from somewhere and was keeping her trembling inside under wraps. "You mean the separation? Of course."

"Of course?" he drawled lazily, his mood having taken a lightning change of direction. "I wouldn't have said there was any 'of course' about it. But what am I? A mere man."

Melody eyed him warily. No one could accuse Zeke James of being a mere anything.

He stared back at her, his uneven mouth lifted in the appealing curve she knew so well. Why did he have to be so—so *everything*? she asked herself with silent despair. Why couldn't she have fallen in love with a nice Mr Average—someone *she* found attractive but who didn't have the rest of the female race champing at the bit? Someone she could have felt was truly hers?

But she hadn't. Bottom line. And maybe it wouldn't have made any difference to how she was feeling if she had. Maybe she would still feel she had to go it alone even if her man had been a nondescript nine-to-fiver with as much sex appeal as the average gnat. But she didn't think so.

Zeke refilled their glasses as the waiter whisked their empty plates away. Christmas carols were playing softly in the background, and outside the restaurant windows the small courtyard the room overlooked had been transformed into a winter wonderland, the one tree it contained proudly displaying its new clothing of glittering white. The flakes of snow, as thick and luscious as in a child's painting, were still falling fast, and already an inch or so carpeted the ground.

Without really thinking about what she was saying, she turned to Zeke. "The snow's settling fast. As soon as you've eaten you ought to think about leaving."

The hour's drive to their big sprawling manor house on the outskirts of Reading would take double the time in this weather, and the Ferrari—beautiful though it undoubtedly was—wasn't ideal for Arctic conditions. He could easily get stranded in the middle of nowhere.

Zeke's smile was little more than a quizzical ruffle. "Can't wait to get rid of me?" he murmured.

He was at his most sexy in this mocking mood, but Melody refused to be charmed. "That and the fact you could well find yourself stuck in the middle of a snowdrift somewhere. The wind's getting up—or hadn't you noticed?"

"I'd noticed."

Melody shrugged. "Don't say I didn't warn you."

"Considering you've done nothing *but* warn me about things since first thing this morning, I wouldn't dream of it."

He was still smiling, but she hadn't imagined the edge to his voice and it did nothing to reassure her he had decided to accept defeat. She felt a wave of intense weariness sweep over her for a moment. She didn't want to have to fight him. She felt so emotionally bruised and battered she just craved peace of mind, and she wouldn't achieve that until she was far, far away from Zeke. Once she had got herself together and or- ganised a few essentials she intended to disappear for a few months. She wouldn't take a penny of his fortune to support herself—she had worked for her living in bars and restaurants before, and she could do it again, and she'd already thought about setting herself up as a dance teacher in the future.

The waiter appeared again with their main course, but suddenly her appetite was gone and she had to force herself to eat. It didn't help that Zeke was watching her like a hawk with its prey, his eyes boring into her as though he was trying to dissect her brain. Which he probably was, she reflected darkly. He would be looking for a chink in her armour—it was the nature of the beast.

"You're struggling." As Melody glanced at him, Zeke motioned with his fork at her own plate. "Tired?"

She nodded. The effort of leaving the hospital and not least this confrontation with Zeke, which she had been hoping to avoid until she was stronger, had taken more out of her than she would have thought possible. The doctors had predicted that she would experience bouts of extreme exhaustion in the early days of her release, but she hadn't expected to feel so completely wiped out. All she wanted to do was to crawl into bed.

"Want to skip dessert for now?" he asked softly.

She didn't know quite what he meant by "for now", but was too weary to take him up on it. She had eaten more at one sitting than at any time over the past weeks, and the champagne had done its bit to drug her too. Dessert was beyond her. She nodded again. She could lay her head down and sleep right now.

Zeke lifted his hands. The waiter appeared at his side and within moments they were leaving the restaurant. She had known she was going to find it difficult to stand up and walk—her muscles still weren't functioning as they once had, and she got stiff easily although her physiotherapist had assured her that was just a temporary thing—but in the event

Zeke's firm hands at her elbows and the way he took charge smoothed the way. Nevertheless, she was painfully aware of her pronounced limp as they left, and wondered what he was thinking. He had always said she had the grace of a young gazelle—well, no more, Melody thought wretchedly.

Once in the foyer of the hotel, she stopped and faced him so he was forced to let go of her arm. He was wearing an expensive dark grey suit and a pale peach shirt and tie and he had never looked more attractive. The dark magnetism that was at the centre of his appeal was so strong she could taste it. Numbly, and with formal politeness, Melody said, "Thank you for lunch. It was very nice. And although it may not have seemed like it I appreciate your kindness in meeting me from hospital today—although it wasn't necessary. I hope you have a good journey back to Reading."

Zeke's jaw was a tight line, but his voice was easy when he said, "You need to rest. I'll get the key to the room."

"I can do that—" She stopped. She was talking to herself. He was already striding to the reception desk.

Too tired to summon up the annoyance she felt his high-handedness deserved, she watched him exchange a few words with the pretty receptionist before pocketing the fob for the room. Then he was back at her side, taking her arm as he said, "I've ordered tea and cake from Room Service for four o'clock. That'll give you two or three hours' sleep, okay?"

Not okay. *So* not okay. What was he *doing*, taking charge like this after everything she'd said? "Zeke—" she began.

"Don't cause a scene, Dee. Not with all these nice people round about. You don't want to spoil someone's Christmas, do you?" The mockery was mild, but with a hidden barb in it.

Short of wrenching herself free, which she had no confidence she could accomplish, anyway, Melody found she had no option but to walk with him to the lift. She didn't want Zeke accompanying her to the room. The foyer had been a fairly neutral place to make their goodbyes, with plenty of people around; her room was an altogether different proposition.

As it turned out it wasn't a problem, because once the lift had deposited them at the requisite floor and Zeke had walked a few yards down the corridor and opened a door Melody found he had no intention of leaving straightaway.

He stood aside for her to precede him, but she stopped dead on the threshold of what was clearly a suite of rooms. "This isn't my room. I didn't book this," she gasped. "I asked for a standard double." And *that* had cost an arm and a leg.

"You've clearly been upgraded," he said silkily, drawing her into the large, luxuriously furnished sitting room, complete with real Christmas tree dressed in festive red and gold decorations, before her wits could return.

When they did, she swung to face him accusingly. "This is your doing." She glanced round wildly, as though the manager of the hotel was going to pop up like a genie out of a bottle. "I want my own room. I want the one I booked originally."

"I understand from the receptionist that was snapped up minutes after I transferred to this when we arrived," Zeke said with unforgivable satisfaction. "Look on it as your Christmas good deed. Those folk probably wouldn't have been able to afford this penthouse, which was the only other available accommodation when I asked, so us having it has meant a happy Christmas for someone else. It *is* the season of goodwill."

Melody said something very rude in response, which shocked them both. And then the full significance of his words hit her. "What do you mean, 'us'?" she bit out furiously. "This is my room and I'm staying in it alone—and I'll pay for it." Somehow.

"Payment in full has already been made," Zeke replied, seemingly unmoved by her anger.

"Well, it can be darn well unmade."

"And cause the hotel staff a lot of extra paperwork and hassle?" Zeke clicked his tongue aggravatingly. "You seem a little short of the milk of human kindness, if you don't mind me saying so. Hasn't the spirit of the festive season touched you?"

She had never come so close to hitting someone before, which shocked her further because she had never considered herself a violent person. Gritting her teeth, she took an audible deep breath. "I want you to leave, Zeke. Right now."

She had expected him to argue, so it took the wind out of her sails when instead he said mildly, "Once you're safely in bed. And don't worry that I'm going to leap on you and have my wicked way. I can see you're dead on your feet, sweetheart."

It was the way he said the last word which drained her of all resistance. Horrified that she was going to burst into tears, she said tersely, "I'm going to the bathroom," and walked as purposefully as she could manage across the room.

The suite consisted of a further three rooms—one a small study, complete with every device needed to keep in touch round the world for a visiting businessman or woman, and two bedrooms, both with *en-suite* bathrooms and decorated in the same creams and hazy greys and golds as the sitting room.

Walking into the cream marble *en-suite* of the second bedroom, Melody shut the door and stood for a moment with her eyes tightly closed. It was a sheer effort of will to open them and walk over to the long mirror. She groaned softly as she peered at her reflection. Her summer tan had long since faded after the months in hospital, but she had been careful to keep up with her cleansing and moisturising routine in spite of everything. Today, though, her skin looked pasty and almost grey with the exhaustion that was racking her body, and her green eyes looked enormous in her thin face. Not a pretty sight; no wonder Zeke had wanted to cut the meal short—she looked like death warmed up.

She had seen her case on the luggage rack in the bedroom as she'd marched through, but rather than go into the bedroom she stripped down to her bra and panties before pulling on the big fluffy white bathrobe which was one of two hanging on the back of the bathroom door. It drowned her, but that was all to the good, she decided, pulling the belt tightly round her slim waist. It concealed everything she needed to conceal from those piercing ebony eyes and that was all that mattered.

He was waiting for her when she padded barefoot into the sitting room, and as she said brightly, "All ready for bed, as you can see, so you can go now," his gaze swept over her from head to foot. She found she was doubly glad of the voluminous robe as her traitorous body responded, the rosy peaks of her breasts hardening.

Gruffly, Zeke said, "You look tinier than ever in that thing. Was the hospital food really that bad?"

She shook her head. "It was me. I didn't have much of an appetite, I suppose. I'll soon put the weight on again now."

"Tiny, but beautiful." His voice was husky now, his face telling her what his words didn't. "Enchantingly so, in fact."

It was this she answered when she murmured, "Please go, Zeke. I can't…" She swallowed hard. "Please leave."

"I know, I know." He took her hands in his, pulling her against the broad wall of his chest and nuzzling the top of her head with his chin. "You need to rest. You've done too much for your first day out."

In spite of herself Melody smiled. "You make it sound as

though I've just been released from prison," she whispered, her voice muffled against his shirt. Which was how she felt, actually. And then she pulled away, the smell and feel of him too wonderfully familiar. She wanted to wrap her arms round his neck, to feel his lips on hers, to beg him to forget everything she'd said and hold her tight. "Please go," she said again, her voice trembling.

He lifted his hand and stroked a strand of silky hair from her cheek. She thought he was going to kiss her, and when he merely brushed her brow with his lips knew a moment's agonising disappointment.

"Sweet dreams," he said very softly. "Don't forget the tea and cake around four."

She nodded, not really believing he would go like this, that he would leave her. She watched him cross the room and open the door into the corridor outside, all the time expecting that any moment he would swing round and come back to her. But he didn't.

The door closed. She was alone. Which was exactly what she had demanded.

Chapter 5

Melody stood staring across the room for some moments, fighting the urge to run after Zeke and say...

Say what? she asked herself wearily. That she had changed her mind? But she hadn't. Not about leaving him. All her reasons held good for that, and had perhaps deepened in the past hours since she had seen him again. She loved him too much, and his power over her had always scared her a little deep inside the private place in her mind where uncomfortable truths were buried. She had to get far away from him. That was the only way.

She swayed a little, so tired she could barely remain upright, and then made her way into the bedroom where her case had been left earlier. Shrugging off the robe, she climbed into bed, wanting to think about her and Zeke, to reaffirm to herself the rationale that vindicated her decision, but so exhausted her brain simply wouldn't compute. She couldn't think. Not now.

The swirling snow outside the bedroom window had bathed the room in soft evening shadow, despite it being only a little past one o'clock, and the bed was supremely comfortable after the hard institutional one she had endured for the past three months. Within seconds her breathing was even and deep and she slept a dreamless sleep.

She was completely unaware of the big broad figure that entered the room a few minutes later, standing just inside the doorway until he had satisfied himself her sleep was genuine, at which point he walked softly over to the bed. Zeke stared down at his sleeping wife for several long minutes, his gaze caressing the fragility of her fine features as she slept, and the breakable quality of the shape under the coverlet.

When he noiselessly closed the drapes against the worsening storm outside the cosy cocoon of the hotel his cheeks were damp.

Melody wasn't sure exactly what had dragged her out of the depths of a slumber so heavy her limbs were weighed down with it. She lay in a deep, warm vacuum, a charcoal twilight bathing the room in indistinct shapes as she forced her eyes open. She felt blissfully, wonderfully relaxed.

For a moment she had no idea where she was, and then the past few hours came rushing back at the same time as voices somewhere beyond the bedroom registered. Male voices.

She couldn't remember closing the curtains. She stared towards the window, her brain still fuzzy, but then as familiar deep tones registered she sat up in bed, shaking her hair out of her eyes. *That was Zeke's voice.* She glanced at her wristwatch but it was too dark to make out the time.

Her heart thudding fit to burst, she threw back the coverlet and reached for her robe on the chair at the side of the bed, pulling it on with feverish haste. After switching on the bedside lamp she again checked her watch. Four o'clock. Tea and cake. Room Service. But that still didn't explain what Zeke was doing here—unless she had imagined it, of course.

Zeke was very real when she opened the door to the sitting room. Too real. Melody's senses went into hyperdrive as she registered the very male body clad only in black silk pyjama bottoms. Not that Zeke had ever worn pyjamas to her knowledge.

It was clear he'd just had a shower before answering the door. His thickly muscled torso gleamed like oiled silk where he hadn't dried himself before pulling on the pyjama bottoms, and the black hair on his chest glistened with drops of water. He was magnificent. Melody had forgotten just how magnificent, but now she was reminded—in full, glorious Technicolor.

She swallowed hard, telling herself to say something. *Anything.* But her thought process was shattered.

"Hi." His smile was ridiculously normal in the circumstances. "Did the knock at the door wake you? It's our tea and cake."

She tried, she *really* tried to rise to the occasion, as one of the sophisticated beauties he'd dated before he'd met her would have done, but she knew she'd failed miserably when her voice held the shrillness of a police car siren. *"What are you doing here?"* she yelled. "You're supposed to have left."

His expression changed to one of wounded innocence, which was all the more unbelievable in view of his attire— or lack of it. Before he could voice the reasonable and utterly false explanation she just *knew* was hovering on his lips, she continued, "And why is the tea and cake for two, considering you ordered it hours ago?"

"Ah…" He smiled, a smile of singularly sweet ingenuousness. "I can explain."

"Please do," she said with biting sarcasm.

"I never intended for you to be alone on Christmas Eve, so I thought I'd stick around for a while, that's all."

He raked back his hair, which had fallen quiff-like across his brow, and she was reminded how much it suited him that bit longer than he normally wore it before she hastily pushed the thought aside. "I didn't invite you to stay," she glinted angrily. "And why are you dressed—" perhaps *un*dressed would have been a more appropriate description "—like this?"

He glanced down at the pyjama bottoms, as though he was surprised at the obviousness of the question, and then met her furious gaze with a serenity that sent Melody's stress level up a few more notches. "I was having a shower when Room Service came with the tea and cake," he said patiently.

Melody hung on to *her* patience by a thread. "Why were you taking a shower in my hotel room?" she said tersely. "And how come your pyjamas are here?"

"I was taking a shower in *my* room—you notice this suite has two bedrooms?" His tone was such he could have been talking to a total dimwit. "And I went out and bought the pyjamas and a couple of other bits while you were asleep. I assumed you'd prefer me to wear something to answer the door in the sort of situation that just occurred," he added, his tone so reasonable she wanted to hit him.

Glaring at him, she wondered how she had lost control of things. It had all been so straightforward earlier that morning. Leave the hospital. Book into the hotel. Go to bed and hibernate Christmas away. And now look at what a ridiculous position she was in—her estranged husband sharing a hotel suite with her and standing practically naked a few feet away.

And looking hot. The little voice in the back of her mind was ruthlessly honest. In fact he was fairly smoking. Zeke had always been very much at ease with his body, and it enhanced his flagrant masculinity tenfold. Wretched man.

Pulling herself together, Melody hardened her heart as well as her expression. "You said you were leaving earlier," she said stonily. "And I expected you to do just that."

He gave her a crooked smile as he sat down on one of the sofas in front of the glass coffee table where their tea and cake were waiting. "No," he corrected softly. "I never did. I know that because wild horses couldn't have dragged me away. I would have preferred us to go home and discuss what needs to be discussed there, but that clearly wasn't going to happen. So—" he shrugged broad muscled shoulders and Melody's mouth went dry "—I adapted to the circumstances as I saw fit."

"Hence changing the room to a suite?" she said stiffly.

"Quite. We may as well be comfortable for as long as this charade continues." He grinned happily. "These cakes look fantastic. I've always been a sucker for chocolate cupcakes and fondant fancies—and that's a lemon drizzle cake, if I'm not mistaken. We missed dessert, so come and tuck in." He was pouring two cups of tea as he spoke.

Melody hesitated for a moment. She wasn't going to give in, and there was no way Zeke was sharing this suite tonight, but the assortment of cakes *did* look tempting, and surprisingly— for the second time that day—she found she was actually quite hungry. She would have preferred Zeke to be fully dressed, but as he seemed more interested in the food than in her...

She sat down on the opposite sofa, accepting the cup of tea he handed her with a nod of thanks and selecting one of the little pink-and-white Genoese sponge fondant fancies hand-decorated with sugar daisies. It melted in her mouth, and when Zeke offered her the cakestand again she took a piece of lemon drizzle cake, filled with rich buttercream and lemon curd, refusing to acknowledge how cosy this was.

Outside the snow was coming down thicker than ever, and as she glanced at the window Melody's stomach did a pancake flip. It was too late to send Zeke away. He'd never make it to Reading now, she acknowledged silently. Okay, so maybe he *would* have to stay after all, but strictly on her terms—and that included his and hers bedrooms first and foremost.

She glanced at him from under her eyelashes. He was sitting eating with every appearance of relaxed enjoyment, and after she had declined more cake had made short work of what was left on the cake stand. The man was impossible—utterly impossible.

He glanced up and caught her looking at him, and as always when he smiled at her in a certain way her blood fizzed. "Remember when you made that clementine, saffron and polenta cake in Madeira?" he murmured softly. "I haven't tasted anything so good as that before or since. You promised you'd make it again back in England, but you never did."

The memory of that day at the villa in Madeira swept over her. It had been their last holiday before her accident and they'd had a magical time: horse-riding along the beach, scuba-diving, sunbathing in the shade of the trees around their private pool and spending each soft, scented night wrapped in each other's arms. They had bought the small juicy clementines at the little local market close to the villa, and she had followed a recipe which Aida—Zeke's daily from the village—had written down for her. Melody was the first to admit she wasn't much of a cook—Zeke was actually much better than her, and had a natural flair with food that made most dishes he served up truly sensational—but the cake had turned out surprisingly well and Zeke had been lavish with his praise.

They had eaten the moist, wonderfully tangy cake after dinner with their coffee, sitting on the villa's balcony in the richly perfumed air as a glorious sunset had filled the sky with rivulets of scarlet, gold and deep violet, and afterwards, content and sated, had made love for hours in their big, billowy bed. He'd told her she was exquisite, a goddess…

Enough. The warning was loud in her head. That was then and this was now, and the girl who had lived in a bikini practically the whole holiday was gone. She had never considered herself particularly beautiful, but had always had confidence in her firm, graceful dancer's body, able to hold her own in that regard with the jet-set who congregated around Zeke like moths to a flame. What would they say now?

People. Melody's green eyes darkened. Always people. When she thought about it now, she had never felt she had Zeke completely. There had always been people in the background making claims on him. Even in Madeira there were friends who came by for dinner or barbecues—beautiful people, rich, funny, intelligent, fascinating. She had told herself she had to expect that; he was nearly forty years old, for goodness' sake, and he had built a life for himself that had to continue when she had come along. It would have been totally unreasonable to expect anything else. And she hadn't minded then—not much, anyway. Only sometimes she'd felt on the outside looking in.

"What's the matter?" He was staring at her. "What is it?"

She came back from the past to find she must have been looking at him without seeing him. "Nothing," she said quickly. "My mind was wandering, that's all."

"Wherever it had wandered it didn't seem to be a good place from the look on your face." His gaze narrowed. "What makes me think it was something to do with us?" he added softly, leaning back in the sofa as he surveyed her through glittering black eyes. "It was, wasn't it? What was it?"

Her senses registered the way his powerful muscles moved as sleekly as an animal's, and she was reminded again how magnificent his body was. The first time she had seen him naked she had been in awe of his male beauty. She still was.

"Melody?" he pressed silkily, in a way she knew meant he wasn't going to let the matter drop. "Tell me."

Suddenly she threw caution to the wind. "I was thinking about how in the whole of our marriage, apart from on our honeymoon, we were constantly surrounded by people wanting a piece of you," she said flatly. "Weekdays, weekends—it was always the same. Looking back, I've sometimes thought I was just one of many hangers-on in your world."

To say she had shocked him was an understatement. She watched as his fiercely intelligent mind considered what she'd said. "You were never, ever *just* anything. As my wife you were up there with me one hundred per cent. Or at least I thought you were." He had sat up straight as he'd spoken, every line of his body tense now. "Obviously I was mistaken."

She wasn't going to let him lay it all on her. "You never asked me what I wanted, Zeke. Not really. And I admit for my part I should have spoken up, but I was overwhelmed by it all." *By my incredible fortune in marrying you. By the impossible fact that you loved me.* "And I'm not saying I didn't enjoy it, because I did, but I never really felt—"

"What? What didn't you feel?"

"That I fitted in, I guess." She shook her head, biting her lip. "Maybe you were right when you said I never thought we'd last. I was never conscious of thinking that, but once you said it I realised there was an element of truth there. And it wasn't just because of my grandmother and her attitude to men. Not wholly. It was because I sort of slotted into your life without you having to make any changes, with me hardly making a dent in your way of going on. And if I disappeared out of it again the same would apply. Nothing would really alter. I'd barely make a ripple as I left."

Zeke was staring at her as though he'd never seen her before. "You *can't* believe that," he said eventually, clearly stricken. "How many times did I tell you I loved you? That I had never loved anyone else? Did you think I was lying?"

Melody paused before answering. She was aware she had opened a can of worms, but there was no going back now. "No, I know you loved me," she said slowly. "But why wouldn't you when I was doing everything you wanted? Being what you wanted? And it wasn't all your fault. I'm not saying that. I loved seeing how the other half lived and being part of that world. It was exhilarating and crazy and a million things besides. But—" Another silence while she searched for words to explain the unexplainable. "But there's another world too—a real world. A world devoid of rose-coloured glasses."

"Meaning what, exactly?" His voice was grim, his body tense.

She shrugged. "I suppose I mean that outside the Zeke James bubble people struggle to pay their bills each month, they work nine to five just to make ends meet, they strive all their lives and never really make it. They can't just pick up the phone and have half a dozen people ready to jump through hoops and pave the way for whatever they want. They've never experienced walking into a store and being able to buy whatever they like without looking at the price tag. They have bad days, they get sick, they—they have accidents."

She stopped abruptly. She wasn't putting this very well. What she wanted to say had nothing to do with wealth and fortune. Not really. It was about Zeke belonging to her and she to him. "I can't explain it very well," she added lamely.

"Are you blaming me for succeeding in life?" Zeke asked, his voice as even as a sheet of glass. "Because you'll wait one hell of a long time for me to apologise for that. I pulled myself out of the gutter inch by inch, and I saw enough to know I'd rather slit my own throat than go back to it. Try living in a succession of rooms with the one person who's supposed to love and look after you but who forgets you're alive most of the time. Sleeping in filthy beds, eating half-mouldy food because if you don't you'll starve and no one will give a damn. Having no idea what a bath is but knowing other people out there don't smell like you and your mother and her pals do. And when you're finally dumped into care, longing to go back to that life, bad as it was, because it's all you've ever known and you're scared out of your wits."

As if he couldn't bear looking at her he stood up, turning away and taking a deep breath. For a moment his back was ramrod-straight and the muscles in his shoulders hard and tense. Every line in his body proclaimed how much she'd hurt him.

Horrified at the wounds she'd uncovered, Melody murmured, "Zeke, I'm sorry. I didn't mean… I'm sorry."

He swung to face her and she saw the iron control was back. "It doesn't matter." His face was relaxed, calm, but she knew he wasn't feeling like that inside. "It was a long time ago. But don't tell me I haven't experienced life, Dee. I wasn't brought up in what you call the Zeke James bubble. Blood, sweat and tears got me to where I am today—that and Lady Luck. But I'll tell you one thing." He moved over to where she was now standing, his dark eyes fixed on hers. "I could give it all up tomorrow and walk away without a backward glance or an ounce of regret. You talk about my world, but let me make one thing perfectly clear. It doesn't own me. I own it. There's a difference. One hell of a difference."

Melody stared into the rugged face. She wanted to believe him but she didn't know if she did. And, anyway, did it really make any difference one way or the other? It was all relative.

This close, she was aware of the fresh soapy smell emanating from his body, of his still-damp hair falling into the quiff which was somewhat boyish and incongruous against the hard tough features. It strengthened his overwhelming maleness in a way that caused her heart to pound as the intimacy of the moment deepened. She felt the pull of his attraction drawing her.

He reached out and sifted a strand of her hair through his fingers, letting it fall back into the shining curtain on her shoulders as his eyes caressed her face. "You look good enough to eat," he said huskily. "Far more delicious than fondant fancies and infinitely more satisfying."

Melody knew what was going to happen, and she also knew he was giving her time to move away, to break the spell which had fallen. The sitting room was lit only by a couple of lamps Zeke had switched on, and the soft mellow glow was enhanced by the swirling snow outside the window and the twinkling white lights on the little Christmas tree. It was cosy and snug, safe and warm, and the power of his sensuality wrapped round her as she gave herself up to the magic of his kiss.

His bare arms folded round her waist, tugging her into the cradle of his hips as he purposefully deepened the onslaught on her senses. She felt her breasts respond as the towelling robe pressed against the wall of his chest, their tips hardening and swelling as the blood heated in her veins.

His tongue probed the warmth of her inner mouth and the effect on her was electric. A little moan escaped her throat, vibrating against his mouth and causing Zeke to groan in return as her arms wound round his neck, her fingers sliding into the black thickness of his hair.

Now his mouth was hungry, demanding and wonderfully, achingly familiar as every nerve in her body sensitised. His grip tightened around her waist, his hips grinding against hers as he moved her against him. She arched in unconscious abandonment, unaware the folds of the robe had opened as her belt had loosened. And then she felt his warm hands on the bare flesh beneath the thin wispy bra she was wearing and she froze.

"No." Her voice was high with panic as she jerked away, pulling the robe back in place and jerking the belt tight.

Zeke was breathing like a long-distance runner and he had to take a rasping breath before he could speak. "It's all right." He wouldn't let her escape him completely, drawing her back into his embrace with steel-like arms which allowed no protest. "We can take this as slow as you want."

"I don't want it at all." Melody's mouth was dry and she licked her lips and swallowed painfully. "We can't—"

"We can." He kissed her again—a mere brushing of her trembling mouth. "We're man and wife, Dee, and you've just proved you want me every bit as much as I want you." It wasn't arrogant or triumphant, just a simple statement of fact. "We are one and you can't fight that."

She shook her head dazedly, a hundred and one conflicting emotions tearing her apart. If they made love, if he saw her naked, he couldn't fail to be repulsed. And she couldn't bear that. She wanted him to remember her as she had been—to picture her in his mind as smooth-skinned, nubile, inviting. She was doing this for him as much as her. She *was*. He had married her when she was perfect. Why should he have to learn to adapt to anything less? She was finding it hard, but what would it do to a man like Zeke? No, this was the only way. It had to end now. Swiftly, cleanly, unhesitatingly—like the surgeon's scalpel. She had to remain strong. She couldn't weaken.

"No, Zeke," she whispered. "We're not man and wife any more. Not here, in my head."

"I don't believe that." He still continued to hold her, but now the circle of his arms was relaxed. "Not for a minute, a second. So don't waste your breath trying to convince me when all you're really doing is lying to yourself, okay? Now, go and pamper yourself—have a long soak in the tub and cream and titivate and whatever else women do when they're getting ready for a night on the town. I'm wining and dining you tonight, and I've got tickets for the theatre."

Melody stared at him aghast. "I'm not going out."

"Of course you are. We're not going to let a bit of snow beat us. This is London, not the arctic."

"I don't mean that." And he knew it. "I'm staying here."

"Why?" The ebony eyes challenged her. "Why is that?"

Melody fell back on one of the oldest excuses in the book—the one that came just after *I've got a headache*. "I've got nothing to wear," she said. It was true. Her suitcase contained the leggings and T-shirts and other comfy clothes she had worn in hospital once she was allowed her own things, but absolutely nothing suitable for the sort of evening Zeke had described. All her evening things were back at their house.

He grinned. "No problem." Releasing her, he walked over to the Christmas tree and she saw that at some point during the afternoon a host of beautifully wrapped parcels had appeared beneath it. "You can have a couple of your Christmas presents early," he said cheerfully, extracting two parcels from the pile. "I bought a size below your normal measurements, so hopefully they'll fit. Try them on and see."

Utterly taken aback, Melody stuttered, "When—? How—?"

Zeke paused as an array of emotions—wariness, delight, embarrassment—flitted across his features. "I did a little shopping when you were asleep," he admitted. "I'd left your Christmas presents at home. I thought—" He shook his head. "Well, you know what I thought. I didn't expect we'd be spending Christmas in a hotel in the city."

"Zeke, I can't accept these." It seemed absolutely brazen to take anything from him in the circumstances. "You must see that."

"Why not?" he said easily and without heat.

Melody wasn't fooled. She'd seen the flash of granite in his eyes.

"I just can't," she murmured helplessly. "I haven't got anything for you, for a start. It—it wouldn't be right."

He slung the parcels on a sofa and reached for her again, refusing to let her go when she tried to pull away. One hand took hold of her face gently, lifting her chin so his midnight-dark eyes stared straight into hers. "You being able to walk out of that place today is all the present I'll ever want. In those first few days I didn't think you were going to make it. I was terrified and I couldn't do anything. Something like that has a way of sorting out the priorities of life, believe me. So, you're my Christmas gift this year."

"Zeke—" She was struggling not to cry. "I can't—"

"I know, I know." He pressed a quick kiss on her mouth. "You don't want to hear it, but tough—it's the truth. Now, take your presents and go and make yourself even more beautiful, if that's possible. Because we *are* going out tonight, Dee. Even if I have to dress you myself." He smiled, but Melody knew he wasn't joking. "Which, incidentally, is the option I prefer."

Knowing she ought to be stronger, but still melting from the beautiful things he'd said, she continued to stand looking at him for a moment more. Maybe going out was the best idea after all. Certainly a night in together would be dangerously cosy with Zeke in this impossibly seductive mood.

As if to confirm her thoughts Zeke kissed her again, as though he couldn't help himself—a kiss of slow sensuality. She had wedged her arms between them, flattening her palms on his powerful chest in an effort to push away from the hot desire which had immediately gripped her. It had always been the same; he only had to touch her and she was lost. His mouth moved to one shell-like ear, nibbling it before progressing to her throat and finding her pounding pulse. His rapid-fire heartbeat under her palms revealed Zeke's arousal as blatantly as the silk pyjama bottoms, and for a split second the old thrill and delight that she could inspire such desire in him was there, before a flood of cold reality doused the feeling as effectively as a bucket of icy water.

He didn't know what she looked like under the robe. He hadn't seen the scars and puckered skin.

Melody jerked away so violently she took him by surprise. "Please don't," she said brokenly. "Please, Zeke." She gathered up the parcels he'd thrown on the sofa and moved to the door, turning in the doorway to say, "What time do I need to be ready?" as she nerved herself to look at him.

He hadn't moved, and her breath caught in her throat at the sheer male beauty of his magnificent body. The velvet eyes swept over her and there was no annoyance in his face. His voice was deep and warm and very sensual when he said, "I've ordered cocktails here in the room for seven before we go."

She nodded stiffly, holding the tears at bay through sheer willpower as it came to her that she had never loved him so much as she did right at this moment. He was everything she had ever wanted—would ever want—and she was going to let him go. She knew it. She just had to make him believe it before she went insane trying.

Chapter 6

Once in her own bedroom, Melody shut the door and plumped down on the bed, the parcels in her lap. She stared down at them through the mist of tears clouding her vision. Rubbing her hand across her eyes, she sniffed. *No crying. Not now. Not until this is over.* She couldn't give in. She had to be strong.

The short pep talk helped. She had always known life after the accident, particularly the first few days and weeks, was going to be hard. For all sorts of reasons.

She nodded to the thought. No just because of learning to cope with the world outside the hospital cocoon. She realised this confrontation with Zeke had always been on the cards from the moment she'd made up her mind their relationship was over. If she could have done she would have simply disappeared out of his life; she didn't want to argue or discuss or rationalise, but she had always accepted she would have to.

The fingers of her right hand moved slowly over the rings on her left, but she refused to brood on the day when she had chosen her engagement and wedding rings. Instead she opened the presents Zeke had given her. The silver shot-silk trousers were exquisite and the cream-and-silver tunic top more so; she didn't dare contemplate what they must have cost, but the designer label shouted exclusivity.

She wished he hadn't done this. Shutting her eyes for a moment, she let her shoulders slump—but it didn't help the tension gripping her nerves. She felt as though any minute now she was going to shatter into a thousand pieces, all the benefit of the afternoon sleep she'd enjoyed ruined.

Bath, she told herself, slightly hysterically. She'd wash the last of the hospital out of her hair and skin. Strange how the faintly antiseptic smell permeated everything, not matter how many creams and perfumes you applied. But she was free of all that now—free of the endless routine and doctor's visits and lack of privacy. So why did her heart feel even heavier, like a ton of bricks suspended in her chest? She had to pull herself together. She couldn't let Zeke affect her like this. If she wasn't strong now it would make things even harder in the future. This was just one night. She could get through that.

Leaving the clothes on the bed, she walked into the *en-suite* and began to run a bath, using a liberal amount of hotel bath oil until the water was a mass of perfumed bubbles. Slipping off the robe, she divested herself of her bra and panties before sliding into the foam until only her head was visible. It was only then, when her limbs and body were concealed, that she began to relax in the delicious silky warmth.

After the months in hospital there was an element of bliss in being able to luxuriate in the scented bubbles without fear of one of the nurses knocking on the door and asking her if she was all right. Not that she hadn't appreciated their kindness and concern—she had—but she had felt stifled at times.

How long she lay there she wasn't sure, but after a while the thought that time was getting on caused a little panic, and she quickly washed her hair and climbed out of the bath. In the old days she and Zeke had often unwound after work by taking a bath together, the room lit by candlelight and a bottle of their favourite wine in hand. It had been a great start to the evening—especially as their intimate sojourns in the massive sunken bath in their *en-suite* had invariably led to something else. They'd often eaten late by candlelight in their bathrobes.

But that was then and this was now, and trips down memory lane were both dangerous and weakening.

Melody's mouth twisted with pain and she pulled on her robe, jerking the belt tightly round her waist. There was no going back and it would be emotional suicide to try. She could no longer live up to Zeke's expectations—his and all the rest of the showbiz crowd they mixed with. And she didn't want to destroy herself attempting to do so. Oh, she didn't doubt most people would be very polite and sympathetic to her face, and some of them would even be genuine. But she had come up through the ranks and she knew how it was, how bitchy and calculating ambitious beauties like Katie could be. She couldn't live with the waiting. Waiting for one woman, more special or more clever at getting what she wanted than the rest, to draw Zeke in.

She wound her hair into a towel and then looked at her reflection in the mirror. Maybe that woman would never appear—perhaps Zeke would be strong against all the come-ons and remain faithful—but that was almost beside the point. It was *her* who would damage what they had if she stayed with him. She knew that now. Jealousy and suspicion were terrible things, and she couldn't expect Zeke to live with them and her, because that was how it would be. She had found out a lot about herself in the past weeks, and even more since she had seen him again today, and she wasn't proud of it. But it *was* reality.

Maybe if she didn't love him so much, or had had a different upbringing, or a thicker skin… She shook her head and turned from the bereft face in the mirror. Too many maybes. The accident had thrown up a whole host of gremlins buried deep in her psyche, and the only thing in the world she was sure about right now was that she had to step out of her life and begin again somewhere far away. And she could do that. She *would* do it. And then perhaps she could sort out her head. Given time. Find the courage to fight the deadening apathy that dominated her outlook on the future when she looked down long years without Zeke. In fact she'd have to. End of story.

She dressed quickly, relaxing infinitesimally once she was covered up. She didn't think Zeke would barge into the bedroom unannounced, in view of all that had been said, but…

She dried her hair into a sleek shining curtain either side of her face before applying her make-up. She kept it simple—just a touch of eyeshadow and mascara to enhance her green eyes and a warm plum-coloured lipstick for her lips. Nevertheless, the effect was almost startling after not wearing make-up for so long. Titivating had been the last thing on her mind in hospital, but now she looked at herself in the bedroom mirror and decided she would do the same every day.

Part of her rehabilitation, she thought with grim humour, remembering the words of the consultant when she had last seen him. He had been so kind, Mr Price. Grey-haired and fatherly, but a man who called a spade a spade, albeit with compassion and gentleness. "I've mended your body, Melody, but it's up to you to do the same with your spirit. I know this has knocked you for six, but there's the rest of your life to live now—which is more than some of my patients can look forward to. I don't understand everything you're feeling, but when you are ready I'd like you to see a colleague of mine who can talk things through with you as many times as you need."

She'd looked down at the name and telephone number he had given her. Dr Greg Richardson. Swallowing hard, she had whispered, "Is he a psychiatrist?" already knowing the answer. They all thought she was losing it, that she'd cracked.

Mr Price's voice had been soft when he'd answered. "He is someone who works with people who need a different kind of healing to the one I can give. Look at it like that. He's a good man. More than that, he's a friend of mine and I know you would benefit from seeing him. Don't dismiss it out of hand, Melody. And..." The good doctor had paused, waiting until she had met his steady gaze before he'd continued, "Don't make any life-changing decisions in the next little while. Give yourself time. It might be a cliché, but time is a great healer."

"You're talking about Zeke," she'd said woodenly.

This time the pause had been longer. "Partly, yes."

Mr Price had meant well. Turning away from the mirror, Melody took a deep breath. And she knew he hadn't agreed with her decision to end her marriage. Emotion flooded in, overwhelming her. But he didn't understand. How could he? He was a doctor first and foremost. He didn't have a clue about the entertainment industry other than what he experienced when he watched TV or went to the cinema or theatre. Showbiz was another world, a world within the everyday world, and since she had entered it after leaving dance school she had relished every second. It had been hard, exacting, unforgiving, sometimes unfair and often capricious, but it had enabled her to do what she loved most—dance. Or what she had loved most until she had met Zeke. From that point he'd become the centre of her world.

She had had it all. She bit her bottom lip with small white teeth, her eyes cloudy. And the gods didn't like mere mortals who tasted paradise on earth. How many times had she thought it was all too good to last? Well, she had been right. It hadn't lasted.

Melody stared blindly across the room, straightening her shoulders as she took several deep calming breaths. And now she had to adapt to the cards she'd been dealt. It was a simple as that. Everything was changed, but there were millions of other people much worse off than she was. She could not, she *would* not give in to the numb, grey, terrifying depression that kept trying to draw her into a mindless vacuum. There was life after dancing. There was life after Zeke.

"Melody?"

The knock at her bedroom door made her jump out of her skin as she came out of the maelstrom of her thoughts. Her hand at her chest, she steadied herself. Then she walked to the door and opened it, a cool smile stitched in place. "I'm ready."

He looked fabulous. Dinner suit, hair slicked back, magnetism increased tenfold. "Hi," he said softly. "Cocktails in the sitting room? They're all ready."

"Lovely." Her voice was a little breathless but she hoped he wouldn't notice. She needed to project coolness, if anything.

"You look…" He smiled and the warmth in his eyes increased her heartbeat to a gallop. "Good enough to eat," he finished huskily. "But then you always do."

"Thank you." Even to her own ears her voice sounded ridiculously prim. "The clothes are very nice."

"But I forgot to give you this when I gave you the other things earlier." He handed her a package, beautifully wrapped like the previous ones. He seemed totally at ease and not at all bothered by her lack of enthusiasm at the gift.

"What is it?" Melody asked flatly, refusing to acknowledge to herself how wildly attractive he was.

He took her arm, leading her through into the sitting room before he said quietly, "Open it and see."

"I—I don't want it. I mean, you've given me enough. I can't accept anything else. Not—not when I haven't got you—"

"Open it." He interrupted her stumbling words coolly, and when she still made no attempt to obey him he casually pushed her down on one of the sofas and sat beside her, undoing the ribbons on the large box. "It won't bite," he added.

As he lifted the lid, Melody gazed down at the silver boots the box contained. The soft leather was worked with tiny crystals in a curling design that wound from toe to heel in a thin line on the outer side of each boot, and she would have known immediately—even if she hadn't seen the name on the box—that they'd cost an arm and a leg. She didn't remove the boots from their bed of tissue paper, raising her eyes to Zeke before she spoke. "I can't accept these. I mean it, Zeke. I don't want anything else."

He sat back a little, folding his arms over his chest as he surveyed her with an air of deceptive meekness. "Why not?"

"I shouldn't have taken the clothes," she said by way of answer, feeling churlish but knowing she had to make him see.

"But you did," he pointed out gently, "and these are part of that gift." His eyes lowered to the black leather boots she was wearing, which were definitely more serviceable than anything else and couldn't compare to the exotic creations in the box.

Melody's mouth tightened as her chin rose. She knew what

he was thinking, but he either took her out in her old boots or not at all. "I'm sorry, Zeke. They're beautiful, but no."

The mockery in the black eyes showed he was fully aware of what she was thinking. "No problem," he said lazily. "If you change your mind before we leave they're here."

"I won't." She stood up abruptly. Sitting so close, she could smell the expensive sensual aftershave he favoured, and it was playing havoc with her thought process.

Zeke rose too, walking across to where a tray holding two glasses of her favourite cocktail—sapphire martini—was waiting. He handed her one of the frosted martini glasses full of the chilled gin and blue liqueur. "No toasts tonight, but I hope you enjoy the evening," he said softly. "We're eating after the theatre, if that's okay? I thought it would give us time to work up an appetite after all that cake."

Melody took a sip of the cocktail. The very blue, very sweet liqueur tasted slightly of lavender, contrasting wonderfully with the spicy gin, and giving her the kick she needed to be able to smile and say fairly normally, "That's fine. I'm not hungry."

"We'll have to work on getting that appetite of yours back. I was always amazed at how much you could eat."

Melody stared at him. "I was a dancer," she said flatly. "I burnt off the calories. Everything is different now."

"Not everything." He leant closer.

With her heart thudding, Melody waited for his kiss. As his lips closed over hers they tasted of the bittersweet cocktail and a warm thrill of pleasure quivered down her spine. When Zeke exerted his charm it was as potent as mulled wine, heady and intoxicating. He was irresistible and he knew it.

He broke the kiss for just a moment, to place their glasses on the coffee table, and then took her in his arms again, holding her lightly against him as his mouth teased at hers. She found herself swept into the world of sensuous delight Zeke evoked so easily, and as she responded to him his arms tightened around her and his lips demanded more intimacy. She abandoned all reserve—for a crazy moment she couldn't do anything else, didn't *want* to do anything else. This was Zeke and she adored him; for a few blissful seconds that was all that mattered.

It was Zeke who finished the embrace by gently withdrawing, although he still continued to hold her, his eyes as black as night as he stared down at her flushed face.

Melody felt light-headed and slightly dazed, her eyes cloudy with desire as she struggled to compose herself. Part of her was shocked and embarrassed at how easily Zeke could break through her defences; another part of her had known this would happen. Zeke was a very physical man; he'd always wanted to touch and hold and kiss her and she had wanted it too.

"You and I haven't changed," Zeke said huskily. "Surely you understand that now? Nothing could come between what we have. We're meant to be together. You must believe that."

It would have been so easy to melt into him again and just agree, to let her need of him—his strength, his security, his overpowering maleness—take control. Over the past months she had been fighting constantly—fighting to get better, to control the negative thoughts that hit at all times of the night and day, to accept the fact of a future without Zeke.

Easy, but not right. That was the hard truth.

Melody stepped away from the warm circle of his arms. She looked at him and swallowed, hating what she had to say but knowing it must be said. "It's over, Zeke," she said, very quietly but with a finality he couldn't fail to recognise. "I have accepted that and you *have* to. If you love me, you'll let me go. I can't be in your world any more. It might sound dramatic, but I know how much I can stand and that would be the final straw. It would destroy me here, inside. I have to make a new life for myself and find out who I am now."

"You're my wife," he said thickly.

If she hadn't been feeling so wretched Melody could have smiled. That was so Zeke. Black and white. He had never seen shades of grey. Not trusting herself to speak, she shook her head slowly, her eyes on his dark face.

"It's Christmas Eve." He leant forward and kissed her again—a hard, confident kiss, strong and sweet. "And at this moment in time you are my wife and we are going out to enjoy ourselves. We're not thinking beyond that. No more about the future, not even tomorrow. Tonight we're living in the moment, one minute at a time, and that's all that matters. Okay?"

The kiss had left her breathless and shaken, but with an effort she forced a smile. Their last night together. It was going to be bittersweet, but why couldn't it be a night to remember? A step out of time? Zeke knew how she felt, she'd made it crystal-clear, so it wasn't as if she was masquerading under false pretences. And it would be something to remember in the lonely months and years ahead.

He had retrieved their glasses and now she drank deeply of the cocktail, knowing she'd never be able to drink it again because it would be forever linked with this last night and the pain which was piercing her through.

"There's canapés and champagne waiting in our box at the theatre, so if you're ready?" Zeke said softly as she drained her glass. He took her arm, his touch firm but gentle.

Melody took a deep breath. Her first real venture into the

outside world since the accident and she was certainly plunging into the deep end, she thought wryly. There was bound to be people they knew at the theatre—people who were aware of her injuries and who would be watching her with scalpel-sharp eyes. Hopefully once they were in their box there would be a degree of privacy, but until then... She squared her shoulders and lifted her chin. "Ready."

It was a lie. She would never be ready. And she was scared, so scared, but she could do this. It was just one night after all.

Zeke pulled her coat round her shoulders, his touch sending tiny bolts of electricity down her nerve endings. It was always the same. Even when he inadvertently touched her it registered every time.

Just before they left the room he turned her round to face him, slowly raising her left hand with her wedding and engagement rings to his lips. He kissed her wrist first, his mouth warm against the silky flesh where her pulse beat, and then turned her hand over and kissed the rings, his lips caressing and gentle. "You've nothing to fear from me," he said very quietly. "I promise you that. I will never hurt you."

She made a small ineffectual sound in her throat, pulling her hand away as she stepped back a pace.

"So defensive." The words were almost a sigh, and for a moment she thought she detected sudden pain in his dark eyes before he blinked and it cleared.

"I thought we were leaving?" She spoke flatly, carefully keeping her facial expression calm. She couldn't afford to let her guard down. Not for a moment.

"We are." But he didn't move.

Melody stared at him warily, swallowing against the tightness in her throat. There had always been something uncivilised about Zeke, and tonight it was in every movement and expression—a sensuousness that was almost animal-like in its instinctive earthiness and male power.

And then he smiled, opening the door. "Let's go."

Chapter 7

It had stopped snowing when they left the hot-house comfort of the hotel, stepping into a frozen winter wonderland that had transformed the city streets into something magical.

The gritters had been hard at work keeping the main roads serviceable, and the hotel staff had had the foresight to clear a path from the hotel door to the main thoroughfare. Nevertheless, Melody was glad of Zeke's firm hand at her elbow as they hailed a taxi.

The snow hadn't seemed to deter the last-minute shoppers making use of some of the big stores which were still open. The white pavements were alive with folk heaped with bags and parcels, and an unusual air of gaiety pervaded the scene. It was as though a white Christmas had evoked the excitement of a child in even the most hardened city-dwellers, and for a little while the wonder of the festive season had swept away everyday problems and difficulties. Everyone seemed happy.

Zeke settled her close to him in the taxi, his arm round her shoulders, and she didn't pull away although his touch made her as tense as a coiled spring. It was strange being out in the hustle and bustle of life again after her long stint in the hospital, but it wasn't that which tightened her nerves, although he must have thought so because he murmured, "Relax. We're doing this together, okay? I'm here. I've got you. This is going to be a pleasant evening, that's all."

"I'm fine," she lied firmly. "Absolutely fine."

The sound he made in his throat expressed what he thought of that, and as he bent and kissed the top of her head with a swift, featherlight touch she thought she heard him sigh again.

Melody stared out of the window without really seeing the brightly lit shops and crowds, overwhelmed by a mixture of emotions—fear and panic and, not least, love. His solid muscular body was against hers, filling her with the old familiar feeling of safety and belonging. When she had met Zeke she'd realised she'd been searching all her life for the security he provided. For the first time she'd felt she had a chance at the things lots of people took for granted. He would take care of her. But now that was relegated to a memory—a beautiful dream which had been sweet while it had lasted.

They didn't talk on the way to the theatre, but every so often Melody felt his lips brush the top of her head. It took all of her willpower not to twist and lift her face to his, and only the knowledge that it would be immensely unfair to give him any hope prevented her from reaching for him. She had seen sadness mingled with desire in his eyes the last time she'd met his gaze, but she knew he still hadn't accepted their marriage was over. And he had to. For both their sakes.

Zeke helped her out of the taxi once they reached the theatre, but she was still vitally conscious of her less than elegant exit, and despair at her clumsiness was paramount as she stood on the icy pavement. Mr Price had told her that she was too hard on herself more than once. "It is the dancer in you who exaggerates what you see as ungainliness," he'd insisted. "Other people would not notice."

She had blessed him for his kindness, but had known it was just that and not the truth. She had watched the smooth, controlled walk of the nurses in the hospital, of visitors, everyone, and marvelled at all she had taken for granted before the accident. But then she supposed everyone was the same in her position. She wasn't unique.

She breathed in the crisp, bitingly cold air, which due to the snow was devoid of the taint of the city for once. *Okay, best foot forward,* she told herself with silent irony as Zeke slid an arm round her waist. And they might not meet anyone they knew, anyway.

And pigs might fly!

They were barely inside the foyer when a gushing voice caused them to turn. *"Darlings…"* Angela Stewart was an actress of some standing and, Melody suspected, one of Zeke's old flames—although he had never said and she'd never asked. But there was something in the way Angela was with her made Melody feel the tall, willowy blonde resented her beneath the effusive front she presented. *"So* lovely to see you." Angela's sharp blue eyes swept her from head to foot before the actress gave a *mwah* of a kiss to the air either side of their faces, her carefully tousled hair stiff with hairspray.

Melody braced herself. "Hello, Angela," she said carefully, trying to breathe through the fog of heavy perfume the blonde was wearing. Angela was the last person she'd have chosen to see.

"How *are* you?" A red-taloned hand touched Melody's arm lightly. "We were so *devastated* when we heard about the accident, you poor, poor love. And you a dancer too. So sad."

"She's wonderful—aren't you, sweetheart?" Zeke's voice was cool, with an edge that made Melody hope Angela didn't prolong the conversation.

Angela's escort—a tall, distinguished man who could have doubled as Richard Gere—must have thought the same thing, because he took her arm after nodding at Melody and Zeke, saying, "Our party's waiting to take their seats, Angela."

Angela jerked herself free, looking straight at Melody. "All those months in hospital must have been tedious for you. I bet you can't wait to get back in the swing of things again," she drawled softly. "But you must take it a day at a time, sweetie. You look a little tired and peaky."

"Melody has the resilience of youth on her side," Zeke put in smoothly. "Remember how that used to feel, Angela? Now, if you'll excuse us…"

They were seated in their box before Melody spoke. "You shouldn't have said that," she murmured as Zeke poured the champagne which had been waiting for them. "She'll never forgive you. I'd be surprised if she ever speaks to you again."

Zeke grinned, offering her the plate of canapés. "Sounds good."

Below them the stalls were filling up, along with the balcony and the other boxes. The musical drama they were seeing was the latest big thing, and tickets were like gold dust. The theatre itself was an old building, with a high, ornate domed ceiling and an air of genteel Victorian splendour, and the central heating was equally archaic and not quite man enough for the unusually cold evening.

Like a magician producing a rabbit out of a hat, Zeke placed a thick, imitation fur throw across her legs. "Is that better?" he murmured softly.

"Where did that come from?" Melody asked, surprised.

"I know this theatre from old. It's too hot in the summer and cold in the winter, but its charm cancels out such inconveniences." Zeke topped up her champagne as he spoke, his voice warm as he added, "Relax and enjoy the show. You're doing great. I'm proud of you, my darling."

It was the look in his eyes rather than what he said that caused her to flush and gulp at her champagne. She had forgotten how he made her feel when she was with him—no, that was wrong. She bit her bottom lip. She hadn't forgotten, had merely tried to bury the memory along with a host of others. And he would never understand, not in a million years, because she didn't understand it herself. It was just this sort of thing that made it imperative she walked away from him now, while things were still civilised between them. She couldn't bear to experience a slow whittling away of such moments as their relationship went sour.

Was she crazy? She sipped her drink, staring unseeing across the theatre. Probably. Almost definitely. And certainly cowardly and weak and spineless.

She looked at him out of the corner of her eye and his dark gaze was soft on her face. "Thinking again," he stated ruefully. "I would like to flick a little switch in here—" he touched her brow lightly "—and turn your head off for a while. How can I do that, my sweet wife? How can I make you live in the moment?"

She shrugged, pretending a nonchalance she didn't feel.

"I only know of one sure way, but that's impossible in here," Zeke went on contemplatively. "Impossible to do properly, anyway, and after waiting so long..."

Melody took another hurried sip of champagne, deciding silence was the quickest way to end this disturbing one-sided conversation. She pretended an interest in the stalls below.

"Remember how it was between us?" He stretched his long legs, sliding one arm along the back of her seat, so close his body warmth surrounded her as his quiet, smoky voice wove a deliberate spell. "Those nights when we didn't fall asleep until dawn? The taste of pure ecstasy, long and slow and lasting. You're mine, Dee. You'll always be mine, as I'm yours. There's no other way for either of us now we've feasted on perfection."

"Don't." Her breath caught in her throat, his words causing a chain reaction in her body she was powerless to control. And he knew it, she thought helplessly.

"Don't?" His husky voice drifted around her like a sensuous cloud. "Don't speak the truth? But the truth will set you free. Isn't that what they say? And you're not facing the truth. Not yet. Our lifestyle, my work, other people—that's all on the perimeter of *us*, you and me."

He was confusing her, blurring the edges. She shook her head, on the verge of getting up and leaving. It was the dimming of the lights that forestalled such an action, but she sat stiff and taut as the show began, every nerve and sinew in her body stretched to breaking point.

In spite of her acute distress, the drama being enacted on stage began to work its magic after a while. The special effects were spellbinding, and the heroine's voice enchanting, but it was the dancers who took most of Melody's attention—especially the lead female, who was as supple and graceful as a young gazelle. It was bittersweet watching the girl, and at first pain overshadowed her perception, but then she felt herself swept into the performance to such an extent she had to bump back to earth when the interval arrived.

"Well?" Zeke's eyes were waiting for her as the lights brightened. "Enjoying it?" he said gently.

Melody nodded, still half lost in the performance. "It's brilliant—absolutely brilliant. And I'm not criticising, but—"

"But?" he pressed her when she stopped abruptly.

"I'd have arranged that last dance number differently. It would have been far more poignant if the lead dancer was taken by the underworld after it finished rather than pulling her out at the beginning. The scene lost something without her present."

Zeke nodded. "I agree."

"That way the roles of Cassandra and Alex could have been tweaked to make them more involved in the struggle, rather than being almost observers." Melody stopped abruptly, aware of the half-smile on Zeke's face. "What?"

"Nothing." Zeke turned as a waitress appeared with a plate of fresh savouries and coffee which he'd obviously arranged to have brought to their box. After tipping the girl handsomely he closed the door after her, enclosing them in their own private little world again. He solicitously plied her with the delicious morsels, and unlike previously his conversation was now easy and amusing, requiring little in response from her.

To her immense surprise Melody found she was enjoying herself in spite of the nerves still making themselves felt in the pit of her stomach. She had dreaded battling her way to the crowded bar in the interval—a place where many of their contemporaries liked to see and be seen—and with that obstacle dealt with, the pleasure of being out on the town after all her weeks incarcerated in the hospital was foremost.

Zeke handed her a cup of coffee, his thigh briefly brushing hers, and immediately she tensed. He was wearing a clean, sharp aftershave that blended well with his own personal male scent, and he had always looked exceptionally good in a dinner suit, his particular brand of hard, rugged sexiness emphasised by the formal attire. "This is nice," he said in a contented murmur, his brawny shoulder against hers.

It was. Too nice. Melody said nothing and the comfortable silence changed, becoming uncomfortable. Still she didn't break it. Zeke sipped his black coffee slowly, his face calm and inscrutable. She had no idea what he was thinking. Not that she ever had. The thought troubled her with its truth and she chewed it over, worrying at it like a dog with a bone.

Was it because he deliberately kept his thoughts from her and because he was enigmatic, private? Or—and here her fingers clenched on her coffee cup—because she had never taken the time to find out his innermost feelings and desires? She had been so occupied with her career, with making good, surviving in the glitzy, showy world they inhabited, that she'd been content to skate on the surface of their marriage while everything had been easy and harmonious. Her amazement that he had chosen her as his wife, that it was all too good to be true, had induced a feeling that she must be careful not to rock the boat and it had been simpler not to delve too deeply.

Children, for instance. She glanced at his chiselled profile, her heart thudding. When they'd spoken of a family she had sensed he wanted children soon, but she'd never really talked to him about that, preferring to relegate it to somewhere in the hazy future. From the way he'd spoken earlier, when the two little Japanese girls had prompted things, it was clear he wanted to be a father—probably needed to create a family unit more than most men due to his upbringing. He would want to give his own children everything he'd never had. Why had she never realised that before?

Because she hadn't taken the time to consider; she had been too busy keeping up with how she felt the wife of Zeke James should be. It symbolised everything which had been wrong in their relationship before the accident and most of it was down to her. But it had been impossible to bring her insecurities into the open because they'd been buried too deep, locked way in the small, scared child part of herself. But she wasn't a child any more. She was a grown woman, and she had to come to terms with her buried fears and emotions before she could function properly as a person, let alone a wife.

She was a mess. Melody sipped at her coffee as tears pricked the backs of her eyes. Zeke didn't deserve to be landed with a nutcase like her. He wouldn't divorce her. He'd made his commitment and he would never go back on it—that was the sort of man he was. So it was up to her to end things and let him find happiness in the future with someone who was his equal—something she'd never felt from day one.

When his hand moved her face to look at him she was too late to blink away the tears. He surveyed her steadily, his black eyes velvet-soft, but the solid strength that had first attracted her was very evident. "It will be all right." His thumbs brushed away the telltale moisture. "Now you're back with me everything will slot into place, you'll see."

She shook her head very slightly. "No, Zeke. It won't."

He looked at her gravely. "Do you seriously think your scars will have any impact on my love for you? Apart from increasing my admiration for the way you've fought to overcome your injuries? Just how shallow do you think I am?"

"I don't think you're shallow." She swallowed hard. "And I've come to realise this is about me, not you. I should never have married you. I shouldn't have married anyone—not until I knew myself. Not until I understood where my problems were."

His face was expressionless. "And do you know yourself now?"

"I'm beginning to." She moistened dry lips. "And I didn't realise what a headcase I was."

"No, not a headcase." His voice was calm, level. "Merely vulnerable and afraid and unconfident. You have always been those things, Dee. This is no surprise to me. You are also courageous and sweet and generous, with the softest heart of anyone I have ever known. The positives outweigh the negatives big time. If you're going to examine yourself, do it properly."

She stiffened a little. "You think you know me so well?"

"I know I do." His smile was almost pensive.

"You're very sure of yourself, aren't you?"

"I have to be," he said quietly. "For your sake as well as mine. The accident has brought to the surface issues which would have been dealt with slowly, over a matter of years, if it hadn't happened. But it has happened. And maybe it's for the best."

She stared at him, hurt beyond measure. "How can you say that?" she accused thickly, the physical and mental agony she'd suffered over the past months rising up in a bitter flood. "I've lost everything I've worked for all my life."

His face tightened, but his voice was still calm and controlled when he said, "No, Dee. You have lost the ability to dance as you once did. That has been taken away from you. But that's all. You can still see and hear and smell and touch. Your mind hasn't been damaged, your intellect is still as sharp, and you can make decisions about where you want to go and what you want to do and carry them out without being dependent on others to enable you to move or walk. There are plenty of people—some of them in that hospital you've just left—who would give ten years of their lives for that alone. You have everything to live for."

Anger replaced the hurt. "You're accusing me of self-pity?"

He looked at her intently with those ebony-dark eyes. "Your words, not mine," he said quietly as the lights began to dim once more. He settled back in his seat, his face inscrutable.

Melody barely heard the orchestra strike up. She sat staring towards the stage, fighting hot, angry tears and telling herself she hated him. *Hated* him. How dared he say all that to her after all she had been through? Didn't he understand how this had changed her life? Didn't he care? She had been right to insist on a divorce—this proved it.

The curtain rose, but it was a few minutes before she focused on the drama being enacted on the stage. The drama in her own life was paramount. She could feel Zeke's eyes on her now and then as the musical progressed, but she didn't glance at him once.

The anger and outrage subsided after a while, and a quiet but insistent little voice deep inside was telling her that Zeke was right. Right, but cruel and hard and unfeeling, she told herself bitterly. How could he say he loved her and talk to her like that?

It was another twenty minutes before she could bring herself to acknowledge that Zeke had said what no one else would dare to say, because he felt she needed to hear it. In all the time she had known him she had never seen him be anything but ruthlessly honest and direct. It was just that the searing truthfulness had never been directed at her before—or not with such severity, anyway. Nevertheless, if this was tough love she didn't want it.

By the time the last curtain call was finished, to rapturous applause from a very satisfied audience, Melody felt like a wet rag. If she had just endured twenty sessions with a therapist without a break she couldn't have been more exhausted or emotionally drained, she thought, as the lights rose and people began to stand up. It was as though in the past few hours since leaving hospital the door in her mind where all her insecurities and issues had been under lock and key had been flung wide open, and she was having to deal with the resulting cans of worms in one fell swoop. Some Christmas Eve, she thought wretchedly.

She must have looked as spent as she felt, because Zeke's voice was genuinely concerned when he said, "We can skip dinner out and order Room Service when we get back to the hotel, if you would prefer that? It's probably more sensible with the weather."

Melody nodded. The thought of an intimate twosome was scary, but she got clumsy when she was tired, and anything was preferable than falling flat on her face in every sense of the words. "If that's okay?"

He kissed her, a slow, gentle kiss, and she didn't have the energy to protest. "Come on," he said softly. "Let's go home."

If only they were, Melody thought suddenly, swallowing at the constriction in her throat. If only this was a year ago, when everything had been all right. But *had* it been? Really?

She was stiff when she rose from her seat, and concentrating on walking as best she could helped to quell the lump in her throat. They had barely left the box when Zeke drew her into his arms and kissed her again. It was a very confident kiss, strong and sweet, and his fingers massaged the base of her spine as his mouth worked its magic. He didn't hurry. He took his time.

Melody felt breathless and shaken when his mouth left hers, and his eyes were smiling as they stared down into her wide green ones. "My brand of physiotherapy," he said smokily, his features shadowed in the dim light in the corridor in which they were standing. "And it's very exclusive."

A thrill of unexpected laughter went through her. "Have you been qualified for long?" she murmured.

"I'm a novice," he admitted softly. "I need a lot of practice." His finger outlined her lips. "Practice makes perfect. Isn't that what they say?"

Her mouth went dry. With an effort she held the smile. "Whoever 'they' are, I'm sure they've got a point." She extracted herself from his arms. "We'll be the last ones out of the theatre if we're not careful."

Zeke grinned. "Suits me."

It suited her too. The last thing she wanted to do tonight was make polite conversation with any more Angelas. The trouble with Zeke being so high-profile was that wherever they went he was recognised by someone or other. Not that he could help that. And it didn't matter—or it hadn't mattered much in the past, anyway. It was different now.

"I don't like being the last at anything," she said, determined not to get embroiled in another weakening embrace, and when Zeke took her arm without another word and led her to the stairs she knew he had taken her none too subtle hint.

The taxi Zeke had booked to take them to their dinner venue was waiting when they walked out of the theatre, the icy cold taking Melody's breath away. Enclosed in the cosy cocoon of their box, she had forgotten the sub-zero temperature outside for an hour or two. He drew her firmly into him as they walked across the pavement, helping her into the taxi and giving the driver their new destination before settling beside her. He slid his arm along the seat at the back of her, a familiar action—and why it should result in her heart hammering in wild, panicked beats she didn't know. She was too weary and emotionally spent to protest when he drew her head onto his shoulder, besides which it was achingly familiar.

"Christmas Eve," he murmured above her head, his voice soft. "Your favourite night. The night of miracles."

So he'd remembered. She had told him the first Christmas they had been together that Christmas Eve had always been special to her in some way she couldn't explain. All through her lonely childhood and even lonelier teenage years the day had held an elusive wonder her circumstances couldn't dispel or negate. It seemed a time for miracles, the restoration of lost dreams and hopes and aspirations, and she had never ceased to be affected by it.

Except for tonight. The thought pierced her through, but it was true. Tonight she was bowed down by reality and she had nothing to look forward to—no expectancy or belief that there was a ray of light at the end of her particular dark tunnel. She simply didn't have it in her to trust she wouldn't spoil what they had if she stayed with Zeke. She couldn't live with the doubt and uncertainty, the wondering, the fear it would turn sour and he'd be driven into someone else's arms. Someone with beauty and grace who was whole and happy and unscathed by life. A girl who could return his love with all her heart and trust him implicitly.

This was going to be their last night together. She nodded mentally to the thought. Somehow she would slip away tomorrow, find somewhere—anywhere—to stay. She had one or two friends who lived in this area. One of them would take her in. It wasn't the best time to turn up on someone's doorstep—Christmas Day—but she couldn't help that. She had to escape Zeke. She had to make him *see*. Zeke wasn't for her. And she didn't believe in miracles any more.

Chapter 8

Amazingly, in view of her misery, Melody must have fallen asleep, because the next thing she knew was the taxi stopping and Zeke's voice saying they were back at the hotel.

"Come on, sleepyhead." His voice was tender, indulgent, as he helped her out of the car. "How about you change into something comfortable when we get to the suite? Maybe have a warm bath first? It'll take Room Service a while to deliver once we've ordered so you'll have plenty of time."

She glanced at him as they walked into the foyer, knowing her limp was more pronounced tonight but unable to do anything about it. "I think I'll go straight to my room," she said tightly. "And I'm not hungry. I'll skip dinner, if you don't mind."

"Hungry or not, you need to eat."

"No, Zeke. I don't. I told you—I'm going straight to bed."

They had reached the lift, and once the doors closed he faced her in the carpeted little box, his voice dangerously soft.

"Dinner is compulsory, Dee. Unless you want me to choose for you, I suggest you look at the menu."

"For goodness' sake." Truly exasperated, she glared at him. "What are you going to do? Force-feed me?" she said irritably.

"If necessary." He nodded. "Exactly that."

She could see he wasn't joking. "I'm not a child, Zeke."

"Then don't act like one. You have been seriously ill and you're still recovering. You need good food and plenty of it."

This was ridiculous. "I think I'm quite capable of knowing when I want to eat, thank you very much," she said tartly.

Zeke raised his eyebrows as a smile flickered across his sexy mouth. The action said far more than words could have done and aggravated her further. Did he have to be so irritatingly chauvinistic? Melody thought waspily. And so certain he was always right?

She gave him what she hoped was a quelling glare and stared at the lift door as though it was the most interesting thing on the planet, knowing it was useless to argue. Nevertheless she was bristling like a furious little alley cat, determined not to give ground, when they opened the door to their suite. Whether Zeke was right or wrong didn't matter. It was his peremptory attitude that had got under her skin.

The lights from the Christmas tree and the couple of lamps Zeke had left on made the sitting room dangerously cosy as they took off their coats—a miniature home from home. Zeke slung his jacket on a chair, loosening his bow tie and opening the first two or three buttons of his shirt as he walked across to the coffee table where the room service menu was sitting. "Now," he murmured smoothly. "I think the steak will do me nicely. How about you? And the raspberry and limoncello trifle sounds good. I'm starving."

Melody plumped down sulkily on one of the sofas. She

wouldn't have admitted to a living soul that her mouth had watered as he spoke. "I had beef for lunch," she said stiffly.

"How about oven-poached salmon with fennel and beet-root?" Zeke suggested amiably. "That's a light alternative and not so rich as most of the other dishes. Perfect to tempt the appetite."

She shrugged, knowing she was acting like the child he had accused her of being but not knowing how else to protect herself against the temptation he presented. He looked more hard and sexy than any man had the right to look, and his lazy air and lack of aggression didn't fool her one bit. "I think I will have a bath," she said flatly, as Zeke picked up the telephone, leaving the room without waiting for him to reply.

Once in her bedroom she shut the door and leaned her weight against it, wondering for the umpteenth time how she had got herself into this situation. "It's just one night," she whispered. "Nothing has really changed." Her plans hadn't altered, and Zeke couldn't keep her married to him by force when all was said and done. She just had to keep her head and by this time tomorrow she could be somewhere else— *anywhere* else. Her soft mouth dropped unknowingly and she levered herself upright with a shuddering sigh.

She wanted to be a million miles away from Zeke, and yet she longed to be where she could see and watch and touch him every minute of every day. How was that for inconsistency? And she couldn't let him see or even sense what she was feeling. She was no match for him at the best of times and his formidably intelligent mind and finely honed senses—attributes which had caused him to rise like a meteor in the world he inhabited—were at their most astute when concentrated on a problem he needed to solve. And at the moment she had no doubt that was how he viewed this situation. He hadn't even begun to accept their marriage was over, everything about him proclaimed it, and so she had to remain strong and focused.

Melody didn't linger in the bath, drying herself thoroughly and slipping into a pyjama vest top and matching loose trousers and then pulling on the fluffy bathrobe for added protection. She hadn't heard a sound from outside her room but as she opened the bedroom door she could hear carols being sung. A carol concert was in full swing on the TV as she entered the sitting room, young choir boys singing "Silent Night" with a purity of tone that was inexpressibly poignant.

Zeke was sprawled on one of the sofas, his long legs stretched out in front of him and a glass of brandy at his elbow. He looked broodingly tough and fascinatingly sexy, and Melody's mouth went dry at the sight of him. His eyes opened as she walked into the room and he straightened slightly, indicating his drink with a wave of his hand. "Like one?"

She shook her head. "I've had more than enough today, thanks," she said, pleased her voice sounded so normal when her heart was pounding like a drum. "I haven't had any alcohol for the last three months, don't forget."

"I haven't forgotten one second of the last three months, believe me. The time's engraved on my memory for ever. Sheer hell."

He had moved so she could join him on the sofa but she deliberately sat facing him on the opposite one, pretending an interest in the cathedral where the concert was being filmed as she tucked her feet under her legs, curling up and pulling the robe over her toes. "It's very beautiful," she said quietly. "There's a timeless quality to such places, isn't there?"

"Why have you shut me out so completely?" His voice wasn't accusing, in fact it was verging on conversational, and for a moment the words didn't register. "I mean, I'd really like to know."

"Zeke, please don't start this again. It's no good."

"For such a soft, gentle creature you can be as hard as iron when you want to be," he said thoughtfully.

Stung, she met his gaze. "I'm not hard."

"Not with the rest of the world, no. Just with me. Why is that? What is it about me that makes you believe I don't bleed when I'm cut? That I don't feel like other people?"

She drew in a deep breath. "I know the last months have been hard for you too. I do know that. But that doesn't make any difference to now."

"Do you blame me for the fact I wasn't with you when it happened?" he asked quietly. "That's completely understandable. I hold myself responsible. I could have—should have—prevented it. I let you down and it's unforgivable."

Shocked beyond measure, she stared at him. "Of course I don't blame you. How could I?"

"Very easily," he said flatly, leaning forward so his hands were clasped between his knees, his dark gaze tight on her pale face. "We were supposed to meet for lunch that day. I would have been with you but for that problem that arose. If I hadn't cancelled, put a damn business meeting before my wife—"

"Stop it, Zeke," she whispered, horrified. "The accident was nothing to do with you. It was me. For a brief moment of time I didn't think. It's as simple as that. Probably countless thousands of people have momentary lapses of concentration every day. I was just in the wrong place at the wrong time to have mine. But it wasn't your fault."

She had forgotten they'd been supposed to meet at a little bistro that day, before he had called and made his apologies; the trauma of the accident and the following days and nights of unconsciousness had wiped it from her mind. But even if she had remembered she would never have imagined he blamed himself for what had happened. Zeke was such a logical man—so rational and clear-headed. She couldn't believe he had been condemning himself all this time. The fault had been hers and hers alone.

He stood restlessly to his feet, shaking his head. "I don't see it that way but we won't argue about it." His eyes held hers. "I'm not going to let you go, Dee. Not after nearly losing you three months ago."

It was the hardest thing she had ever done in her life to look back at him and speak the painful truth. "You have no choice. It takes two to make a partnership and I can't do it any more. I need…" She paused, knowing her voice was shaking but unable to keep the tremours from showing. "I *want* a divorce, Zeke. Our lives are set to go down different paths now. Surely you see that as much as I do? We can't go back to the way things were. It's over."

Two small words that cut like a knife through all the intimacy they had shared, the good times, the laughter, the joy and pleasure. She watched his face change, becoming set and rigid, as though he'd pulled a mask into place hiding any emotion. "And what I want and feel counts for nothing?"

Melody unconsciously gripped her hands together, struggling for composure. "I'm doing this for you as well as me—"

"Don't give me that." He didn't shout, but the tone of his voice stopped her mid-sentence. "That's too easy a get-out and you know it. Never once today have you asked me what I want or how I'm feeling. You've simply stated you're walking and that's that. No discussion, no compromise, no nothing."

She could see why it appeared that way to him, but how could she explain it was sheer self-survival driving her? She had always felt out of her depth in Zeke's world, but before the accident she had known she was out of the ordinary in one way—her dancing. She was good, more than good, and it had been the foundation of who she was—for right or wrong. Now that foundation was gone, smashed by a ten-ton truck...

The ball of pain in her stomach that had nothing to do with her accident and all to do with leaving Zeke contracted suddenly, as though a steel fist had been driven deep into her solar plexus. Without picking her words, she whispered, "When I was a little girl I was always on the outside looking in. I didn't get invited to parties or to tea with anyone. No one waited to walk home from school with me or called for me at the weekends to go to the park or play at their house. Of course looking back now I know it was because my grandmother never let me have friends round and she wasn't friendly with the other mothers, but then I thought it was me. That the other girls didn't like *me*—thought me odd because I hadn't got a mother and father like them. Perhaps they did or didn't. I don't know. But then I found that when I danced the rest of the world didn't matter. I lost myself. I wasn't me any more. And my grandmother encouraged it, knowing how much it meant to me. She did do that for me."

"While effectively screwing you up in every other way."

Taken aback by the bitterness and outrage in his voice, Melody shook her head quickly. "No, no she didn't. She—she did the best she could—the same as we all do, I suppose. She didn't have to take me in, she could have let me go into care, but she didn't. And she had been hurt—badly. I think she loved my grandfather very much, and certainly she never got over him. Her way of dealing with it was to hide her pain behind a façade of being tough. And she had lost her daughter too—my mother. She had a lot to cope with."

"You're making excuses for her. You always do," he said softly, the harshness gone from his voice.

"I'm trying to explain." The unexplainable. And opening up like this terrified her. But he deserved this at least.

"Dee, you're more than a dancer. You've always been more than a dancer." He'd come and crouched in front of her as he spoke, his trousers stretched tight over muscled thighs.

The temperature in the room rose about twenty degrees and all coherent thought went out of Melody's head. She stared at him, knowing he was going to kiss her and wanting it more than she had wanted anything in her life.

The polite knock at the door to the suite followed by a male voice calling, "Room Service," came as a drenching shock. Zeke reacted before she did, standing up and walking across the room while Melody made a heroic effort to pull herself together.

The man bustled in with a laden serving trolley, quickly and efficiently setting the small table in a corner of the room with cutlery and napkins, lighting the two candles in a silver candelabrum which he'd brought with him and placing it in the centre of the table. "Would you like me to serve the food, sir?" he asked Zeke, after he'd opened the bottle of wine Zeke had obviously ordered and offered him a taste before pouring a little into two large wine glasses.

Zeke glanced across at Melody, who was still sitting on the sofa. "No, we'll be fine. Thank you, and happy Christmas."

He slipped the man a tip which made the waiter's, "And a very merry Christmas to you, sir, madam," positively euphoric as he left, and as Melody joined him at the table Zeke pulled out a chair, unfolding her napkin and placing it in her lap as she sat down. "May I serve the first course, madam?"

Lifting the covers off two delicate white-and-silver bowls,

he revealed creamy, steaming soup which smelt divine. "I didn't order this." Melody glanced into his dark face.

"I thought we'd do it properly." He slid a fresh crusty roll onto a small plate next to her soup and then took his own place at the table. "Eat," he ordered softly.

The soup was as delicious as it smelt, and the salmon which followed equally good. Zeke talked of inconsequential matters with a comfortable ease which relaxed Melody in spite of herself, teasing her a little and making her laugh, his humour gentle and self-deprecating. Lulled into a mellow state of mind by Zeke's lazy air, the light yet satisfying food and the wine she sipped almost unconsciously, Melody found herself drifting in a haze of well-being. She felt calm and peaceful inside, she realised with a little shock of self-awareness. For the first time in months. It was such an alien sensation.

By the time Zeke brought out the desserts Melody was sure she couldn't eat another thing, but the Madeira cake spread with lemon curd, dosed with limoncello liqueur and topped off with raspberries and a mascarpone custard was the perfect end to a perfect meal and she ate every morsel. Replete, she finished the last of her wine, and when Zeke got up from the table and pulled her over to one of the sofas, sitting down beside her, she didn't protest.

"It's midnight," he murmured after a moment or two, his voice smoky-soft. "Happy Christmas, darling."

Darling. He shouldn't call her darling, she thought, but then she pushed the reasoning behind it away, not wanting anything to intrude on the moment. She watched as he reached into his pocket, bringing out a small package which he handed her, kissing her once very lightly. "What is it?" she said suspiciously.

"Open it and see."

"Zeke, I didn't want anything—"

"Shush." His mouth was harder, more insistent, and this time the kiss left her entire body trembling when he raised his head. "Open it," he said again, his voice husky.

The eternity ring was exquisite: sparkling diamonds and emeralds set into a delicate ring of white gold. When Zeke slid it onto her finger it nestled perfectly between her wedding ring and engagement ring, which was a beautiful thing in itself, with emeralds clustered round a magnificent diamond. Melody stared down at the glittering stones, anguish vying with other emotions she couldn't even bring a name to. She pressed the palms of her hands onto her eyes, hating herself for what she was doing to him.

Zeke gently brought her fingers away from her face by grasping her wrists, his dark eyes gazing into her tormented ones when she stared at him. He had aged in the past three months, she realised with a little shock of mortification. Time had become ingrained in the features of his face, the way it did when someone had suffered unbearable bereavement or loss. Had he unconsciously let go of her? In some deep recess of his mind had he known what they'd had was over? Was that it? Knowing Zeke as she did, he would have fought such a feeling. He would have felt he was letting her down.

"I love you," he said simply. "That's all this means. I will always love you. This feeling isn't optional. It's not something I can turn on and off. When you came into my life I thought I was doing all right, that I was autonomous, cool—call it what you will. Your arrival was unexpected and unsolicited. I wasn't looking for for ever. I don't think I even understood the notion until you stood on that stage and danced your way into my heart."

Her breath caught in her throat. "I can't dance any more."

"But you are here. That's all that matters." He lowered his

head until their lips were millimetres apart. "You have to believe that, Dee, because I don't know how to convince you beyond saying it and showing you how much I love you."

With a soft exhalation she accepted his mouth on hers. She fell against him, needing his strength, his maleness, his overwhelming virility, all the qualities she'd missed so deeply. He kissed her heavy eyelids, one after the other, pressing them closed as though he knew she needed to shut everything but the feel and taste of him out of her mind. Melody found herself in a velvety darkness made up entirely of what his body was doing to hers, her desire mounting as he deliberately deepened the kiss until the reality of the touch and taste and smell of him was irresistible, a fire which burnt everything in its path. She wanted him. She ached with it.

He picked her up in his arms, carrying her towards his bedroom. He manoeuvred the door open and carried her over the threshold as gently as if she were a china figurine. Kicking the door shut behind him, he walked into the dark bedroom, lit only by the soft shadowed glow of a bedside lamp he must have left on earlier.

Melody tensed as he laid her down on the bed, but instantly he was beside her, wrapping his arms round her in a gesture intended to reassure and comfort. There was no force, no urgency, his mouth caressing her lips with small kisses that gave pleasure without demanding a response.

Her breasts were pressed against the hard wall of his chest, and slowly and repetitively Zeke began stroking her back, his mouth moving all over her face in the same swift kisses as his fingers carefully worked down her spine from her tense shoulders to the seductive flare of her hips. Gradually she relaxed again, her body curving into his as his lips returned to her mouth and he kissed her more deeply, his skilful hands and mouth evoking the burning desire she remembered from the past.

When he removed the robe she was barely aware of it, and then he pulled the pyjama top over her head, caressing the silky skin of her throat and shoulders and nuzzling at the hollow of her collarbone before kissing her breasts one by one. She moaned deep in her throat when his mouth seized one nipple, giving it exquisite attention before moving to the other, and now her hands moved feverishly over his flesh, pulling the shirt away from his body so she could run her fingers over the hair-roughened muscle rippling with each movement he made.

Her mouth moved where her fingers had explored, her tongue curling round a copper nipple that beaded at her touch. She could taste a faint saltiness on his skin, the smell of lemon from the soap he used mingling with a more earthy scent. She had told him once in the early days of their marriage that she thought he was beautiful and he'd laughed, saying only women were beautiful. But he was wrong. He *was* beautiful, his body as powerful and perfectly honed as the statues of the old Greek gods that graced Mount Olympus.

"I've missed this," he murmured huskily. "Not necessarily the sex but being able to hold you, to know that you're there, that I only have to stretch out my hand to touch you."

She knew what he meant. There were some things more intimate than the act of intercourse—small actions between a couple that spoke of a relationship, of sharing, of being committed.

"Mind you, sex is great," he added in a hoarse whisper as her hand felt for his arousal, finding the taut flesh between his legs and stroking it. "I'm not advocating celibacy."

The dark shadows gave her the confidence to flow with what was happening, and when he removed her pyjama bottoms and the rest of his own clothes her arms reached for him, pulling him on top of her. She wasn't allowing herself to think. If she thought her conscience would force her to stop this, unfair on him as it was, because this one night wouldn't change anything. And so she didn't think. She just felt and touched and tasted.

Now he was naked her hand circled and caressed his huge erection again, knowing she was inflicting a pleasure-pain as he groaned and caught her wrist. "We're going to take this slow and easy," he breathed raggedly. "We've waited too long to rush things, but I'm only human, Dee."

His eyes glittered like an animal's in the near darkness, his face planes and hollows, and she reached up and placed her palms along either side of his face. Although he had shaved earlier the stubble already coming through gave his skin a rough, sandpapery texture that was at odds with the boyish quiff falling across his forehead. "Tonight it's just me and you," she whispered breathlessly. "No past, no future, just the present. I want to make love to you, Zeke. I want to feel you inside me again."

"Not as much as I want to be there." He kissed her again, a kiss she more than matched, but when she tried to guide him into her again he removed her hand. "Later," he murmured. "We have all the time in the world."

He began to touch and taste every inch of her body, teasing her with a slow sensuality that had her mindless and panting beneath his ministrations. Her skin became sensitised all over, the feminine core of her throbbing and swelling as she twisted and quivered under his mouth and hands.

Their lovemaking was as good as it had ever been, and the feelings were the same, but different. Before she had imagined they knew all there was to know about each other. Now she felt she didn't know herself, let alone Zeke. But one thing she was sure about was that she wanted him, and she wanted him because she loved him. She would always love him. She knew that now. It was part of what had terrified her after the accident. Maybe deep inside it had always terrified her. Love gave the beloved such power, such control. It had broken her grandmother, probably her mother too, and it would break her if she stayed and let it happen.

And then all reasoning became blurred again as desire took over—a desire only Zeke could quench. He moved slightly and she felt the tip of his masculinity at the mound between her thighs. He moved again and entered her just the tiniest bit, causing her legs to wrap round him as her body urged him closer and she arched her hips.

His mouth found hers once more, his lips warm and firm, and as his tongue thrust a path into her inner sweetness he possessed her to the full, the sensation extremely satisfying. He waited one moment, while her body adjusted to the swollen hardness of him, and then began to thrust strongly, building their shared excitement as the pleasure became almost unbearable in its intensity.

When the moment of climax came Melody thought she would shatter into a million pieces, her muscles contracting so violently that Zeke reached his peak a second later, his body shuddering as he groaned her name. And when the pulsing of their flesh quietened he collapsed on top of her, burying his face in the curve of her throat as he murmured her name again, his voice tender and soft.

It was a while before he half lifted himself on one elbow, studying her flushed face as he said lazily, "Wow. If this is what a period of abstinence does, it's not all bad." He smoothed a lock of hair from one cheek, his tough light. "You're something else, woman."

"You're not so bad yourself," she managed fairly normally, thankful his mood was so relaxed and light-hearted. She couldn't have handled any more soul-searching right at this moment. A part of her knew that Zeke would see their making love as a means of putting everything right between them, but she would deal with that when she had to.

He pulled the duvet over them both, tucking her against him with his arm round her shoulders. "How can even a hotel room become home when you're with the person you love, whereas our house was just bricks and mortar with you gone? It's made me realise I could live in a mud hut and be perfectly happy if you were there."

Melody forced a creditable laugh. "I can't see you in a mud hut—not unless it was fitted with internet access and enough mod-cons to let you keep your finger on the pulse."

There was a moment of vibrating silence before Zeke shifted, lifting her chin so he could meet her eyes. "Is that so?" he said lazily. "If someone heard that who didn't know me they'd think I was a control freak."

She never had known when he was joking, and she didn't now. She looked at him for several long seconds before she saw the twinkle in his eye. "Oh, you," she murmured weakly, snuggling into the side of him.

"Actually, you've got me all wrong." He kissed the top of her head, his voice rumbling deep inside his chest where she pressed her face against his torso. "Like I said to you before, my work doesn't control me. It never has. I do what I do because I enjoy it and because it has been fulfilling on the whole. Sometimes a situation has gripped me and I've put too much effort in for too little reward, but not often. Other times I've made mistakes. Like the time I cancelled a certain luncheon engagement because of a crisis that I thought only I could solve. Biggest mistake of my life."

He paused, his voice wry when he said, "Maybe there has been a touch of control freak there after all, but no more."

A leopard couldn't change its spots, and why should Zeke change, anyway? She had known what she was getting into when she'd married him after all. But things had been different then. She had been different. And she couldn't go back to how she'd been.

Suddenly all the reasons why it had been madness to sleep with him again were there, panic coursing through her as she realised what she'd done. She wasn't aware that she had tensed or changed her position in any way, but she must have done, because his voice was deep and expressionless when he said, "What's the matter? You're retreating again."

She wriggled out of his arms, swinging her legs over the side of the bed as she said, "Don't be silly. I—I need the bathroom." She looked for her pyjamas, but the items of clothing scattered on the floor all looked the same in the shadows. The thought of walking to the *en-suite* naked was unthinkable. What if he put the main lights on or followed her? But she couldn't sit there all night. The thoughts flowed with the swiftness of terror. And if she started scrabbling about for her pyjamas she'd look ridiculous.

"Dee?" He touched her back and she flinched. "Have I said something? I was trying to be honest."

"It's fine." Even to herself her voice sounded brittle. Knowing she had to do something, and fast, she stood up and practically ran to his bathroom, shutting the door behind her and leaning against it for a moment before grabbing the white towelling hotel robe from the back of it and sliding it on. Jerking the belt tight, she shut her eyes in relief, her breath expelling in a deep sigh. She was safe. He hadn't seen her.

She had known Zeke would follow. When a tap came at the door her eyes opened. "Dee? Are you okay?" he called softly.

She pulled the belt tighter. "Yes, I'm fine."

"I don't believe you." His voice was strained.

"I'm all right, I promise. I just need a minute, that's all. Please, Zeke. I'll be out in a moment."

There was a pause, and she could almost hear his mind whirring. Then his voice came quiet and steady. "I'll get us a drink. What would you like? Wine? Fruit juice? Or coffee, tea, hot chocolate? There's plenty in the fridge as well as hot drinks."

Numbly, she forced her lips to move. "A coffee. Thanks."

"Don't be long." A pause. "I miss you already."

She waited until she was sure he'd gone and then turned on the light, staring at her reflection in the mirror over the wash basin. A wild-eyed, pale-faced woman stared back at her and she barely recognised herself in the haunted features.

What had she done? *What had she done?* And what sort of message had sleeping with him sent to Zeke? No, Zeke, I don't want to stay married to you. Oh, yes, Zeke, you can take me to bed. No, Zeke, there's no future for us. Oh, yes, Zeke, the more intimate we are the better.

She sat down on the edge of the bath, her fingers pressing tight into her closed eyelids as though she could shut out the memory of the past hour, erase it from her mind by an iron will. But of course that was impossible. She'd done some stupid things in her life but this went far beyond stupid. Infinitely beyond. It was cruel and selfish and unreasonable and totally unforgivable. He would hate her now and she didn't blame him.

She was still berating herself when another tap came at the door. Zeke's voice was light, with a thread of steel. "If you don't come out, I'm coming in."

Her hands tightened on the edge of the bath and then she stood up, opening the door. "I was just coming."

"I thought you'd prefer coffee in the sitting room," Zeke said coolly. He was wearing the black silk pyjama bottoms and nothing else, and he looked hard and tough and sexy, his hair ruffled and his eyes ebony-dark as they scoured her face. "And then perhaps you can tell me why you left our bed like a scalded cat. I was under the mistaken impression it'd been great."

His words caught her on the raw, but at least the dose of adrenaline provided the strength she needed to face him. "Firstly, it's not our bed. It's yours," she pointed out, sailing past him and making her way into the sitting room. "Secondly, I did not leave like a scalded cat or a scalded anything."

She glanced at the coffee table, where coffee and a plate of biscuits were waiting, a sofa pulled close, and then walked across to the window, opening the curtains and looking out. It was snowing again—beautiful, starry flakes that whirled and danced as though they were enjoying their brief life to the full.

She was aware of Zeke coming up behind her and then his arms enclosed her. Her back rested against his chest and his chin nuzzled her hair. "Okay, let's have it," he said softly. "I've got the message that all is not yet resolved."

She didn't know how to say it. "I—I don't want you to get the wrong idea," she said lamely, hating herself.

"Lady, I don't know if I'm on foot or horseback," he drawled with dark amusement, "so the wrong idea's the least of it. That *was* you I made love with a while ago, wasn't it? You haven't got a clone who doubles for you now and again?"

"What I mean is—"

"What you mean," he interrupted, turning her round to face him but still keeping her in the circle of his arms, "is that in spite of having your wicked way with me you are still holding to this ridiculous notion of a divorce. Correct?"

She couldn't tell if he was furious and hiding it extremely well, or if the slightly sardonic attitude was for real. Zeke was a master of the inscrutable. Warily, she nodded.

"Okay. So you've got that off your chest. Drink your coffee."

He had to take this seriously. "Zeke, you have to understand—"

He stopped her with a breath-stealing kiss. "Come and have your coffee and biscuits. And then we're going to talk some. We should probably have talked before we finished up in the bedroom, but I never did profess to be perfect."

"There's nothing to say," she protested helplessly.

"There's plenty. Let me put it this way, Dee. Until you can convince me it's over, it's not over."

Melody stiffened in defence of his arrogance, her hands pushing against the wall of his chest. "Let me go."

"Sure." She was free immediately. "But you still have to convince me. You're part of me, Dee. One half of the whole. I have certain rights. You married me, remember?"

"You talk as if you own me." She was shaking inside, his closeness a sweet torment, but she knew if she didn't attack she would be lost. "Do you know that? Is that what you believe?"

"Only in as much as you own me," he said softly. "It works both ways. You gave me your love and so that's mine—as my love is yours. The difference between us is that I trust you. I trust you with everything I am and everything I have. But you're not there yet, are you? There's still a question mark hanging over my head like the sword of Damocles. True trust involves commitment, becoming vulnerable, Dee. It can make you feel exposed and frightened. Oh, yes, it can. Don't look at me like that. Do you think you're the only one who's scared rigid at the enormity of what true love and trust involves? But it's worth it. In the long run, it's worth it."

She shook her head, unaware of the tears coursing down her face until he stepped forward and stroked the moisture away with his fingers. "It's going to be okay," he reassured her very quietly, his eyes dark and steady. "You're a good person and so am I. In fact I'm a great person. We're destined to be together."

It was so silly that she had to smile, as he'd meant her to. "I don't want to hurt you," she whispered, in such a low voice he could barely hear her, "but better that now than later. This—us—it's impossible, Zeke."

He drew her over to the sofa, pushing her down and handing her a coffee made from the complementary tray left in the room. "This is your night." He put a biscuit in the saucer of her cup. "A night that laughs at the impossible. Only believe."

That was just it. She couldn't. Melody put the cup to her lips, not even noticing the milk was the long-life sort that she hated. She couldn't believe any more.

Chapter 9

They sipped their coffee in silence, eating the biscuits automatically. Melody didn't want to talk and start the process of discussion again. There was nothing more to be said. She was so tired—not the physical, bone-weary kind she'd experienced earlier, but tired in her spirit. Arguments and counter-arguments—she had been going over them in her head for weeks alone in her hospital bed. There was nothing new Zeke could say that she hadn't already considered. She was all reasoned out.

"Let's go and build a snowman."

If Zeke had said *Let's take a trip to the moon tonight,* Melody couldn't have stared at him with more amazement. "What?"

"A snowman." He pointed to the window. "The hotel has a tiny courtyard that the restaurant looks out on, with a tree and some bushes in it. We could build a snowman." He grinned at her. "Let's live dangerously. What do you say?"

"We couldn't." She shook her head. "Everyone's asleep. It's probably locked. They wouldn't allow us to do that."

"There'll be someone on Reception." He pulled her to her feet. "I fancy being out in the fresh air for a while."

So did she. Months of being shut in the antiseptic confines of the hospital had been stifling. "They'll think we're mad."

"They're entitled to their opinion." He bent his head and kissed her once, hard. "Get dressed in warm clothes. Unless..." he paused as something occurred to him "...you're too tired?"

He meant unless her legs were paining her, Melody thought. And they were, a little, but not half so much as they had in the hospital, when she'd had nothing to think about but how she felt. A feeling of recklessness took hold. "No, I'm not tired."

"Come on then. We'll build our very own Frosty for posterity."

"I hate to remind you, but it'll melt within days."

"Ah, but the memory won't," he said, as they left the sitting room for their respective bedrooms. "And I for one happen to believe that all snowmen come alive the moment they're alone. He'll make the most of his short sojourn here."

"You're crazy," she said, laughing. This was all very un-Zeke-like. "Absolutely crazy. Do you know that?"

"No, just grateful." His voice was suddenly serious. "A few months back they were telling me to prepare myself for the worst on that first night they got you into hospital. That kind of experience has a way of making you sort out what's important in life and what's not. You think everything is under control, that you have the future mapped out in nice neat compartments, and then you realise it can change in a moment of time. We're so fragile, us human beings. We break easily."

"Especially in an altercation with a lorry," Melody put in dryly, not wanting to continue along that route. "There is something to be said for the olden days, when it was just horses and carts and Shanks's pony. A wheel over your foot wouldn't have been so bad."

"I guess." He smiled, the glint of laugher back in his eyes. "Although I got kicked by a horse as a child and it's less than pleasant. I was black and blue for weeks."

There were so many things she didn't know about him. Why it was suddenly so important that she hadn't known about the boyhood incident Melody didn't know, but it was. She turned, opening her bedroom door, and once inside the room dressed quickly in several layers.

The hotel staff would think they'd taken leave of their senses, she thought, as she finally pulled on her thick coat and a woolly hat and scarf. But this beat the many nights in hospital when she'd watched each long hour creep by while the rest of the world slept. Everything was so black in the early hours when you were wide awake and hurting, so hopeless and daunting.

Perhaps she had thought too much? She nodded mentally to the notion. But how could you turn your mind off when sleep wouldn't come? She had refused sleeping pills; she had been on enough medication in the initial days following the accident to last her a lifetime. So drugged up she remembered nothing.

So stop thinking now. Again she nodded mentally. What had that little Irish nurse with the bubbly personality used to say to her? Oh, yes. "Go with the flow." And if the flow tonight was behaving like a pair of kids, so be it.

Zeke was waiting for her when she left her room, and once in the lift he dropped a feather-light kiss on her nose. "You look about ten years old in that hat." He flicked the bobbles with one finger. "All bright-eyed and bushy-tailed."

She smiled. Zeke just looked drop-dead gorgeous. "And is

that good or bad?" she asked lightly, openly fishing for compliments.

"Oh, good—definitely good. I was half expecting you to
change your mind about the snowman, to be honest." He
smiled. "You're always such a stickler for not rocking the boat
and playing safe. I didn't think you'd dare face the hotel staff."

Was she? She stared at him. Probably. Another ghost from
her childhood she'd brought with her into adulthood. Her
grandmother had definitely been of the old brigade who believed children should be seen and not heard. Part of what had
attracted her to Zeke in the beginning was his absolute refusal
to accept boundaries, both from outside and within. "Life isn't
a bowl of cherries in spite of what the old song said," he had
told her once. "It's what you make it, and to win you have to
take life by the throat sometimes and force it into submission.
Rolling over and playing dead gets you nowhere."

She hadn't known if she agreed with him at the time, but
tonight she knew she did. Keeping her voice light, she said,
"It's not exactly on a par with climbing Mount Everest or
journeying down the Amazon, is it? Building a snowman!"

"It's all relative," he declared firmly. "One man—or woman's—snowman is another person's Mount Everest."

The lift doors opened into Reception and he took her hand
as they walked across to the desk where the night staff, a porter and a receptionist, were sitting. They looked up in surprise. "Can I help you, sir?" the receptionist asked politely,
professional to the core.

Zeke smiled sweetly. "We want to build a snowman," he
said blandly. "In your courtyard. I trust that's okay?"

The receptionist blinked, but recovered almost immediately. She knew who Zeke James was, and it had caused quite
a buzz that he was staying at their hotel with his poor wife

who had nearly died in that awful accident three months ago. The manager had made it quite clear that whatever Mr and Mrs James wanted, they got. "Certainly, sir," she purred smoothly. "Michael will unlock the door to the courtyard for you. Is there anything you need to—" her pause was infinitesimal "—build your snowman?"

Zeke considered for a moment. "A hat and scarf would be great. And perhaps a carrot and something for his eyes? You know the sort of thing. Oh, and something that'd do for buttons."

The receptionist nodded efficiently, and Melody had to bite her lip to stop herself laughing. This was going to be such a good story for the girl among the other staff. The eccentric millionaire to the hilt. She could bring this one out at dinner parties for years to come.

When the said Michael escorted them into the courtyard, which was three or four inches deep in snow, it had stopped snowing. The night was bitterly cold, but crisp and exhilarating, and although the odd window or two which overlooked the courtyard in the hotel glowed dimly, most of them were in darkness. "I'll go and sort out those items you wanted, sir," the porter said, obviously tickled pink by the proceedings. "Lost property should provide the hat and scarf. In these days of political correctness I'd better ask—is the intended snowman male or female? I wouldn't like to presume the gender."

Zeke smiled. "I think we'll build one of each. How's that?"

"Right you are, sir. Very wise, if I may say so."

As the man bustled away, Melody caught Zeke's eye. "They think we're oddballs. You know that, don't you?"

His smile widened, his voice serene. "I prefer idiosyncratic myself—and why shouldn't we make the most of it? We've had plenty of winters where it's been damp and wet and miserable in this country. This is—" he paused, staring up into the dark sky above them and then at the white crystallized tree the courtyard contained, made beautiful by its blanket of glistening snow "—special. A night in a million, don't you think?"

He was right. It was. The whole night was special. Special and poignant and unbearably precious. Melody pulled her gloves farther over her wrists. "Let's get building," she suggested matter-of-factly, praying he hadn't noticed the tears pricking at the back of her eyes. "Our offspring are waiting to be born."

She wished she hadn't said that as soon as the words were out of her mouth. It suggested a permanence which could never be now. But he didn't appear to notice, and soon they were busy with the job in hand. It was hard work, but fun, and she didn't think she had laughed so much for years. The porter returned with the things they'd asked for and then stayed to help for a while. They learnt he had a wife and eight children and twenty-four grandchildren, which was a little staggering, and that every Christmas they all descended for Christmas Day lunch and tea.

"It's mayhem," he said cheerfully. "Absolute mayhem. But the missus is only truly happy when the brood's around. Some women are like that, aren't they? Natural mothers."

Melody smiled and nodded, but his words had struck a chord in her which had been bothering her for a while. Before the accident she had always assumed that eventually she and Zeke would have children, but she had been content to put it to the back of her mind. The act of bringing a child into the world was a huge responsibility, she'd told herself in the rare moments when she'd dwelt on the possibility, and both parents had to be ready for it otherwise it could cause havoc between a couple.

Like it had between her mother and father. Her father had left without even seeing his child, abandoning her mother because he couldn't or wouldn't grow up enough to be a father and husband. And she knew her grandfather had blamed her grandmother for being too tied up with their daughter and neglecting him. Her grandmother had told her that herself. *And so, deep in the hidden part of her, she had reconciled herself to not having children. That was the truth of it.*

She stopped what she was doing and stared at Zeke. And now the very thing she'd decided against was a torment of what she had lost. She wanted his babies. She wanted to have a part of him. Why hadn't she realised it before it was too late? Why hadn't she faced some of those issues and brought them to light? And how could she have been so mixed up for so long without knowing it? Surely other people weren't like her?

"What?" Zeke had been busy rolling a head for the first snowman but now he straightened, his breath a white mist in the freezing air. "What is it? What's the matter?"

Melody came out of the maelstrom of her thoughts, forcing a smile. "Nothing," she said lightly. "I was just wondering what those little girls we met earlier will say when they see our snow couple in the morning. Perhaps we should build two little ones too. They'd like that. A snow family, like them."

His eyes narrowed in the way they did when he knew she was prevaricating, but with someone else present he didn't press the issue, and soon they were engrossed in building again. The porter left to find them hot drinks after half an hour, and the two of them worked on in the crystal-clean air.

It took two hours, and several cups of hot chocolate provided by the amenable Michael, but eventually the snow family were finished.

The receptionist came to take a look, smiling at the four

figures. "They're kind of cute," she said, stifling a yawn. "Especially the children. Shame they won't last for ever."

Zeke grinned. "Thanks for providing the necessary extras." He turned to Michael, who had joined her. "I hope we haven't kept you from more important things."

The porter smiled back. "What could be more important than a family at Christmas? Even if it is a snow one!" he said quietly. "Happy Christmas to you, sir. Madam."

The two hotel staff went back into the warmth, leaving them to survey their handiwork for a moment or two. "That was quite profound," Zeke said lazily. "I think Michael has hidden depths." He took her arm. "Come on, let's get you back inside."

Although her face was rosy with the cold, Melody didn't feel chilled in herself, and she found she didn't want the magical interlude to end. It was Christmas Day, and later in the morning she would walk out of Zeke's life for ever. The break would have to be final, clean and sharp. There could be no meeting up for civilised lunches or dinners, none of the "we're still good friends" scenarios people they knew indulged in. The past hours had shown her that.

Zeke was irresistible. To her, anyway. To be with him was to want him in every way possible, and so the only option was to remove temptation once and for all. It was quite simple, really.

As they stepped into the heated confines of the hotel from the bitterly cold air outside she shivered convulsively, but the sudden chill was in the essence of her rather than the change in temperature. The night would soon be over.

"You've got cold." Zeke's voice was concerned. "We stayed out too long. I wasn't thinking. I'll run you a bath when we get back to the suite. You need to get warm."

"No, it's fine." How did you tell the man you loved with all your heart you were leaving? Perhaps you didn't. Maybe the best thing to do was to disappear when the opportunity presented itself? It would avoid the trauma of a final goodbye.

Coward. The accusation was loud in her head and she couldn't argue with it. She was a coward. If she wasn't, she would take the gamble of staying around and seeing what happened.

They reached the lift, and as the doors were closing Zeke curved his arms round her waist. "We're both cold," he murmured huskily. "How about a shower for two, like the old days?"

Her heart stopped and then raced, but through the panic something was clear. She couldn't hide any more. This had always had to happen for him to accept what she had been trying to tell him. He had to see her as she was now—scars and all. She'd had a romantic, idealised idea of leaving him with the image of how she had been—but, Zeke being Zeke, he was never going to let her go if she didn't bare all. Literally. This was necessary, essential. *But, oh, please, don't let me see his face when he looks at me,* she added silently. She wouldn't be able to stand it.

She bent her head, her forehead resting on his wet jacket. "Your room or mine?" she whispered, keeping her voice steady.

"You choose," he said softly, hugging her tight.

"Yours." That way she could leave and find sanctuary in her own room when she needed to. An escape route.

He lifted her chin, kissing her long and hard on the mouth. They were still kissing when the lift doors opened, and he kept his arm round her as they walked into the sitting room of their suite. "Let's get these wet clothes off you," he said softly, helping her shrug off her thick jacket and taking her hat, scarf and soaking gloves before pulling off his own. Then he took her cold hand, leading her out of the sitting room and into the corridor towards his bedroom without speaking.

Once inside he went into the bathroom and turned on the water in the shower cubicle. When he returned to the bedroom Melody was standing exactly where he had left her, limbs frozen in fear and embarrassment at the thought of undressing.

"Now to get you all warm and snug again." He pulled off his jeans, T-shirt and jumper as he spoke, discarding his socks and pants and standing stark naked before her with a supreme disregard of his nudity. He had always been very comfortable with his own body, which didn't make this any easier.

Whether he sensed how she was feeling, Melody wasn't sure, but he didn't attempt to undress her as she had been expecting. Instead he turned and went back into the bathroom, calling over his shoulder, "Come and join me when you're ready. I'll make sure the water's not too hot."

She remained perfectly still for a moment, and then feverishly began to disrobe before she lost her nerve. The bedroom was dimly lit by the same bedside lamp as before, but the bathroom light was stronger, more unforgiving. Once she had shed her clothes she forced herself to move the few steps to the bathroom, her legs wooden. *Get it over with,* she told herself. *Just do it.*

Zeke was in the shower with his back to her, and the air was already steamy because he'd left the door ajar. She stepped into the shower and he turned immediately, wrapping his arms around her. He was already warm and her skin felt icy cold in comparison.

"Just get acclimatised for a minute," he said huskily, his

hands massaging her slender back and shoulderblades. "You'll soon warm up, I promise. You're frozen right through."

Locked together as they were, Melody felt she'd had a moment's reprieve. The spray poured down mostly on Zeke, and after a minute or two he turned her round so the water hit the back of her head in a tingling flood. His hand reached for the shower gel and he poured a little into his palms, lathering it before running his hands over her shoulders and down her arms in firm gentle movements. "Nice?" he whispered throatily in her ear.

Her nerves were pulled as tight as piano wire, and for the life of her she couldn't reply. He turned her again, his long fingers stroking the white foam across her breasts in slow, sweet languid caresses meant to arouse her, and—in spite of her thudding heart—she felt her nipples tighten under his light touch. Feeling her response, he cupped her breasts in his hands, his thumbs drawing circles round the rosy-pink peaks until they were swollen and aching and she had to bite into her lower lip not to moan out loud. He was so, so good at this.

"So delicious," Zeke murmured huskily, his mouth finding her eyelids, her nose, and then her lips in a scorching kiss. "Feeling warmer?"

Unable to speak, Melody managed to nod her head, memories crowding in of times in the past when they had showered together—intimate, precious times. Times of loving and laughter.

With his eyes holding her wide green ones, Zeke lathered his hands again, running them slowly across her belly and then over the rounded swell of her bottom as he moved her sensuously against his hardness. She knew he must have felt the scars at the bass of her spine, but he didn't pause before sliding his fingers over her skin to find the golden curls at the apex of her thighs, his gaze never leaving hers.

Slowly she began to relax, the warm water and his caresses bringing a pleasure that quenched the panic. The worst scars were grooved in the tops of her legs, and standing wrapped together as they were he couldn't see them. For now that was all that mattered. The moment would come, but not just yet.

She reached for the shower gel, her voice soft as she whispered, "My turn," longing to run her hands over his body.

"By all means." His voice was thick with passion and his body demonstrated how much he wanted her, his breathing ragged and his manhood as hard as a rock.

Melody began by soaping the hair-roughened expanse of his muscled chest, flattening her palms over his nipples and rubbing the hard little nubs slowly as she watched his reaction. She took her time, loving the feel of his male flesh, and when her hands slid lower his stomach muscles bunched. Then she found the steely length of his manhood, causing him to gasp as he pulled her closer. "Hell, Dee," he muttered thickly.

"I haven't finished," she protested faintly, wanting him as much as he wanted her and knowing she couldn't wait either.

"Sweetheart, I appreciate the fact you think I'm a control freak, but believe me, I know my limitations," Zeke said shakily, reaching behind him and turning off the shower. He propelled her out of the cubicle, grabbing two towels off the bath rail and wrapping one round Melody and the other one around his hips.

He pulled her into the darkened bedroom, turning and taking her into his arms as he kissed her hungrily, the towels sliding from their bodies as they fell on the bed. Their bodies were still damp, their hair dripping, but nothing mattered but sating the fierce desire burning between them.

Zeke's hands moved over her feverishly, as though he couldn't get enough of the feel of her, his lips finding the warm pulse in her throat, the rounded swell of her breasts and their swollen peaks, the velvet skin of her belly. When he entered her their bodies moved in a perfect rhythm, building their shared sensation until his final thrust sent them spinning into another world—a world of ecstasy and untold pleasure and splintered light. Melody clung to him, not wanting the moment to end, knowing it would be the last time they'd be like this.

"I love you." He moved slightly, relieving her of his weight but still keeping his arms round her as he fitted her into his side, pulling the duvet over them.

"I love you." She could say that and mean it, but her voice was thick with the knowledge that she was going to lose him. "So much. Always remember that."

Zeke fell asleep quite quickly, but although she was utterly exhausted Melody couldn't doze off. She lay in his arms, warmly relishing the closeness as her thoughts tortured her. They had made love for a second time and he still hadn't seen what the lorry had done to the once perfect body he had so adored. She had thought the moment had come, and although she had been terrified there had been an element of relief there too. But she'd had yet another reprieve.

She shivered, the slight movement causing Zeke to tighten his embrace in his sleep, but after another moment she carefully extricated herself from his arms and crept out of bed. The hotel room was warm and her hair was almost dry already, but again she felt a shudder run through her.

Quietly she left his bedroom and made her way to her own after picking up her clothes. Once there, she pulled on a pair of leggings and a warm thigh-length top, brushing her hair into submission and then securing it in a high ponytail at the back of her head. Then she walked over to the window and looked out.

It was five o'clock in the morning on Christmas Day. The night hours were almost over. In a little while children all over the country would be waking up to see what Father Christmas had brought them. Houses and flats and apartments would be filled with excitement and noise, and later families would gather together for Christmas lunch. Mothers would be harassed and flushed from working in the kitchen and keeping over-exuberant offspring from raiding their selection boxes, fathers would be playing host and plying visitors with pre-lunch drinks, and grandparents would be arriving with that extra-special present their grandchildren thought Father Christmas had forgotten.

It was a day of busyness and joy and elation, of eating and drinking too much, playing silly games and watching TV. That was normal, the way people did things—only she had never had that experience as a child. Her grandmother had been of the old school. One small stocking hung on the mantelpiece, containing an orange, a monetary gift and a small toy, had been her lot, and Christmas Day had been like any other day except they'd had turkey for lunch followed by Christmas pud. They had spent it alone, and although her grandmother must have received Christmas cards she couldn't remember any. Certainly there had been no decorations nor a tree. After her grandmother had died and she'd been invited to friends' houses for the Christmas break she had been amazed at the furore and excitement, at the sheer pleasure everyone got from the day. It had been a revelation of what Christmas could be.

Why was she thinking of this now? she asked herself, gazing out over the snow-covered buildings beyond the hotel, their rooftops white against the black sky. The past was the past and it didn't do to dwell on it. Her grandmother had done her best and she had always known her grandmother loved her in her own way. She had been fortunate compared to some. Zeke, for instance.

She moved restlessly, suddenly aware of why her thoughts had taken such a turn. Deep inside she had always known Zeke was her chance of experiencing what other people took as ordinary family life. There had been a part of her that had hoped they could create their own world within the world—a place where children could be born and loved and protected, where all the things they'd both missed in their childhood could be given to their babies. She had hoped, but always not quite convinced herself.

And she had never believed she was good enough for him. So she had held back on total commitment, subconsciously waiting for the time when the bubble would burst. She had always been striving towards an unattainable pinnacle of perfection, and although he had taken her as his wife and loved her she hadn't felt she was the best person for him.

Maybe if she had known her mother and father it would have been different—or her mother at least. She had always felt there was so much missing in her background, and her grandmother had been chary about discussing anything. Even the briefest sojourn into the past had brought such bitterness and pain on her grandmother's side she hadn't felt she could press for more. And so she'd grown up wondering, all the time wondering, without any answers about the people who had given her life.

Melody closed her eyes, wrapping her arms round her middle as she shook her head slowly. All this wasn't really relevant to what she was facing now. She was a grown woman of twenty-seven and she had to move on. She had to leave Zeke—go somewhere far away, get a job and carve out some sort of a life for herself. Her thoughts ran through her head, a silent litany. She had told herself the same thing so many times in the past three months, willing herself on.

She couldn't change her mind now. She opened her eyes, beginning to pace the room. She couldn't—didn't dare—let herself imagine anything different, because where would she be then? This way she knew what she was taking on and there was a strange comfort in that, somehow. She'd survive.

She stopped abruptly, feeling as though the walls of the room were pressing in on her. She had always hated small spaces. That had been part of the nightmare of staying in hospital—the feeling of absolute confinement. She needed to get out and walk. It was the only way she could think.

She didn't hesitate. Grabbing a pair of socks from her case, which she still hadn't unpacked, she walked silently into the sitting room and found her coat, hat and scarf, pulling on her boots which were still damp from the snowman exercise. Her gloves she left. They were so sodden she was better off without them.

Slipping the key to the suite in her handbag, she opened the door to the corridor outside and made her way to the lift. When the doors glided open at Reception her heart was thudding. She didn't know what she was going to say to Michael or the receptionist. But as luck would have it Michael was nowhere to be seen and the receptionist was on the phone. She walked quickly across the tiled floor and out of the main doors, giving a sigh of relief when she was in the street.

The cold took her breath away after she had warmed up so nicely, but she walked on. The snow banked either side of the pavement so there was a path in the middle, and she had no trouble reaching the main thoroughfare. She hadn't expected any traffic, it being Christmas Day, but already the city had awoken and yawned life into its inhabitants, and there was the odd person walking here and there, and cars on the roads.

Melody walked with no clear idea of where she was going, taking care to tread carefully. In spite of everything a little frisson of exhilaration curled down her spine. This was the first time she had been out under her own steam—properly out—since the accident, and the independence was heady. It felt good to be part of the human race again.

Although it was still dark, the streetlights combined with the effect of the snow lit up her surroundings perfectly well. She pulled her hat farther down over her ears—it really was bitterly cold—and marched on, wondering why she didn't feel tired. She had felt exhausted yesterday afternoon, and again in the taxi coming back from the theatre, but now she felt as though she could walk for miles.

In spite of coming outside to consider her position with Zeke and what she was going to do, she didn't think as she walked along. She merely breathed in the icy air, luxuriating in the way her face was tingling and the feel of the morning on her skin.

She was alive. She hadn't died under the wheels of that lorry and she wasn't paralysed or confined to a wheelchair. She was lucky. She was so, so lucky. Zeke had been right, and Mr Price too, when they'd said she was better off than lots of the other patients at the hospital.

It was possibly only half an hour later when she realised she needed to sit awhile. Walking in the thick, crunchy snow was more difficult than on clear pavements, and now that the first flush of elation had dwindled exhaustion was paramount. Mr Price had warned her against doing too much initially, she thought ruefully. It would seem he knew her better than she knew herself—which wasn't difficult.

Hyde Park stretched out to the left of her, the trees a vision of Christmas beauty with their mantle of glittering white, but, deciding it was sensible to stay on the main road, she resisted the impulse to wander in. Instead she brushed the snow off a bench on the pavement overlooking the park and sat down.

A young couple meandered by, wrapped in each other's arms, the girl's ponytail tied with bright red tinsel, a thick strand of which was looped round her boyfriend's neck like a scarf. They smiled at Melody, the girl calling, "Happy Christmas!" before they ambled on, giggling as they stumbled in the snow.

They probably hadn't gone home yet from some Christmas Eve party or other they'd attended, Melody thought, watching the pair walk on. She suddenly felt aeons old, their carefree faces emphasising her staidness.

She'd never really gone to parties—not until she had met Zeke, that was. Her grandmother hadn't approved of what she'd classified "aimless frivolity", and even at dance school and in the years following she had preferred to spend any free time practising her dance moves rather than anything else.

No, that wasn't exactly true. Melody frowned as the thought hit. She had always felt guilty if she considered going to parties or get-togethers, knowing the sacrifices her grandmother had undoubtedly made to provide the money for her to follow her chosen career. Add that to the fact that she'd invariably felt like a fish out of water, and had tried to hide herself away in a corner on the rare occasion she'd been persuaded to accompany one of her friends to a shindig, it was no wonder she hadn't been asked much. She'd never felt quite able to let her hair down.

And then Zeke had swept into her life, turning it upside down and challenging all the rules she'd lived by. Her heart thudded, panic uppermost, but she wasn't sure if it was the thought of walking away from him that caused the churning or the fact of how stupid she had been in not making the most of these past few hours when she could still touch and caress him. Why was she sitting on a bench in the middle of a London street when she could be in his arms? Time was so short.

Her toes clenched in her boots but she remained sitting where she was and gradually the panic subsided. She was here because she needed to think. She had been thinking non-stop since the accident, but not coolly or unemotionally. Anything but. She had been jolted to her core and every single thing in her life had been shaken.

It might have been better if she'd been allowed to cry, to sob and howl the frustration and pain at what the accident had taken away from her out of her system, but she had learnt early on that crying unsettled and disturbed the nursing staff. She supposed it had disempowered them in some way, made them feel they weren't doing their job, and because they had all been wonderful to her she'd repressed her grief and got on with the process of building her body. It had satisfied them at least.

A gust of wind feathered the snow on a tree inside the park, missing the ones on either side. She stared at the cascade of white as the cold chilled her skin.

How many times had she asked herself, why her? Why had she had this happen to her? Why had the one thing in her life she was any good at been taken from her? But it was useless thinking like that—as useless as that tree complaining to the wind. *And it wasn't even true.* She was beginning to see that.

Melody was getting cold, but she still sat, her thoughts buzzing. Dancing had been her whole life from as long as she could remember, but that didn't mean she wouldn't be good at something else if she tried. She just never had. Although she might not be able to dance any more, she could teach. At the back of her mind she had always imagined herself doing that one day, just not so soon. She'd thought she would ease herself into it, not have it presented as a *fait accompli*. But why fight it? The accident had happened. End of story.

And Zeke? Could Zeke possibly fit into this new life?

It was as though a separate part of herself was speaking, forcing her to confront the real issue.

It was one thing to decide their marriage was over in the clinical unreal surroundings of the hospital, where life was measured in the regimented hours of an institution, quite another when she was presented by Zeke himself. Dancing had been a vital part of her life, but Zeke—Zeke had been her world. From the first date they'd enjoyed each other's company more than anyone else's, and the intimate side of their relationship had been everything she could have wanted and more. He'd been affectionate and tactile on a day-to-day basis too, often sending her texts out of the blue to say he was thinking of her, and meeting her out of work for lunch or in the evening when she wasn't expecting it.

Her mind grappled with the memories pouring in now she had allowed the floodgates to open. Making love till dawn. Walking on the beach at midnight at the villa in Madeira. Zeke at the stove, cooking breakfast as naked as the day he was born. The list was endless, and after keeping such a tight rein on her mind for the past months she was now powerless to stop the tide. She simply sat, her head spinning and her thoughts bringing a spiralling vortex of emotion that made it difficult to breathe as the sky lightened and dawn began to break.

A new day was dawning, but Melody was anchored to the

past, and in spite of her brave thoughts about the future she simply couldn't see a way forward which included Zeke. Their life had been in the spotlight, and because of who he was and the business he'd built up so painstakingly it would continue to be. And something fundamental had changed in her.

Could they function together as a couple, with Zeke living his life and her living a completely different one? Separate not just in their work but in their social life too? She didn't think so. It was a recipe for disaster, however you looked at it.

And so she continued to sit under a pearly white sky, a small figure all alone, huddled up on her bench.

Chapter 10

"Now, I could be wrong, but something tells me you could do with a nice cup of tea, dear. You look frozen to death."

For a moment Melody couldn't focus on the small plump woman who had sat down beside her on the bench, an equally small and plump dog flopping at his owner's feet. She stared into the rosy face vacantly. "I'm sorry?" she murmured.

"I walked by this way a little while ago—my Billy still has to have his morning constitutional whether it's Christmas Day or not—and I saw you then. It's a mite cold to be sitting for long, isn't it, dear?" The bright brown eyes were penetrating, but kind. "You all right? You look all done in."

Melody tried to pull herself together. Now she had come back to the real world she realised she was absolutely frozen to the core. Her reply of, "I'm fine, thank you", was somewhat spoilt by the convulsive shiver which accompanied it.

It seemed to have decided her Good Samaritan. The little woman clucked her tongue before saying, "I always have a cup of tea once I get in, and my place is just across there, dear. Why don't you come in and warm up before you get yourself home?"

"No—no, thank you." Melody forced a smile as she stood up, only to find she was as stiff as a board. "You're very kind but I'm perfectly all right. I—I was just sitting awhile."

"You don't look all right, if you don't mind me saying so." Obviously plain speaking was the order of the day. "You're the colour of the snow. Look, my name's Mabel, and I'm not doing anything until my son comes to collect me and Billy later this morning for Christmas lunch at his place. Lovely house he's got—all modern and open-plan, I think you call it. Wouldn't do for me—too much like living in a barn—but it suits him and his wife and the kiddies and that's all that matters. Anyway, I've got an hour or two to kill, and I could do with the company, to tell you the truth. I don't usually mind being on my own—my Billy's good company, bless him— but Christmas Day is different, isn't it? I miss my Arthur then. He died a couple of years ago and I still can't get used to it. Fifty years we were married, and childhood sweethearts. That still happened in my day. Not like now." This was followed by a loud sniff which eloquently depicted Mabel's opinion of present-day romance.

Melody moistened her lips, ready to refuse the invitation when she caught the fleeting expression in Mabel's eyes. The loneliness connected with something deep inside her, and instead she found herself saying, "If it wouldn't be any bother I'd love a cup of tea. I didn't realise how cold I'd got."

"That's right, dear." Mabel was aglow, standing up and yanking Billy—who had settled himself down for a nap—to his feet. "Nothing like a cup of tea for sorting things out— that's what I always say. The cup that cheers—that's what my Arthur said."

Mabel's house turned out to be a well-kept terraced property with an air of faded grandeur and photographs of family adorning every surface in the neat little kitchen-diner Melody was shown into. It was as warm as toast, an Aga having pride of place in the old-fashioned fireplace, and two-cushioned rocking chairs complemented the scrubbed kitchen table and four chairs tucked in one corner. There was a serenity to the house, a quietness that spoke of tranquillity rather than emptiness, which was immensely comforting. Melody had a strange sense of coming home.

"Sit yourself down, lovey." Mabel pointed to one of the rocking chairs as she spoke. Billy immediately curled up in his basket in front of the range and shut his eyes, as though to say, duties performed; do not disturb.

"Thank you." Melody sat, somewhat gingerly, and wondered how on earth she had ended up in a total stranger's house on Christmas Day morning, when Zeke was fast asleep in their suite at the hotel. At least she hoped he was asleep. Yes, he would be, she reassured herself quickly. And even if he wasn't it was too late to worry about it. She was here now.

Mabel bustled about making the tea, and when the little woman warmed the teapot and then added two teaspoonfuls of tea from a caddy before pouring hot water into the pot Melody wasn't surprised. Teabags, somehow, weren't Mabel's style.

"Here you are, dear." Mabel passed her a cup of tea with a thick slice of homemade shortbread in the saucer. "Now, why, if you don't mind me asking, was a bonny-looking girl like you sitting all by herself on Christmas morning, looking as though she'd lost a pound and found a penny?"

Melody had to smile. No one could accuse Mabel of beating about the bush. She took a sip of the scalding hot tea and then set the cup in its bone china saucer. "I don't know what to do," she said simply. "Or which way to turn."

Mabel deposited her dumpy little body in the other rocking chair and smiled placidly. "A trouble shared is a trouble halved—that's what I always say. So why don't you tell me all about it?" She took a bite of her own shortbread and indicated for Melody to try hers. "Get yourself on the other side of that, lovey, and tell me what's wrong."

"It's a long story," Melody said hesitantly.

"Then all the more reason to get on with it straight away."

The logic was irrefutable.

An hour and several cups of tea later, Melody was wondering how on earth she could have given her life story to a virtual stranger. Not only that, but she was feeling more relaxed and at home in Mabel's house than she'd felt in years.

Mabel hadn't interrupted her as she'd told her about her childhood, her teenage years, meeting Zeke and all the trauma following the accident. She had simply listened. Billy had twitched in his basket as he'd chased imaginary rabbits, making little growling noises in his sleep now and again as his paws had moved convulsively, but otherwise the kitchen had been quiet and still with no distractions.

"So…" They had sat in silence for a good ten minutes or more, and Melody was half asleep when Mabel broke the peace. "What are you going to say when you go back to the hotel?"

Melody stared at her new friend. "I don't know. What should I do?" Even to herself her voice sounded beseeching.

"I can't tell you, dear, but then you know that. This has to be your decision and yours alone. Only you know how you feel."

Disappointed, Melody straightened in her chair. "I can't stay with Zeke," she said tonelessly, pain tearing through her.

"Can't or won't?" Mabel asked calmly. "There's a difference. My Arthur and me lost five babies before we had our son. After the fifth, I said I couldn't go through it again. Arthur didn't argue with me, bless him, not even when I decided I couldn't stay here, in this house, with all the memories it held. I wanted to make a fresh start somewhere far away, I told him. Australia, perhaps. I had a brother who'd emigrated and he was doing all right. Or New Zealand, maybe. Anywhere but here, with the little room upstairs decorated as a nursery and the empty cot that had been waiting for a baby for umpteen years."

Melody was wide awake now, hanging on to Mabel's every word.

"And so I made my plans. Arthur was an engineer, very well qualified and the top of the tree in his own particular field, so we could have gone anywhere and he'd have been sure of work. My brother sent me information on some lovely houses close to where he lived, and a colleague of Arthur's had always said if we ever thought of moving he wanted first option on buying our house, so we didn't even have to worry about selling it. We said our price and he didn't quibble. Arthur gave notice at work, and everything was set for emigrating at the end of May. I remember May twenty-eighth was the day we were going to set sail. Funny how some things stay in your mind, isn't it?"

Melody nodded, transfixed by the drama of the long-ago happenings of the little woman in front of her.

"It was a lovely spring that year—soft and warm and days of endless sunshine all through April. Girls were wearing summer dresses and everyone was happy. Everyone but me.

All our plans had gone smoothly, and Arthur had a good job lined up in Australia, but I knew it wasn't right. I wanted to go, I needed to go, but it didn't feel right deep inside—here." Mabel touched her heart. "You know? I was running way. I knew it but I wouldn't admit it. And I had good reason for wanting a fresh start—heaven knows I did. I felt I couldn't bear the future if I stayed. The same cycle of hope and then crushing disappointment when my body let me down again."

Mabel leaned forward, taking one of Melody's hands between her own. "I felt such a failure, you see. Every time it happened I felt I'd let Arthur down and it was affecting our marriage. I wasn't the girl he'd married, we both knew that, and although he said he loved me just the same, and that as long as he had me it didn't matter if the children didn't come along, I didn't see it that way. I'd even thought about leaving him. He had three brothers and they all had big families, and Arthur was so good with the children—their favourite uncle. I thought if I left him he could have children with someone else."

Mabel shook her grey head, making her permed curls bob. "I was very mixed up. Confused and hurting and trying to be strong."

"Like me," Melody whispered, and Mabel squeezed her hand. "What happened? Did you get as far as trying out Australia?"

"Arthur's mother came round to see me one morning. It was at the end of April and the sun was shining. I opened the door to her and burst into tears. She stayed the whole day and we talked and talked. I'd lost my own mum years before, and I wasn't one for sharing my troubles with anyone—especially anything private-like. She said something very wise to me that day, and it was a turning point, bless her."

"What was it?" Melody was holding her breath.

"That the only thing to fear is fear itself. I fought the idea at first, telling myself I wasn't afraid, that it wasn't as simple as that. It's amazing how many reasons you can find to justify yourself when you try. But of course she was right. I was frightened of the future, of trying again, of failing, of losing Arthur's love—a whole host of things. And fear has a way of undermining every foundation in your life, of clouding every issue, especially love and trust. It blinds you."

"And so you stayed," Melody said softly. "You didn't leave."

Mabel nodded. "It wasn't a bed of roses, mind. I had to work at it every day. The worries didn't go overnight—they were too deeply ingrained, I suppose—but slowly I saw light at the end of the tunnel, and when I became pregnant again a few months later I believed it would be different and it was. Our Jack was a big strapping baby, with a pair of lungs on him to wake the dead and a smile as wide as London Bridge."

Melody smiled. "I'm glad for you, I really am, but your circumstances were different to mine."

Mabel let go of her hand, but her eyes were tight on the young face in front of her when she said, "Different circumstances, lovey, but same cause. From what you've told me your Zeke isn't about to change his mind about you because of a few scars. Not now, not ever. And you're running just the same as I tried to do, although I was going farther than you—across the other side of the world. But you could go that far and it'd be the same mistake. Because you can't outrun the fear. You take it with you. When you were talking earlier you called yourself a dancer, but that's not quite right, dear. Dancing was something you did, but it didn't sum up who you are. You're made up of a thousand and one things that make the whole, and by the sound of it that whole is what your husband loves. Same as Arthur loved me."

Melody gazed into the wrinkled face that was so kind it made her want to cry. "Zeke said something along those lines," she admitted quietly, "but I thought he was just being the dutiful husband and trying to say the right thing to comfort me."

"There's nothing wrong with that—a bit of husbandly comfort," Mabel said stoutly. "But it doesn't mean he didn't mean it. I came to realise that what doesn't break you makes you stronger, as a person and as a couple. That sounds trite, lovey, but I can say it because I've proved it. Young folk today have grown up having everything in life as instant as the coffee they drink, and when something happens that needs a bit of backbone to deal with it half of them are befuddled as to how to cope. You're not like that, and I don't think your Zeke is either."

Melody thought back over the past twenty-four hours and the hundreds of little ways Zeke had shown he loved her, and wiped a tear from her cheek. "But he hasn't seen what I look like now," she whispered. "And there's so many women out there that throw themselves at him."

"That's the fear talking again." Mabel leant forward and patted her hand briskly. "Now, I'm going to make us another cup of tea and a nice bacon sandwich before you go. Me and Arthur always used to start the day with a cup of tea and a bacon sandwich, but I've got out of the habit since he went. And Melody—" Mabel held her gaze, her voice soft "—don't expect to cross all your bridges in one fell swoop, dear. You'll have good days and bad days, but you'll win through—same as I did. It seems to me that your Zeke needs you every bit as much as you need him. Have you considered that? All those women you talk about were throwing themselves at him for years before he met you, and he didn't fall for any of them, now, did he? Believe in him, lovey. Have faith. Christmas Day is a better day than most to start doing that, don't you think?"

Melody nodded, only half convinced. She suddenly realised she needed to see Zeke again, to look into his face when he said he loved her, into his *soul*. She watched Mabel bustle about the kitchen without really focusing on her. But even that wouldn't be enough. He had to see her as she was now, and it was then she would know. She loved him so much she would be able to read what he felt about having a crippled wife. She would always walk with a limp now, always have a jerky gait, and in the immediate future there were weeks of physiotherapy in store, with possible complications in the way of arthritis and so on as she got older. Their world had been a place of beautiful people—starlets, celebrities, the rich and famous. And botox and plastic surgery when the edges began to fray.

She glanced at her watch and was amazed to see how the time had gone. It was nine o'clock. Zeke might be awake now, wondering where she was. She had to get back to the hotel.

She gulped down her bacon sandwich, anxious to be gone but not wanting to offend Mabel after all her kindness, and then hugged the little woman before she left the house.

It was bitterly cold outside, but the morning was bright, a high mother-of-pearl sky and a pale sun giving brilliance to the snow-covered world beneath. The city was properly awake now, and although it was not as busy as usual on the main roads, Melody passed lots of pedestrians picking their way along the icy pavements, some with children in tow on new bikes or scooters, which their parents were endeavouring to manipulate through the snow, panting and puffing as they urged their offspring along.

Melody was halfway back to the hotel when she caught sight of Zeke in the distance—a tall, hatless figure head and shoulders above most other folk. Even being so far away she could see his face was as black as thunder. He was angry, furious. Her heart buffeted itself against her ribcage and she stopped, watching him get nearer. He hadn't seen her yet, and she didn't know whether to wave or not. In that first moment of panic if she could have disappeared through the floor out of sight, she would have. He was clearly beside himself.

She had always tried not to upset him in the past. Confrontation of any kind had always crushed her. Not just with Zeke, with anyone, she acknowledged rawly. She had always needed people's approval, or at the very least their acceptance, and to achieve it she had sometimes stifled her own opinions or desires. Somehow the accident had changed that, and she mustn't go back to how she had been. She didn't want to do that. She straightened, her slim shoulders going back as her chin lifted.

Zeke saw her in the next instant, and even from fifty yards away she could see the relief which flooded his taut features. She swallowed, feeling her heart rate skip up another couple of notches, and began walking towards him, wondering how her life had become this constant plunging spiral of emotion. She wanted some kind of normality again. Life would never be humdrum if she stayed with Zeke, she knew that, but their day-to-day existence had been if not ordinary then part of a pattern. The times when they had been alone had not been as many as she would have liked, but there had been the nights locked in his arms when he had been all hers. If only that could happen again.

She didn't know what to expect when Zeke met her. Certainly not the blank face and the voice empty of all expression when he took her arm, saying, "Let's get back to the hotel." He suited his long stride to her shorter one, but that was the only concession he made as they negotiated their way along the snowy pavements which were lethal in places.

Melody looked up at him from under her eyelashes, her gaze registering the lines of strain round his mouth and eyes. She had been right. He was angry, but he had been worried too—as she would have been if their positions were reversed. But she'd had to get away for a while, selfish though it had been, although she couldn't expect Zeke would understand that.

"I'm sorry," she said in a small voice. "I went for a walk to think. I—I didn't mean to be so long."

"Some four hours in all, according to the receptionist who saw you leave the hotel," Zeke said silkily.

Melody winced. She would have preferred him shouting at her than his dangerously controlled soft tone. It never boded well.

"And it didn't occur to you to ring me and let me know you were all right?" he continued. "Or even turn your mobile on so I could contact you? But, no, why should it? You're totally in Melody world, aren't you? I'm merely your husband, that's all."

Melody bit her lip to stop herself firing back. He had every right to be mad. "I was fine."

"And I knew that by what? Telepathy? I had no idea where you were when I found you'd gone a couple of hours ago. I've been scouring the streets looking for you and trying to ignore the fact that the river is very deep and very cold."

"You didn't think—" She stopped, appalled he could imagine she would take her own life. "You couldn't have imagined..."

"I didn't know what to think, Melody."

The very fact he had used her full name told her he was beside himself—that and the rigidity of his features.

"I can't reach you, can I? That's the nub of the issue," he ground out flatly. "You've shut me out more effectively than I could have imagined. There's no room for me any more. We're not a couple. Perhaps we never were. Maybe all I imagined we had was just wishful thinking on my part."

She didn't know what to say. That she had hurt him to the core was very clear, but if Zeke held power over her when he was his normal confident, intense and demanding self, it was multiplied a hundred times to devastating effect in his hurt vulnerability. "I—I thought I could get back before you woke up," she said weakly, the excuse sounding lame even to her own ears. "And I didn't mean to be out for so long, but I met someone—an old lady with her dog. We—we talked for a bit."

"Really? And this old lady and her dog were such riveting company that it completely slipped your mind you had a husband who might—just might—be a tad worried that you had up and disappeared in the middle of the night to goodness knows where?"

"I can't talk to you when you're like this."

"*You* can't talk to *me*?" He gave a harsh bark of a laugh but didn't slow his footsteps or look at her. "You're priceless, do you know that? Absolutely priceless. Only you could say that."

She felt sudden tears burn her eyes, but blinked them away furiously. How ironic that just when she had begun to think they might have a chance he'd decided they were through. He had had enough and she couldn't blame him. She'd acted like a crazy woman over the past months and she couldn't— hand on heart—promise him she was any less scared of the future. He didn't have to put up with this, and why would he?

By the time they reached the hotel her legs were aching

badly from the unaccustomed exercise, but she would have walked on hot coals before showing it. They had just entered the lobby when Melody saw the Japanese family, coming from the direction of the dining room, the two little girls clutching beautifully dressed dolls and chattering away to each other. The mother smiled at Melody as they approached, clearly remembering their conversation the day before. "Santa found his way, as you can see," she said serenely, secure and content in her role as wife and mother. "And the reindeers must have enjoyed the carrots because they were all gone this morning."

"That's good." Melody stopped and admired the children's toys before saying, "Have you seen the snow family that came in the night? I think Santa must have brought them too."

"Oh, yes, they were delighted." As the father walked on with the children, the mother turned, her voice soft as she said, "Someone has been very busy."

The two women exchanged a smile before Melody and Zeke walked towards the lift, and as the doors opened Zeke said flatly, "How come a stranger gets your smiles?"

Taken aback, she stared at him. "I'm sorry?"

"It doesn't matter." He pressed the control panel, and as the lift swept them upwards he thrust his hands deep into the pockets of his trousers, his gaze on his shoes.

"Zeke, please let me explain. Can't we talk at least?"

"Wait." He raised his head, pinning her to the spot with his ebony eyes. "Wait till we're in the suite."

The few seconds until they were standing inside the sitting room seemed like hours, but then Zeke shut the door behind them and Melody forced herself to turn and look at him. His first words took her completely by surprise. "Is there someone else?"

"What?" She stared at him in utter bewilderment.

"Have you met someone else?" he repeated stiffly.

"Me?" Her voice was a squeak, and she cleared her throat before she managed, "Of course not. How on earth could I have met someone else when I've been in hospital for the last three months? I've only seen doctors and other patients."

"Stranger things have happened."

"Well, not to me." She struggled to keep her voice steady while anger streaked through her. How could he think that? How *could* he? "And I resent the question."

He stared at her intently, and what he read in her face must have reassured him on that point at least because she saw the granite features relax. "I'm sorry but I had to ask. It would have explained a good few things—not least why you felt it necessary to creep away on Christmas morning and disappear for umpteen hours whilst making sure you were incommunicado."

"It wasn't like that," she protested weakly.

"Actually, that was exactly what it was like."

She watched him take a deep breath and realised he was having difficulty holding on to his self-control. He wanted to yell at her, to shout. He calmed himself with a few more deep breaths and she marvelled at his willpower. "What I meant was I didn't deliberately not call you," she said tentatively. "I simply didn't think."

"Great. That makes it much better," he said with grim sarcasm. "I'm so unimportant I didn't even register on your radar."

"Stop being like this." Her voice came out sharper than she had intended—probably because she was desperately trying to keep cool so she could think about what to say, how to reach him. "I hate it when you're this way."

His eyes went flint-hard. "Like what?" he said slowly and

deliberately. "Like I'm angry or hurting or scared rigid? Like I lie awake every night trying to make an impossible situation possible again, knowing I'm up against an adversary who holds all the cards because I love her? My life is falling apart and everything's disintegrating. I am going quietly crazy and I can't concentrate on anything but us. But I mustn't show it. Is that right? Well, tough. I'm human, believe it or not."

Melody's heart stopped. Zeke was always professional, the consummate business tycoon. No matter what happened he didn't let it interfere with his work. She hadn't really thought about how her accident was affecting him because she had been too caught up in her own pain and grief, but if she *had* given it thought she would have expected he was carrying on as normal, engrossed in the daily exhilarating and hectic whirl that made up his show business empire. But that hadn't been the case at all. And he had already admitted he was blaming himself for not meeting her for lunch that day, as they had originally planned. The guilt of that must have been playing on his mind too. He'd been tormenting himself every bit as much as she had.

She swallowed against the painful lump in her throat as her heart kick-started and then pounded against her ribcage so hard it hurt. How had she missed the fact he was suffering too?

Because she had been so wrapped up in herself, a separate and merciless part of her mind said honestly. So immersed in her battle first to survive and then to claw her way out of the deep fog of despair and depression. And Mabel was right. It was fear which governed her life now. Somewhere in the midst of those first weeks she had let it master her and it had remained in control ever since. It had coloured every thought, every decision.

She had hurt him. Badly. She had pushed him away when he

had needed her as much as she had needed him. She had even stopped him visiting her in the hospital. What had he said? That he had resorted to driving to the hospital car park at night just to be near her. Why hadn't she realised he'd been asking for help too? How could she have got it so terribly wrong?

Melody stared at him. He hadn't taken the time to shave when he had found her gone, and his hair looked as though he had run his hand through it a few times—probably in anger. And he had lost some weight over the past months. Altogether he looked harder, sexier and more devastatingly attractive than ever. She loved him, she thought wretchedly. She loved him more than life itself and she had torn them to shreds with her blind stupidity.

She drew in a steadying breath. "I'm sorry," she said simply. "I've done everything wrong and I don't blame you if you're sick and tired of me, if you hate me."

"Hate you? I love you!" He was shouting now, and it was a relief. "I love you so much I'm going crazy, woman. What the hell do you want from me, anyway? Tell me, because I'd really like to know. Tell me what to do and I'll do it, damn it."

Just hours ago she wouldn't have been able to answer him truthfully—especially when he was glaring at her with such deep intensity the black of his eyes glowed like hot coals. "I want you to keep loving me because I love you and I can't do without you." There—she had said it, and now the fear was rising up, strangling her, as the enormity of what she'd done washed over her. She stared at him, waiting for his reaction.

Zeke didn't move or even blink for an endless moment, then his whole body relaxed with a deep exhalation. "Come here," he said softly, opening his arms. "We need to talk. I have to understand and you have to open up. But first I need to hold you and convince myself you're really here and not at the bottom of the Thames or in some other guy's arms."

He held her for a long time without speaking, and although she had wrapped her arms round his waist Melody was aware her heart was pounding like a drum. This was the moment of truth—or at least the next little while would be the moment of truth. Because their talk could only end in one way, and when it did, when they made love, he would look at her scars. They both knew that. The thought made her feel physically sick.

"Okay." He drew back a little, but only to lead her over to the sofa. "I'm going to call Room Service before anything else. What do you want to eat and drink?"

"Nothing." The thought of food was enough to choke her.

Zeke picked up the phone and ordered coffee and croissants for two before coming to sit beside her. "Tell me where you went this morning first," he said softly. "We'll get onto the whys in a minute. I want to know exactly where you've been."

"I walked for a while, and then sat on a bench and an old lady came and talked to me. She invited me to her house for a cup of tea," Melody said numbly. "She—she was kind."

"Then I'm grateful to her," he said expressionlessly.

"She told me about her life, how she lost several babies and then went on to have her son. The time…it just went. I didn't realise. I—I think she's lonely in her own way."

He nodded. "And do I take it this conversation was a two-way thing? That you told her about our problems?"

She was touched he said "our", when he could, in all honesty, have said "yours". It was her turn to nod.

"This is not a criticism, more of an observation," Zeke said carefully. "You could spend four hours talking to this old lady about how you were feeling, but you can't share it with me?"

Melody couldn't let that go unchallenged. "I didn't spend

four hours with her. It was two at the most—probably only one and a half. And I *have* talked to you about everything."

"No, Dee, you've talked *at* me, when you have talked at all. You've given me a list of reasons why the thought of staying with me is impossible—none of which I buy, incidentally. In fact you couldn't come up with a reason for us to split because there isn't one. From day one I knew we were going to be together. I told you that often enough. But you never believed me, did you? It never sank in. Even after two years of marriage."

She stared at him, her eyes huge in her white face. "I wanted it to be true." She swallowed painfully. "I really did."

"But you never *believed* it," he said softly. "No matter what I said or what I did you didn't believe it."

She couldn't deny it. Some inbuilt survival instinct had prevented it. If she had let herself accept she was the only one for Zeke—his "dream woman", as he'd often described it—the risk would have been too great. Once she had relied on him to that extent she'd never have recovered if it all went wrong. Her voice was a tiny whisper when she said, "I suppose I couldn't believe someone like you would want someone like me for ever."

Zeke's fingers took hold of her face and his dark eyes stared straight into hers. "What do you mean, someone like you? You're beautiful, exquisite, unique—the best there is. And the amazing thing, the thing I couldn't get my head round at first, is that you're as lovely on the inside as the outside. The first time I met you—when you were late for the audition, you remember?—I wanted you physically. You danced as though every bone in your body was fluid, flowing with the music, and it was the most erotic thing I'd ever seen. And then you stood in the middle of the stage and refused to be intimidated by my questions or by me. A little firebrand, gusty and defi-ant. And then I heard you talking with the other girls and I found out the reason you were late was because you'd taken pity on an old woman who was devastated by the loss of her cat. Those other girls couldn't understand it. There wasn't one of them who would have done the same. I couldn't understand it. You were an enigma. I had a job to believe you were real."

"Me?" Fascinated as she was by his description of her, she found it hard to believe he was talking about ordinary, run-of-the-mill Melody James.

"Your soft centre is something I have no defence against, my love," Zeke murmured huskily. "It melts me, it ties me up in knots, it makes me want to be a better man than I am and to believe that good can triumph over bad—that Father Christmas really does exist, and that roses round the door and happy-ever-after is there for the taking." And then he smiled. "Don't look like that. Don't you know how much I adore you?"

No. No, I had no idea. "Of course I do."

"Liar." It was without heat. "Sweetheart, you penetrated my heart as easily as a knife through warm butter. I won't pretend there were times when I was frustrated I couldn't do the same with you. But I'm a patient man."

Zeke? Patient? He had many attributes, but patience wasn't one of them. And he did have her heart. He always had.

Something of what she was thinking must have shown in her face, because he smiled again, his voice soft when he qual-ified, "Semi-patient at least—for you, that is." He bent and pressed a kiss on her mouth, pressed another to the tip of her nose and onto her forehead, before settling back and survey-ing her with ebony eyes. "So, tell me why you banned me from visiting you in hospital, and why your solicitor told my solicitor you want a divorce," he said levelly, no inflection in his voice. "And why, after we made love—twice—you still felt the need to escape and put some distance between us."

Chapter 11

The arrival of the coffee and croissants a moment or two after Zeke had demanded she talk to him delayed the inevitable by a few minutes. Melody didn't want to eat or drink, but she did both to gain a few precious get-your-facts-straight moments. The coffee was too strong, and the croissant she forced down didn't sit well with Mabel's bacon sandwich, and when she had finished Zeke's eyes were still waiting for her to begin.

Her heart was thumping in her chest, staccato-beating in her ears, because she knew she had to get this right. She had to make him understand why everything she had done since the accident was wrong. All her past had come together when she'd woken up in that hospital bed, and from that moment she had been in a vacuum of fear and confusion, sucked into a dark and terrifying merry-go-round of hopelessness.

She cleared her throat. "I haven't been thinking clearly over the last weeks." To give him his due, he didn't raise his eyebrows in the quirky, sarky way he did sometimes. Neither did he make any of the hundred and one responses he could have made in the circumstances. He simply sat looking at her. She didn't know if that made it easier or harder.

"I've realised this—my freaking out in the hospital and asking you for a divorce and everything—is because…" She paused and swallowed hard. "I was frightened you wouldn't want me any more now I'm—I'm disfigured." She rushed on quickly before he could speak. "Not that you have ever done or said anything to make me think that way. I know it's me. Mabel—the lady I met today—said I was letting fear rule me, and she's right. It's just that I know you appreciate grace and beauty more than most. Partly due to your—your beginnings and everything, and there's nothing wrong with that. But— but I'll never dance again. I'm…different now."

"Sweetheart, your legs were messed up. I know that's one hell of a big deal for you, because dancing is your life, but I can help you through it. This doesn't have to be the end of using the fantastic gift you've been given, just rechannelling it. I've got a couple of ideas about that, but they can wait. The main thing I have to convince you of right now is that your grace and beauty has never depended on your dancing. You are grace and beauty. Those qualities are in every word you speak, the way you are, every look and movement you make. The lorry couldn't take them away from you, don't you see? You're my sweet, generous, incomparable baby—my darling, my love."

She was falling apart, her eyes blinded by her tears, and when he took her in his arms again she fell against him, need- ing his strength and security as never before as she sobbed against his broad chest.

"What?" He bent his head to her, her incoherent words punctuated by convulsive shudders. "What did you say?"

"I—I—" Melody made a huge effort and sat up, taking the

handkerchief he gave her. "I don't see how you can think of me in that way. It's like you're talking about someone else."

"Then you'll just have to take it on trust until I can convince you," he said softly. "And if it takes a lifetime I'll do it. You're mine, Dee, every bit as much as I am yours. You are the only person I could have possibly ended up with, and if we hadn't met—if we'd missed each other somehow—I'd have gone on as I was. Happy in a way, fairly okay with myself, but with a huge reservoir inside me which would have remained untapped. I've heard it said that there are several people in the world that someone can love if they meet them, but it's not that way with me. You saved me. That's the only way I can put it."

He had never told her this before—not in so many words— and yet now when she thought about it she realised his whole way with her had demonstrated it from the beginning. She smiled tremulously and blew her nose, shaking back her hair from her damp face, and then lifted one trembling hand to his face. "I love you," she said very quietly. "I always have and I always will. There will never be anyone but you for me."

He smiled a singularly sweet smile as his hand covered hers. "Then there's nothing we can't overcome."

She nodded, relaxing into his embrace as he reached for her but knowing deep inside that she was still frightened by what lay ahead. She hated that she felt that way, but she couldn't help it.

He tilted her face to meet his, covering her lips in a fierce kiss of such hunger that she immediately responded to the deep, unspoken need. His mouth was still hard on hers as he stood and picked her up in his arms, carrying her into his bedroom as he crushed her against him. Lying her on the bed, he bent and stretched out beside her, but he didn't immediately begin to undress her or himself, wrapping his arms round her in a gesture intended to comfort as he kissed her again.

The kiss deepened, becoming one of such explosive warmth that sexual feeling flowed through her as hot and smooth as melted honey, and she sighed in pleasure, curving into him as though she would fuse their bodies together. He pulled his mouth away for a millisecond to fill his lungs, and then the sensual onslaught began anew as he tangled one large hand in her hair, continuing the magic of his kisses as his lips travelled over her cheeks, her closed eyelids, the arch of her fine brows before returning to reclaim her mouth once more.

He kissed her for a long time as his hands roamed over her body on top of her clothes, cupping her breasts and shaping the plump mounds with his palms as his thumbs teased her nipples into hard peaks. Winter sunlight spilled onto the bed from the large window, splintered yellow against her closed eyelids which enclosed her in a world of pure sensation.

She was aware of him divesting himself of his clothes, although his mouth barely left hers, and then he expertly removed her top and her lacy bra. His mouth moved from hers, lingering for a moment over her collarbone as his lips stroked the silky skin, and then he reached the soft fullness of her aching breasts.

Melody moaned throatily as his mouth fastened on one erect nipple and he gave it loving attention before moving onto its twin. "Exquisite," he murmured softly. "Such wonderfully large rosy nipples. You taste of molasses and roses, do you know that? Sweet and scented and deliciously ripe. I want to devour you. I can't get enough of you."

He continued to please her with lips and tongue until she dug her fingers into his muscled shoulders, murmuring something incoherent even to herself. It seemed impossible so much feeling, such emotion, could be contained in her body without her splintering into a million pieces.

"I want to kiss every inch of you," he whispered, his mouth returning to her lips for a moment. From being fluid she stiffened as she felt him peeling off her leggings and lace panties, but almost immediately he was lying against her again, holding her close so her breasts came into tender contact with his chest. The friction of his body hair against her engorged breasts was tantalising, but reality had caused her to become tense in his arms and she didn't know how to pretend. She didn't actively resist him, but the thudding of her heart now had nothing to do with sexual desire and all to do with panic.

He kissed her once more before he said, very softly, "Dee? Look at me. Open your eyes. Look at me, sweetheart."

She couldn't. Ridiculous, but she couldn't. She was too terrified of what she might read in his face. Kindness and pity would be worse than distaste.

"Please, sweetheart." He stroked a strand of silky hair from her brow. "Look at me."

Slowly she forced her eyes open. He was smiling. Funny, in all her nightmares she hadn't considered that, but she might have known Zeke would surprise her.

"The worst is over," he said, sheer love shining from his eyes. "You've faced your fear and now we move on. You won't believe you're more beautiful and desirable to me than ever for a while. I understand that. But your scars aren't ugly to me, darling. They remind me I'm the luckiest man in the world, because I came close to losing you and I was spared the unthinkable. I couldn't have gone on without you. I know that."

Her eyes traced the contours of his face, taking in the velvet black eyes, the sloping lines that created his firm mouth, the straight solid shape of his nose. She searched each feature, looking for the barest hint of disgust but there was none. He was just her Zeke, her babe. She had always called him that, babe, although she didn't know why. She had certainly never felt inclined to do the same with anyone else.

Her hands had been knotted against his chest, but now they slowly uncurled as he kissed her again, his tongue rippling along her teeth until she opened to him. He wrapped the long swathe of her strawberry-blond hair around his fingers, tilting her head back slightly as he ravaged her mouth. Each movement he made exploded more desire in her veins, radiating throughout her body with a drowsy warmth that was voluptuous and sensual. She had missed him. She had missed him so much, the longing for his presence and body so intense she'd had to shut it out of her consciousness or go mad with the need. But now there was no need to fight the passion and love and desire. She could give in to those deepest inner needs.

She closed her eyes, curving into his hard male frame and sighing with sheer ecstasy as she drifted off into a place of bliss.

Chapter 12

Melody stretched slightly, drowsily aware she was enclosed in a cosy cocoon. She cuddled deeper into the animal warmth that was the source of her satisfaction, her limbs heavy and relaxed. Quite when she became aware of the fact that a hard muscular forearm was curved over the dip in her waist she wasn't sure. It could have been minutes or hours. But suddenly she was wide awake, her eyes opening.

"Hi." Zeke's voice was lazy and his kiss was deep and slow. Her green eyes stared into ebony. "I fell asleep."

He grinned, apparently not in the least put out. "That you did," he agreed smokily. "Which was a first for me."

Melody didn't know where to put herself. The culmination of months of anguish, worry and heartache and she had fallen asleep under Zeke's lovemaking. She hadn't meant to. She had been there with him every inch of the way—or so she had thought. "I'm sorry," she murmured helplessly. She remembered him kissing her after he'd undressed her, reassuring her, and then… "I must have been more tired than I thought."

His grin widened. "But you've had a nap," he pointed out softly, enfolding her in a tender yet hungry embrace, his hands stroking down her spine from her shoulders into the concavity of her tiny waist and to the seductive flare of her hips as his tongue drew an arc round the curve of one ear before his teeth gently closed on the lobe. "And it hasn't been that long. I bet the coffee is still warm in the pot out there."

They didn't put it to the test. They explored each other with sensual and hungry abandon, loving each other with a need which did away with any thought of shyness or restraint. Zeke's fingers slipped down the length of her, defining her neatly rounded bottom with a languid caress as he pulled her into the hard strength of him. Even when his hands moved over the base of her spine and the tops of her legs she didn't flinch, putting her hands to either side of his face as she pulled him down to meet her in a kiss that was as fierce as it was gentle.

The blood in her veins rushed to nourish the surface of her skin, a rosy glow turning her flesh translucent and releasing her intimate perfume. By the time he levered his body over hers she was aching for him, the feel of his arousal an aphrodisiac in itself. She couldn't contain the desperate little whimper of desire that broke from her lips, needing him deep inside her, wanting the feeling of oneness, of closeness.

With one sure thrust Zeke entered the silken sheath that welcomed him, Melody's muscles tightening to lock him into her. The rhythm of their shared passion mounted, and with each movement Melody felt they were reaffirming those vows they had taken two years ago, but with a special meaning now. Then they had been madly in love, giddy and intoxicated with the thrill of the newness of it all. Now they had come through the fire and their joining was all the more intense and passionate because of it. It was as though their very souls were merging and they were equal in their drawing strength from each other, their entwined bodied fitting together in a manner as old as time and as sweet.

Zeke filled her completely, the sensation extremely satisfying as he built their rapture until she thought she would float right out of her body into somewhere beyond time. When the culmination came its violence sent them both over the edge of reality. In all the times they had come together—times of deep passion and erotic exploration and need—it had never been so cataclysmic, and she knew he felt it too. He held her hard against him, his body trembling with the aftermath of their lovemaking as he kept her intimately joined to him.

"I love you." His voice was deep and warm and very sensual. "More than life itself."

"I love you too," she whispered shakily.

He searched for something in the depths of her eyes and then kissed the tip of her nose. "You're addictive, do you know that? Before I collected you from the hospital I promised myself I'd take it nice and easy. I'd just be there for you, no pressure, no strain, taking it as slow as you wanted. And now in the space of a few hours I've made love to you three times. My only excuse is that for the last three months I've lain awake each night in our bed wishing you were there with me, remembering how it was, driving myself crazy."

He withdrew from her body but his arms came around her, binding her to him in a constrictive circle as he whispered, "I can't believe you're here now. When I woke up earlier and found you gone…"

She cupped his rugged face with her small hands, kissing him hard. "I'm sorry," she said gently. "I won't do that again. I promise. I'm here now."

He kissed her back, even harder, stroking her warm flesh

as he moved her against him. "In mind as well as body?" he asked quietly. "And don't pretend to make me feel good. I need to know how you're feeling if we're going to beat this thing."

In reply she curved her body around his, delighting in the way they fitted together. "I'm here," she repeated firmly. She slid her fingers over the damp skin on his back, powerful muscles responding under her touch before she stroked her way round to his flat belly, teasingly following the line of hair which arrowed downwards before flaring dramatically out again and providing a thick dark cradle for his masculinity. When her hand circled and caressed the erection her touch had brought forth, she smiled at him seductively. "Fancy making that four times you've forced your wicked way on me?" she murmured throatily, kissing the corner of his mouth tenderly.

This time their loving was long and slow and infinitely satisfying, and when they had come back from the world of intimate light and sensation, Melody lay in her husband's arms, her whole body so relaxed it felt boneless as Zeke pulled the duvet over them. The events of the past twenty-four hours and not least the weeks of misery and anxiousness before Christmas had caught up with her, but she didn't want to sleep again. She just needed to be with Zeke, to feel him, look at him, touch him. She felt as though she had been on a long, dangerous journey and come home. Softly, she murmured, "You said you had some ideas about what I can do in the future earlier?" She twisted to face him. "What are they?"

He cupped her buttocks and pulled her tightly against him, his mouth taking hers in a long kiss. When at last he released her lips he still held her close. "That I have," he agreed huskily. "How about I go and fetch us a drink and we'll talk? There's wine in the fridge."

She grinned at him. "Isn't it a bit early in the day for wine? It isn't even lunchtime yet."

"Not at all. It's Christmas Day. Ordinary rules don't apply. Besides, it'll give you an appetite for lunch—which, incidentally, I suggest we have here in bed. In fact I see no reason for us to get up today, do you?"

She gazed at him, loving him and thanking God that Christmas Eve had worked its magic and brought her to her senses. "None at all," she said softly.

The wine was icy cold and delicious when he brought the bottle and two glasses back to bed, along with the rest of the presents from under the tree in their little sitting room. She opened her presents in his arms, delighting in the dainty little gold wristwatch, gossamer-thin silk nightdress and negligee, her favourite perfume and other gifts, all perfect and chosen with love. But it was the eternity ring nestled between her engagement and wedding ring her gaze kept returning to. The ring was exquisite, but it was the statement behind it that made it precious beyond words. He had bought it when she had rejected him, spurned his love and refused to listen to him, because he loved her and was determined love was eternal. And it was. Oh, it was.

"Before I make my suggestions about the future, can I just say they are meant to fit in with you having my babies?" Zeke said softly as she snuggled down in his arms again.

Zeke's babies. She could let herself believe it would happen now. She smiled at him, radiant in a way he hadn't seen before and so beautiful she took his breath away. "That might happen sooner than you think," she said serenely. "We've made love four times in the middle of my cycle and I haven't been taking the pill since I've been in hospital, so..."

"You wouldn't mind?" he asked, a touch anxiously.

She touched his face lovingly. "Would you?"

"I can't wait to have you barefoot and pregnant," he said with deep satisfaction. "And it would fit in well with certain changes I've made in my own life in the last little while." He smiled at her frown of enquiry before kissing her.

He reached for their wine glasses, topping them up and handing her hers before he said, "A toast to the new owner of Media Enterprises—David Ellington."

She stared at him in amazement and shock. "You've sold your business?" David Ellington was a mogul billionaire.

"Lock, stock and barrel," he said cheerfully, taking a gulp of wine. "I should have been with you the day of the accident instead of chasing my tail over some damn crisis or other. It was a wake-up call—a terrifying one. I vowed the night of the accident that if you pulled through I'd reassess what was important in my life. So I did. It didn't take much thought."

Melody was horrified. His empire was hard-won. He had built it up brick by brick and she knew he was immensely proud of what he had achieved. "You shouldn't have done that," she whispered. "Can't you change your mind?"

"Too late." He smiled at her. "And it's *exactly* what I should have done. You confirmed that yourself yesterday. You told me you needed to make a new life, separate from the hectic entertainment business we've been involved in, something that would cut out the excess of parties and other functions that took up so much of our time. Independently of you I had come to the same conclusion. It would have happened sooner or later once we'd decided to start a family. The accident merely precipitated things. You were right when you said there were too many people wanting a piece of me, but wrong when you thought you were just one of them. That was never true, however you felt. I didn't feel it was the moment to tell you I'd sold up yesterday—there were other things to sort out first. But when I said to you I could give it all up and walk away without a backward glance or any regret, it was because I had done exactly that. My world was never the business or the contacts I'd made or the power games. Not after I had met you. You are my world, Dee. We've spoken about a family but if the children didn't come along for whatever reason I would still consider myself blessed among men. You're my sun, moon and stars. The centre of my universe."

He touched her stricken face gently, stroking down her cheek and round her full lips with the tip of his finger. "I'm glad it's gone, Dee. Truly. It was a stage of my life which was enjoyable while it happened, but I want to move on with you. It's also made us a great deal of money," he added with male satisfaction. "More than enough for us to do anything we want for the rest of our lives." ·

She could still hardly take it in that he had actually walked away from his empire. But if he had told her instead that he intended to sell she would have thought he didn't mean it, she realised now. Was that why he'd made it a *fait accompli*? She would have felt guilty, felt he was only doing it for her, and would have attempted to persuade him they could go on as they had been. Maybe he knew her better than she knew herself? On second thought there was no maybe about it.

"Thank you," she murmured softly.

Suddenly she felt as if a huge weight had been lifted. No more premières and red carpets and first-night parties. No more relentless rounds of functions and shows and receptions where you couldn't wear the same dress twice or the knives would be out—always in the back. Of course some of the social occasions they'd attended had been fun, and overall she had enjoyed herself and relished being on Zeke's arm as his wife, but the accident had changed something independent of the damage to her legs, and she wouldn't have wanted to step onto the merry-go-round again. And now she didn't have to. But at a huge cost to Zeke.

"What will you do?" she asked him tremulously, not knowing if she wanted to laugh or cry. He wasn't the kind of man who could sit and do nothing.

"Again, let me qualify," he said, settling her more comfortably in the circle of his arms. "This all has to fit in with what I see as my main job of being a husband and father, okay?" He waited for her nod before continuing, "I have a couple of ideas, and they could run alongside the treatment programme your doctors and I have worked out, which will take one day out of the week every week for some time but could result in practically full mobility after six months or so, and excellent long-term prospects. There's a Swiss doctor I've got on board who specialises in your sort of injuries—there's no one to beat him, not even in the States—and he's confident you'll be walking normally by this time next year."

She half lifted herself on one elbow and kissed him with single-minded intensity and sweetness. Just knowing he was ready to stand and fight with her was everything, and whether she regained all she'd lost didn't matter so much now.

Zeke lifted strands of her hair and twined them round his fingers as he kissed her back just as strongly, and then he dropped a kiss on the end of her nose as he drew back a little. "First idea," he said matter-of-factly. "We look for suitable premises and open a drama school for under-privileged youngsters. It would be the real McCoy, for kids from nine or ten upwards, so we'd need to employ teachers for the normal subjects as well as those specialising in drama and dance and so on. It could be a boarding school for those who wanted it, and a home 365 days of the year for others who need it. Children who have been kicked from pillar to post, kids in the care system or in dysfunctional homes. They'd all have to have a leaning towards acting or singing or dancing, but once they were with us they'd be there until they chose to leave. And the home part of the place would be exactly that—not an institution. A place of security and unconditional support."

The sort of place he would have longed for as a confused and troubled boy, Melody thought, her understanding causing her to swallow the lump in her throat. Oh, Zeke, Zeke.

"Of course you'd be in charge of the drama side—the hiring of staff and so on—and I thought you might want to be hands-on teaching dance? We'd need an establishment with plenty of grounds for a swimming pool, tennis court and so on, and a house separate from the school for us would be essential. I've no real idea of the mechanics of it all, but I know people who could make it happen as long as the funding was in place."

"And we could afford to do that?" she asked softly.

Zeke smiled. "Several times over, sweetheart." He guided her glass of wine to her lips and took a sip of his own before he went on, "There are other options, of course. You might like to travel for a year or two once your treatment is over— a world tour, staying over for as long as you like if a particular place takes your fancy. Or we could run our own theatre? Something in that line? Or you could run a traditional dancing establishment?"

Melody came straight back to the idea that had fired her imagination. "This drama school—wouldn't it be a huge undertaking to do it properly?"

"Massive," he agreed. "The dance side would involve performance, choreography, management and dance theatre, including the history of dance and related arts, aesthetics and critical studies, production, music accompaniment and composition, and that's without the drama side. Acting, directing, technical aspects, backstage crafts and writing for the stage would all be necessary, along with practical theatre."

He paused for breath and Melody stared at him in wonder. "You've really looked into this, haven't you?"

Zeke nodded. "It would be a total life change, Dee. But one which would fit with family life if it was done properly. We would afford to get the best folk for the children on board, people of like mind, and I thought—" He stopped abruptly and she saw a muscle clench in his square jaw.

"You thought?" she pressed quietly.

"We could make a difference. Not to every child, perhaps— I am a realist—but for the ones we give direction and purpose to it would be worth it. But it's only an idea."

She buried her face in his neck for a moment, overwhelmed at the turn their lives had taken. This was perfect, so utterly perfect. And only Zeke could have thought of it.

"Dee?" His voice carried a note of anxiety. "You don't have to say anything until you've thought about it. It's a big deal—"

She stopped him by winding her arms around his middle as she lifted her face to his. "I love you, I love you," she said, over and over again so he would know. "And I can't think of anything better. Think of it, Zeke. Children who have nothing, given a foundation and a pride in the gift they have. Do you really think we can do it? Provide them with a home and hope?"

"Of course." The words were pronounced emphatically, a declaration, and she knew in that moment he would make it happen.

She reached up and placed her mouth on his. It wasn't often

she made the first move, and his reaction was immediate and fierce as he crushed her into him, kissing her with a hunger that touched her to the core. He kissed her for a long time as they murmured incoherent words of love, drawing strength from each other. "I can do anything with you by my side, but without you I'm nothing," he muttered desperately. "Never leave me like you did this morning—without a word, a goodbye. I thought I'd lost you. I need you, sweetheart. You've got no idea how much."

"I think I have, because I need you every bit as much," she whispered brokenly. "I've been so miserable. Not because of the accident and knowing I'd never dance again, but because I thought I had to let you go. You're my world, my existence."

He gave a choked laugh. "So we've both been tearing ourselves apart because we love each other?"

She smiled tremulously. "Maybe we aren't the smartest kids on the block," she admitted weakly. Joy, like warm honey, was spreading through her body with healing reassurance. She could believe this. She could trust him. She had wasted weeks of her life letting fear dictate her actions and rule her mind, but no more. She must have been crazy—stark, staring mad—to imagine Zeke would look at another woman or walk away from her. He wasn't like her father or her grandfather. He was unique and all hers. Her husband, her love, her life.

They held each other tightly until the crescendo of emotion descended to a more controllable plane, and after one more long, lingering kiss she snuggled into him with her head on his chest. "I booked in to this hotel for a few days," she whispered drowsily, after a minute or two of listening to the steady beat-beat of his heart beneath her cheek. "We can spend them all in bed, can't we? Have all our meals here?"

She knew he was smiling. She could read it in his voice

when he murmured, "Sure thing," as his hands wandered soothingly over her skin, stroking her neck, her shoulder, her back in light caresses. "We've got some time to make up and I can't think of a better place to do it. Besides, plenty of sleep, plenty of exercise—of the most beneficial kind," he added, squeezing one rounded buttock to give emphasis to his words, "along with good food and drink is just what you need. This is our time. No one knows where we are, the phone won't ring, and my mobile's switched off. There'll be no taps at the door apart from Room Service."

"Mmm." Heaven on earth. Melody closed her eyes and felt herself gradually drift towards sleep. Zeke's breathing had become slow and steady and she knew he'd fallen asleep, but one arm was draped over the dip in her waist and the other hand was tangled in her hair as though even while he slept he needed to know she was secure and within his grasp.

She thought of the snow family in the courtyard and smiled dreamily. Last night had been magical and infinitely precious, but they had the rest of their lives to look forward to now. Nights locked in each other's arms and days spent together as they worked to bring hope to children who expected none, who were damaged like Zeke had been. This was a new chapter, a new beginning, and when the babies came— Zeke's babies—they would be loved as neither of them had been loved when they were young. Their children would grow up strong and secure in their parents' love—she and Zeke would make sure of that—each one knowing they were precious and unique.

Zeke stirred slightly, drawing her even closer as he murmured her name in his sleep, and as she floated into a warm, soft, safe place she knew that to him she was everything—the only woman he could ever love, complete and whole. And because he thought she was beautiful she was.

Sleep crept up on her, and in her hazy contentment she thought of Mabel and her wise words. She would go and see the old lady again, and take Zeke with her this time. She felt they were meant to be good friends, and the loneliness she had sensed in the brave old soul could be channelled to some extent. Children loved a grandmother figure, and always responded to dogs too. She could see Mabel joining them for days out once the school was up and running, and she was sure the old lady would play her part in counselling hurting little hearts the same way Mabel had comforted her that morning.

She slept, and the two of them continued to lie wrapped closely in each other's arms—two hearts that beat as one, two minds intrinsically linked for eternity with that most powerful and sweetest of bonds, true love.

They had come through the fiery furnace. They were home.

★ ★ ★ ★ ★

TEXAS TYCOON'S
CHRISTMAS FIANCÉE

Sara Orwig

Thank you to Krista Stroever.
Also, with love to my family, who are my world.
Love and thanks to Maureen.

Chapter 1

Festive lights twinkled on Reunion Tower and across the sprawling metropolis of Dallas. Nick Rafford barely noticed his view. While he enjoyed guests at his party celebrating his return after being in Côte d'Azur the past three weeks, his attention focused on Grace Wayland, his caterer.

He had never seen her until tonight. His secretary had made arrangements for the catering company to do this Christmas party. From the first glimpse, Grace had surprised him.

Memory flashed back to the moment his butler had announced Grace's arrival and shown her into the penthouse study.

Rising to his feet, Nick suffered a jolt to his system as sea-green eyes met his gaze. For an instant she seemed equally startled because color drained from her face and her eyes widened. It was fleeting, vanishing when she regained her composure.

Grace Wayland's plain black dress should have caused her to fade into anonymity. Instead, he was riveted as she crossed the room and held out a slender hand to shake his.

When his hand closed over hers, the contact sent a sizzling current. She stood only a few feet away and hot attraction engulfed him. Mere seconds or a minute—he didn't know how long their gazes remained locked. Breaking the spell, she said in a low voice, "I'm Grace Wayland."

Her name was enough to bring him out of his daze, causing his second surprise of the evening. Brilliant green eyes mirrored his own anger. He had anticipated a different response, expecting her to fawn over him, to do all she could to please him with this party. Curious about her cool manner, he studied her.

"And so I meet one of the Raffords," she added.

"You knew who I was before my secretary called about this party?"

"Of course," she said, removing her hand from his, warmth lingering from the slight physical contact. "I imagine you've heard about me, just as I certainly have you. We have something in common—Michael. That's who this is about, isn't it?"

Nick kept his features impassive, hiding his surprise at her bluntness. "I figured I'd be the one to bring up Michael. My party isn't the place or time for a discussion. Will you be available if I come to your office Monday?"

"Fine. I'll be free around nine. How's that time?"

"I can be there at nine," he said, having already cleared his Monday calendar in anticipation of meeting with her.

"I assumed Michael was why you paid an exorbitant fee to get me to cater tonight. You could have saved yourself money by coming to me directly to book the party," she added, her voice dropping to a whisper.

He shrugged. "You were highly recommended and I thought this was a way to meet. Tonight, my focus is on my party," he said, suspecting it was going to be difficult to keep his mind on his party or his guests with Grace around. As he'd answered her, he noticed her full, rosy, inviting lips.

"When it comes to Michael, to my baby, I doubt we have anything to discuss," she declared.

His surprise over her responses deepened. Mixed reactions were churning inside. He wanted to remind her that her "my baby" remark had been inaccurate, but he restrained himself from antagonizing her unnecessarily. His annoyance battled his attraction. Once more, their gazes collided, the heated moment stretching until she broke the spell.

"I have your instructions regarding the party. My help is waiting in the van to bring in the food and get ready."

"I detect reluctance about catering for me," he said.

"This job will be good for my business," she replied, the barrier of coolness still in place.

"Summon your help. I'll have someone show you around," he said, while he considered her professional, noncommittal answer. Nick walked to the intercom to talk briefly to his butler, who responded in seconds. As Grace left with him, Nick watched her walk out, noticing her long legs and narrow waist.

Casually, while guests arrived and mingled, he checked on the arrangements, finding food, setups—every aspect of the preparations—flawless and accomplished with no disruption to him.

Later in the evening he stood with his two closest friends. He was only half-listening to their conversation while he watched Grace replenish a dish on his dining table.

"I don't blame you for paying little attention to us," Tony Ryder, Nick's tall, curly-haired friend, said. "Where did you find her? The hors d'oeuvres are excellent, but I don't think it would matter how the food tasted if she came along with it. Is she the manager?"

"Manager and owner. It's a small business I heard about, so I thought I'd try it."

"Right," remarked Jake Benton, his blue-eyed gaze flicking to Grace and back to Nick. "How soon are you taking her out?"

Nick shook his head. "I don't think so. So how has the basketball game been while I've been away?"

"Team missed you," Jake said. "Hope you're not too out of shape after a month off."

"Given the amateurs we are and playing twice a month at best, I don't think my missing a couple of games will matter except for the score of our team," Nick remarked, and his friends laughed.

"Great party, Nick," a tall, blue-eyed man said as he joined the three. "Missed you at the last game."

"See, Gabe agrees. The team needs you," Jake said.

Nick faced Jake's younger brother. "I don't think I'm all that important. I'm not giving up my trips for basketball with the three of you," he added, and the others grinned.

As they talked about their hobby, Nick tried to keep his attention on his friends. They had known him long enough that they would notice if he continued to watch Grace. Both Tony and Jake were as close to him as brothers. Gabe was close also, since he had grown up with them. Nick knew he could trust all three if he told them about Grace, but he didn't care to discuss Michael with anyone.

He didn't want to discuss his nephew with Grace either, but he had to. Later during the party, when she was in the kitchen, he strolled in to find her refilling a tray of hors d'oeuvres.

After a glance at him she returned her attention to the job at hand. "I hope everything is satisfactory."

"More than acceptable," he replied, watching her long fingers move, deftly arranging bruschetta, mini quiches, enticing

tidbits on the tray. Even though her hands bore no rings, he
already knew her single status. He caught a whiff of an unfa-
miliar, exotic perfume. Too much about her enticed him to
the point he forgot his mission for minutes at a time. When
had he found a woman as distracting as Grace?

"You're very good at this, yet you've only been doing it a
few years," he said, taking a tasty cheese phyllo she had just
placed on a silver tray. Replacing it immediately, she continued working.

"As I expected, you've inquired about my background,"
she remarked without looking up. The light glinted on gold
highlights in her silky brown hair worn clipped in a loose bun
on her head. "I've worked in restaurants or in catering since
I was in high school." Her long brown lashes hid her eyes as
she worked.

"So this catering business of yours, is it a childhood wish
come true?"

"Not exactly, but close," she answered. Big green eyes jolted
him as they had at his first encounter. The crystal, vivid green
beneath the long lashes was a stunning combination. Each
look burned with a simmering animosity. He had to concede
to himself that her beauty complicated his mission in spite of
having nothing to do with the problem between them.

"You've done an excellent job tonight. You've impressed
my friends."

"Thank you," she answered.

He left, fighting the urge to flirt with her, because that
would be the road to disaster. He remained astounded by her
aloof manner. He had never anticipated it. Her coolness made
him reassess his view of her. Her poise and self-assurance denied her impoverished background. While she demonstrated
little gratitude for his business, the catering had been executed

with perfection. She loomed a more formidable foe than he had imagined.

"I don't have any idea what the deal is, Nick," Jake said, walking up to him. "Anyone can feel the sparks when you and your caterer are together, yet the looks she gives you contradict that."

"You've forgotten," Nick said. "I told you about my brother and this baby he supposedly fathered."

"I remember," Jake said, turning to look again at Grace. "So this woman is the guardian?"

"Yes. I keep expecting Dad to revert to his old self and forget this nonsense about wanting a grandchild in the family, but so far he hasn't. He wants the baby to have our name and be in his life. He doesn't expect or want to have complete custody."

"He's older, Nick, and he's had a brush with mortality. That can change a man."

"This is totally out of character for him. Dad's thinking isn't as clear as it was before the last heart attack."

Jake sipped his drink and frowned slightly. "On other subjects or just this one?"

"I'll admit, mostly this one, but I'll repeat, this interest in a baby is so unlike him."

As a mutual friend approached, Nick turned to greet him and the conversation switched to golf, yet Nick couldn't lose his continual awareness of Grace. Occasionally, he looked into her green eyes and each time, electricity zigzagged through him. Certain he had the pertinent facts about her, he had been surprised there was no man in her life.

Thinking she would be impressed by the family wealth, he was still surprised by her frosty manner. His stubborn father would not back down. If she was uncooperative, they would be in for a battle, and he was the one in the middle who would have to do the negotiating. Normally, where a beautiful, sin-

gle woman was involved, he would be happy to step in, but
in the current situation, he opposed what his father wanted.
Maybe Grace herself would settle the whole thing and for
once in his life, the old man would have to accept not getting what he wanted.

Nick's spirits lifted only slightly. He hated to break the
news to his father, who was frail now and in failing health.
Eli had spent a lifetime getting his way and didn't take it well
when he couldn't. Monday morning, Nick would discover
where they stood.

A piano player filled the evening with music and conversation grew louder after everyone had eaten their fill.

In spite of enjoying his guests, Nick kept track of Grace,
who remained in the background assisting and directing the
cleanup. He had been watching her talk to one of her staff but
then a guest took his attention and the next time he looked
for Grace, she was nowhere in sight. The catering staff had
disappeared as well. He excused himself and strolled through
the crowd, entering an empty kitchen.

He saw an envelope with his name neatly typed on the
front. The bill was inside and she had gone. He tapped the
envelope against his palm. She hadn't been the woman he
had expected. What would an appointment with her Monday bring?

Shivering from the cold winter night, Grace drove away
from the high-rise condo where Nick resided in an exclusive,
gated area near downtown Dallas. She heaved a sigh of relief.
Visions of dark chocolate-colored, thickly lashed eyes bedev-
iled her. Nick Rafford was charismatic, overwhelming, sexy,
and accustomed to getting what he wanted. Each time she had
been near him tonight there had been a disturbing electricity

between them. What woman wouldn't feel tempted around a man that attractive?

She had tried to hide her initial shock when she had entered the room to meet him. It was the first time she had seen one of the Rafford men in person. She had seen pictures and knew Michael had their black hair and dark eyes, but in person, she noticed more. Michael and his uncle had the same straight nose and thick eyelashes, a dimple in the right cheek. The seven-month-old baby under her guardianship bore a strong resemblance to his uncle. Michael had good genes.

As she drove, she recalled glimpses of Nick smiling, laughing with friends, shaking hands, talking earnestly. He was breathtaking, handsome, too appealing. His white shirt with flashing gold cuff links and navy slacks added to his commanding appearance and there had been no mistaking his arrogance. The man made it obvious that he expected to have his wishes granted.

What did Nick really want? Was he coming after Michael? Another chill ran down her spine. Yet the coldness vanished as she continued thinking about Nick. No one could stay chilled remembering Nick.

She didn't want the Raffords in Michael's life. She admitted to herself she was terrified they would take the precious boy from her. She'd had him from the moment he left the hospital after his birth and loved him as if he were her own son. She mulled over the strong resemblance to his uncle. His incredibly handsome uncle.

Her fears had heightened when she had stepped into Nick's ritzy condo with its glass walls in the living area and panoramic views of the city. The opulent furniture and lamps were expensive. The kitchen had been state-of-the-art and when she had stepped into a spacious bathroom, the mirrors, plants and sunken tub with gold fittings had been as luxurious as the rest of the condo. She remembered seeing a spread about his home in a Dallas magazine. Imported marble, a New York decorator, priceless antiques, original oils, a lavish backdrop that added to his aura of wealth and power.

She wished she could shake Nick out of her thoughts, hoped even more that she would never see him again.

When she entered her small ground-floor apartment, she greeted her aunt, who was babysitting Michael.

Dressed in a gown and robe, Clara Wayland brushed brown hair away from her sleepy green eyes. "How was it?"

"The job went well. He seemed pleased."

"And?"

"And I have an appointment with him at my office Monday morning. Otherwise, I'm as uninformed as ever about what he wants. Well, maybe I know a little more, since I've actually met him. I'll tell you about it after I change clothes and look in on Michael. How was he tonight?"

"An angel. A happy baby who went to sleep about nine."

"I've missed him."

"You always do," her aunt said as Grace went into her bedroom, shedding clothes and changing into cotton pajamas and a robe. She tiptoed over to look at the crib, fighting the urge to pick up the sleeping baby and hold him in her arms. A chill gripped her. There could be no good reason Nick Rafford wanted to meet her. None. She didn't want him near Michael. She gazed at the baby, so aware of the startling resemblance to Nick. She leaned down to brush Michael's cheek with a light kiss and caught a whiff of baby powder. "You're mine now, sweetie. Not the Raffords'," she whispered.

She rejoined Clara, who had fixed cups of hot chocolate. "Monday morning, you can call your lawyer to go with you," Clara said.

"I won't need a lawyer to just talk to the man. Tonight is the first we've met."

Clara sighed. "I need to remember that you won't let him intimidate you or frighten you into doing something you don't have to do."

"I don't think that will happen," Grace said. "He was courteous. Obviously, he wants something concerning Michael. He hired my catering service to scope me out."

"Don't borrow trouble," Clara said.

"When Bart Rafford kicked Alicia out, he didn't want anything to do with his baby. He denied the baby was his. I can't imagine the jet-setting multimillionaire uncle has any interest in Michael. His brother never did and since Bart wasn't killed until Michael was three months old, he had time to meet his son if he'd wanted."

"Does the uncle have a wife and children?" Clara asked.

"No. Nick is single," Grace said, remembering his dark brown eyes on her as he grasped her hand in their handshake. "He's in society pages, so that's how I know he isn't married. He's busy and has a reputation as shrewd in business. From what Alicia told me, at that time, the grandfather had no interest in Michael and I've heard the grandfather's health has failed lately. An ailing grandfather, a single uncle—those are the only relatives. I can't figure out what, but they want something from me concerning Michael. I'll learn what it is on Monday morning."

"Please call me the first chance you get. I'll be worried about you."

"Don't fret," Grace said, smiling at Clara. "Legally, Michael is mine."

"Grace, the Raffords have an enormous fortune. You wouldn't stand a chance of stopping them if they—"

"Don't think about it," Grace said.

"You're right." Clara smiled. "I think I'll turn in. I wish you'd sleep in your room and let me take the sofa here."

"I'm fine. Thanks for staying tonight."

"I love to see Michael. You're the daughter I never had. My boys are scattered and still single—Chet in Germany. Miles in Japan. I've given up on my own grandkids, but thank goodness I can be with Michael."

"Chet sent you plane tickets and you'll be in Germany with him for Christmas."

"That's not like having them here," Clara said. "I worry about leaving you and Michael alone for Christmas."

"Don't be silly. You'll have a wonderful time and Glenda is already lined up to babysit Michael for me. I don't worry when he's with either one of you."

"She's reliable and she loves him, too. Glenda and I have been friends since we were five years old. She's like a sister to me," Clara said, repeating what Grace had heard many times before.

"Her family is coming Christmas day, so that's worked out," Clara added. She smiled at Grace. "Thank heavens I have you and Michael. I count my blessings every day." Clara hugged Grace and headed for her room. At the door she paused. "Bart Rafford killed in a ski accident. You wonder what would have happened had he lived."

"I suspect it would have been just the same as it is now."

"He never saw his son." Shaking her head, Clara left.

In minutes Grace was stretched beneath covers on the sofa. She lay in the dark, thinking about Nick's party, going back to the first moments, now etched in her memory. She couldn't forget Nick or anything about him. Nor could she keep from worrying about his purpose in seeing her. She wasn't giving up Michael no matter what, but the Rafford money and Nick's reputation as a ruthless, shrewd businessman worried her.

★ ★ ★

At nine Monday morning Nick was ushered into Grace's narrow, plain office. Looking dynamic, he dominated the space. Was it his take-charge attitude or his mere physical presence that sped up her heart rate? When she looked into his eyes, a current zinged to her toes. He was sinfully handsome and it was easy to see why women were drawn to him. She had watched him Friday night, occasionally hearing conversations as she passed him, and knew he could turn on the charm. With an effort she tore her gaze from his dark eyes.

As he glanced around, she became acutely conscious of her office with its cramped space and old furniture in the aging building. She operated on a shoestring, yet her business was growing, a plus, she reminded herself constantly.

"Good morning," she said, greeting Nick without offering her hand.

"Good morning," he replied, giving her a faint smile. "Red becomes you."

"Thank you," she replied. She was certain the compliment rolled off his tongue without thought, yet she couldn't keep from being pleased. He extended the envelope that had contained her bill and she guessed it was her payment.

"Here's for the party. You did a bang-up job and there were a lot of compliments on the food. You should get more bookings from my friends." His hand was well shaped, his fingers long, his white shirt cuffs hiding his wrists.

"Thank you. Some guests asked for my card. I appreciate the opportunity of your business," she replied. Approval would have been satisfying from any other customer, but his solemn expression and the intensity of his dark eyes took away pleasure. His presence screamed a mission. "Please have a seat."

He sat in one of the small chairs and she pulled one around to face him, too aware of his proximity. Unsettling, he threatened her well-being. Adding to his overpowering presence, his thickly lashed dark brown eyes were piercing.

"I've come to talk about Michael."

She drew a quick breath. "From the first I figured that was why you wanted to meet."

"That's right. My father is in poor health. In the past year he's had two heart attacks. Illness has changed his outlook on life. He'd like to meet you and Michael."

Her heart lurched and she locked her fingers together as she fought a sense of panic. The Raffords' power loomed. She imagined that the father was even more formidable than the son because of his years developing influential friends. Taking a quick breath, she attempted to maintain a calm demeanor.

"Are you aware that your brother signed away his rights to Michael?"

"That's what I've been told."

"He did that in the last weeks of Alicia's life. She tried to get everything lined up so Michael would be financially provided for and have a guardian until he's grown. I can't imagine your father simply wants to see the baby. I'd guess there's more to it than that," she added, hoping for a denial. When Nick didn't give one immediately, her dread increased.

"He doesn't intend to take Michael from you, but he wants to get acquainted with his grandson," Nick said. "I'll repeat—illness has changed my father's values. His grandson has become important to him. I'd like to arrange a meeting and it would be easier on my dad if you could get together at his house," Nick continued. Her gaze dropped to his mouth and slightly sensual lower lip. What would it be like to feel those lips against hers?

Startled by her train of thoughts, she returned to the moment. She could not keep from having a faint glimmer of hope from Nick's remarks. "If your father is that frail, he surely can't want Michael in his life much of the time. It doesn't sound as if he is in any shape to care for a baby."

"He's not, but he can afford to hire care. Frankly, while you have a growing, successful business," Nick said, glancing around her office, which she could imagine he was contrasting with his own and his father's, "my father can do much more financially for Michael than you can."

"Money really isn't everything," she replied. Her chill intensified. Nick sat relaxed, looking as if he was the one in charge. His tone of voice carried a note of steel, indicating she could be in for a bitter, ugly fight with a powerful man. "I love Michael and when I'm not with him, my aunt, or her closest friend, keeps him. My flexible schedule allows me to spend a lot of hours with Michael. Did your parents spend hours with you?"

"Touché," Nick said with a trace of amusement. "No, they did not."

"I've read about you and your father in the society pages of the paper and local magazines. Your father has had several marriages and many women in his life. It was the same for your brother when he was alive. Who did you spend the most time with—nannies?"

"Nannies, the chauffeur, boarding school," Nick replied, confirming her guess. She wondered about his life and could see how his relationships might be shallow and brief. Some people would envy Nick's childhood, but she thought it was inadequate. She didn't want Michael to grow up in any such manner.

"Face the facts, you're limited in the life you can provide for Michael," Nick stated. "You should give some thought to what you're turning down here. My dad wants me to set up a meeting where he can talk to you about Michael. Just talk. You should be willing to do that, because there is nothing threatening in meeting. Far from it," Nick added, self-assurance lacing his tone. He remained at ease, as if assured of the outcome of this conversation.

She bristled. "Your brother wanted nothing to do with his baby. Where was your father at that time?"

"I've told you, my father is a changed man."

"This transformation is a little late and it's difficult for me to believe he's actually changed. Michael's mother, Alicia Vaughan, was my best friend my entire life. Before she died, she told me about Bart. When she was pregnant, your brother was blunt and coldhearted with Alicia. The last time Alicia saw him, he called her foul names while insisting he wanted nothing to do with 'her brat.' He sent her on her way in tears in a rainstorm. That night was when she had the wreck that eventually ended her life. She almost lost Michael because of the wreck. After what occurred, I can't see any reason to take Michael to your father."

Nick leaned forward, placing his arms on his knees, his navy suit jacket falling open. A gold cuff link glinted in the light. He was close, distracting her with fleeting thoughts about how handsome he was. She found it difficult to get her breath, impossible to resist looking again at his mouth. What was the man like when he was not on a mission? She had seen glimpses of that last night.

"My father has aged a lot in the past year. He's in failing health—I think he's hanging on for Christmas and he wants to see his grandson. Can't you at least meet with him? What harm could there be in that? You need to think about this, because you might be a lot better off and the baby certainly would. My father is enormously wealthy. Don't cut Michael off from a better life."

The words were persuasive, as well as the man. She felt a flutter of sympathy that vanished when she remembered Alicia sobbing in the hospital bed, hooked to tubes, hanging on to life. At the same time Michael, who was delivered a month early because of the car wreck, had been in neonatal intensive care. All caused in part because of how cold and harsh Bart Rafford had been to her friend.

"Michael was orphaned because of your brother. Alicia begged him to recognize his son. He could have said no without being hurtful about it. I see no point in taking Michael to visit your father. He's had his chance to have the baby in his life. He could have come forward when Alicia was pregnant or right after that last time she saw Bart."

Grace stood and Nick came to his feet immediately. She was aware of his height and that aura about him conveying his control. He stood close to her, and once again she was more conscious of Nick than anything else. His features were impassive and she had no idea whether he was irritated, disappointed or mapping his next move.

"Just because my brother was hurtful doesn't mean you should be. If you're frightened about Michael, don't be. My father can't take him from you, because he's not well enough to do so."

"I think I've made my feelings clear," she said, unable to get Alicia out of her mind or stop worrying that while Eli Rafford wasn't well, he was a man who had enough power to achieve his goals.

"You can live with your conscience over your decision?"

"Better than I could if I agreed to take Alicia's baby to see your father. Does he have any idea how cruel his son was to my friend? Or does he just want Michael in his life and he doesn't care what happened to Alicia? Bart used her and then discarded her."

"I think most women my brother 'used' were extremely willing as well as pleased at the time," Nick remarked drily, stirring Grace's indignation "Your friend wasn't forced to have an affair with him."

"She realized what a mistake she had made." Grace stepped away from Nick to head toward the door. "I think we've finished our conversation."

"Don't be so quick to toss away Michael's future. Suppose this catering business doesn't last? Then what?" Nick asked, honing in on her deep fear. "You know how to reach me if you change your mind," he said. As far as she could tell, he didn't seem distressed, but she suspected he could easily hide his feelings.

"I can tell you now—I won't change my mind."

Nick gave her a cool, satisfied smile as if he expected her to capitulate to his wishes. "When you do rethink Michael's future, just call." Nick hesitated, his gaze undergoing a subtle change that warmed her. He gave her a glance that caused her heart to skip a beat.

"Too bad we didn't meet under other circumstances," he said in a deeper tone, this time setting her heart racing. As he left, closing the door, she let out her breath.

"But we didn't," she said to no one, surprised by his last remark which, for a brief moment, had taken her away from the problem. How much more difficult it was to deal with the situation when the messenger was a charismatic, sexy man like Nick.

She felt completely wrung-out, as if she had been sparring with a formidable foe. She didn't imagine she had seen the last of the Raffords. Men with wealth such as theirs did not accept defeat easily.

Was she cutting Michael off from a myriad of marvelous opportunities that Eli Rafford could provide? That was exactly what had sent Alicia to see Bart. Would Alicia have jumped at this chance and think Grace was being a poor guardian? Grace simply feared the Rafford patriarch would take Michael from her, but she needed to give Nick's request more consideration before she totally slammed the door on the Raffords. Eli Rafford could insure Michael's future. After a few days, it still wouldn't be too late to contact Nick and agree to his wishes.

The thought chilled her more.

She wanted no part of Eli Rafford and she couldn't imagine that he merely intended to see Michael a few times. She suspected he wanted his small grandson. And he would want to give him the life he had given Nick—nannies, chauffeurs and boarding schools. As far as she was concerned, she could give Michael vastly more because he would have her loving care and attention.

She walked around her desk and looked up her attorney's phone number, afraid she would need help to fight this battle. Frightened and concerned, she was certain it wasn't over and that she had not seen the last of Nick.

Chapter 2

Nick drove his black sports car away from the strip mall where Grace rented space for her office. Relief dominated his feelings as he glanced at his watch. His lunch appointment with his closest friends would get his mind off this problem for the time being.

Jake and Tony were already waiting and soon Gabe Benton joined them. Over hamburgers, Nick realized the lunch was not pushing his problem out of mind.

"Nick, I don't think you heard a word I said," Jake stated.

"Sorry," Nick answered. "It's Dad and what he wants. Long story, but the three of you know about the baby that might be Bart's. Dad has a bee in his bonnet about getting the baby into the Rafford family."

"And that's not what the baby's guardian wants," Tony guessed.

"Money talks. I can't imagine your dad hasn't made her an offer or had you make her an offer," Jake remarked. "That's the usual MO for all our dads."

"She's not interested."

"Is this the new caterer you had?" Tony asked.

"As a matter of fact, yes."

"Simple. Just marry her," Jake suggested with a twinkle in his eyes.

Nick gave him a look. "I'm not marrying anyone to get something for Dad. I'm not marrying for years, period. All you guys will be married before I am."

"The hell you say," Tony replied. "Name your price, I'll bet you're married first."

Nick relaxed, enjoying the good-natured exchange and getting his mind off his problem. "I will be the last. One million in the pot."

"Oh, no. I'm definitely going to be the holdout. I'll bet a million and I will win," Jake said.

"I'm guaranteed to win," Tony stated.

"You guys—betting a million over getting married. I could be the winner because I'm the youngest, but my money is going elsewhere," Gabe said. "Count me out of this."

"All right," Nick said. "We have a bet. Last one to marry gets one million from the other two—namely, I will collect from both of you."

"Deal," Jake said as Tony nodded. "It's sweet," Jake added. "Gabe is our witness. I don't expect this bet to be over for years."

"You guys are in it now, and it will be years," Nick said, smiling and relaxing.

Their conversation shifted to sports and for half an hour he didn't think about Grace, the baby or his father. It wasn't until he told his friends goodbye and left that he went back to thinking about his father's demands.

"Might as well get this over now," he said to himself, dreading breaking the news to his father. He changed direction and headed to his father's palatial estate. When he entered the grounds, he called his dad's nurse to let her know he was coming.

Circling splashing fountains, assorted statues and well-tended beds of flowers, Nick drove around the mansion to the back, sitting in the car long enough to call his office and tell them when he would be in.

He pushed the bell at the back and the door was opened by a gray-haired uniformed woman he had known since childhood.

"Good morning, Miss Lou," Nick said, smiling at her.

"Morning to you, Mr. Nick. Your father will be glad to see you."

"I have doubts about that. I'm telling him something he doesn't want to hear."

She laughed. "None of your escapades now!"

"There hasn't been any such nonsense since I went off to college," he said, laughing with her.

She chuckled and shook her head. "He's in the library. He'll be glad to see you. I think he's lonesome. He talks to me a lot more now."

"Then he shouldn't be so lonesome. You're good company," Nick said, smiling at her. He walked down the broad terrazzo-floored hall to enter the spacious room that included three walls of shelves filled with books and pictures.

His father was in a chair near the bay windows and his nurse turned to smile at Nick as she stood.

"Good morning."

"Hi, Megan. Morning, Dad," Nick said, crossing the room. "Megan, you can stay. I won't be here long," he said, but she shook her head.

"I have some things I can do," she said.

Nick watched the petite auburn-haired nurse as she left through the open door into the hall. Nick sat facing his father, who was dressed and had shaved, wearing a cardigan over his shirt and with his feet in slippers. He was a thinner version of his old self and more gray had spread through his thick black hair. Nick knew he resembled his father and wondered if this was how he would look someday.

"How are you this morning?" Nick asked.

"Same as last week. I take it you've talked to Grace Wayland."

"Yes, I did. I went to her office today to discuss Michael."

"So when do I get to see my grandson?"

"Dad, because of Alicia, Grace has very strong feelings about us. She resents Bart's treatment of Alicia, especially Alicia's last visit with Bart."

A pained look crossed his father's face and his gaze shifted to the windows. Nick noticed a muscle working in his dad's jaw while he crushed the corner of his open cardigan in one hand. "I'm sorry I didn't talk to Bart more at the time. I made a mistake in not taking an interest from the first."

"Grace is bitter over her friend. She sees no point in bringing Michael to see you."

"Damn it, Nick! You can be persuasive. Why didn't you talk her into a meeting?"

"Well, maybe my heart wasn't in it. Stop and think a minute about it. We're not certain this is Bart's child."

"He told me that it probably was his baby. Early on, I didn't feel strongly about it, but my life has changed. I want to see my grandson. This is vital to me," his father snapped, some of the old force returning to his voice. He stood and walked to the mantel to brace his arm on it. "I want that child in the family. I intend to see that he has the family name." Eli turned to stare at Nick. "Doesn't she realize it will be better for Michael?"

"I pointed out to her that you can do a lot more for Michael than she will ever be able to," Nick said patiently, knowing there would be more to come because his father never gave up on something he wanted badly.

"She's not thinking about the baby."

"That doesn't matter if she refuses to allow you to see him. Bart signed away his rights. He gave up any claim. Add to that, Grace's bitter feelings over the treatment her friend received from Bart."

"I suppose she blames Bart for Alicia's wreck."

"She probably does," Nick said, mindful that Grace did blame Bart. "Dad, give it up. Someday I'll give you grandchildren. Besides, you've told me that you never wanted more children, nor did any of the women you married. It's a late point in life to decide you want to enjoy a grandchild."

"Nick, damn it, I intend to give my grandson his heritage of the Rafford name and in some manner to rectify what Bart did."

"You'll send your blood pressure higher worrying over this," Nick said gently. "Right now, you're not completely well. You can't deal with a grandbaby. You really never have wanted to have babies around."

"No, I haven't. I just want to see the little boy. I want him legally an heir—and I've told you that you will get the bulk of the estate no matter what happens. I wouldn't think of cutting you out of most of what I possess, but there is enough for him to have a trust. After all, Nick, he is your nephew."

"It's difficult to relate to a baby I've never seen, with a deceased mother I can't recall meeting." Stretching out his long legs, Nick folded his hands, giving his father time to vent his frustration.

"Bart handled things badly, but I'm aware of this family's responsibility—"

"Dad, you don't have a responsibility. Bart signed his away totally."

Eli scowled, glaring at his son. "I want this baby in our family and I can do so much for him."

"Grace Wayland doesn't want you to. She doesn't want you to meet him. She refused to see you. I'm sorry, but there it is."

"The hell you say? You walked out and gave up? You don't give up when it's something you want."

"Understand, Grace was adamant about it. She's incensed over her friend. She isn't going to be talked into it."

"Well, then I'll bribe her into it. Did you tell her I would set up a trust for Michael?"

"I told her you could do many beneficial things for him. I pointed out to her that you can do far more for Michael than she can and it didn't move her. She doesn't want nannies or chauffeurs or boarding schools for him."

"Damn it, what's the matter with the woman? She's in business for herself. You told me she came from a poor background with no college education in the family. How can she turn up her nose at money for the baby?"

"She's unhappy with the Raffords," Nick reaffirmed patiently.

"Alicia came from that same poor background, but she appreciated money."

"I can imagine," Nick remarked drily, thinking his brother got tangled up often with women after his money. "In a way, it's refreshing to meet a woman who doesn't put the dollar first."

"Refreshing? It's damned stubborn. She's letting emotions cloud her judgment and she isn't giving the baby a fair shake."

"She was unmovable," Nick said, hanging on to patience. "Maybe if I try again in a few months she will have thought it over and softened up about it."

"Nick, time is important to me. It grows shorter by the day."

"Your doctors say you are doing fine. Let's wait a few weeks—Christmas is coming and maybe the holidays will change her mind. I'll talk to her again sometime," Nick said, astounded at the words coming out of his mouth. He didn't want to argue with Grace Wayland again, but his sympathy went out to his dad. "I'll try again soon. We won't give up." When he stood, Eli crossed the room.

"I don't want to give up. This is my grandson. I'm sticking to what I want, to know him and give him our family name."

Nick nodded. "I tried, Dad. I better go. I have an eleven-o'clock appointment. I'll let myself out."

On his way out, Nick checked in with the nurse and the staff, then left. Relieved to have broken the news to his dad, he wondered whether his dad would give up. Nick didn't want to argue further with Grace. With a little time maybe his dad's feelings about the baby would cool, although Nick knew that was probably wishful thinking. His dad was like a dog with a bone over something he wanted and couldn't have. He would go after it and hang on like crazy.

Nick shifted his thoughts to business, running over the information he had been given for a morning appointment to discuss a land acquisition in the Dakotas. Wrapped in thoughts about business, he continued to the twenty-story building in downtown Dallas that housed the Rafford energy company.

Business occupied Nick for the rest of the day until late afternoon, when his direct line rang and he saw it was a call from his dad.

"I knew it," he said under his breath, wondering what scheme his father had hatched during the day to pressure Grace about the baby. His father wouldn't discuss it over the phone, so Nick promised to drive out and see him after work.

He replaced the receiver and spent another hour working before closing up.

As he walked through his secretary's station he smiled. "See you tomorrow, Jeananne."

"Have a good evening," she answered.

"Thanks, I will," he said as he left, wondering if his father was going to make another plea that would mean dealing with Grace. He couldn't imagine any other reason for the request to drive out and see him again. They went months without seeing each other. Twice in one day had to mean something was brewing.

Nick drove through the estate, up the winding driveway past the statuary and fountains. He continued to the back, the easiest way in, greeting the staff and heading this time for his father's favorite living area.

Still in his cardigan and slippers, Eli smiled. "Thanks for coming. I want to talk further about this problem of Michael."

"I figured you did."

"Would you like to join me in a drink? I have a fine bottle of red wine."

"Sure, Dad. Let me," Nick said, crossing the room to the bar where a bottle of red wine had already been placed on the counter with two crystal glasses beside it.

He uncorked the bottle to pour the Pinot Noir.

"So how are profits this month?" Eli asked.

"Better than last month," Nick answered, picking up their drinks. "I have a land deal in North Dakota that will be good I think."

"I don't worry that you'll ever spread yourself too thin even though you do take risks."

"You recognize you have to take risks," Nick said. "I learned that from you."

"Here's to success," Eli said, lifting his glass of wine.

Nick sat in a navy wing chair facing his father and lifted his glass. "I'll gladly drink to that. So what's up?"

Eli smiled. "I'm aware how persuasive you can be when you want to be. I'm going to do a little arm-twisting myself. Nick, I want my grandbaby in my life. I'm counting on you to see to it that my wish is granted."

"I've tried. With Bart signing away his rights and declaring that he wanted nothing to do with the baby, there's little I can do."

"You made tentative overtures about my seeing Michael. I want Michael legally my grandson and to have my name. I intend to get what I want."

Now Eli sounded like himself and not a frail, aging man. Nick wondered where the conversation was going and what his dad had in mind.

"I talked to my lawyer today. Harvey came out to the house after lunch. I hate to do this, Nick, but I don't think you're taking me seriously or are convinced about how much I want my grandson in my life."

"Wrong. I'm definitely taking you seriously," Nick said as he braced for another odious assignment.

"Well, you will now. As of this afternoon, I have two new wills. One leaves the bulk of my estate, the houses, my possessions to you with a trust for Michael and five million when he reaches twenty-one. The other will leaves my sizable fortune to charity with the exception of this house and one million to you."

"You're cutting me out of your will," Nick said, shocked and staring at his father.

"I hope not. I don't want to have to use that will. If you get Grace Wayland to agree to allowing me to legally have Michael declared a Rafford and to let me know him, I will shred that will and you will get the bulk of everything I own.

Otherwise, Nick, your inheritance is cut. You won't starve or be broke—you're a multimillionaire already—but I'm worth a lot and I'm sure this will give you an incentive."

"Damn it, Dad, I can't move that woman to do what she doesn't want to do or legally doesn't have to do," Nick said. He was barely hanging on to his temper, exasperated with his father's unreasonable demands.

Eli smiled. "Think about it. You have monumental achievements. Women like you, Nick. I can count on you. Make no mistake though, I mean what I say. Harvey has the wills and my instructions."

"So exactly what do I have to get her to agree to? Let me get this clear. You want more than a visit with the baby."

"I want him in the family. I want her to willingly go to court with us and give him the Rafford name."

"Damn it," Nick said. There was no point in arguing and the sooner he got out of his father's presence, the less likely they were to get into a real battle of wills. He stood. "Under the circumstances, I better start making plans. I'll think over what you want," he said, glancing at his watch. "I have to go, Dad. I'll see what I can do."

"I'm sure of your success, Nick." Eli raised his glass in the gesture of a toast.

"You haven't met Grace Wayland. She has strong feelings about our family."

"You'll convince her otherwise. I've never seen the woman you couldn't wrap around your little finger."

Nick shook his head and left. As he drove to his condo, he mulled over the turn in his life. His father meant what he'd said. Nick knew it was no idle threat. And he didn't want to toss away a fortune and give up. Not without a fight.

The problem loomed a full-scale battle. Grace hadn't wanted

to let his dad see the baby, much less actually let him become part of the family.

Nick thought of her green eyes flashing with fire. The prospect of seeing her again was two-edged. He hadn't been able to get her out of his mind since they met. On the other hand, he had little relish for the struggle to win her over. He had tried reasoning with her. Now he'd just have to try charming her.

He concentrated on driving while he began to map out his next move.

Grace ran over the bookings for the coming week. Christmas was approaching and she had a long list of parties. She glanced up to see her assistant.

"Nick Rafford is here," Jada announced.

"Tell him to come in," Grace said. "I'll get this over with quickly."

"I don't think I'd be in a rush," Jada said, smiling.

Grace was certain he would try to talk her into yielding on her refusal to meet with his father. She'd hated the jump in her pulse when he had called for this appointment. She was just as annoyed now that she experienced a tingling awareness of him as well as being unable to avoid thinking about how she looked. And she had talked too long to him today on the phone. What should have been a five-minute call had turned into half an hour before she realized how much time she was spending.

While she placed papers in a file cabinet, Jada announced Nick.

"Grace, here's Nick Rafford."

Hoping she didn't reveal the physical reaction, the hitch in her breathing at the sight of him, she motioned toward a chair. He was the most handsome man she had ever known. "Please have a seat."

"Thanks. Ever the businesswoman," Nick said, smiling with a flash of white teeth that were as flawless and winning as the rest of his appearance. As before, his dark eyes kept her spellbound until she realized she was gazing back, with silence spreading thickly between them.

"So what brings you to my office?" she asked, trying to be brisk and cut the breathlessness from her voice. How could the man stir such a reaction by nothing more than his presence? She was amazed by his effect on her. Men didn't set her heart racing and make her insides tingly. Nick had never flirted with her and they barely knew each other, yet her response to the sight of him was unmistakable. Worse, he heightened her consciousness of herself, her plain navy skirt and shirt, the shortness of the skirt that didn't reach her knees. Again she was mindful of her drab, simple office, something she seldom had given a thought about until Nick.

"I assume this is your busiest time of the year, unless June weddings bump Christmas to second place," he said. He looked relaxed as if in total command of the situation in spite of having been soundly dismissed in their last meeting.

"Good guess. This is the busiest season and June is second."

"That's what I figured. The last time I saw you I made my case. I'm here on a different errand. This time I want to drop family matters. I'm doing what I would have done if we'd met under different circumstances. Namely, I'd like to take you to dinner—strictly a man and a beautiful woman he would like to know better. Just an evening out with nothing else going on for a few hours."

She laughed. "You're doing this to soften me up for another argument about Michael."

Amusement lit his dark eyes and heightened his already overwhelming appeal. "Maybe, but that isn't my intention for this one night. You're an attractive woman," he said quietly, causing her more palpitations. "You're single. I want to take you out. Are you free tonight?"

She wanted to answer yes, accept his invitation and have an exciting night with a handsome man who lit fires in her. At the same time, common sense screamed to avoid any close contact with him. He wanted her most precious possession—Michael.

Nick Rafford was accustomed to winning big battles, acquiring what he wanted when pitted against more formidable opponents than a single woman guardian. She had no illusions about his invitation, but that didn't take away the temptation to accept.

"I can see the wheels turning. Stop worrying about my motives." He leaned forward and picked up her hand, placing his thumb on her wrist. "Your pulse is racing, as is mine." His strong fingers were warm, a steady, light pressure that made her heart beat faster. His brooding dark eyes held a promise of sensuality. "Say yes, Grace," he coaxed in a husky voice. "I'll take you home tonight any time you want. Let's have a few hours together. The night promises fireworks. How about I pick you up around seven?"

"Yes," she whispered, "if my aunt is free to keep Michael. I'll contact her," she said, retrieving her phone from a pocket. When Grace broke the connection, she nodded. "I'm free. I expect you to keep your promise of taking me home if I ask."

"I swear. I've never gone against a woman's wishes concerning a relationship."

"You can't describe dinner together as a 'relationship.' I'm barely acquainted with you," she said, aware now his thumb traced lightly back and forth on her wrist and her palm, faint strokes that wreaked more havoc.

"I gave you a truthful reply to your statement. Hopefully, a reassuring one."

"This is one of the nights this month that I have open.

There aren't too many of them." When she withdrew her wrist and stood, he came to his feet. "Speaking of business, I should get back to work," she said.

Once again she thought she detected amusement in his torrid gaze. He stood close enough for her to notice his inviting aftershave. Without thinking, she looked at his mouth. Would they kiss tonight? She could feel the heat rise in her cheeks at the prospect of Nick's kiss. It had been a long time since she had gone out with anyone.

"Selfishly, I'm glad there's no man in your life right now."

"There isn't and hasn't been for a while. For the past seven months, I've been too busy with Michael. Before that, for years my time has gone to learning the catering business and then starting up my own."

"Sounds as if you're overdue for a night on the town. Let's make it a bigger deal and start at six. Will that be too soon?"

Her mind raced, because six would mean closing early. Yet how long had it been since she had gone out for the evening other than to cater? A few hours with a handsome, sexy man. No diapers, no responsibilities, no rushing to keep a party running smoothly. Anticipation bubbled in her.

"Six will be fine."

"See you then," he said, and left.

As she went back to the task at hand, her mind kept returning to Nick. Was she making a huge mistake by getting better acquainted with him?

She went to find Jada. "Since we don't have anything booked tonight, I accepted Nick's dinner offer."

Jada squealed with delight and wrung her hands in glee. "Sweet! You're going out with Nick Rafford! He is the handsomest man I've ever seen! How awesome!" Her ponytail bounced as she danced.

"Jada, he's Michael's uncle. He probably has ulterior motives."

Jada waved her hands in the air. "Of course he doesn't. And if he does, you'll be able to cope. Go seduce him and marry him."

Grace had to laugh. "I barely know him. Besides, the man has publicly been quoted as a confirmed bachelor and his father had multiple marriages. Also—marry Michael's uncle?"

"A legal guardian is not a blood relative. You certainly aren't a blood relation even though you're the only mother Michael knows."

"I'm having dinner for the first—and maybe last—time with Nick. What I came to tell you is that he wants to go early, so about two let's close up and get out of here. Everything is set for tomorrow night, isn't it?"

"Yes, and if he asks you out again, I can handle the Whitman party just fine. We have our help ready and I can take care of the Lansing party."

"I'm certain you can, but I'll be around. He hasn't asked me out tomorrow night."

"He will," Jada said with a grin. "I'm just sure he will."

Grace shook her head. "I'm going back to my office. I've had as much enthusiasm as I can stand," she said, wondering what Jada would be like when she fell in love.

By two the office was closed and Grace drove to her aunt's to see Michael for a while before going home. She was thankful she wouldn't have to hear another person bubbling over her dinner date—her aunt would do no such thing.

She gave Clara a hug and then turned to pick up Michael as he stretched out his arms and cooed, babbling "Ma-ma."

He smelled of baby powder and formula as she hugged him and he clung to her. He was warm and soft, cooing and babbling. She was sure she loved him more each day that passed.

She looked beyond him at her aunt. "You're sure about tonight?"

"Absolutely. Are you certain about going out with Nick? If they try to take Michael from you, I wouldn't be able to stand it. He's a grandson to me."

"Don't worry. Do what I do. Remind yourself that I have the papers Bart Rafford signed giving up Michael. I have the letter he gave Alicia, and the attorney has Bart's recorded testimony giving up his rights to his son. I have Alicia's will where her wishes for Michael are clear."

"Thank goodness she lived several weeks, long enough for the arrangements to take place."

"I think she was hanging on partially because of settling who cared for Michael," Grace said. She sat on the floor and put Michael down to play with him. "I'll be here for about an hour if you want to do anything."

"I might run to the neighborhood grocery. I won't be gone long," Clara said.

"Take your time. Michael and I will have fun," Grace replied, clapping her hands and then putting Michael's tiny hands together.

She continued to play with the baby after Clara's return until Clara finally pointed to the clock. "Grace, I hate to interrupt, but soon Michael will be getting hungry and you're going to have to go home to change now if you want to be on time."

"I have plenty of time," Grace said, getting to her feet and picking up Michael. She talked to him as she carried him with her to the door and then turned to hand him to Clara.

"Aunt Clara, are you sure you want him tonight?"

"Yes, I am. He's a sweet baby and easy to have. You don't have many nights out for anything that's just fun for you. You go enjoy yourself, but be careful. The Raffords are powerful, ruthless men with money and resources."

"I'll be careful. He promised just an outing with no talk about Michael or families."

"Talk is easy and Nick Rafford is accustomed to manipulating people far more experienced than you are."

"I'll be careful, I promise," Grace said as she left.

At her apartment she showered and dressed in a wine-colored dress with a plunging vee neck and long sleeves. She brushed her hair up, looping and pinning it with a few free strands. Finally she stepped into high-heeled pumps and did a brief inspection in the chipped mirror. "You're out of your league," she said to herself, thinking of Nick. Her gaze fell to Michael's framed picture on a table and she picked it up. "I love you," she whispered. "I don't want to lose you." She kissed the picture lightly, the glass cold against her lips and then she retrieved a tissue to wipe off the slight smudge.

When the doorbell rang, she picked up her coat and purse, glancing around the empty room that seemed a haven. With her pulse quickening, she went to meet Nick.

Chapter 3

Nick's smile melted her fears and reluctance. On her doorstep beneath the porch light stood over six feet of handsome male, impeccably dressed in a charcoal suit that had likely cost more than her last month's profits. Even white teeth, creases bracketing his sensual lips, a seductive approval in his gaze—all enticed. Packaged for seduction, he radiated confidence that increased his physical appeal. Behind him a sleek black limo waited.

Small wonder she was weak-kneed and shaken, hot and definitely bothered. As well as speechless.

"You look gorgeous," he said with warmth in his dark brown eyes.

"Thank you. You appear quite handsome yourself, but I'm sure you're accustomed to hearing that."

"This is the first time I've heard you say it. I'll admit, I'm pleased," he said. "Do you want to tell your aunt and Michael goodbye?"

"Michael is at Aunt Clara's house," Grace said, wondering

if he had planned on getting to see Michael tonight, but it was his father who wanted to meet Michael. She couldn't imagine that Nick cared in the least about a baby nephew.

"In that case, are you ready for a night out?"

"Yes, I am," she answered truthfully, smiling at him. He touched her cheek lightly with his forefinger.

"That's better. I haven't seen many smiles—something I intend to change tonight."

"The issues between us are not conducive to merriment."

"That definitely has to change. Let's get started."

She nodded and slipped into her worn black coat, closing the door behind her. A cold wind whipped her and she pulled her coat collar closer. "It's dark so early now," she remarked, shivering in the cold.

"You'll be warm in a second."

"I've never ridden in a limo, a fact that I'm certain doesn't surprise you. While you, on the other hand, have ridden in them since before you can remember."

A chauffeur opened the door and she climbed inside the luxurious interior, thinking it was an enormous waste of space for just two of them. While she noticed the lavish conveniences, her attention shifted to Nick. He sat near her, partially turning to face her and stretching his arm along the seat. Wind had caught a lock of his midnight hair and blown it over his forehead, heightening his appeal.

"You could live in here," she observed, only half aware of what she said because her attention was on Nick. "With the exception of a bed and bath, this is a mobile home."

His amused expression made her realize how inexperienced she must sound. "I can see why you're not in a topcoat," she continued. "Your limo is toasty warm." She slipped out of her coat and had started to pull it around her shoulders until Nick took over the task. His warm fingers brushed her nape, creating sizzles. "So tell me about this life of yours, Nick. It's vastly removed from mine."

"Not unlike your own life, except I'm not starting up a business. We both work to accomplish our goals," he said, his eyes taking leisurely inventory of her features, pausing on her mouth with a directness that caused her lips to part as she inhaled quickly. "We make decisions. We deal with people and accounting." He continued his bland list while his satisfied expression brought heat to her cheeks. He could see the effect he was having with nothing except a sensual visual survey. "We're both single. We both live in Dallas."

"You make it sound plain and simple, but it's not. I've seen local papers and magazines," she said, hoping she gave a sensible reply. She felt trapped in a web of sensuality that he spun effortlessly. Trying to focus her attention solely on their conversation and break his spell, she looked away.

"I go to parties. I imagine you do, too," he continued.

She smiled at him. "When I do, I don't get my picture taken."

"Something I can forgo," he stated.

She glanced out the window as they drove through downtown Dallas, where holiday lights multiplied the feeling of a fantasy evening.

"So, Grace, what do you want in life? Dallas's largest catering business? A chain? What's your ultimate goal?"

"I want my own successful restaurant or restaurants," she said, sharing her ambition with him and surprised at how well he could convey an illusion of intense interest in her life, something that cajoled information from her. "Since my first job I've worked in restaurants. I started with my aunt and uncle, who had a modest restaurant that was reasonably successful. When Uncle Pete died, Aunt Clara sold the restaurant and retired." Grace was aware as she talked that she had Nick's undivided attention. His steady gaze gave her the sense that he was spellbound by every word she said. She could see that such concentration would cause people to reveal more to him.

"A restaurant is open six or seven days a week, requiring long hours and demanding work, I would imagine."

"So how many hours a week do you put in?" she asked, suspecting he worked longer hours often.

He smiled. "You make your point. Now what do you do for recreation?"

"Now my pleasure is in taking care of and playing with Michael. He's a delight. Compared to yours, my life is simple. While we have things in common, we live in different worlds. I don't ride in limos and jet off to Europe."

"From the first, you've surprised me. I expected someone entirely different."

"Maybe you had preconceived notions about Alicia as well as me. While you, on the other hand, filled my expectations completely."

"Ouch. That means predictable and a few other undesirable descriptions."

"Not necessarily. I had the advantage of hearing beforehand about you from the media," she said.

"Don't believe the tabloids. Except the confirmed-bachelor part. My father has married enough to scare me from that forever."

"I'm sure." Glancing outside, she gave him a questioning look. "Where are we going?"

"Since you haven't had a night out in a long time, I tried to think of something special. We're taking my plane to Houston, where we'll board my yacht. When you're ready, we'll fly back the same way."

"Your yacht," she echoed, unable to believe she was headed for the experience he outlined. An evening on a yacht in the Gulf with a handsome multimillionaire. How had she tumbled so abruptly into a magical night that she would never forget in her entire life? Her excitement soared over the prospects. "You meant what you said when you told me something special," she remarked. Her anticipation caused her to flash him an eager smile.

"Ah, your smile—that makes my efforts worthwhile. Regrettably we got started in a manner that prevented many smiles from either of us," he said softly. "You have a smile that should get you the world," he added, his eyes warm.

"I think your flattery probably makes more gains than my smiles have," she answered lightly, aware they were treading on dangerous ground by flirting.

"I figured you would have a sitter for Michael and have to get home tonight."

"I definitely have to get home tonight," she said quickly, wondering if seduction was in his planned schedule. He grinned, an infectious, disarming grin that caused the temperature in the limo to climb.

"I'll get you home whenever you're ready to leave. Both flights are short. Sometime we can do something more spectacular and take a little longer."

"You're so certain we'll be friends despite having a life-changing disagreement between us."

"We'll see about that 'disagreement,' but not tonight. Tonight is your special night to get away from the demands of caring for a baby. No matter how adorable he is, a night out is long overdue."

She watched as they took the road for the airport. In minutes they drove past hangars across the tarmac and stopped. Nick went ahead, turning to offer his hand, holding hers as she stepped down.

Another cold wind struck her. Nick held her coat while she slipped her arms into it and pulled it close. He took her arm and they hurried to the waiting jet. Even through her coat, his firm touch stirred electricity.

She boarded another luxurious conveyance. Nick sat in a chair only a few feet from her. His raven hair, ruffled by wind, tumbled over his forehead. Watching him rake his fingers through his hair, she had visions of running her own fingers through the thick, wavy strands. The more tousled he looked, the more his appeal heightened. How easily he evoked a lusty reaction in her. Annoyed with herself, she couldn't resist watching as dark hairs sprang away from his hand.

In seconds she was buckled into the comfortable seat, facing Nick, her coat taken by an attendant who had also asked for her drink order.

Offered various cocktails and wine, she had chosen a glass of Pinot Grigio when she would have preferred a cup of steaming coffee, but that had not been in the offering. True to what Nick had predicted, she warmed rapidly and by the time they were airborne and the myriad lights of Dallas twinkled below, her chill had vanished.

"You were telling me about your life until our conversation was interrupted," he reminded her.

"I've told you what my big goals are. What are yours?" she asked, hoping to direct their conversation to his past. "I can't imagine what you want when you already have everything."

"No one has everything. I have goals—to increase business, to be a success at it."

"I'd guess there's something in your life that you want that's far more specific. What drives you, Nick?" she asked, aware that when she said his name it seemed more personal than with anyone else she ever talked to.

She caught a fleeting expression of something she couldn't define—surprise? Amusement? "Perhaps you don't want to tell me," she added quickly, unaccustomed to prying into people's lives.

"I'll answer any question you ask," he said. The words couldn't hold a double entendre, but they achieved that result with her anyway.

"I want to become a billionaire," he answered with a flat tone that made her realize this was important and a goal that surprised her. "Actually, I'd like to make more than my dad has. Maybe that's competitive. If so, it's the way he raised me to be."

They paused in the conversation as the attendant returned with a bottle of wine, uncorked it and let Nick give his approval before pouring the pale wine and serving it. As soon as they were alone, Nick leaned closer and lifted his glass.

"Here's to a fabulous escape for you."

"I'll toast that one," she replied, touching his glass lightly with her own. Her gaze was captured again by Nick's as they both raised their glasses for a sip. In midnight depths she detected a look that conveyed unmistakably that before this evening ended, he would kiss her. Her pulse jumped. The prospect heated her and she wanted him to. If he reached for her this moment, she would go into his embrace eagerly.

As if he discerned her thoughts, his gaze became heavy lidded, erotic.

Realizing where they were heading, she made an effort to end the spell, sipping her wine and looking away. Mentally, she searched for the broken threads of their conversation to pick up where they stopped. "You were telling me your goal, which I cannot fathom."

"It seems simple to me," he replied, leaning back again.

"You're already a multimillionaire. It boggles my mind to have so much wealth and strive to obtain more."

"Actually the money is not the exciting part. The battle to

acquire riches, as well as manage a fortune so what you have makes more, feeds my ambition."

"You need a challenge," she said, realizing what motivated him. Fear emerged from the discovery, because Eli's goal concerning Michael and her rejection pitted Nick against her in an unmistakable contest.

"Life's more interesting when fighting for something and infinitely more satisfying when I win."

"Perhaps that's the main part. You plan to win."

"Absolutely. Who plans to fail?" he asked, stretching out long legs that were only inches from touching her.

"Now you worry me. That drive definitely applies to your mission for your father," she stated solemnly.

Instantly Nick straightened and placed his hands on the arms of her chair, hemming her in and commanding her total attention. His face was only inches away and she could barely breathe.

"Not necessarily. Tonight, absolutely not. I talked about my life goal. I didn't have a thought in my head about my father. While we're together, my entire aim is to get to know an enticing woman," he added, lowering his voice, his expression as warm as a caress, making her insides jelly.

"All right, Nick," she whispered. "I believe you." She could not avoid shifting her gaze to his mouth. She wanted to kiss him. Mindful that was an unequivocal path to disaster, she longed to press her lips to his.

Their pilot announced an approach to Hobby in Houston, breaking the spell.

Nick flicked a knowing glance at her as he leaned away.

She gulped air into her empty lungs. He was a spellbinder. Effortlessly, he had crumbled her resistance and she reminded herself to get a better grip on her responses.

The minute they emerged from the plane, she shed her

coat and realized why Nick hadn't worn a topcoat. Warm coastal air enveloped her and she smiled in delight. "Ah, this is grand," she said.

"Excellent. I want the entire evening to be grand," Nick said, and she smiled at him.

They boarded the chopper that whisked them to his luxurious white yacht floating on dark water. The magical atmosphere increased, Nick weaving a spell that could mesmerize her completely.

After meeting the captain and part of the crew, Nick held her arm. "Let's go to the top deck for a drink and we'll dine. Afterward I'll give you a tour."

"Sounds perfect," she said.

They rode in a glass elevator that revealed a view of a sweeping staircase, floors beautifully outfitted and enormous pots of exotic plants. When the doors opened, she stepped onto a deck that increased her sense of unreality. A small band played and she saw a table set, centered with a crystal vase holding bird of paradise blooms tucked between white orchids and plumerias.

"Nick, it's paradise here. Warm weather, a yacht, the lights reflecting on the water. The docks and coastline are decorated for the holidays—various colored lights as if this is part of a colossal party," she said, turning to smile at him.

"I'm slipping," he said. "Water, flowers, yacht, lights—I was in hopes I'd be in that list somewhere."

Feeling giddy, she laughed. "You, sir, are the pièce de résistance," she admitted, tossing caution overboard.

"That's infinitely better," Nick stated, turning her and taking her into his arms to dance to the ballad the band played.

Startled, she followed his lead. In spite of the slight space between them, she detected his inviting aftershave. Through the fine wool of his suit jacket and his shirt, she felt the warmth of his arm. His hand holding hers heightened her sensory reaction.

"I'm in a dream tonight. You've succeeded beyond my wildest hopes. I never guessed I'd spend an evening like this."

"I'm more than pleased and if you think you're the only person having a great time, you're wrong."

She smiled. "For a few hours, there is no tomorrow and no routine life," she said. "Only paradise and a handsome charmer," she admitted, conscious she played with fire. Raging fire. Even so, she refused to allow caution to reemerge.

The music ended and Nick led her to their table. "I have champagne."

"It has to be followed by coffee when we eat. I'm not into wine and champagne and magic."

He smiled as he opened the champagne with a pop and poured it into slender flutes. He offered the bubbling drink.

"Nick, this yacht is moving," she said, startled by the realization that they were sailing.

"Don't be alarmed. We're traveling only a short distance along the shoreline and then circling back. I thought you'd enjoy seeing the lights and it would be more pleasurable than remaining anchored."

The fleeting question arose: could she trust him and accept what he promised?

As if he discerned her thoughts, he spoke. "I promised we'd go back whenever you want. If you're uneasy, we can return now and eat at one of the restaurants," he said, and she felt foolish.

"I just don't know you very well."

"Say the word and we'll return right now."

She shook her head. "Thanks, but no. I'm just unaccustomed to getaways like this."

"Text your aunt, tell her where you are," he said. "I think

you'll feel better. I'll talk to the band." He walked away and, losing her qualms, she followed his suggestion, grateful that he had made it.

When she finished the message, she took her drink to the rail. After a few minutes Nick joined her.

"Feel better now?" Without waiting for her answer, he continued, "Is everything all right at home?"

"Yes. Michael is sleeping and my aunt is getting ready to watch her favorite show."

They stood, chatting about nothing in particular and watching lights along the shore slip past until she realized they were moving slightly away from land, angling toward the turn he'd indicated.

During dinner, while each course was lavish, culminating in succulent lobster, her appetite was diminished by the charisma generated by Nick. "I haven't relaxed and enjoyed myself like this in months," she remarked, looking at him and smiling. "Actually, in this manner, never. I know you know how to relax. You have a reputation in the media."

"In the tabloids. I hope you aren't relying on those for your info about me."

"Definitely not! I'm relying on my own observations. My friend Alicia never mentioned you. I don't think she ever met you."

"No. In hindsight, I might have been better off if I had met her."

"You probably wouldn't believe me if I told you she hadn't had many relationships with men. She was in love with a guy right after high school. That lasted a year. Then there were a couple more. She ran around with friends who were male, but nothing serious, nor did she sleep with them."

"You sound as certain as if you were talking about yourself."

"I am. We grew up together in bad circumstances. Both

our families were poor. Worse, her father died when she was seven. Mine died when I was eleven. Alicia and I were as close as sisters, in fact, closer than I am to my own sisters. And she only had one brother who was killed three years ago. Alicia and I shared our hopes and disappointments. When she met your brother, he swept her off her feet. His money impressed her. She also liked him."

"Money impresses a lot of women. Women liked my older brother and vice versa. No problem there."

"I'm sure you receive the same reactions."

"I didn't from you," he reminded her. "That's where you threw me a curve. Principle before money? I never expected that response when I talked to you Monday morning."

"Michael is more important than money to me. I've spent nearly my whole life without money."

"That's why you should have been so awed and willing," Nick remarked.

"No. Michael is my son now," Grace replied, hoping to reinforce her position. "I took Michael home from the hospital after he was released from neonatal intensive care. His premature birth was terrifying. Now it would scare me more because I love him so much and feel as if he's my baby."

"He's actually my brother's baby—at least according to what I've been told."

"He is definitely your brother's child," she stated, realizing Nick's food was as forgotten as her own. "I knew my friend almost as well as I know myself. I've told you there were no other men in her life when she met your brother. Actually, Michael looks as if he's your son. When you see Michael, you'll know your brother was his father."

Nick's eyes narrowed. "We bear a resemblance? I'd never thought of that. I look like my father, so that means Michael might. That isn't something you can fabricate."

"Or exaggerate. I'm sure you'll eventually see for yourself. He looks like your son. No one could possibly disagree."

Nick gazed into space and she wondered why the discovery had silenced him. Had he figured this was another man's baby and dismissed his father's wishes? She didn't know what ran through Nick's mind, but the news that he and Michael bore a strong family resemblance troubled Nick.

He frowned slightly as he turned back to her. "Michael doesn't look like Bart? Did you ever meet Bart?"

"No, I didn't, but I saw a snapshot of him. I don't think Michael resembles Bart. Bart had hazel eyes, brown hair."

"Bart and I are actually half brothers. We had different mothers."

"That's something I didn't know."

"Bart and I had our own lives and were busy. Time slips away." Nick lapsed into silence again. A short while later he looked at her plate.

"Neither of us is eating. There's a great dessert."

"I'll pass, although everything is delicious."

"We can have the dessert later. C'mon, and I'll give you that tour," Nick said, standing and coming to take her arm.

As he showed her the upper decks, Nick kept the conversation on ordinary events, shared interests in movies and books. When he led her into his master suite, her senses spiked and her nerves became raw. She looked at the luxurious burnished-wood built-in furniture, rich brown leather upholstery, and a wide king-size bed covered in satin.

"Here's where I sleep when I stay on board," Nick said. His voice lowered, developing a husky note. Again his words were harmless, but his tone, his gaze when she looked up at him, his hand lightly on her arm—all combined to have her picture herself lying on his bed in his embrace.

When he turned her to face him, her heart thudded. His

hand on her arm was one more casual contact that should have been meaningless but instead was sizzling. She didn't want this fiery attraction that kept her breathless with him, yet there was no denying it. She wanted his kiss, could actually feel herself lean slightly toward him. His dark eyes warmed, his lids partially closing as he gazed at her mouth. She gathered her wits and her will.

"Nick, we should go back. Maybe dance now," she whispered, making an effort to turn away. Her heartbeat galloped in anticipation. Before the evening was over they would kiss and that knowledge played havoc with her nerves. Desire heightened, plaguing her.

"If that's what you want," he said.

They returned to the upper deck, where he drew her into his arms to dance, holding her lightly, gazing at her as they moved together in complete unison.

Hours later, as they stood talking quietly at the rail, she turned to him. "This is a bewitching night, Nick. You shouldn't make it so unforgettable and enticing."

"Why not? We can have a life separate from the problems caused by my father."

"Actually, I don't think we can," she said. "And it's time to start back home."

"Whatever you want," he said, smiling at her as they left the rail.

Within the hour they were airborne and Nick was entertaining her with more tales from his past.

It was almost three in the morning when his limo stopped at her apartment complex and Nick walked her to the door. "Give me your key and let me open the door."

Wordlessly, she handed over the key. He pushed open the door and held it for her to enter, following her inside and closing the door while she cut off the alarm. She turned to face him.

"Thank you, Nick. The evening was a dream come true— a night I'll remember for a very long time."

"It's not over yet," he said in a husky voice, slipping an arm around her waist and drawing her closer. At his hungry look, she glanced at his sensuous mouth, wanting to step into his embrace and kiss him, to be kissed. Yet once she did, her life might not ever be the same.

"Nick, this is dangerous, foolish," she whispered.

"Shh, it's only a kiss. It's meaningless—a goodbye, a touch. A kiss won't change our lives or the future."

"You are so sure of yourself," she said quietly, the tension growing between them. The warning inside grew dimmer. She couldn't look away from Nick's dark eyes, couldn't move away from him. Could he hear her heart pounding? Or feel her pulse racing?

Lightly, his fingers drifted along her throat, then up to her ear and in her hair while his arm tightened around her waist, drawing her closer.

"Nick, we shouldn't," she said, but her protest was weak, more of an invitation. She was losing ground, succumbing to desire. She inhaled and stepped back, out of his embrace. "You're not going to charm me into giving you what you want. You wanted this night to be about getting to know each other."

"I've kept my promise. I haven't pushed you about Michael."

"You did what you promised," she acknowledged. "I had a wonderful time, but now you need to go."

He gazed at her in silence and she could see the craving burning in the depths of his eyes. He nodded. "I'll take you to lunch Tuesday and we can talk."

He turned and was gone, the door closing quietly behind him.

She stared at the door. Every inch of her yearned to call him back, to step into his embrace and kiss. Kisses that she suspected would be as spellbinding as the entire evening had been. Desire scalded her. She wanted him with a hunger she wouldn't have believed possible.

She had done the right thing by keeping a distance between them. Then why was it so unsatisfactory and why did she long to be in his arms?

Sleep was lost for most of the remainder of the night. The time with Nick replayed in her mind while longing heightened instead of diminishing. She had to forget Nick, go on with her life, keep Michael safe from the Raffords, but it was difficult to think of never seeing Nick again. Lunch Tuesday. He wanted to talk about Michael. She could refuse, stop this before it went any further. Nick's dark brown eyes and the way he had held her when they danced tormented her until she finally drifted to sleep and dreamed about kissing Nick.

Chapter 4

At home Nick swam laps in his pool, trying to cool his raging libido. He ached to kiss Grace, too aware she had wanted to kiss. Her green eyes had conveyed lust and she had come close to succumbing. He was determined to win her over. Too much rested on the outcome of his dealings with her. He was accustomed to getting what he wanted and he intended to with Grace.

Meanwhile, he wanted her with an urgency that surprised him. He thought about her constantly and he couldn't recall doing that with any other woman.

Grace was different. Why? Was it solely the money that he would win or lose? She was a beautiful woman, but his life was filled with other entrancing women. Was it just because she was a challenge when he so seldom found a ravishing woman who resisted him?

Whatever the reason, getting his inheritance was essential. Tuesday, he intended to walk away from that appointment with a promise from her to let his dad meet Michael. With his father's health so frail, time was of the essence.

★ ★ ★

She had to move lunch Tuesday to two o'clock. She had spent the early hours getting dressed, finally selecting a simple navy suit and silk blouse. Then she had spent the rest of the morning reminding herself to resist whatever Nick asked.

Nick insisted on picking her up at her office, so she waited at the door. When Grace saw his black sports car approach, she stepped outside, hoping she hid her own feelings, because her racing pulse and butterflies in her stomach were unwanted. Adding to her flutters, Jada had been bubbly the entire morning over the lunch appointment. With a deep breath, Grace approached the curb.

When he stepped out to open the door for her, she had another jump in her pulse at the sight of him. Lunch in the middle of the day on a Tuesday shouldn't be filled with magic in a romantic surrounding. She hoped to be practical and firm, and resist whatever he suggested, because this meeting was clearly an effort to get what he wanted from her.

"Hi," he said, the gleam in his brown eyes causing a gush of warmth. "Busy day?" he asked.

"Very. Hopefully the afternoon will be quieter. Thanks again for a Saturday night that was relaxing and memorable. It was great to get away a few hours."

He flashed another smile. "For a moment there I hoped the reason was personal, not merely to get out for a few hours. We proved we don't have to battle constantly. I want to find some common ground."

"Common ground where Michael's future is concerned is entirely different. You can't undo the damage your brother did. Your family had every chance. We've been over that," she said, resentment curling sourly.

He drove to a popular place, where they hurried in the brisk, cool wind from his car into a restaurant that had grown quiet when the noon crowd had thinned. Near a fireplace that contained the last glowing embers from a fire, Nick sat across from her. Today he was in a brown sweater over a white shirt, looking casual, handsome and exciting.

After ordering, he smiled at her. "You look great. Very efficient, very businesslike, so desirable."

"Thank you, but the latter is not on our agenda."

"For now, forget the argument between us. You know what I did Sunday and yesterday?"

"How could I possibly have any idea?" she asked, amused by his question.

"I spent far too much time thinking about you and Saturday night. And wanting another night out."

"Nick, we can't pursue a relationship," she said, clinging to caution while another part of her wanted to smile and agree. "Of course, I know you're trying to get me to cooperate one way or another."

"I'll admit I'm trying to win you over, but not exactly for the purpose you're thinking now. There are some personal, ulterior motives here that do not involve my father," Nick said, his voice deepening and the expression in his eyes conveying unmistakable desire.

Her breath was erratic. "Stop flirting, Nick. We have no future—with family or without family."

"That doesn't have to be. I know you enjoyed Saturday night. I want to go out again. And once more, it has nothing to do with the future or my nephew or my father. Grace, you kept me at arm's length on Saturday night. I intend to change that."

Spellbinding words, yet was it a ploy to get his way? If he seduced her, she would succumb to everything he wanted. Now was the time to resist him, to ignore her tingling, breathless reaction, turn a blind eye to his handsome looks, hold fast to rejection even though everything in her screamed to accept, flirt with him and go with the moment.

"You're a dirty fighter, Nick. You know there's a chemistry and you've emphasized the attraction."

"What man wouldn't?" he asked in a low voice. "You're beautiful, Grace. I'm a warm-blooded man and I like being with you."

His words heightened her reaction, melting animosity and caution. "Wisdom tells me to avoid a wide-eyed, heart-thumping acceptance of your offers," she whispered.

"Maybe wisdom, but nothing else."

"You know I react physically to you. We react to each other, although I suspect you have this response from a lot of women. But with me, you have a strong ulterior motive."

With his gaze locked on her he raised her hand, brushing a kiss on her palm while his thumb was on the vein in her wrist. He watched her intently. "See there," he said in a husky voice. "Your pulse is rushing. Far faster than normal. As is mine. If we were alone now, you'd be in my arms."

"Nick, stop this," she said, hearing words spoken in a tone that sounded more like an invitation than a denial.

"I want to take you out tonight, including eating together," he said. "Say yes, Grace. Your assistant has already told me she can cover the party for you because it's a small one with a client you've had before."

"You just go barreling ahead to get what you want," she said.

"You weren't discontented Saturday night. You've gone with me twice now and you're in no worse situation for spending time with me, so what's the harm in accepting? Especially when it shows that you want to accept."

She laughed. "You don't give up, do you?"

"Not with you, because you want to go with me. How's

seven tonight?" He leaned closer. "We'll make it a short, early evening and do whatever you'd like to do. If I promise again no discussion about Michael and my dad, how's that? Now a yes," he said.

"Yes, against wisdom and caution."

"We have unfinished business."

"You promised—" she started to say.

"I'm not referring to Michael or Dad," he said.

Their waiter approached and Nick released her hand, watching her while green salads were placed in front of them.

Through lunch, Nick flirted and charmed and she forgot the problems for moments at a time until she would realize how much she responded to Nick. Each hour spent with him made her want to be with him even more. In spite of knowing that, she craved the excitement he brought into her life. Women could not resist him and in too many ways, she was no different from the others. She had capitulated easily to his dinner offer. She couldn't believe their time together meant anything to him except a means to get Michael. For her it was one more unforgettable evening instead of a few quiet hours playing with Michael and then spending the remaining time going over books for work. Just once more and then a firm, unyielding refusal. Could she really stick to that plan when Nick turned on the charm?

"I would like to talk about Michael *now*, though." Nick reached across the table to grip her hand again and her heart skipped a beat. His hand was warm, enveloping hers, causing havoc with her nerves.

"There really isn't anything to get to. My feelings haven't changed."

"Listen to me," Nick urged quietly. "You've been logical, not too emotional over this issue. Just come meet my dad and let him see and hold his grandson." Dark brown eyes bored into her while his thumb ran back and forth over her wrist, creating distracting flutters.

"How simple you make it sound," she said, her voice breathless, almost a whisper.

"It's harmless, Grace. My father is very ill. His heart is in bad shape and he's getting more frail. At least let him meet Michael and hold his grandson. Is that too much to ask?"

She withdrew her hand from Nick's. "You make it sound so easy, yet I always remember Alicia and her wishes."

"Alicia dealt with Bart. That's a whole different issue. Don't punish my father for stupid, cruel things my brother did."

"Your father could have stepped in."

"At the time my father knew nothing about Bart's rejection. Christmas is approaching—the season of giving. It's going to be damn bleak for my father. Bring the baby over and meet my dad and let him satisfy himself just seeing Michael. I'm not asking to take Michael or change his name or anything else right now. Just let Dad see him and hold him. Give him this, Grace."

She looked away, torn by Nick's plea and aware that she couldn't be that selfish over Michael, yet fearing the Raffords' power and Nick's ulterior motives. She thought about Michael and how much he resembled Nick. Once Eli Rafford saw the baby, he would never want to let him go because of that resemblance. To Eli, Michael would be Nick all over again. She was certain the remarkable resemblance would make a difference in Eli's attitude.

"Once your father sees Michael, he will never want to let him go."

"Grace, my father's days may be limited. He isn't well. He can't take Michael from you. This is only a meeting. I promise," Nick added quietly.

She looked into unfathomable brown eyes that told her

nothing. This man had a reputation for being ruthless in business. Was she being naive, gullible and taken in by a charmer who had plotted every move to take Michael from her?

"We can make it short," Nick added.

"All right, Nick," she said, staring at him intently. There was no change in his expression, reminding her that he could hide his emotions completely.

"Thank you for agreeing. You'll see how much it means to him."

"You better keep your word."

"I've promised. Don't be so fearful. It'll be all right. My father can't take your baby and if you're worried that I'll try to talk you into marriage, I have no intention of bringing either a wife or a baby into my life. My freedom is important and, at this point, I don't care to become a daddy. I'll make the arrangements. When will you be free?"

She pulled her phone and checked her calendar. "I'm booked solid since it's getting so close to Christmas. I can turn the parties over to Jada either Thursday afternoon or Friday afternoon."

"I'll make arrangements with Dad for Thursday afternoon," Nick said.

"I should get back to the office. You've gotten everything you want, so we can go now," she said with a sharp note in her voice.

"Not everything."

As they left, she was conscious of his height, his body so close to hers and his hand on her arm. He had gotten everything he wanted, yet he had sounded reasonable in his requests. Time would tell. She prayed she had no regrets.

Nick kept the conversation light, but worries were already besieging her when they drove back to her office. He got out quickly and came around to open her door. "Thanks for lunch, I think," she added, emerging from the car.

"How's two o'clock Thursday afternoon?"

"That will be fine. Michael may fall asleep, but that's all right."

"I'll pick both of you up at your place. Thanks for this. You'll see, after you have this first visit with my dad, you won't be sorry about your decision."

"We'll see, Nick. Thanks for lunch." She turned to walk briskly away, her back tingling because she guessed Nick stood and watched her. She dreaded meeting Eli Rafford, suspecting her trepidation would only grow. Inside her office, she turned to watch Nick drive away. She hoped she was doing the right thing.

Thursday seemed eons away and then it was upon her. She left work early to get Michael ready only to find Clara had already bathed him and laid out clothes.

"He's been fed and I think he'll fall asleep soon," Clara said.

"If you'll watch him a few more minutes, I'm going to change clothes," Grace said, hugging Michael and giving him a kiss before handing him to Clara.

"Sure. Take your time. I'll get Michael dressed in his sailor suit."

Grace changed to tan slacks and a matching silk shirt, then brushed her hair and clipped it at the back of her neck. She returned to Michel's room to find him seated on a blanket, playing with his toys and cooing.

"He looks adorable," Grace said, her worries returning.

"I know this meeting was probably inevitable, but I just pray your legal rights are binding. Once this man sees his grandson, he'll want him more than ever."

"Nick insists that his dad simply wants to see Michael and hold him. Clara, I hope I'm not making the mistake of my life."

Clara frowned and looked at Michael, who was playing with a rattle and happily babbling unintelligible words. "Me, too, Grace. I know Nick Rafford has pressured you into this meeting. A visit sounds harmless, but once Eli Rafford sees his grandchild, I hope the resemblance to Nick doesn't reinforce his goal to give Michael the Rafford name. Or more. Eli Rafford may be frail, but he has the money for nannies and all kinds of help. He could try to take Michael and pay people to care for him round-the-clock." Nannies and staff would raise Michael instead of relatives. Clara shuddered while Grace's chill deepened.

"That's what I fear," Grace said. "They have the money to do as they please. I made an appointment to talk to my attorney in the morning."

"Thank heavens," Clara declared. "You can't fight the Rafford money, Grace. I'm afraid Nick Rafford is showering his attention on you for a reason."

"Hopefully, this afternoon will be only what Nick said, simply letting the grandfather see his grandson. That doesn't give Eli any rights, no matter how much he wants them."

"Just remember Alicia, what she went through and how she tried to cut them out of Michael's life. The man's son was selfish and dreadful."

"I know. It's pointless to tell you to not worry. I'll call you as soon as I get home."

As she glanced at her watch the doorbell rang. "Come meet Nick," she said, picking up Michael.

It was time.

Nick stood immobilized, one of the few times in his life he was consumed by shock. He forgot people, surroundings, his purpose in coming. His total attention was on the baby in Grace's arms—a baby who was a mirror of his own baby pictures.

Stunned, he stared into big, dark brown eyes with black lashes, a thick head of baby hair as jet-black as his own, the same shaped ears.

"Oh, my God," he whispered. "He could be mine."

Grace spoke, but her words didn't register with him.

"Bart never saw his son, did he?" Nick asked finally.

"No, he didn't, but that was his choice," Grace replied. "Nick, come inside and meet my aunt."

Nick inhaled deeply, stepping inside, unable to take his gaze from the baby, realizing instantly his father was in for a shock. It occurred to him that his father would never give up the battle now to get Michael legally into the Rafford family with the Rafford name.

"Aunt Clara, this is Nick Rafford. Nick, my aunt, Clara Wayland."

Nick turned his attention to the woman standing beside Grace. Her green eyes were glacial and her mouth was closed tightly as she nodded, making it obvious that she didn't approve of him or want Grace taking Michael to meet his dad.

"I've heard about you and your care for Michael," Nick said, smiling at her, certain the smile would not be returned.

"Michael is Grace's precious child now. He loves his mother very much."

Nick could feel the waves of dislike and anger from the woman. "I appreciate her sharing Michael today and letting my dad meet his grandson. That is going to mean the world to him."

"Michael can't possibly be that important since your family shunned him totally at birth and when his life was hanging by a thread."

"Something my dad is sorry about now," Nick said quietly,

knowing she was immersed in anger with the Raffords. "Mrs. Wayland, my father has no intention of taking Michael from Grace. Today, he wants to meet his grandson. Just see him."

"It isn't today that worries me," Clara snapped, and Grace placed her hand on her aunt's arm.

"It's all right. I'll go with Nick now. I'll call you when we get back. Thanks for your help today."

She buckled Michael into his carrier and Nick picked it up as Grace gathered Michael's bag. She brushed a kiss on her aunt's cheek. "Don't worry," she whispered.

"I'm glad to have met you," Nick said politely and left, waiting outside for Grace to join him.

"Sorry, but she's worried and upset."

"If I could be boiled in oil, she would have seen to it. Or a few other dreadful ways to get rid of me. Sorry to worry her so much. She could have joined us."

"Heaven forbid. She wouldn't want that and neither would you or your dad. Or any of us. She'll calm down if your intentions are really what you say."

"They are. Now I know why you looked so shocked when you first met me. I thought it was the hot chemistry between us, but, sadly that wasn't it at all. You were stunned by my resemblance to Michael," he said.

"Yes, I was surprised when I first saw you."

"Michael himself nails the Rafford paternity—except Michael looks as if he's my child instead of Bart's. There's no earthly reason to ask for a DNA test if we could. This baby is a Rafford through and through as far as appearance goes. He couldn't look more like my baby pictures. And I have a picture where I'm dressed in a sailor suit like the one you have on him today. That's going to jolt Dad."

"I didn't think of that. Should we go back and change?"

"No. I'm not going another round with your aunt."

Grace chuckled. "You? Scared of Aunt Clara?"

"I've faced opponents in boardrooms who didn't look that hostile. I'm thankful she wasn't armed."

"Aunt Clara wouldn't hurt a fly. I'm shocked. You're intimidated by Aunt Clara."

"Don't rub it in. I'm amazed she hasn't spent every second trying to convince you not to go with me today—or the last time, for that matter." Nick glanced in the rearview mirror at Michael in the backseat. "I don't know anything about babies, but I'm guessing this is a very happy baby."

"He's a darling. He is a happy baby."

"I would be, too, if you were taking care of me," Nick said, and she smiled.

"Sorry, you don't qualify," she answered lightly.

"I think I'll let the nurse and my dad know about the family resemblance before we spring Michael on my dad. This is going to be a shock."

"And make him want Michael all the more."

Nick glanced at her. "Don't start worrying. Dad will be pleased I'm sure and I don't know if he can want to know Michael any more than he does right now. You can't imagine how pleased and grateful he is that you've agreed to this. You'll see," Nick said, keeping to himself what would occur. His father would take one look at Michael and get an account set up, get presents for Christmas and want all sorts of things that involved the baby. "Just remember my dad is elderly and doesn't work anymore, which used to take a lot of his time and attention. He has no women in his life and I'm not around that much. Michael will be his main focus. That doesn't mean he wants to take the baby from you. I promise you that. Dad never was into children or babies."

"He is now," she said, and her tone sounded sharp.

They rode quietly until passing through the gates to his father's estate.

"Do you have a home besides your condo?" she asked.

"Yes. I have a condo in Houston. I have a home in Colorado and a ranch in West Texas. I lead a relatively unpretentious life."

"It sounds as if you do," she remarked drily. "Yachts, businesses, women, houses, condos. So simple."

"Modest compared to what I could do if I wanted to."

They wound up the driveway that gave a full view of the front of the mansion and he heard Grace's intake of breath. "This is a castle. Who lives here besides your father?"

"His staff, which now includes his nurses. There are currently two who live here and they take different shifts. I detect worry in your voice."

"How can I fight this?" she said.

"Perhaps you won't have to," he declared, but the words carried a hollow ring. His dad would fight with his whole being to get this child declared a Rafford.

He hoped that when Grace saw the house and met his father, she would come to her senses and realize what Eli could do for Michael. And now, Nick thought his father would do more. The two wills plagued Nick constantly. More than ever, he felt he had to get Grace to cooperate as quickly as possible before his father got really attached to Michael.

At the moment, Nick wanted to gnash his teeth in frustration. Grace had to capitulate. He reminded himself that she had so far.

He pulled to a stop in front, wanting to take Grace through the most impressive entrance. The more awed she was, the more cooperative she might become. He pulled out his cell phone. "Just a minute, Grace. Let me talk to the nurse and maybe Dad."

He made the call, giving her time to take in her surroundings, the vast wings of the house, the massive statuary and fountains in front, the immaculate flower beds with an array of colorful winter plants.

When he finished, he put away the phone. "Well, let's go introduce Michael to his grandfather. Michael will never know the storm swirling around him."

"I hope not. And I hope I survive it."

"You will," Nick said, wondering if she could be rethinking her stand on keeping Michael out of the Rafford family.

Nick stepped out to open her door and pick up Michael. He took Grace's arm. "My dad's no ogre in spite of the wild tales about his business deals."

"I think you're talking about yourself there."

He chuckled as they crossed to the massive door. He heard the chimes and then the door swung open.

Chapter 5

As the door swung open and a butler faced them, intimidation enveloped Grace. She was certain that was the intention of Nick and his father. She couldn't imagine anyone ever reaching a point where they took this magnificence and wealth for granted. She reminded herself that Nick had been born into it.

"Good evening, Mr. Rafford. Your father is waiting." The butler glanced down at the baby in the carrier, and Grace heard his swift intake of breath, but his expression didn't change.

They stepped into a mammoth marble hallway where Nick set the baby carrier on a side table. The hall ceiling soared three floors, and an enormous crystal chandelier hung above her head. Ahead, two staircases wound up to the next level.

"I'll get Michael from his carrier now and take his jacket off," she said, busying herself. Her fingers were cold and stiff and she dreaded the meeting with Eli Rafford. She wished now she had never succumbed to Nick's charm or agreed to anything involving him, although she suspected it wouldn't have stopped Nick or his father and it might have made matters worse.

She picked up Michael, holding him close, wanting to keep him in her arms and never hand him over to Nick or his dad.

"Ready?" Nick asked, and she nodded, raising her chin and hoping she looked far more calm and self-assured than she felt.

Along the hall they passed open doors on rooms with magnificent furnishings. How could one frail man live in this mansion? She suspected the staff was huge.

He stopped in front of a closed door. "Dad's in here. Grace, I'm going to tell him we're here. I think Michael will really surprise my father and I don't want to give his heart too big a jolt."

"Of course," she said, and waited. Nick reappeared and motioned to her, taking her arm and walking her into the room.

"Grace, I want you to meet my father, Eli Rafford. And this is his nurse Megan Sayer. Dad, Megan, meet Grace Wayland and Michael."

The tall brown-eyed man standing beside a wing chair smiled at her. "Thank you for coming and bringing Michael, Miss Wayland," he said in a strong voice. He didn't look as infirm as she had envisioned from Nick's description. "I appreciate it very much."

The petite nurse standing nearby gave her a friendly smile. "He's been looking forward to this for quite a while."

As she greeted both of them, Grace crossed the room on a thick Oriental rug. "Here's Michael, Mr. Rafford," she said.

He looked at the baby and she saw his eyes narrow. "He is you," Eli said, glancing at Nick and then back to the baby. Eli sat in the chair. "That's an uncanny resemblance. He looks like your son, Nick. May I hold him, Miss Wayland?"

"Yes, of course. Please call me Grace."

"He does look like you, Nick," Megan said as she spread a baby blanket over Eli's lap and Grace walked forward to give Michael to his grandfather.

"My grandson," Eli Rafford said, and there was no mistaking the awe in his voice. "This is my grandson."

Grace noted that Eli seemed to have a firm grip on Michael, and Megan stood close at hand. Michael played with the buttons on Eli's sweater while he babbled.

"He's happy," Megan said.

"He's a wonderful baby," Grace added.

"Have a seat, Grace," Nick said. "Let's have something to drink. Want pop or a cup of hot tea or coffee?"

"I'll have hot tea," Grace replied, sitting in a chair near Eli. She handed Michael one of his toys, which he promptly began to chew.

"He's adorable," Megan said. "The resemblance to you is amazing, Nick. He could pass for your son. I'll see about your drinks," she said, crossing the room to an intercom.

"I'm trying to get used to the resemblance," Nick said, sitting across from her.

"I'm so pleased," Eli said, smiling broadly. "I don't know that much about babies. I'll let you have him back, but what a thrill this is. Would you allow me to have a photographer take a picture of Michael with Nick and me?"

"Of course," Grace replied, guessing that was probably the beginning of a lot of requests.

"I would treasure it. I can't tell you what pleasure you have given me by allowing me to get to know Michael. Nick, I can't believe this child doesn't belong to you."

"It gave me a shock to see him, too," Nick said.

As both men looked at Michael, Grace's worries deepened. Eli's expression was the same as he might convey to a beloved relative even though he had never seen Michael before today. The wonder in Nick's eyes equally upset her. There would be no turning back now. Michael would be drawn into this family in spite of her efforts to avoid any contact. She had contemplated taking Michael and moving away, but her business was growing with repeat clientele. And from Alicia's dealings with the hostile Raffords, she had never thought they would be a problem. Now worries grew with each encounter.

"As I understand from Nick, you are in the catering business and your aunt takes care of Michael a lot of the time."

"Yes. I've been fortunate and Aunt Clara adores Michael. She has no grandchildren and she considers Michael a grandchild," Grace said, hoping to convey how much a part of her life and her aunt's Michael was.

"Nick wanted me to promise to keep this conversation simple and not intrude on your care of Michael, but I would like to offer to set up a small account that you can use for whatever you need for him."

"Dad, we agreed to avoid this today," Nick reminded his father.

"That's fine, Nick," she said quickly. "I appreciate your offer, Mr. Rafford," she said to avoid an argument. She had no intention of using Rafford money to care for Michael.

"Excellent! And you must call me Eli. I can't physically do much with a baby. I never did as much as I should have with my own sons, but there are other ways to play a part in his life. Also, I had my secretary get Michael some toys." Eli reached behind his chair to pull out a sack and hand to her. "You can give him what is appropriate now and let him have the others when the time is right."

"Thank you," she said politely, taking the sack from him to glance at each toy, finding both elaborate, expensive toys as well as simple ones. "Your secretary either knows babies or asked an expert because these are all suitable. Since Michael chews on everything, I'll wash them before I give them to him. Thank you. I'm certain he'll have fun." For a moment she thought of Alicia with a forlorn sense of loss for what her friend would miss, causing her to think again of Bart Rafford and the grief his selfishness had caused.

A staff member brought drinks and a plate of cookies that no one touched while Eli Rafford asked nonintrusive questions about Michael and her business and told her a little about his boys when they were young. Michael stretched out on the blanket with his toys and in a short time was asleep.

"Our conversation doesn't prevent his napping," Eli observed.

"He can sleep through most anything," Grace said, aware of Nick's gaze on her as they talked. Megan had left and Grace assumed she had been present to make certain her patient didn't receive too big a shock over Michael.

Grace could see the tall clock standing across the room behind Nick. It was almost two hours later when Michael began to stir. "I think it's time to take Michael home now," she said, knowing the baby would be hungry and need to be changed.

"Grace, I can't tell you what this meeting has meant to me," Eli said. "I'm so grateful. I know you have a busy schedule, but I hope you will come again and bring Michael with you."

"I'll be happy to," she said, thinking the visit had been easy and in some ways, it seemed right for Michael to be with his grandfather and for Eli Rafford to know his grandson.

"I'm delighted to meet his mother—which you are now and always will be." He extended his hand and she shook it, feeling a firm grip and looking into dark brown eyes that hid everything as much as Nick's.

Nick buckled Michael into the carrier and gathered the sack of toys while Eli handed an envelope to Grace. "Inside you'll find the papers for the account I've opened. Everything is there, but if you have questions, feel free to call me. I have too much free time in my life now," he said. He walked to the door with them and leaned forward to brush a kiss on the top of Michael's head. He turned to Grace. "Thank you," he said.

"I'll see you again, Eli," she said, certain she couldn't possibly avoid it. Nick took her arm and they left.

In the car he glanced at her. "Thank you. That meant a lot to my father."

"Did you know he had opened an account?"

"No, I didn't, but I wasn't in the least surprised. I know my dad. He's manipulative and hell-bent on getting what he's after. He wants to know Michael. It's important to him and he thinks in terms of what he can do with money. This is his only grandson. He'll shower Michael with gifts."

"I feel as if I'm sinking in quicksand. The quicksand of the Raffords. I catered your party. I've spent an evening out with you, have gone to lunch with you, have met your father and let him meet Michael. It keeps growing, Nick, when I didn't want any part of your family, frankly."

"We're not monsters."

She noticed a muscle worked in his jaw. "No, you're not, but you both are men accustomed to getting what you want."

"Was it so bad today?" he asked.

"No, of course not, but I don't want your father's money."

"Don't turn it down. Take it. He doesn't need it and you can do something for Michael with it. Don't hang on to principles and grudges that would keep something good from Michael."

"I suppose I'm thinking of Alicia, who was closer to me than my sisters."

"Where are they?"

"Doreen works in Vegas and Tanya in Los Angeles. I haven't seen them for several years."

"While Bart and I went our separate ways, we were closer than that."

"Had your brother been half as receptive as your father, so

much heartache could have been avoided and Alicia would still be alive. I can't keep from thinking about it."

"And I can't help what Bart did. Neither can my father. Bart was younger, had a different mother and, frankly, I always thought he was a spoiled brat about a lot of things. In ways we were close but we differed, too. And we looked nothing alike. I can't get used to the baby's resemblance to me. He shocks me every time I look at him. The whole world will think he's mine."

Nick drove to her apartment, carrying Michael inside. "He's fallen asleep again," Nick said, surprise in his voice.

"It was the car ride. He won't sleep long because it's past time for him to eat. I didn't want to get out a bottle at your dad's and stay to feed Michael." She glanced at Nick. "Well, you did it, Nick. Now I've been to your dad's and he's met Michael and he's definitely in Michael's life."

The minute she looked into Nick's eyes, her knees became jelly. Desire was fire in depths of brown. Her mouth went dry and she felt breathless.

"You want to kiss as much as I do," he whispered as he stepped forward and slipped his arm around her waist to draw her to him.

She stiffened, because she was crossing another line that she could never undo. And then she was lost to the moment. "Yes," she whispered, winding an arm around his neck, gazing up at him. "Damn you, Nick, for coming into my life," she added.

"I'm glad I did." His mouth came down forcefully, parting her lips as his tongue went possessively into her mouth. Heat flashed like wildfire. She tightened her arm around his neck and kissed him in return, her tongue stroking his and fanning the flames.

He clasped her close against his hard length while his other hand tangled in her hair and removed her clip. Caution vanished, consumed by passion. She thrust her hips against him, moaning softly with pleasure.

"I've wanted this since I first saw you," he whispered, and returned for more, kissing her deeply as he leaned over her and she clung to him.

His hand slid down her back. She wanted him more than ever.

The beat of her heart increased while her breathing became hoarse. Sensation blazed into a roaring inferno.

How long they kissed she didn't know. When his hand slipped lower, down over her bottom, she had to call a halt. With effort she pulled away, opening her eyes as if drugged. She desired him with an intensity that she had never known before.

"Nick, we need to stop," she whispered. Her breathing was as ragged as his. His mouth was red from kisses and her lips throbbed. She longed to step back into his embrace and continue what they'd started, but she had to end it now or she would complicate her life badly.

"I want you," he said, framing her face with his hands.

His words wrapped around her, a statement that rang with feeling. "You want something from me," she said. "This is about Michael more than you and me."

"Not this," Nick denied in a husky tone. "This has nothing to do with family, baby, or anything except a man wanting a desirable, sexy woman."

His words were a melting caress, creating havoc with her guarded intentions.

"It doesn't matter whether that's true or not. Any relationship between us is doomed. Alicia got embroiled with a Rafford and it cost her life. That thought is constantly with me."

"I've said it before—I intend to prove that I'm not Bart."

Nick's arm slipped around her waist to pull her to him. "I'll never treat you the way he did Alicia. I want you in my arms in my bed and I'm determined to get what I want," he said.

"Sorry, Nick. That isn't going to happen. Your father will never give up now with Michael, but I'm not getting more deeply involved. Not with you or your family. The Raffords had their chance."

"I'm not talking about getting what my father wants. Damn it, I want you, Grace." He swooped down to kiss her again, his arm encircling her instantly and pulling her tightly against him as he kissed her passionately.

She grabbed his upper arms to stop him, but the moment his tongue thrust deeply into her mouth, her rejection transformed into need.

Passion heightened. She wound her fingers in his thick hair at the back of his head while her other hand ran across his broad shoulder. She wanted to touch and feel, kiss and be kissed.

Instead, she broke away. "Nick, stop this. We have no place in our lives for love. None whatsoever," she said, as if trying to convince herself.

His gaze traveled slowly over her features, weakening her resistance. Gently, he combed strands away from her face.

"You'll change your mind," he whispered.

"I can't," she replied, hoping she could keep him out of her life. Part of her craved the opposite. She couldn't succumb because it would be a disaster.

"Thanks again for today," he said, and turned, pausing to look at the sleeping baby. Then Nick walked out, closing the door quietly behind him.

She stepped to the window to watch him, his long, purposeful strides proclaiming his confidence.

★ ★ ★

Friday morning Nick called to arrange an afternoon appointment at her office. As they talked, he could feel the coolness in her tone of voice. Finally, she yielded and agreed to see him at her office late in the afternoon.

The moment he strolled through the door, every nerve in his body came alive. Consumed by lust, he had suffered hot, erotic fantasies that tormented him. Efforts to put her out of his mind had failed. Longing streaked in him, heating him, driving his purpose in meeting out of mind.

When their gazes locked, he could feel the sparks and she obviously experienced it, too. And just as apparent, she fought it. She sat in silence behind her desk, a convenient barrier between them.

Nick pulled a chair closer to her desk, to face her. "Thanks for seeing me," he said, sitting back to notice with satisfaction that a flush rose in her cheeks. Beneath a matching suit jacket, her vee-necked rose blouse revealed the beginning of lush curves. He longed to walk around the wooden desk and take her into his embrace. Instead, he sat quietly facing her. "How have you been?"

"Fine, Nick," she answered, and he thought she looked more gorgeous than ever. He wished she would come sit near him.

"Do you have Christmas plans?" he asked.

"I'll spend it with Michael. It'll be quiet, but fun."

"What about your aunt? Won't she be with you, too?"

"No. She leaves Monday to be with her son who is in Germany. I'll just be with Michael. So what does your father want now?" she asked.

"You're so certain my visit concerns him," Nick remarked drily.

"Doesn't it? I know you don't have designs of your own

on Michael, so it has to be your father. If you just wanted to see or be with me, I don't think you'd call for an office appointment."

"You're right. My father would like to see Michael again."

As she looked away, her hands locked together on the desk. Her knuckles whitened, an obvious indication she was unhappy with his request. "You told him he could see Michael again," Nick reminded her gently.

Her gaze settled on him, glacial green that conveyed her irritation. "I know I did. That doesn't make me want to."

"Honor the request of an aging, failing grandfather."

"Stop playing on my sympathy," she flung back at him.

"I'm just stating the truth," Nick replied. While she kept her features impassive, he could see the battle raging inside her.

"Very well," she said, relenting. "I know I told him he could see Michael."

"Thank you, Grace," Nick said. "Christmas is next weekend. Come visit Christmas Eve. Have dinner with us and stay over Christmas morning. Then you can go home and have your Christmas with Michael. That way, I'll enjoy Christmas."

"I think that's way more visiting than I intended when I told your father we would see him again."

"Look, you don't have plans. You've already told me that. This may be Dad's last Christmas. Michael's presence would give him so much joy. Your presence will give *me* pleasure," Nick added, wanting her to agree. He wasn't looking forward to Christmas Eve and morning with his dad, something they never used to do, yet something he felt duty-bound to do now.

"Nick, I don't care to spend my Christmas with your dad."

Nick stood and walked around the desk, pulling her chair out and grasping her waist to draw her to her feet. Frowning, she opened her mouth, he guessed, to protest. He took advantage and leaned down, covering her mouth with his.

Momentarily, she was stiff in his arms and then she yielded, wrapping an arm around his neck. His body heated with white-hot desire as he leaned over her and kissed her hungrily, pouring out the lust he'd felt in her absence. He savored the kiss, the softness of her mouth, the sensual feel of her tongue. Her body was curvaceous, lush and warm against him. He tangled his hand in her hair, which had been pinned on her head. He didn't care. He intended to kiss away her remoteness and elicit a response and an acceptance from her.

He could feel her heart thumping against his, hear her soft moans that raced through him like lightning. He wanted to lay her down on her desk and make love to her now, but that was impossible.

Instead, he tore his mouth away to look at her as she gasped. Her eyes slowly opened. "Spend Christmas with me," he demanded. "You'll be alone otherwise. I want you there with me. Will you?"

"Yes," she whispered, looking dazed. Fire now replaced the frost in her green eyes. Her lips were red, full, an enticing temptation. He dipped his head again to kiss her, stopping any words.

She arched against him, holding him tightly while her fingers tangled in his hair. He throbbed with need and was hard, ready. They had to go slowly, because they were racing headlong into a depth that would complicate and heighten the friction between them.

"Stop, Nick. We're in my office," she gasped. She gulped air and her protest was weak, but he stepped away.

She smoothed her hair that had too many strands pulled loose to put back in place. As he watched, she took it down and shook her head. He reached out, winding his fingers in her silky, thick hair.

"Your hair is beautiful, Grace," he whispered. He leaned

forward to brush a kiss on her throat. "I want to bury my hands in it."

"Nick, my assistant could come in."

"She won't. I asked her to see to it that you're not disturbed," he whispered, trailing kisses to her nape and hearing her intake of breath. He placed his hand against her throat and could feel her racing pulse, which gave him a stab of satisfaction.

He straightened, dropping his hands to his sides. "You agreed to Christmas Eve with me and Christmas morning."

"I know," she whispered, her reluctance obvious.

"I promise to see to it you have a good time."

"You can't possibly promise that," she said without conviction in her voice. He couldn't keep from smiling at her.

"It'll be a Christmas to remember forever," he said.

"Watch what you promise," she warned, the frost returning to her gaze. "Now you go back and sit where you were unless you're leaving."

He gripped her hand. "Come here." Circling the desk, he held a chair facing his. "Sit here and stop keeping the damned desk between us. I want to talk to you before I go."

"Have you always spent Christmas Eve and morning with your father?" she asked as she sat, her question surprising him.

Pulling his chair closer to hers, Nick shook his head. "No. There were a lot of holidays when he would go off to Europe with my current stepmother. I stayed with a friend," he answered without thinking about his reply. His thoughts were on Grace because her disheveled appearance made him think of hot sex. Her hair tumbled around her face, cascading across her shoulders, a thick, wild mane that was a sensual invitation.

Her lips were just-been-kissed red. Desire glowed in the depths of her gaze, making it difficult to think about their conversation when what he wanted to do was draw her back into his embrace and continue kissing her.

"You never had to stay at the boarding school?"

"No. When I was young, I think Dad arranged with a friend's family to get me invited, probably showering them with presents for taking me in. When I was older, I had friends who would invite me because they knew I wasn't going home."

"That's dreadful, Nick," she said, staring at him as if he had sprouted two heads. "I'm amazed you spend your Christmases with him now if he abandoned you that much on holidays in your childhood."

Nick shrugged. "I didn't until these last two years when his health failed. And now he's lost Bart. I guess I love the old man and I feel sorry for him. He's having a tough time. I don't have anything to gain by going off and leaving him alone for Christmas. That would be selfish on my part. What he did is his own worry. What I do is mine."

"That's good of you," she said in a strange voice, studying him intently. He wondered whether he had won her over slightly with his reply and hoped that was the reason behind the sharp stare.

"Christmas Eve with us will be better than staying alone with a baby who'll sleep a good deal of the time. Also, Dad would like to have a professional photographer out to get some Christmas photos with Michael."

She had to laugh. "Nick, a *professional* photographer? As I told your dad, it's fine with me—as long as I get a picture, too. That will be wonderful and something I could never afford."

"See?" he said. "Dad's money can do things you like," he reminded her lightly and she wrinkled her nose at him. "How about I pick you up around five o'clock on Christmas Eve?"

"Make it half past five, please. I have a lot of party-planning to do, and I won't have Clara to help with Michael."

"Half past five it is. Excellent," he said, wishing the weekend started tonight and he could be with Grace. "I'm looking forward to this holiday, something I definitely was not doing until a minute ago."

The pink deepened in her cheeks. "Don't be ridiculous," she replied lightly.

"Before I go, there's one more thing. It's important and before you give me an answer, take a few days to think about it. I expect you to refuse my request, but give it consideration." The minute the words were spoken, she stiffened and he could feel an invisible barrier rising between them. Her frostiness returned, along with a wary look in her eyes.

"What's that, Nick? What else do you want of me?"

"My dad would like Michael to legally have the Rafford name," Nick stated.

She locked her fingers together in her lap. "He doesn't waste time. No. That would basically give Michael to your family."

"No, it won't. Just a legal last-name change. The name does not put him in my family and Dad knows that. Think about this request before you decide. I can see the refusal in your expression. Consider what I'm telling you. Dad will set up a trust for Michael. Right now, he will open an account that you can use for him. This would help you out with the baby and pay for his college. No giant fortune, just a reasonable sum to see that he's educated."

"Stop, Nick," she ordered, looking into his dark eyes. "I don't want Rafford money. I don't really need it. I'm not changing the baby's name from Vaughan, Alicia's name. You're on a futile mission and wasting your breath. Neither threats nor bribes will win me over."

"I'm not going to threaten you with anything," he said, smiling at her and causing her slight frown to vanish. "Look, why deny Michael the benefit of this? Michael is a Rafford—why not let him have the name?"

"The Vaughan name is a tie to his mother."

"Do you really want to take this away from Michael?"

"I don't think I'm taking anything from him," she argued. "I'll take care of Michael, send him to college, and I don't need your father's money."

"My father is a generous man," Nick said quietly, wondering if she had any concept of the fortune she was refusing. It was an effort to hold on to his patience. Who turned down money and a deal like the one his dad was offering? "We're not talking small change here," he couldn't resist tossing out.

"It doesn't matter," she said. "I won't do this. He wants Michael to be a Rafford. Next thing, he would want Michael to stay with him. He can hire nannies easily. Then he'd want to keep Michael and move me into his mansion, unless he tries to just get rid of me."

"You're jumping to conclusions."

"No, I'm not," she stated. "Your dad is after my baby. End of discussion, Nick. We won't argue through Christmas Eve over this issue, will we?"

"No," he said, wondering if he could keep his word on that one. "I'll tell Dad your answer. He'll have to abandon the idea for now."

"For now and forever." She stood and he came to his feet. He had achieved an important part of his quest. He would get to spend Christmas Eve and morning with her. The prospect pleased him and he intended to use the time to win her friendship. In the meantime, he'd have to deal with his father's disappointment. Not that his father would relent in his pursuit of the name change.

★ ★ ★

Nick postponed telling his dad until the next day. His father's anger worried Nick because it couldn't be good for his heart. He had to think of some way to convince Grace to agree.

Michael Rafford. How simple it would be, yet Grace had been adamant. Nick raked his fingers through his hair, mulling over ideas, finally beginning to settle on one that he had originally rejected instantly.

Three nights later in the club dining room with one of his close friends, Nick mentioned his plan. Jake Benton's jaw dropped and he stared at Nick.

"I think your brain has stopped functioning."

"I've thought about it. A marriage of convenience—I legally adopt my nephew. We end the sham marriage after Dad's gone. The marriage puts a crimp in my life for only a little while."

"Suppose your dad recovers fully and is here another twenty years? You'd be married to a woman you don't love and vice versa, raising your brother's child. The last wouldn't be bad, but the other terrible. Don't do it."

"We could divorce. She'd get the benefits of the Rafford money because she would be part of the family."

"You'd have to share the fortune."

Nick shrugged. "Not really. I'll be Dad's heir because I'll agree to make Michael and Grace my beneficiaries. She's not a gold digger or she would have gone after Dad's money when she had the chance. If something happens to Dad and then to me—I don't have heirs anyway."

Jake tilted his head, his deep blue-eyed gaze intent. "I guess you have a point there. Michael is Bart's child, so that would be good. You'll make your dad happy."

"Yes. If I can talk Grace into this."

"She'd be crazy to turn you down."

"She's independent as hell and fighting to keep us from latching on to Michael. She's scared of losing him."

"She's his mother and he's actually been her baby from the start from what you've told me," Jake said. "I guess I can see how you came up with the idea, but a loveless marriage is scary as hell. Marriage is scary as hell. Look at our dads and their failed marriages and the misery it gave everyone."

"It'll be a cut-and-dried business deal," Nick said, thinking about Grace's kisses. "Sort of."

"Not exactly cut-and-dried," Jake replied in a sarcastic tone. "I saw her. Sparks were flying between the two of you when you didn't know each other. There won't be anything cut-and-dried about a marriage to her. She's hot," Jake said. "You'll sink like you're in a tar pit."

Nick grinned as he shook his head. "I don't think you can compare her to a tar pit, and you're right about hot. No, I guess it might turn out to be exciting."

"Watch out, Nick. You're going to complicate your life terribly. You'll also lose a million dollars in that bet we made."

"I can stand the million. I don't want to lose my dad's fortune."

"I don't blame you. No matter how old they get, our dads can't stop trying to manipulate everyone around them. That's one reason you and Tony and I got to be close friends—shoved together first by our dads and then sticking together because we all had the same kind of dad—driven, controlling."

"If you stop and think about it, we're probably somewhat that way ourselves now."

"I hope to hell not," Jake said, with a dark look at Nick. "Are you telling Tony this harebrained scheme of yours?"

"If I see him, I will."

"Well, I don't think any of us, you included, can say a marriage of convenience would work. Even to a woman like you have in mind. We three know firsthand the likelihood of a successful marriage. At least in the circles we've moved in. I suppose if you go into it with low expectations, you won't be disappointed."

"I have high expectations of getting back in Dad's will. That's my prime goal. Grace and I should be able to develop a workable arrangement and she won't be hanging on me, falling in love with me."

"Suppose you fall in love—I don't need to ask that one. You won't. I know you as well as I know myself. No such thing will happen. We were disillusioned long ago."

"If you're through eating, we might as well head to the poker game. Tony may be there by now," Nick said, drinking the last of his water and standing. As the two men left the luxurious club dining room, Nick fell into step beside Jake in the hallway.

"By the way, are you going to the private horse sale at the Jenkins ranch next month?" Nick asked.

"I wouldn't miss it. Tad Jenkins has the best horses around."

"I agree. We'll be bidding against each other," Nick said, and Jake grinned.

"I won't bid if you start first and you don't if I start first— how's that?" Jake suggested.

"Sounds okay. Every horse he sells will be prime horseflesh."

"You'll miss it if you're on a honeymoon."

Nick shook his head. "Nothing will interfere with my attendance at that sale. I can work a wedding around it."

"Does the little lady ride?"

"I have no idea, nor do I care. I have other plans for my time spent with her," Nick said and Jake laughed.

"Good luck with your crazy scheme. I hope you know what you're doing. I'm one step closer to winning our bet."

"I know what I'm doing. Now if I can just convince Grace," Nick said, deciding Christmas Eve would be the time to propose.

Chapter 6

Monday before Christmas, Grace kissed her aunt goodbye. Clara would not be back to Dallas until after the first of the year.

"Have a wonderful time with your son," Grace said, hugging Clara. "Glenda will be here part of the time to help with Michael, so you enjoy yourself."

"I will, but I'll miss Michael. You take care," Clara said solemnly. "I'll worry about you Christmas Eve. I know Eli Rafford wants Michael and will keep after you until he gets what he wants."

"Stop worrying. I won't let that happen. An immediate worry is what do I give them for gifts. Both men have everything they want," she said, having spent the past week wondering about what to give Nick.

"You'll think of something. You've already given Eli Rafford the best gift possible in taking Michael for Christmas. Take care of yourself and Michael," Clara said again. "And I want one of those copies of the Christmas photographs."

Grace gave her aunt another hug and watched her hurry to her car. She turned away, thinking about what to give the Rafford men—impossible task.

That night and the days and nights to follow, Grace was busy catering Christmas parties until Christmas Eve arrived. The booked parties were over until the day after Christmas when they started up again.

It took the afternoon to get ready to go to Eli Rafford's for the night. As she packed, the butterflies in her stomach grew worse. She dreaded dealing with Michael's grandfather while excitement mounted over being with Nick again.

She picked up Michael, smoothing his thick black hair. He was dressed in a navy jumper and a white sweater. She kissed his cheek. "You look adorable," she told him, smiling at him as he cooed and babbled. "Now please don't spit up on my sweater," she said to him, turning to look at both of them in an oval mirror. Her hair was clipped behind her head and she wore a red sweater and red wool skirt—maybe a poor choice with a baby. She glanced down at him. "Remember, no formula on this sweater, please. This is your first Christmas, sweetie."

She looked around her tiny living room, at the Christmas tree placed on a table to keep it away from Michael, who crawled well now. She had a few presents under the tree for him, but he was too little to open his gifts. She could imagine the toys that awaited him from his grandfather.

The doorbell rang and she hurried to face Nick, whose intent gaze knotted her insides as always.

"Merry Christmas," he said, smiling at her while she motioned for him to come inside. He stepped in, filling the narrow hallway and moving into the living area. "Ah, you're all ready for Christmas," he said, walking to her tree. In a black topcoat over his suit, he dominated her small living room, which seemed to shrink in size when he entered.

"Our tree isn't fancy, but he's too little to know what's happening. He's beginning to crawl, so I had to keep it out of his reach," she said, while putting on Michael's coat and then buckling him into his carrier.

"Good idea. Dad had a child's fence put around ours. We have a nanny for the evening to help you with Michael, so you can eat in peace and quiet. If it's all right with you, we'll let her give him a bottle if he wants one while we eat."

"Thank you. That's fine," she said. She would be present to make certain Michael was taken care of, yet it would give her a chance to enjoy eating without interruptions. If Michael was awake, she rarely got through a meal without being disturbed.

"I didn't think you'd object, since we'll all be right there. She came with high recommendations," he said, smiling. He turned to her and her heart missed a beat.

"I'm sure she did," she said. "It will be a nice change."

Nick walked up to place his hands on her shoulders. "I've missed seeing you."

"Nick, there's not much point in us seeing each other."

"I don't know about that. We have Michael between us. I have a feeling we're in each other's lives for a long time to come." Her heart drummed as she looked into his warm dark eyes. "You look beautiful, Grace," he said in a husky voice.

"Thank you." She gazed up at him, thinking he looked energetic, sexy, appealing.

In turn, he looked amused as he studied her. "I'd rather stay right here with you," Nick said in a deep voice. "My dad is waiting, though. He's been counting the minutes until it was time to get you. Otherwise, we wouldn't rush back."

"But since he is waiting, we should go. Besides, Michael

will eventually stop sitting quietly and amusing himself in his carrier."

"Do you have an overnight bag packed?" Nick asked, picking up the carrier with Michael and glancing around.

She slipped into her long black coat. "Yes, a bag for each of us and a small box of toys and things for Michael."

Nick took the bags from her hands, shouldered them, picked up Michael and opened the door. Carrying the box of toys, she turned off the lights, locked up and left with him.

"Christmas Eve," she said.

"We'll always remember spending it together," Nick reminded her. "Have you been busy constantly?"

"Yes. The past hour has been my quietest for the entire week."

"I can imagine. I could have rescued you from that, whisked you away until tonight. Next time, let me know."

"Thanks, but I had work to do. We've had parties booked day and night, so I couldn't have escaped had I wanted to."

"Get ready for a party yourself. Small party, that is. Dad is as excited as a kid about tonight."

"It's a grand holiday," she said.

"This is definitely the best part," Nick said.

She remained in the grip of excitement as they drove through the estate grounds once again. A cold front and a dense fog were settling in and it was cozy in Nick's car. Michael cooed in the back as they wound up the driveway. The minute they stepped inside, she drew a deep breath, reminded again of the Raffords' wealth and power.

The mansion had been turned into a winter wonderland. Trees with myriad lights sparkled at spaced intervals along the great hallway.

"Nick," she said, halting to stare at the enormous tree standing between the two curving staircases. It had to be at least twenty feet tall and decorated with hundreds of twinkling ornaments. "This is fit for royalty."

"My father probably thinks he *is* royalty," Nick remarked drily. "It's just a big tree."

"Maybe to you, because you've grown up with trees like it. To me, it's magical, amazing. How I wish Michael knew what he was seeing. It's magnificent."

"That's not the family tree. It's in the great room and that's where we'll spend the evening."

Garlands of greenery and red ribbons draped the banisters of the winding staircases. "Michael, look," she said to the baby in his carrier, "Isn't it beautiful? Nick, this is enchanting. I'm sorry he's too little to know what's here."

"He will next year," Nick said, and she gave him a startled glance. She hadn't thought in the long term about Eli and Nick remaining in her life. The thought of them becoming permanent in her life had just become more real.

"I brought presents in that bag you're carrying," she said.

"You didn't need to. Michael would have been enough of a gift."

She walked beside Nick, overwhelmed again by her surroundings, wondering why she had ever thought for a second that she wouldn't be diminished, made to feel insignificant the minute she entered the mansion again.

They passed through the wide double doors to the great room, where Nick told her most receptions and formal parties were held. Another huge tree, this one white, was festooned with ribbons and more sparkling ornaments and bows. She stopped in front of it in awe. "What fantastic Christmases you must have had," she said, momentarily forgetting what he had told her about his childhood holidays.

"Some years I wasn't here," he reminded her, and she turned to stare at him.

"I'm sorry, Nick," she said. "Now I think it was best that Bart didn't marry Alicia, not that he ever had any intention of doing so. Michael would have grown up in the same manner."

"Good evening," came a voice behind them and she turned to see Eli Rafford enter the room. He crossed over to shake her hand and then looked down at Michael as Nick removed the baby from his carrier.

"Ah, he's a fine-looking boy. Thank you so much for coming. I've looked forward to this since you accepted my invitation. I think he's grown in the past few days."

She smiled as Nick took her coat to hand it to a staff member who had materialized quietly. Grace took Michael from Nick, watching while Nick put her presents around the foot of the huge tree along with a mound of gifts already under the tree. She looked at the luxurious Christmas trimmings and thought about her own meager decorations and single, small tree and wondered how Michael would feel about his two families. She was certain the Raffords were in her and Michael's life to stay. Unless Eli tried to get rid of her.

She glanced up at Nick, who turned to look into her eyes with a questioning expression.

"I'll take Michael's things to the nursery where Vanessa, the nanny, is," Nick said, picking up a bag and leaving.

"Oh, my word!" For the first time she noticed stockings hung on the mammoth fireplace, one for each of them, including one with her name and one with Michael's.

"We have stockings."

"Of course we do," Eli said, chuckling. "It's Christmas. They are hung for Santa. Now, let me hold my precious grandchild," he added. "Come sit near us, Grace, and tell me more about Michael."

After placing Michael in Eli's arms, she sat close in a wing chair. As frail as Eli appeared when he was standing, his arms looked strong and his hands large, and he seemed to have a firm grip on Michael, who was happily playing with a teething ring.

Nick returned to sit near them, facing her. As she talked, she was aware of Nick listening, watching her with a faint smile on his face. Once she caught him studying her legs and when he glanced up and their eyes met, his were hot, filled with so much desire that her heart skipped.

"The photographer should be here right away. Thank you for consenting to pictures."

"It'll be great to have Christmas pictures of Michael," she responded.

It was only minutes later the photographer was announced and for the next hour, pictures were taken and then the photographer packed his equipment and was gone.

"Michael is a happy baby," Eli observed. "What a marvel he is. A special baby. Your sharing him with us this Christmas is the greatest possible Christmas gift."

"It's good for the two of you to know each other," she said. Under different circumstances, she would have been delighted to find the grandfather and uncle in Michael's life. As it was, her fear of Eli had been pushed aside slightly for this evening.

When Michael became wiggly, she spread a small blanket on the floor and put some of his toys on it, setting him down. He sat happily playing before beginning to crawl around. She scooped him up. "He's getting around better every day. He likes to explore."

"Let's go meet the nanny and I'll show you Dad's new nursery. Excuse us, Dad. We'll be back shortly."

As they entered the hall, Nick reached out to take Michael from her. "I'll carry him. You've probably carried him for hours."

"Actually, yes I have. I don't mind yet because he's not too heavy."

"Sometime I'll give you the grand tour of this house."

She laughed. "I hope I don't get lost tonight. And Michael will be staying in my room, right?"

"Unless you want a different arrangement. If you don't want him in the same room, he can stay in the nursery with Vanessa, because she's staying the night."

"I'd rather have him with me when I go to bed. He sleeps through the night, but I wouldn't want him to wake in a strange place with someone he barely knows."

"I figured that. Vanessa will put him to bed in the room where you'll sleep and she'll sit in there with him until you turn in. Then she'll stay in her own room. We have a third floor filled with staff who live here. As you could see driving up, there's as much room as a hotel."

"A very large hotel," she said. "Michael may not be happy going home with me someday when he grows accustomed to what he has here."

Nick gave her an inscrutable look and she wondered what was on his mind. "Why the look?" she asked.

"Just thinking about what you said. You're his mother and you love him. He'll always be happy going with you. Here we are," Nick said, taking her arm while he carried Michael with his other arm. They entered a large, enchanting nursery that reminded her again of the Raffords' wealth. The room held a double bed, a baby crib, dressers, tables, a rocking chair, two other chairs, and was decorated with nursery rhyme decor. A bin contained toys. A tall blond woman stood when they entered.

"Grace, this is Vanessa Otis. Vanessa, meet Grace Wayland, and this is Michael."

"He's adorable," Vanessa said, taking the baby from Nick.

"Hi, Michael," she said to him before smiling at Grace. "When did he last eat?"

"He'll probably be hungry soon because it's been long enough since the last bottle. I brought formula, bottles, baby food, and he takes some finger food. Everything is in his bag."

"I have Michael's bag with his things and I can fix the bottles. I have six younger siblings, so I'm accustomed to babies," she said, smiling at Grace, and Nick waited while Grace gave instructions about Michael's bottle.

When they left, Nick walked beside her. "Are you going to worry about him?"

"No. Vanessa seemed competent, and I imagine she has plenty of credentials, in addition to her own siblings, and has been thoroughly checked out."

"You're right. She has some great recommendations, but I wanted to be sure you were comfortable."

"Actually, I imagine I'll enjoy dinner more. When I'm home, I never sit through a meal without interruptions."

He smiled. "Yet you love taking care of him."

"Of course. I love him. He's precious and I can't wait to get home to him every day. So what's our schedule here, Nick? Are presents opened tonight or tomorrow?"

"Tomorrow morning. We'll have the Christmas meal tonight and Dad will go to bed early. This has been great for him, Grace. He's trying to make it nice for you because he appreciates having Michael more than you can guess."

"It's easy to do this now while Michael is a baby," she said, wondering what the future held. Her problems had diminished with Nick's presence because she was so aware of him. He was close, tempting. She would be alone with him later and the prospect was exciting.

When they joined Eli again, Megan was with him. Dinner was served in a large dining room that could have easily accommodated twenty at the table. It was a lavish spread and the food was delicious, but it was difficult to eat with Nick seated across from her, his smoldering dark eyes on her, holding promises of hot kisses later.

After dinner, Vanessa brought Michael in his pajamas to play in the great room. At his bedtime, she scooped him up, promising to rock him to sleep, and Grace kissed him and let Vanessa carry him to bed. Half an hour later, Eli apologized, saying he had to turn in for the night. Megan held his arm as they left the room.

Nick tossed another log on the fire, crossed the room to close the wide double doors and came back. "Let me show you something," he said.

She stood to go with him and they headed toward the doors he had just closed. He stopped in front of them, but didn't reach to open them and she gave him a puzzled look.

"You haven't noticed," he said, glancing up.

She looked up to see the mistletoe tied with a bright red velvet bow hanging above her head.

He shook his head. "I've been waiting since the last time we were together. We're under the mistletoe." His arm circled her waist and he leaned forward to kiss her, pulling her tightly into his embrace.

"Since when do you need mistletoe?" she whispered, before their lips touched. She slipped her arms around him and stood on tiptoe while her heartbeat galloped.

Pressing against his hard body, she felt his erection thrust against her. She ached for him, wanting him, knowing each time they were together she was becoming more involved with him. This holiday was going to bind her closer than ever. While he kissed her, nothing else really mattered. His kisses fanned desire to greater heights. She needed more, wanted his hands and his mouth on her. All evening the looks he had given her, the slight contacts had increased her longing until she felt she would burst.

"Nick," she whispered, and crushed her mouth to his for more kisses, moaning as her hips plunged against him. He held her tightly with one arm, his other hand trailing down her back languidly, a sensual caress. His hand slipped over her bottom, following her curves and then slid around her waist.

Slipping beneath her red sweater, his large, warm hands pushed away wispy lace and cupped her breasts. She moaned with pleasure as her tongue thrust deeply over his.

She heard his deep-throated groan while his thumbs circled each taut bud. Waves of pleasure washed over her. Eagerly she ran her hands over his powerful shoulders, removing his jacket, to unbutton his shirt. His sculpted chest was rock hard with a thick mat of black curls. She tangled her fingers in black, wiry chest hair, relishing touching him.

He leaned over her, his passionate kisses going deep, heightening her response. Within minutes they had to stop or they'd be beyond stopping. She tore her mouth from his while caressing his chest, her signals as mixed as her feelings.

"Nick, we have to stop," she whispered.

"Why?" he asked, raising his head. He continued to caress her breasts while his gaze slowly devoured her. "You're beautiful," he whispered, his thumbs rubbing each nipple.

Fighting her own desire, she clutched his hands. "No more," she whispered, unable to find a strong voice.

"Why? We're alone. No one will disturb us," Nick said.

"I didn't come here tonight to sleep with you. I'm not ready for intimacy. I'm not making love at your father's house," she said. "Lust isn't the point of this visit."

"It's what we both want," Nick said bluntly.

She stepped back, slipping her bra into place as he watched her. While she straightened her clothes, her heart raced. Nick stood inches away, his hair tangled from her fingers. His shirt was open and his muscled chest captured her attention. His trousers indicated his arousal. He wanted her and he looked seductive, appealing.

Her heart hammered loudly. With an effort to break his spell she intended to stick with what she had told him.

"You and I shouldn't make love. Not tonight. Most likely not ever. I don't care how great the kisses are," she whispered. "We've got Michael, different views and opposing goals between us. I'm not succumbing to desire, because it will only complicate everything between us a thousand times over. We're not in love. We're not in agreement. Your family, you because of your dad, wants Michael. I don't want you to have him. It's that simple, and seduction would be an emotional disaster."

"It doesn't have to be," Nick stated, studying her.

"This has been a nice evening, but we should each go our separate way now."

"If that's what you want, Grace," he replied. As he buttoned his shirt, she struggled to get a grip on her emotions. Resisting the urge to walk right back into his arms and toss aside her declarations, she shook her head, smoothing her hair away from her face.

"C'mon, I'll give you a partial tour and show you where you'll sleep. You and I are in the east wing, where the nursery is." He led her down a large hall.

"How did you ever get used to this?" she asked.

"I grew up in it. Parts were off-limits for play for years. When I outgrew that restriction, I went everywhere. This was my home and I got used to it just like you do your home."

He directed her through an open door and switched on a light. She stood in an elegant suite with decor in shades of brown and tan.

"Here's where I am, should you want to come talk," Nick said. Grace gave him a sharp look to see amusement in his eyes.

"And my room?"

They returned to the hall and entered another suite. The pink and white looked done by a decorator, just as his had, with elegant white furniture and bright pink accessories. Pink and green Christmas decorations adorned the sitting room, which had a decorated white tree standing in a corner. Beyond the sitting room she could see a bedroom. When she stepped to the door, she saw a baby crib on one side of the room. Vanessa came forward with a book in her hand.

"Michael is sleeping. He hasn't stirred since I put him in his bed."

"Thank you so much," Grace said.

"He's a sweet, happy baby. I'll go to bed now," Vanessa said as she headed for the door.

"Thanks, Vanessa," Nick said. "We'll see you in the morning." Nick and Grace strolled to the sitting room where Nick stepped ahead to hold the door for Vanessa. When they were alone, he walked back to Grace.

"I can watch him tomorrow morning."

"Dad will want him with us for the opening of the presents. He's been talking about this for a week and you know he has toys for Michael."

"I can imagine," she said.

Nick reached beyond her and pulled a sprig of mistletoe off the Christmas tree to dangle the sprig above her head. "One kiss beneath the mistletoe," he said. Without waiting for her answer, he kissed her, holding her close.

She remained immobile for a moment, but then wrapped her arms around him, her exasperation vanishing instantly as desire fanned to life again.

She moaned and poured herself into their kiss, returning

his passion, her senses coming to life as longing assailed her stronger than ever.

She had no idea how long they kissed, but she finally ended it. "Nick, nothing has changed since we kissed earlier."

"I'll leave now, but sometime you'll want me to stay. You'll let me make love to you because you want me just as much as I want you. We don't have a battle between us. Because of my dad, you're conjuring up demons. But you and I don't have a real struggle going. Far from it," Nick said, stroking a strand of hair away from her face.

"Nick, you should go," she whispered, his words as seductive as his caresses and his kisses.

He brushed another kiss lightly on her lips, tossed the sprig of mistletoe onto a table and turned, walking to the door where he paused. "If you want to talk, I'm right there. Knock on the wall and I'll come so you don't have to leave Michael."

"Forget any knocking on the wall," she said in amusement. He grinned and left, closing the door behind him.

Looking around the suite, she noticed the mistletoe and picked up the sprig. With a glance at the white tree and its pink decorations, she noticed there weren't any other sprigs of mistletoe. Had Nick put that sprig on the tree?

She peeked at Michael, who was sleeping on his knees facedown on the Co-Sleeper attached to the bed. He wore footed pajamas and had his stuffed bunny clutched in his hand. Filled with love, Grace touched his head. She couldn't keep his grandfather from seeing him or being with him. She wished she could just trust that Eli didn't intend to try to take Michael from her.

When she slid into bed, she guessed Nick would fill her dreams as he had every night for a week.

★ ★ ★

Christmas morning she showered and was dressed in a green sweater and slacks before Michael stirred. "Merry Christmas, love," she said as she picked him up and nuzzled him. He smelled of baby powder and he clutched her shoulder while she carried him.

When she had Michael dressed in his red Santa suit, she left her suite. Nick's door stood open and he appeared. "Merry Christmas," he said, smiling at her.

Casually dressed in a navy sweater and chinos, he looked dangerous, sexy, appealing.

"Merry Christmas, Nick," she said as he walked up to her to kiss her lightly.

"Merry Christmas to you," she said.

"Good morning, Michael," Nick said, and the baby smiled at him.

"Look at you, getting a smile first thing. He barely knows you."

"He knows I'm his uncle," Nick said. "And he's glad to see me, just as I am glad to see you both. Sleep well?"

"Of course," she answered.

"Let's do Christmas. Dad can't wait to give Michael a present. I don't think he ever got excited over either Bart or me on Christmas morning."

"He might have when you were very young," she said.

"We were in his way when he was young. Now, he's changed. His illness has turned him into a different man. Many of those driving goals he had are gone and the people around him get his full attention."

"Michael is probably hungry. He's a very good baby, but I don't want to keep him waiting."

In the kitchen Vanessa waited. As soon as she saw them, she came to take Michael from Grace. "How adorable he is," she said, smiling at Michael. "Michael is happy all the time. I'll feed him and you can eat your breakfast. Mr. Rafford and Megan are in the great room. They've already eaten and have coffee waiting for you in there."

Grace handed over Michael and joined Nick at the table. The cook brought plates of eggs and toast. After they finished, they joined Eli and Megan by the Christmas tree. Little toys filled Michael's stocking and his toys sat at the foot of the tree.

"Santa has been here," Eli said with twinkling eyes. His color was better and he looked stronger than when Grace had met him, causing her to wonder how big an influence Michael was in his life.

Grace left to get her cameras. When she returned, she saw that Eli also had a camcorder and a camera ready, and she laughed. "I think this baby is going to be a celebrity this morning and he'll have no idea what's going on. It'll be a thoroughly documented first Christmas."

Nick smiled. "Dad wants every minute caught. We'll start with Michael though I know he can't open anything."

"No, he would promptly put the wrappings in his mouth." As Vanessa handed her the baby, Grace said, "I'll put him on the floor and let's see if he gets one of his toys first." She set Michael down and picked up her own camcorder. He promptly crawled to a transparent ball filled with plastic butterflies and glittering spheres that played tunes when he rolled it around.

In minutes they were immersed in gifts and Nick handed her a box with a lovely blue ribbon that she intended to take home and keep. It was from Nick and as she opened it, she guessed he had one of the women who worked for him do his shopping.

It was a silver frame that would be perfect for Michael's picture and she looked up, smiling at Nick. "You know I love this. It's beautiful and perfect."

"Great," he replied, his eyes filled with a special look that thrilled her and made her forget they were in a room with others.

"Now I'll open yours," he said, taking a present and sitting near her as he tore it open. Startled, he looked up at her. "Where did you get these?" he asked, surprise in his voice. He lifted out two framed pictures of the last rodeo he'd been in as he rode a bucking horse.

"I'd read about you in rodeos in a Texas magazine, so I called around and finally found the pictures. I hope you don't already have them."

"No," he said, smiling. "I don't, and I'm happy you tracked them down. Thank you," he said, and she had another tingle because his tone made the statement personal, carrying silent meaning. He might as well have been blatantly flirting for the effect he was causing. She watched as he walked to the tree and picked up one of her presents for Eli.

The moment Eli opened the box and removed a scrapbook filled with photos of Michael, he smiled at her. "Grace, what a treasure! You couldn't have possibly given me anything that would please me more. I'm so grateful," he said, flipping through the pages. He looked at her and his eyes filled with tears. "Thank you. This means more than you know," he said, his voice cracking.

"I'm glad," she replied, surprised by his reaction, which was far deeper than she had expected. She could feel the barriers around her heart develop cracks, a dangerous reaction.

It took most of the morning to get through the presents and to watch and film Michael, plus getting snapshots of him with each of them.

Lunch was long and leisurely, and filled with stories from Eli of other generations of Raffords, and then they spent another hour playing with Michael before he fell asleep. While

Michael slept they went to the lavish entertainment room to watch a Christmas movie, which was timed perfectly with Michael's nap that ended as the movie finished.

It was almost five in the afternoon before Grace told Nick she should go home. She thought Eli was beginning to droop. Goodbyes took another twenty minutes. Finally she was in the car with Nick. The day had become overcast, a fog settling in, bringing darkness early.

"You made my dad a very happy man today. You can't imagine how much this meant to him."

"That's good," she said, wondering how Nick truly felt about his nephew. Michael had to have cut into Nick's life and caused upheaval in trying to please his dad's wishes. She glanced back at the sleeping baby. "I think Michael is worn to a frazzle. His brief nap this afternoon helped, but he may sleep through the night now, since he ate just before we left your dad's."

"I imagine Dad is worn to a frazzle, too. He usually has catnaps and he missed them. All in all, the visit was fantastic."

"You sound surprised."

"I'll have to admit, I am. I knew it would be good to be with you, but we had a house filled with people—Dad, Vanessa, Megan and the rest of the staff constantly present. I wanted to be alone with you, but today was enjoyable and I'll admit, I'm surprised by my feelings for my nephew. I've never been around kids, never thought about them. I haven't particularly cared to get to know any if I'm briefly around them. Michael is cute and he can certainly win you over, which is funny, because he can't converse and he drools."

She laughed. "So you like him after all. He's adorable and who could resist him?" she said, her smile vanishing as she wondered if today had simply reinforced Eli's determination to get Michael into the Rafford family and hereafter it would be easier to enlist Nick's help.

"Don't start worrying," Nick said quietly.

"I hate that. You easily guess my thoughts while I never have the remotest idea what's on your mind."

"You should be able to guess exactly what's on my mind," he said, his suggestive tone carrying a sexy innuendo that made her forget the past day, problems and others.

"I want to be alone with you," Nick said, his tone stirring more shivers. "We've spent Christmas without a single kiss."

"We kissed early this morning when I first saw you."

"That one hardly counts," he said.

She didn't want to tell him that even the slight brush of his lips on hers this morning had stirred a heated response. Nick's looks, his presence, his kisses, always brought a reaction. He had to know the effect he had on women.

At her apartment Michael stirred and Nick waited while she fed Michael, changed him and put him to bed.

"He's out for the night this time, I'm sure," she said. "We'll have our little Christmas tomorrow morning," she said, coming back into her living room, which now seemed smaller than ever. Lights glowed on her tree and she wondered if she looked poor to Nick. He would never understand her refusal of his father's monetary offer.

Nick crossed the room to her. "Merry Christmas," he said, taking her into his arms. His gaze lowered to her mouth and she forgot everything else. His tongue parted her lips, thrust deeply into her mouth to stroke her tongue.

Melting, she clung to him, kissing him hotly in return, wanting to rattle him as much as he had her. He had sent her life into an upheaval with his passionate kisses. They were headed for a blowup because of their struggle over Michael. She was entangled with Nick now and there was no turning back on that. All she could do was fight to keep her baby, but she was beyond the point of resisting Nick. Each time they were together he became more important and had a stronger effect on her. When he wasn't present, he was in her thoughts far too much of the time.

Continuing to kiss her, Nick picked her up to carry her to the sofa where he sat down with her on his lap. She could feel his arousal pressed against her, hard and ready.

He cradled her against his shoulder while his hand stroked her hip and slid to her waist. His other hand wrapped around her, his fingers slipping beneath her sweater to take away her bra and caress her breast.

While moaning with relish, she ran her fingers through his thick, short hair, caressing his nape. She wasn't aware of his fingers unfastening her slacks until he shoved them away and slid his hand across her bare belly, his fingers moving lower, touching her between her thighs intimately.

She tried to twist away to protest, but he continued kissing her. She caught his hand to inch him away and he merely drifted to caress her breast. He sat up, gazing at her with a hooded, scorching look that was as sexy as a caress.

Mesmerized, she watched as he tugged off his sweater and tossed it away, leaving his chest bare. Hastily he pulled her sweater over her head.

"Nick."

"Shh," he whispered, cupping her breasts. "You're beautiful, Grace. So gorgeous," he added, leaning down to kiss her breast. His wet tongue circled her nipple and she gasped, closing her eyes, clinging to him while she ran one hand over his muscled chest.

Pleasure rocked her in waves, heightening desire as he could so easily do. He tilted her back against his shoulder while he kissed her on the mouth and his hand slipped low again, going beneath her silk panties.

His warm fingers touched her intimately and she moaned as she arched against his hand, momentarily yielding, taking pleasure in touching him and being touched, knowing she was sinking deeper in her relation with Nick with each second that ticked past, each caress that bound her closer.

"Nick, wait. We're going way too fast and heading for intimacy, seduction, something I absolutely can't deal with," she said, pulling away.

His hot gaze traveled over her bare breasts and she couldn't stop doing the same, with a seeking study of his strong shoulders and chest. Her insides heated, clutched, an ache throbbing low inside her.

With an effort, she lifted her gaze. "Nick, slow down." She wiggled away, standing and pulling her sweater on, tugging her slacks back in place and fastening them.

Nick gripped her wrist. "Grace, come here."

"Didn't you hear me?" she asked as he pulled her toward his lap.

"Sit here with me. Let me talk."

Suspecting that if she sat on his lap they would do little chatting, she still did as he asked, tense and ready to protest the minute he started to kiss her. She was intensely aware of his bare chest, which kept her tingly and wanting him. Lust was rampant. How long could she successfully resist Nick? How badly would it complicate her life if she yielded to him?

"I want to tell you something. My dad does not give up easily," Nick said, and she chilled, fear overcoming desire.

"He's put me in a bind over Michael. If you legally changed Michael's last name, it would not give him to my dad."

"It would be a step in that direction and I don't think your dad will stop there. Do you really think so?"

"I can't imagine that he would ever try to take Michael from you. Especially after getting to know you. My father is not a monster. He's just a man who's determined to get his way when he wants something."

"And he wants Michael with all his being. He has nothing else to focus on in his life now. All his attention is on Michael and wanting my baby to be a Rafford. There's only one real way for Michael to become a Rafford and that's to take Michael from me."

"That's not true. There's another way."

Chapter 7

Dread filled her as she looked into his eyes. Whatever he suggested could not be anything she would want to do. It had to involve losing some of Michael in her life.

"What does your dad intend?"

"You're right that his main goal is to get Michael in the family. He thinks I can accomplish this, so he's put pressure on me because he knows he's helpless to do much."

Her trepidation grew. "I don't want to know, but I have to hear. What are you instructed to do?"

"Bring Michael into the family. At least with the Rafford name and a promise my father can share in his life. Dad threatened me if I didn't accomplish this. He's changed his will."

"Nick, this is so unfair. Your father is ruthless and you're going to be the same way," she said, moving off his lap and walking to her mantel to get some distance from him. A knot had formed in her throat and she had turned to ice. "All right. Tell me about this new will and how your father has threatened you," she said, bracing for what had to be bad.

Her spirits sank as Nick related the terms his dad had given him. When he finished, they gazed at each other in silence. She rubbed her forehead.

"I can't believe he would take your inheritance in such a manner."

"Believe it. My father does what he has to when he wants something. I checked with his attorney, who had been told he could talk to me about the new will."

"So if I don't capitulate, you lose a fortune."

Standing, Nick yanked on his sweater as he crossed the room to her. "I've thought of a solution. Hear me out, because your first reaction is going to be an emphatic no."

"You're not reassuring me. All right, what is your idea?"

"Marry me. We'll have a marriage of convenience."

Shocked, she stared at him momentarily speechless. "You're right," she said finally. "My reaction is a very emphatic no. We're not in love, Nick. You're not a marrying man. What happened to what you said to me—you're a confirmed bachelor. I recall, 'My father has married enough to scare me from that forever.'"

"I'm suggesting a temporary union. It's a marriage of convenience, no deep emotional involvement on either of our parts, but beneficial to both."

"I think 'beneficial' would be describing what you and your dad get. I would gain nothing."

"Of course you would," Nick said quietly, moving a strand of hair behind her ear, his touch mildly distracting even though her attention was on what he was saying. "I'd make it worth your while because I'll inherit the bulk of my dad's estate. Michael will have a trust and as my wife, you would have money to take care of him in any manner you desire. You can have your restaurant. In addition, I'll pay you a million."

Another surprise jolted her. Her head spun at the thought

of what Nick was offering. Her life and Michael's would be altered drastically. "It boggles my mind. I can't imagine that much money being mine. I've been poor my whole life until the last few years and that's been what I've earned by hard work. You see what a simple life I lead. I can't fathom living in the manner you're proposing, much less marrying you. It's worth that much to you to do this?" she asked, unable to grasp how Nick could be making her such an offer.

"My father is enormously wealthy. If I inherit, I'll be a billionaire."

"It's that important to you that you would lock yourself into a loveless marriage?"

"Yes, to you. A union with you isn't exactly a grim prospect, Grace. We have a hot chemistry between us. We could make this work. I'll remind you again, it's temporary."

She rubbed her forehead again. "Nick, my head spins. It's lust between us. There are so many questions about the marriage, much less thinking of the future and Michael and the money."

"Look, I don't want to lose Dad's fortune, I'll admit that. No, we're not in love, but frankly, Dad's health is very poor. He spent years just sleeping three or four hours a night, working on high-pressure deals, partying when he wasn't working. He hasn't taken care of himself and now he's paying a price. His doctors have talked to me. We won't be married forever and you'll come out of it well fixed, Michael taken care of, and you and Michael can lead your own lives."

"That sounds cold."

"Not too cold," he remarked drily. "You and I get along great except for this problem between us caused by my dad. Marry me, let me adopt Michael. That puts him in the Rafford family, but there is no earthly way Dad could or would take him from you if you're my wife."

"I suppose that's true," she said. "Not as long as I stay with you."

"Damn straight. If you don't like being married to me, we don't have to be in each other's faces. There's enough money to do as you please. I'll set up an allowance for you that will be generous and you can do what you want. Keep catering, open your restaurant, stay home with Michael—suit yourself. This will give me Dad's inheritance and give you what you've dreamed of in life. You'll achieve that goal of yours far sooner."

Nick's dark gaze compelled her to want to accept. She moved away from him to break the spell he spun just with his presence.

"Nick, that's a lot to think about. You have to give me some time."

"I will, but remember, time is important. Dad could have another attack or a stroke, and then the deal is off because it would be too late. I hate to be blunt about it, but that's the truth as presented to me by his doctors."

"You would be Michael's legal father," she said, turning to study Nick and wondering how good this would be for Michael.

"I'm glad you're considering Michael, too. While he's only a baby, he has a big stake in your decision. As my child, he would be my heir and I would support him until he's grown." Locks of black hair fell across Nick's forehead and a muscle worked in his jaw, another hint of the intensity of his feelings.

"Of course, I'm wondering what kind of father you'd be."

"I can't make promises about something I don't know about myself, but I've been surprised how much he's wiggled into my life. I enjoyed last night and today with him around. He has a way of winning you over, though it's effortless on his part."

"Yes, he does," she said, thinking about Nick's declaration.

"This marriage between us won't last and I have no inclination to take Michael from you. Michael would be my heir."

"At least you're honest and that's good." They stared at each other and she could feel the clash of wills and see the determination in Nick's expression. He crossed the room to her to place his hands on her shoulders.

"Marry me. It won't be bad and you know it. You'd get what you want. I'd get what I want. Dad gets what he wants. It will be good for Michael and there is no way on earth you'll lose your baby. Dad and I will just be more in your life than otherwise."

"More in my life? Nick, you and I would have an intimate relationship."

"I can't see that that would be bad," he said quietly, slipping his hand to her throat. "We're not in love, but sex promises to be great between us."

"I still can't imagine you suggesting this. You have a lot to lose."

"Not as much as I have to gain," he countered. "My bachelor freedom I can forgo for a while. Grace, once again, this is a temporary marriage. It's not a lifetime commitment."

"You're charming and sexy. You've told me what a confirmed bachelor you are. Suppose I fall in love with you?"

"Hopefully, if that happens, I'll fall in love with you. If I don't, that's one of the risks you take, but there aren't many other risks and people can survive breakups. At the moment we're not in love."

"Intimacy may lend itself to love. I know I can't be detached about someone I'm intimate with."

"Regard it as a risk. I think this marriage will be well worth your while for all the pluses there are."

"You know I can't possibly give you an answer now."

"I'll repeat, don't wait long. I can't see that you have much to lose and you have a world to gain for both you and Michael." Nick drew her into his embrace and leaned forward to kiss her.

She stood resisting him, her thoughts on his proposition, but then his mouth opened hers, his tongue thrust inside and her attention shifted to Nick. He kissed her passionately as if trying to win her over physically, a reminder of the strength of their attraction. Marriage, making love constantly, a million dollars, plus her restaurant. It spun in her thoughts, but his kiss drove away reason. In seconds passion encompassed her.

She wound her fingers in his hair again, standing on tiptoe to kiss him ardently. She ran her hands over him, slipping them beneath his sweater to caress his smooth back, trailing down to his narrow waist.

Nick stepped back, pulling off first his sweater again, and then hers. "This is good, Grace. We do well together." His gaze traveled to her breasts as he unzipped her slacks and let them drop. He unclasped her bra to push it away, cupping her breasts to caress her before kissing her.

His tongue was hot, wet as he circled a nipple and made her clutch his shoulders. In minutes he straightened to kiss her, holding her with one arm banding her waist while his hand caressed her inner thighs. She spread her legs slightly, giving him access.

"You're beautiful. Desirable," he whispered. "Awesome," he added, his words another caress that heightened her desire.

His hand slipped higher and he tugged away her panties before his fingers touched her intimately, stroking her while he continued to kiss her.

Her heart thudded violently and she could feel his heartbeat racing beneath her hand spread on his chest.

She moaned with longing, sliding her hand down, unfastening his pants to get them out of the way and feeling his washboard stomach. Minutes later she pushed away his tight briefs. She took his stiff rod in her hand to caress him.

Sensations showered her, heightening her response and longing. She tugged at his shoulders, spreading her legs wider for him. "Nick," she whispered before kissing him.

She wanted him and she was crossing a line where there would be no turning back. She was also on the verge of accepting Nick's marriage proposal and then they would be making love every night. She would not stop him tonight. If marriage loomed she wanted him now before she made her decision, yet deep in her heart, she was inclined to say yes to Nick and take the breathtaking proposition he offered. Say yes and gain the world for herself and for Michael.

Nick's kisses and caresses reclaimed her attention and she forgot his proposition as she clung to him and returned his passion.

"Are you protected?" he asked, and she leaned away slightly.

"No," she answered.

"I can take care of it." He kissed her again until she forgot about his question or their brief conversation. He swept her into his arms and carried her to place her on the sofa. Picking up his trousers, he removed his billfold, retrieving a packet in foil.

She watched him, marveling at his strong body, virile and fit. He returned to kneel to kiss her, starting at her feet and working his way up until he moved between her legs and let his tongue travel where his fingers had played.

"Nick," she gasped, her fingers tangling in his hair. His tongue dallied across her belly, drifting higher to give attention to each of her breasts, and then he moved over her to kiss her, his weight solid.

She kissed him until he shifted, kneeling between her open legs. His gaze traveled deliberately over her. "You're stunning."

She watched his strong, well-formed hands as he put on the condom and then he lowered himself to enter her, filling her slowly, causing her to arch to meet him.

"Nick." She cried his name again, pulling his shoulders closer, running her hand down over his broad back and his firm buttocks. She locked her long legs around him, in motion with him, carried on a spiral of passion.

Nick slipped an arm around her, holding her, kissing her as he thrust slowly and withdrew, setting her on fire with need.

"Love me," she cried, her hips arching against him. His control held and he continued to pleasure her until her pulse roared in her ears and nothing existed for her except Nick's body pleasuring hers.

Finally his control shattered. He pumped faster, Grace moving with him as her need reached a climax. Carried high, she crashed with satisfaction that washed over her. She held him tightly while he shuddered with his release. His body was sweat covered, as heated as hers.

With a galloping heart, she gasped for breath until he kissed her passionately again, moving with her, slowing now. His breathing was heavy, irregular as her own.

"Nick, how I wanted you." She could never go back to feeling remote from him the way she had before.

"Ah, Grace, you're unbelievable, better than I had hoped, and I expected the world. We'll be great. You can't argue that one," he whispered, showering light kisses on her face while he held her. "This is a Christmas to remember. Make it extraordinarily special. Be my Christmas fiancée."

Christmas fiancée. How tempting Nick could be.

Slowly she cooled and caught her breath while she remained locked in his embrace, one with him and for now, no dissension between them.

"I want you in my bed every night. I would have without

the proposal," Nick said, studying her, and her heart missed a beat over the promise of passion in his eyes. In that moment, she was certain she would fall in love with him. Particularly if he turned out to be a great father to Michael.

She combed raven locks off his forehead and Nick leaned down to kiss her. "Say yes, Grace. It'll be good for everyone. You won't have regrets."

"I'll have a hundred second thoughts and possibly dissatisfaction," she said, certain she would. "But I'll admit, I'm considering your proposal because Michael and I would gain. And it would keep your father from ever taking Michael away from me. I don't think a court would take a baby from the guardian mother, but I'm not a blood relative and your dad is. Plus he has the power and the money to win what he wants. He probably knows judges and has the best attorneys, whereas I can't possibly have the resources to put up much of a fight."

"Lamentably for you, that's right. My dad knows he can get what he wants." Nick rolled over, holding her tightly and keeping her with him as they squeezed together on her sofa.

"Next time we find a bed," he said.

"I have two bedrooms. One is empty now."

"That sounds promising. Can that be an invitation for me to stay?"

She smiled, tracing his lips with her fingers. "I suppose it is since you asked. Nick, I want to talk to my attorney about this."

"Fine. I had a prenup drawn up. It's in the car, so I'll get it before I leave. You can look at it and make changes, but everything you'll get is in the document."

"You're so sure of yourself, it's revolting," she said. "You already have the prenup. Your arrogance has always been obvious."

"But adorable," he said in fun. "I'm sure of myself because

this is a good deal. Grace, I don't give up my bachelor freedom lightly. I've thought about this."

"You want your inheritance as badly as your father wants Michael. Neither of you is accustomed to losing."

"You've managed to resist both of us pretty well so far. Frankly, I'd say you're the winner in this battle."

"Maybe I am," she said, winding her fingers in his chest hair and thinking about their lovemaking. "You're a sexy fellow."

He shifted to look down at her. "I'm glad you think so because you burn me to cinders."

"Ah, the result I intend," she said smugly, wishing with her whole heart she did. "Maybe I'll marry you and make you fall in love with me, you who are so sure of yourself."

He chuckled. "Do that. I'm not protesting. Let's go find your bed before one of us falls on the floor." When he stood and picked her up, she pointed in the direction of one of the open doors.

"I have a baby monitor in there and I can hear Michael anyway, although he rarely wakes in the night any longer."

"And which direction is the bathroom?"

"The door to the right," she said.

He placed her on the bed and brushed a light kiss on her mouth. "I'll be right back," he said, and left.

She stood, turned back the covers on the bed and climbed in, pulling a sheet over her. In minutes he returned, aroused and ready. He slipped in beside her and pulled her into his arms.

"Come here, sexy woman," he said, kissing her. His hand drifted down her back and over her bottom, rekindling desire.

It was dawn when she fell asleep in his arms. She had no idea how long she slept, but she stirred and looked at Nick, who had his arms wrapped around her as he held her close.

The past two days had been unforgettable, tonight's proposition, a shock. She would call her attorney to make sure the sham marriage would be as big a protection of Michael as Nick had said. She suspected it would because she couldn't imagine that it wouldn't completely satisfy Eli and return Nick's inheritance to him.

The risk was falling in love—inevitable with Nick. Would he ever really fall in love with any one woman? Or would he be in and out of marriages and relationships like his father?

One million dollars. Plus Michael taken care of financially for the rest of his life. Plus an allowance. She could not possibly refuse him. With her eyes adjusted to the darkness, she looked at Nick, seeing his handsome features, the thick midnight hair tumbling on his forehead, black lashes feathered over his cheeks.

Their lovemaking had been one more argument on Nick's side. The passion was fantastic, beyond anything she had dreamed possible. She studied Nick's straight nose and prominent cheekbones, his firm jaw. If Nick stayed in her life, she would fall in love—it was absolutely unavoidable. Yet heartbreak was a risk worth taking for everything else Nick promised. She just had to remember to not expect any long-term relationship. A temporary marriage with myriad benefits.

On any given day there were people walking around who were survivors of a broken heart. She would also pull through. He had a prenuptial agreement already drawn up, which was a clear indication of his confidence.

Her life was about to be turned topsy-turvy by the man holding her close. He was still a stranger in many ways, yet she was becoming friends with Nick, getting to know his father and learning some of the family history.

While she gazed at him and thought about their lovemaking, desire returned. Soon he had to be going, but they could make love one more time. She raised slightly to trace the curves of his ear with her tongue.

Almost instantly his arm tightened around her and his eyes opened. She gazed into his dark eyes and felt his arousal as he pulled her closer to kiss her and they loved once again.

It was the first graying of morning when she watched Nick dash to his car and return with a manila envelope. Once he closed the door he handed the envelope to her. "Look it over and give it to your attorney. I'll see you later today. Do you work or stay home?"

"Parties start up today and I'm working tonight. You can come by my office Monday at four and we can talk there."

They stood looking at each other. His warm brown eyes made it obvious he wanted to make love again. "You need to go, Nick. I have to get things done."

He stepped forward to embrace and kiss her. She hugged him tightly until finally she looked up. "You're a lusty one."

"You drive me to lust," he said, caressing her throat. "A few more minutes and we'll be back in bed. All right. I'll be at your office at four." He walked to his car and was gone. She closed and locked the door and went to look at Michael, studying the sleeping baby and thinking about how his life had changed.

She picked up the manila envelope to read the agreement, receiving more surprises with Nick's generosity, because she would get more than he had told her. Michael would have a trust that would assure him a college education and a comfortable life not counting contributions from her. She would be given a generous allowance, one million to be paid, half when they married and half when they separated. She paused at that one, certain that if she married Nick she wouldn't want it to end. She would do everything in her power to make him love her in return.

Michael's cries interrupted her reverie. She slipped the agreement back into the envelope and it was midmorning before she had a chance to talk to her attorney. She drove to his office for an early afternoon appointment that was brief because he urged her to accept Nick's offer if she got along with Nick and thought she could live with him.

She drove back to the office and told Jada that she didn't want to be disturbed for the next hour while she sat in her office mulling over what she was about to do.

Nick arrived promptly at four. Jada, bubbling as ever around him, showed him back to Grace's office. She hadn't told Jada or anyone else except her attorney about Nick's proposal. This was something she wanted to make up her mind about without other influences except a legal opinion.

Nick walked in, his navy jacket unbuttoned and open. He closed her office door and crossed the room to kiss her, a light kiss that turned into a passionate one.

"Nick, we're in my office," she said finally, trying to catch her breath.

"With the door closed. It's private and you're delectable."

They studied each other and he raised one black eyebrow. "Did you talk to your attorney?"

"Yes. He gave me the go-ahead from a legal standpoint."

"Terrific. Now it's whether you want to live with me and take my offer or not." He embraced her lightly. "Will you marry me, Grace?" he asked, and she wondered if the day would come when she would wish those words had been said in love.

"Yes, Nick, I will. And I want the prenuptial agreement."

"Ah, Grace." He let out his breath and pulled her up to kiss her hard, an exuberant, triumphant kiss that started fires and made her want to be alone with him. He wrapped his arms around her to kiss her thoroughly, holding her close. She was committed now and her life had just changed forever.

He released her. "We need to get together to make our plans. One thing—let's wed as soon as possible. I'll help you in every way I can and I'll pay for the wedding so spend what you want."

"Nick, slow down," she said, laughing as his words spilled out.

"I'm excited about this. When can you go with me to tell my dad?"

"Nick, won't he see right through this and know it's a sham marriage?"

"Not at all. He proposed to my third stepmother after knowing her a week. I've been in touch with him and he knows I see you. He'll accept it because it's what he wants. Michael will legally be his grandson. When can you get away to see him? Can you give me time tomorrow afternoon?"

"I have a wedding tomorrow night, but I'll turn things over to Jada and if you'll be here promptly at five, we can go then."

"I'll tell him today. I'll break the news so it's not too much of an emotional upheaval. He'll want to see you."

"I won't be able to stay long."

"That's fine. It shouldn't take long. He'll probably want a party sometime if the doctor allows it. We can do that after the wedding. So how soon can we get married?"

"I haven't thought ahead about this because I've spent my time trying to decide whether my answer would be yes or no. I don't have to have a big wedding. I just have Jada and another close friend, my two sisters, and my aunt."

"You know a lot of people because of your business and I imagine you have some clients you've gotten to be friends with. My dad is going to want the world to know about Michael. Between Dad's friends and mine, we'll have a big guest list."

"Why didn't this family feel that way about Michael when Alicia was alive?" Grace couldn't keep from saying, thinking what a sad turn of events to have them want Michael now after Alicia was gone.

"That was Bart's doing and I've told you, Dad's illness has changed his values. I'm giving you carte blanche to hire people and get everything pulled together quickly."

"How quickly? I want Aunt Clara to be a part of all this and she won't be back for two more weeks."

"Look at the calendar. Mid-January."

"You don't adopt Michael until we're married and I have the first half of my money," she stated firmly. "I've written that in the prenuptial agreement."

Amusement flashed in Nick's eyes. "Fine. Get your calendar. Friday is the last day of December. Let's have a wedding two weeks from that—it would be mid-January, actually almost three weeks away from today. Your aunt will have returned by then."

"Nick, this makes my head spin. Two weeks from this Saturday and a big wedding. My sisters may be in Timbuktu. We are so scattered."

"You contact them and let's get started. When can I have an evening with you?" he asked, his tone changing. Her pulse skipped and she wriggled away to look at her calendar. "Thursday is a rehearsal dinner that Jada can manage. I'll go out with you on Thursday."

"Great. Here," he said, handing her a credit card. "Use this. I'll have my secretary text the names of florists I've used a lot. If you trust me and will tell me what kind of music you like, I can get the musicians."

"Nick, we're doing this and we know so little about each other."

"We know what's important," he said, his expression changing. "I've thought about you all day long," he said. "I couldn't wait to see you," he added, and leaned close to kiss her again.

Wedding plans were forgotten, along with the tingly excitement she felt over her new life.

Desire overwhelmed her and she kissed him, letting go plans and worries. As their kisses heated and longing intensified, she wanted so much more. Reluctantly, she stopped.

"Nick, there's something else. I'd like to wait until we marry to have sex again. Last night was impulsive. I couldn't resist you and your seductive lovemaking. I don't rush into things and I'm charging headfirst into this marriage, definitely the physical relationship. Can we postpone sex until the wedding?"

"I'm not going to like waiting. What's the point?"

"A relationship now and getting ready for a crash wedding. These things will complicate my life at a time of the year when I'm really busy with my business. Plus if I stop working and stay home with Michael—which I will be able to do—I'll be busy getting the catering business taken care of," she said, thinking she was capitulating too fast to everything Nick wanted. He could wait for a physical relationship until the wedding. She didn't want to wait herself, but she wasn't going to be that easy for Nick.

"Whatever you want," he said. "Won't be agreeable, but if it's what you want, we wait."

"Thanks."

"No complaints over last night, are there?" he asked, studying her.

"What do you think?" she asked, running her hand along his thigh. He inhaled deeply and pulled her close.

"When you do that, I'm not keeping hands off," he said before he kissed her. Again, she responded, kissing him with abandon for a few more minutes, wondering whether she could resist him until they said vows. She intended for him to really desire her and she hoped above all, to avoid having him tire of making love before they became man and wife. Last night had been spectacular, fireworks and dizzying sex for her, but she didn't know if he had been as dazzled as she.

Now she poured herself into her kiss, on fire with longing, erotic images of Nick's virile body taunting her.

When she ended their kisses, she caught her breath. "I'm going to have to leave the office shortly for a party we're catering tonight. This is a large, important party and Glenda is keeping Michael for me."

"All right, I'll go. I'm going to miss you."

"Good. I want you to miss me," she said softly, tapping his chest and leaning closer to him. "I want you to miss me and think about me and count the minutes until we're together again."

"I think your wish is granted." He framed her face. "You've given me a fortune with your agreement. I'll make this marriage good for you in return. I just want to let Dad know and I want to have the ceremony as quickly as we can. Then I want to make love to you all night and all day long for at least a two-week honeymoon."

"Sounds wonderful, Nick," she said. "In your past relationships, I'm curious, have you always been the one to walk or have you ever had heartbreak?"

"No heartbreak, Grace. Either I've been the one or it's been mutual. Don't worry about when we part. We haven't gotten together yet."

She smiled at him. "You want this to be great and I do, too. Maybe our marriage will work the way we both hope," she said, wishing again that if she fell in love with him, it would be mutual and he would love her in return.

"What if I ask your father to escort me in place of my dad who's no longer living? Will that be too difficult for him? I really don't have anyone to ask. Clara's sons aren't close to me—I doubt if they'll even attend. Alicia's parents are gone, too. She had fewer relatives than I do, hence I have Michael."

"I'll check with Megan, but I doubt if it will be too hard for Dad. He can hang on to you. He will be overcome with delight that you asked him. You'll see—he will show his gratitude to you in some tangible way for the marriage and for asking him to escort you."

"I don't need that," she replied, and Nick shook his head.

"You're unique, Grace. Stop resisting accepting something good."

"You got what you want. I'm going to marry you. Now you go."

He smiled. "I'll go, but I'll be back and I will think about you while we're apart."

She walked to the front door with him, stepping outside where a chilly wind buffeted her. "I'll wait to tell anyone except Aunt Clara and my sisters until we've told your dad."

"Good."

Nick climbed in his car to drive away and she went to her office to call her aunt.

How would Clara react?

Chapter 8

Nick called his father's house and let Megan know he was coming to the house to see his dad. The next call was to Jake and one to Tony, arranging to meet them at the club where they could eat. He called Jake's brother and asked Gabe to join them. With excitement humming in him, Nick drove away, thinking about the wedding. He would have to decide which of his friends he would ask to be in the wedding party. Tony and Jake definitely. Gabe would have to be included, perhaps as an usher. Who would be best man? He might have to flip a coin, but if he decided in such a manner, he would tell Jake and Tony when he was with both of them. The fortune was his. He had won over Grace. He'd lose his bachelor freedom—the minute he thought about the prospect, he remembered making love to Grace and became aroused. He wanted her constantly. He didn't mind losing his freedom if it meant sex constantly with Grace.

Except no sex until the wedding. Seemed silly to him because she obviously wanted him and she was the sexiest woman